COME THE MISTS
OF CHAOS

DREAMBORN, BOOK II

K.A. VANDERHOEF

FOR ED, AND FOR ALL THOSE WHOSE COURAGE SHINES

BRIGHT IN THE FACE OF DARKNESS.

PROLOGUE

Layna sits cross-legged at the bottom of the pool, fingers wrapped around the grate of the drain cover to ground herself. She releases a bubble of air and watches it rise through the water to the surface between the shadow of Kat and Suzanne's floats. She likes to think that maybe she was a mermaid in a past life, since she's always found it comforting to momentarily escape the world this way. The weight of the water, the rippling sunlight, the stillness. All the sounds from above—music playing on the radio, Suzanne chatting away, Kat's older brother, Gabe, mowing the lawn—are distant and muffled. The world up there is still going on as normal, but down here it feels like she's stepped out of life, stepped out of time. Like she's just an observer from some shimmering alternate dimension.

It's not so much an escape as it is a chance to absorb her life more fully. To see it from a different perspective and appreciate it as an outsider. Up there are problems and worries, drama and decisions, and all sorts of other distractions. From down here, her life looks sort of perfect. And she doesn't want it to change.

She releases her last bubble of air and follows it up, breaking through the water between her friends in extra dramatic fashion as life explodes back into existence around her.

"Ah, a horrifying sea creature!" Suzanne shouts over the hum of the lawnmower, splashing feebly at Layna as if to defend herself.

"Super impressed by your lungs, Layna," Kat says. "You managed to miss Suzanne's entire freak-out about what she's supposed to wear on the first day of high school. I fixed it. You're welcome."

"Super impressed right back, then," Layna says with a giggle, as she grabs onto Suzanne's float and wipes at the wet hair matted to her face.

They start high school next week, and Suzanne has honestly been freaking out for most of the summer. She sees it as a chance to reinvent herself, Kat sees it as a chance to join the varsity field hockey team, but Layna just sees it as a chance for everything to get all messed up.

"First impressions matter, guys!" Suzanne urges, compulsively adjusting the strap of her bathing suit top. Ever since she had to start wearing a real bra earlier this summer, she has been super self-conscious. They had to practically force her to even put on a bathing suit to come in the water with them.

The glass door leading onto the back deck slides open, and Layna's mom reemerges from Kat's house, followed by a very pregnant Mrs. Taveras. They settle back into their deckchairs, now with two glasses of Mrs. Taveras' specialty summer drinks in hand.

"The Morir Soñando is ready whenever you want it, my sweet princesas!" she yells down to them.

"Thank you!" the three girls shout back in unison.

Mrs. Taveras leans over the platter of fruit and cheese on the table between the two deckchairs and clinks Julianne's glass with hers. She says something that Layna can't hear over the noise of the radio and lawnmower, but it makes her mom throw her head back with laughter. Layna feels herself smiling along as she watches them. She will never get tired of seeing her mom's face light up like that. Mrs. Taveras' exuberant personality and sunny disposition always manage to flip the switch.

The sound of the lawnmower dies, and Layna looks left just in time to see Gabe in cannonball formation flying through the air towards them. She is doused in water with her friends as she hears Suzanne shriek in surprise.

"Idiot, you're getting all your gross sweat in here!" Kat yells as Gabe's gorgeous, smiling face emerges from beneath the surface. Droplets trace down his chiseled jawline, and his dark lashes stick together as he blinks the water from his rich, earth-colored eyes. Suzanne immediately wraps her arms across her chest in his presence.

"My sweat deserves to be in here," Gabe replies, as he treads water between them. "I earned this. What have you done all day?"

"It's my birthday weekend. I get to do whatever I want, and what I want is to float in sweatless pool water with my friends," Kat argues.

"Well it's probably my last real summer, so I get to do whatever I want too."

Kat rolls her eyes. All Gabe talks about is joining the military next year after he graduates. Kat pretends to find it annoying, but Layna knows she's afraid for him. Her dad has been deployed enough times for the fear to be real.

"You don't have to go just to impress Dad," she mutters.

"It's not to impress him. It's because it's the right thing to do. World ain't getting any safer. Someone's got to protect all your asses."

"My ass can protect itself," Kat says, splashing him and diving off the float into the water to avoid continuing the conversation. Gabe hops up onto the float with a contented sigh, as though he just won it in battle.

"So, you girls excited for high school?" he says, folding his muscular arms behind his head, his russet skin glistening in the sun as he closes his eyes.

Suzanne steals a furtive glance at his abs. "Yeah, excited," she says distractedly.

"Eh…" Layna replies with indifference.

Gabe chuckles. "It'll be great. Promise."

"I hope so," Layna replies, as she floats onto her back and looks up into the cloudless, blue sky. Easy for Gabe to say when he's going into his last year. It's a lot scarier when it's all still ahead of you. She sighs as she watches a plane flying overhead and starts wondering what her life will be like when she's the one who's seventeen and going into senior year.

She closes her eyes.

When she opens them, the music and the conversation, the sunshine and the future and the hope have evaporated, and she is once again looking out the window of the plane carrying her away from that life she no longer gets to live. The beautiful memory has faded, but its hooks are in her heart, and if she doesn't figure out how to free herself, it will tear her to pieces. But she can't forget either. She can't forget that they are the reasons she's on this plane.

Never in her wildest nightmares is this where she saw herself at the end of her junior year. One of her best friends gone, one in a coma, and herself off to help prevent the end of the universe with an ancient Order of semi-humans who protect the world through their dreams. Maybe if she did see this in her future, they would have kept her in that mental hospital. And if they had, maybe everyone she loves might still be alive and safe. At least for now.

She looks down at the disappearing coast of New Jersey with unfathomable longing. Down there were all sorts of problems and worries and fears. But from up here, the life she once had looks sort of perfect. How she wishes it didn't all have to change. She keeps her eyes on the twinkling lights of the coast until they fade into the night.

PART I

"What is common to all men?
Hope. Because those who have nothing else
possess hope still."

- Thales of Miletus

CHAPTER

Layna is in the dark. The air blankets her skin and tickles at her nose, damp and musty and saturated. She stifles a sneeze as she drops her duffel bag on the stone floor. The sound reverberates off the cavernous space around her. A minute ago, she stood beside Blake in the cramped aisle of a ten-person jet that had touched down in London. Layna assumed they'd be getting a connecting flight to Athens, but as Des grasped their shoulders, the early afternoon sun that shone through the triple-paned windows of the cabin was snuffed out like a candle. Apparently, London was close enough for Des to port them in his weakened state to their final destination.

As her eyes adjust to the darkness, a small, delicate flame materializes ahead of her, flickering from the shallow depths of a basin.

"Where are we?" Blake asks from behind her. It's the first thing he's said since he stormed out of Lady Anora's kitchen in North Carolina. Though no one else was boarding the charter plane with them, Blake went directly to the back seat and shoved his enormous, red headphones over his ears to drown out the world.

Des sat across the aisle from Layna in the front of the cabin and made some pale attempts at conversation—old memories of Heathrow Airport the last time he ever needed a plane to get somewhere, his disapproval of people who applaud upon landing, and the 'lack of bloody legroom' on commercial flights. But after the plane reached cruising altitude, Layna found herself joining Blake in the back. They didn't speak, but Layna was comforted by his closeness. She knows Des isn't the one who decided to make their families believe she and Blake were dead with Lucien's ability of oneirokinesis. But he didn't stop it either. Only Blake could empathize with the unquantifiable solitude that comes with being officially dead. No longer tethered to the world that she knew, she has been mislaid, cast adrift in an imperiled new life that is not her own.

"We are deep underground in the Consulate Chamber," comes Lady Anora's soft reply from somewhere in the darkness.

It was only some eight hours ago that they parted ways in North Carolina, but the velvet cadence of Lady Anora's voice now conjures warring emotions inside Layna. She has come to associate the sound with comfort and safety and family. But now, Lady Anora is not only a source of those associations but a thief of them. It is impossible to reconcile the two versions of this woman she had come to trust so completely.

2

"Underground?" Blake sputters. "Is there at least like a light switch or something?"

Layna hears his quickened breath, and her eyes futilely search the dark for his. Underground is not the most ideal place for claustrophobics.

"Yes…something," Lady Anora murmurs. "Just a moment."

Delicate footfalls echo across the space, and Layna makes out the vague outline of Lady Anora in the faint glow from the basin as she kneels before it. She removes the medallion hanging around her neck— the same one she used to open the door to the athenaeum back at her house in North Carolina—and drops it in the basin with a resonating, metallic clunk.

Blake responds with a pained grunt of impatience as this fails to switch on any light or evoke any change in their surroundings whatsoever.

"The Consulate will arrive momentarily," Lady Anora announces. "I want you to recite to them the Phantom's Prophecy as you read it in the Dream Book, exactly as you did for me. Can y'all do that for me?"

"Sure," they answer simultaneously. Layna didn't miss the formality in her mentor's voice. Lady Anora is being careful with them. Because, of course, her claircognizance gives her an intrinsic knowledge on people she interacts with, and it must have shown her some truth of what she's done to them. Layna is glad for it. Let *her* carry some of this weight she's put on them.

Though Layna has no desire to do anything for Lady Anora or the Consulate right now, at least there is a task. Something for her brain to focus on. The plane ride was an endless hum of numbed agony and suppressed ruminations. All she wanted was to sleep. Not because she felt particularly tired. She felt particularly nothing. But because she thought it might be a solace of sorts to begin exacting her revenge on the umbrae in her dreams. But of course, sleep was not a friend.

Each time Layna began to drift off, she was startled awake by any one of the numerous haunting images from the day. Kat lying unconscious and battered in the hospital bed. Suzanne's hand floating in the water outstretched toward the pocketknife that was useless to save her. Her cries for Layna. Her lifeless stare. The towering umbra slashing through Des' back with its six-foot blade of darkness. Jim down on one knee before her mom, both of them oblivious to what would be Layna's last moments with them, and the tragic lie that would soon befall them. Each searing memory mocked her, doubling down on her pain as it aroused the instinct to run to her mom and best friends for reprieve.

Eventually, Layna gave up on sleep and curled her legs up to her chest so that she could cradle herself. She held on tight long after her arms went numb, as though her own grasp was the only thing keeping her from porting right back home and out of this nightmare. Maybe it was. And just when she thought she wouldn't be able to hold on any longer, Blake's hand brushed hers.

She looked up to find him watching her. His eyes—it wasn't so long ago they were barricaded and unfamiliar—seemed to beckon her into their azure depths. They held her, cradled her so that she didn't have to do it alone. Here, in this life she thought had entirely forsaken her, was an unexpected refuge. Blake hesitantly placed his hand, palm

4

up, on the armrest between them. Layna unfurled her stiff body and placed her hand in his, easing herself back against the seat. The electric tingle of his touch quieted some of the noise in her head, and she didn't release his hand until some hours later as the plane touched down in London.

"They have arrived," Lady Anora proclaims, disrupting Layna's thoughts and the stillness of the chamber.

Layna scans the darkness in vain for the figures of others in their presence.

"Please project yourselves into the Ouroboros. They await your appearance," Lady Anora adds quietly before vanishing.

Layna sighs at her own ignorance. They're here, they're just not *here*. She concentrates on projecting, and the space around her erupts in the fiery light of more than a dozen Nauts. The midnight-blue and sunshine-gold auras blend together and bounce off the swimming, grey barrier of the Ouroboros.

They are standing on the threshold of a vast underground chamber, which Layna can now see is circular in shape and rises at least one hundred colossal feet to a high-domed ceiling. Scattered along the walls of the chamber, high above their heads, are dozens of balconies, each large enough to hold thirty people. But there are no discernible stairs, ladders, or other means of access. Clearly, this place was designed for Nauts.

Through the haze of the Ouroboros, Layna can see markings of glittering gold and countless faded murals interspersed along the walls among the balconies. The murals appear to depict scenes of their ancient Naut ancestors and the Oneiroi who came to Earth to grant humanity the power of dream travel. Four glowing, serpentine figures in the sky, descending over the heads of a crowd of people bearing spears and rocks. Two bowed figures, a man and a woman, kneeling before the Oneiroi. A fire of yellow and blue, a ritual dance, the umbrae. Yin and yang and the serpent—the symbol of their Order. The images breathe life into the mythology of their heritage, and Layna feels an instant kinship with this place.

And the Consulate. Layna momentarily forgets her anger toward them in the face of her awe. She has never seen so many Nauts at once, and the sight of them all gathered together in this mythical, incandescent chamber takes her breath away. They all wear simple robes of gold and indigo to match their auras, aside from Lady Anora, whose robe is white with golden and blue trim. The robe she apparently earned as Senecta, eldest member of the Consulate. They sit in a circle, elevated at least ten feet off the ground as though levitating, which at this point wouldn't surprise Layna in the least. But in fact, each Naut is perched atop a surreptitious throne chiseled from the stone walls and jutting out into the center of the chamber. In effect, it gives the Consulate an intimidating, towering vantage point over whomever their audience may be at the center.

The twelve thrones lie in pairs of two—representatives of each of the six regions of Earth—with each pair situated between six massive columns the diameter of two grown men. Layna's eyes trace the glittering etchings that pour down the columns, across each throne, and spill out onto the floor, spiraling inwards toward the basin at the center of the circle. When random English words pop unsolicited into her mind, she realizes what the markings are—the language of the

6

Oneiroi, the same as the writing in the Dream Book. Upon closer inspection, she realizes the markings are actually made of real gold, poured into the grooves of the carved stone. It dawns on her that this secret society of semi-humans with a whole host of divination abilities must have been able to amass great fortune over their millennia of existence.

From the periphery of the center circle, Layna scans the faces of the Consulate and recognizes Thaddeus, who offers an earnest but pained smile, and Nuru, who nods curtly in greeting. Seven women and five men, most of whom appear to be in the latter years of life, and all of whom have a smattering of dark battle scars around their auras. A few are younger, perhaps middle-aged. Lady Anora settles gracefully into the remaining throne, her long, silver hair now packed neatly into tight braids piled atop her head. The rest of the Consulate members give her the same salute that Layna saw Des give to Nuru on the ship. A closed-fist tap to the solar plexus before raising the hand palm forward, as if about to fire lucetelum.

"Thank you all for your swift response," Lady Anora announces. "I've called this gathering of the Consulate of Augury to discuss the matter brought to my attention by the two newly ascended Nauts who will appear before us today. Layna Emery and James Blakely Knox, please step forward."

Lady Anora beckons them toward the center of the circle where Layna notices a raised platform in the foundation, curved around the basin like a crescent moon. Her stomach does a backflip as she and Blake walk out under twenty-four glowing, watchful eyes, their obtrusive footsteps resonating through the stillness.

7

Layna throws a nervous look at Des, who grabs their duffel bags and falls quietly into the shadows behind the columns. He approaches the only other observer in the room—a young man about Des' age and a nyx like Blake—who sits bent over a desk, intently scribbling away on a glowing piece of parchment. Des gives the man a hearty clap on the back and he nearly jumps out of his chair. He glances up at the smiling, six-foot figure hovering over him, wrings out his hand, and then continues with his manic writing.

As she steps up onto the crescent platform, Layna notices the fire in the basin in front of her is no longer a mere flicker as it was in the homeplane. Here, it is fully ablaze, but it is no ordinary flame. It looks white-hot but gives off no discernible heat, and it fluctuates unnaturally slowly, as though swaying to an unheard, sensual rhythm. Lady Anora's medallion lies at the bottom of the basin with the white side facing up. And in the light of the fire, Layna can see it bears the symbol of their Order, the same as the cover of Oneironautica, the Dream Book.

"Thank you, Layna, Blake," Lady Anora says with a nod. "My fellow Augurs, as you know, Layna and Blake have been training only a short time under the guidance of Desmond Hart with my assisted supervision. The testimony they share with us today will alter our fundamental understanding of the Phantom's Prophecy, and it is of the utmost importance in our ongoing investigation into the coming battle for the life of our universe. Oneironautica has already deemed it time to share the Prophecy with these young Nauts. This occurred within a matter of days since their activation into our ranks."

A round of hushed murmuring rolls across the pairs of Nauts. Layna can sense their appraising gaze, the invasiveness of their extraordinary minds trying to discern her worth. She feels naked, all her thoughts and flaws and dreams and fears laid bare before these people who, whether she likes it or not, are her new superiors. She tries in vain to tamp down the blazing heat rising to her cheeks.

"Now, I assure you that there can be no mistaking the authenticity of what they read, particularly given that both Layna's telesthesia and Blake's oneiromancy directed them to it. I say this because what I am about to tell you is implausible, and though it is something that was foreclosed to my third eye, I can at least confirm that they are speaking the truth. For Layna and Blake, the Prophecy was…altered. For them, there were not two stanzas, but three.

"After I was informed of this, I went back to Oneironautica and read the Prophecy again for myself. As did Desmond. It was the same as it has always been. This means, as far as we know, the alteration exists only for new Activates reading it for the first time. Though we cannot know this for sure until Oneironautica reveals the Prophecy to other Activates. So, for now, it is their testimony alone that we depend upon. This gathering being so introduced, I ask the members to cast their stones as to whether we shall hear from our two witnesses."

Layna watches in captivated silence as each member of the Consulate ports down from their throne in turn, removes an identical medallion from his or her neck, and releases it into the basin. Each medallion is cast with the white side facing up, and as each is added, the hue of the unearthly fire changes to reflect the aura of the Naut who cast it. From gold to blue and back to gold. The final Consulate member

9

to cast her stone sits in the throne paired with Lady Anora's, the nyx representative of Region Six. She is an eccentric-looking, middle-aged woman with spiked hair dyed electric-blue to match her aura. Once her medallion is added, there is a delicate flash, and the fire returns to its pure, white state.

"By unanimous consent, we shall hear from Layna Emery and James Blakely Knox on this matter," Lady Anora declares.

No wonder these gatherings can go on for days, Layna thinks in exasperation. *All that just to decide to hear what they have to say? What an inefficient voting system.*

Lady Anora then addresses Layna and Blake, her grey eyes softening as she looks down upon them. "If y'all would recite to the Consulate what the Prophecy said for you, we would be deeply appreciative."

Blake casts a hesitant glance at Layna before they begin the simultaneous recitation.

> *Bound as one, twin fates are sealed*
> *Neither light nor dark may yield*
> *A balance broke by Phantom's spark*
> *The mists of Chaos beget the dark*
>
> *When of Aether and of Blood*
> *Lends passage to the shadowed flood*
> *The universes distend and rip asunder*
> *The Light of Kosmos forever smothered*
>
> *Once Eskhatos is eclipsed*

Then it can end in only this
Unless Day joins Night and Night joins Day
As one to close the Gateway

The oration is met with deadened quiet and an exchange of shocked glances. The silence lingers, and Layna shifts uneasily on her feet, waiting for some response. One by one, all bewildered eyes swing from Layna and Blake toward Lady Anora. In each gaze, Layna sees the deference to their Senecta, the silent plea for guidance in the face of the unexpected revelation.

Lady Anora clears her throat and continues with the formalities. "Having heard from the witnesses, I ask that we dismiss them to the arena where the others await their arrival, and so that we may open the circle to what I'm sure will be a lengthy discussion."

There is no response. The Nauts are effigies chiseled in stone.

Oh my god, we broke them. We broke the Consulate. The Earth is doomed.

Layna tries to catch Lady Anora's eye, but she notices Lady Anora offering a delicate nod to each member in turn, and she realizes they are casting their votes by inaction. By leaving their medallions untouched in the basin, they are voting in the affirmative.

"By unanimous consent," Lady Anora affirms. "Desmond, would you be so kind as to escort Layna and Blake to the arena?"

That's it? Layna scowls as Des steps forward to lead them away. Why shouldn't they get to stick around and hear what the Consulate has to say? They're the only ones who read the third stanza. The Consulate is dismissing them like a couple of troublemaking children.

Layna nearly laughs out loud at how ridiculous the thought is. Because, of course, they basically *are* children. A couple of dubious teens who have been part of this insane new world for all of a week, who know almost nothing about these mysterious, mystical people or their prehistoric past, what they're capable of, or what the hell they've gotten themselves into. She should feel relieved to pass along the weight of the Prophecy's words onto others more capable of bearing them. She's done her duty. Now let it be their problem.

But the words nag at Layna. They were meant for her and for Blake. Speaking them aloud hasn't surrendered them…they live inside of her.

Des beckons to them impatiently from the edge of the circle. Layna sighs as she relents and heads toward him. But she hears only her own footsteps echoing across the chamber. She turns to see Blake still on the platform. He is facing her as though intending to follow, but he remains motionless, hands balled into fists at his sides and a war inside his eyes. Before Layna can coax him to step off the platform, he spins around to face Lady Anora. "No," he says in a whisper traced with fury.

Lady Anora doesn't seem surprised by his protest. "No?"

"We're not leaving," Blake declares, standing up a little straighter as the circle of god-like figures shift uncomfortably in their stony thrones. "Our lives have been totally screwed up, our families were attacked and then made to believe we're dead, which we probably will be soon since we've been forced to come here and told we have to help fight a war to save the universe—no sorry, *two* universes. And Layna and I are the only ones who read that Prophecy differently, as far as you know. You brought us here so we can help, not to be parrots. So let us help, if we can. Let us stay. We deserve to stay."

Rather than being mortified, Layna finds herself suppressing the urge to run back and throw her arms around him. The thought conjures a memory. Up on the balcony in North Carolina, his body pressed to hers, the beat of his heart and the laughter in his eyes as they learned the power of the lucetelum. She takes care to walk in measured steps back toward the platform, sucking in a breath to settle her nerves as she returns to his side.

"Very well, Blake," Lady Anora replies calmly.

It's not the reaction that Layna was expecting, and from the expressions on the faces of the Consulate, it seems it's not what they were expecting either.

But before any of them can protest, Lady Anora continues, "I ask that the Consulate consider this request and allow the witnesses to remain in the circle for the remainder of this gathering."

In response, five of the unfamiliar members port one by one to the basin and reach straight into the flame to flip their medallions to black. The fire turns from white back to blue, then gold. Blake heaves an aggravated sigh as his shoulders droop in defeat.

"Thank you for casting your stones. We do not have unanimous consent to allow the witnesses to remain in the circle for the rest of the gathering." She pauses, gazing at Layna and Blake as she adds, "Let me therefore offer an amended request. I ask the Consulate to consider allowing the witnesses to remain in the circle for my address before they are dismissed."

After a hesitant pause, all five members who flipped their medallions return to the basin to flip their medallions back to white.

"With unanimous consent," Lady Anora says with a grateful smile, "after having heard from our witnesses, I, the Senecta, shall now offer my address on the matter before we open the circle to discussion," Lady Anora begins. "It is a lesson in humility that we are still learning about a Prophecy nearly as old as the universes themselves. And I know today's revelation was not what we were hoping to hear, as it puts to rest a timeworn debate among the scholars of our Order. The debate, of course, between the old Telikó and Chrónos schools of thought. The scholars of the former espousing the view that the end of the inverse universes would begin on a single aetherworld, and the latter that the end of the universes would take place at a single point in time across all aetherworlds.

"As you all know, the Oneiroi, upon their death, told Hemera and Nyx that the Prophecy would come to pass during the life of Earth. Telikó scholars believed 'of Aether and of Blood' meant it would be human beings who would lend passage to the shadowed flood. That Earth—believed to be imbued with the weakest power as the last world visited by Oneiroi—was doomed to bring about the annihilation of all life in the Kosmos. Some millennia later, Chrónos scholars challenged that view. They believed we were misinterpreting the Oneiroi term as meaning 'blood', when in actuality it meant 'life-force'. Their theory was that all worldlings on every aetherworld would lend passage to the shadowed flood in another universal event like Saa. Just as spontaneous sentience invited darkness into our universe through the limited channels of worldling minds, they believed this would be a similar, larger-scale event that would, essentially, open the floodgates to Erebus.

"Over the past centuries, we have become aware of an exponential growth of darkness in humanity. A proliferation of disorder, of separateness. Of Chaos. Humanity has wholly forgotten who they are. They have forgotten that the light of Aether blazes within each of them as it does everything in the Kosmos. Their self-destructive proclivities are tearing them apart from the inside with physical and mental disease. And the destruction of other humans, other ethereal beings, and the planet itself has become pervasive. Hate, fear, and greed more widespread. The technological capability of humans to wield the power of Chaos to commit mass extermination, more accessible and deadly than ever before.

"All of this has led to a dangerous imbalance that has now given unprecedented strength to Erebus, as evidenced by the various anomalies we've been investigating of late. We believed, according to the Chrónos theory, that these anomalies may be happening across the Kosmos. Alas, today's testimony confirms the Telikó school of thought, as the concealed stanza of the Prophecy actually identifies us by name. *Eskhatos.* The original Oneiroi name for Earth. Once *our* world is eclipsed in darkness, the Kosmos will be ripped apart.

"My brother and sister Augurs, while this does mean that Earth is fated to be the downfall of the Kosmos, it also gives the Nauts of Earth the chance to prevent it. Had the Chrónos theory been correct, trying to mount a coordinated war against Erebus across all aetherworlds would have been a hopeless impossibility. But now, we can at least have hope. Because there are no floodgates that will

15

suddenly spring open. There is only us—our world, our Order. We are the barricade. We must have hope, because we *are* the hope. The only ones who can stand between Erebus and the end of everything. And have hope too because the third stanza does not only identify Earth, it also suggests a way that we may prevent the shadowed flood. This Consulate must discover the meaning of the full Prophecy while our new recruits train here safely in Oneiropolis and our scholars continue to search the mysteries for a way to weaponize. All is not yet lost. I open the circle to discussion and dismiss our witnesses to the arena for orientation." Lady Anora nods toward Layna and Blake.

Des leads them away again, this time without protest, as Layna's head swims with information. Des escorts them down a dark tunnel leading away from the Consulate Chamber into progressively smaller, less elaborate chambers. Their own light casts shadows along the walls and illuminates the chipped murals that continue to stretch out before them.

Layna assumed they would be heading above ground, but as they walk further ahead, she feels the ground sloping downward. They come upon a grand archway lined in gold, which would be much grander if it wasn't surrounded by piles of rubble. On the other side of the archway, the walls change to something more like sandstone, and the murals have disappeared. It takes Layna a minute to realize the square and rectangular gaps in the walls interspersed here and there are old doorways and windows. Though it has now become little more than a tunnel, they appear to be walking through the buried streets of an ancient town.

As they make a sharp left turn, Layna finally asks, "Des, where exactly are we anyway?"

"I was waiting for one of you to ask me that," he quickly replies, grateful for the invitation to speak to them again. "We're a ways below the City of Athens, in the lost city of Oneiropolis. It's what remains of one of the two oldest cities ever built, though human history has remained unaware of its existence. The ruins stretch almost the full length of the city proper built atop it. That was the Consulate Citadel we just left, which stands at the center of the city. Now we're headed to the arena. I think you'll both fancy it."

"*Oneiropolis*? Seriously?" Layna implores.

"Aye, I know," Des replies with a chuckle. "Its original founder is one of our most famous Naut ancestors. We call him The Architect. His true name was Aelius, and he was the Senectus of his time who sought to build a new, grand site for the Order. This was after the original site located somewhere in modern-day Turkey was invaded and destroyed by worldling raiders. Anyway, the ambitious plan ended up costing poor Aelius his life, and the city went unfinished for centuries. By the time it was completed, credit for its creation went elsewhere. But The Architect had fondly referred to his dream as Oneiropolis—quite literally, dream city—and so now we call it that in his honor."

"So, what? Nauts, like, live here?" Layna asks.

"Nah, it hasn't been an operational city in ages. The only part of it that gets used with any regularity nowadays is the Citadel where the Consulate holds their gatherings. But Nauts do come here every now and again for training in the arena, ceremonies, announcements, and the like."

"So it's kind of like our command center...for the whole world?" Layna wonders aloud. "How does everyone understand each other if they're talking in all different languages?"

"Ah, right, that'd have been quite the shock without fair warning. Remember how you could translate the language in the Dream Book lickety-split? It's because Kosmoli—the Oneiroi language—is sort of pre-programmed into our Naut DNA. And once you reach ascendance, as you two now have, the language itself operates as an embedded interpreter in our minds. It's like a satellite receiving a coded message and decoding it before sending it to the language receptors in our brains. So regardless of what language a Naut may speak aloud, you will understand it as English."

"For real?" Layna challenges. "I never have to learn another language? Guess Spanish class was a total waste."

"As far as your communication with other Nauts, no, you don't. But it doesn't work with worldlings—you know, ordinary humans. Both satellites have to be online in order for the translation to go through, so to speak."

Layna gives Blake a halfhearted grin over her shoulder only to find that he doesn't even appear to be aware that she and Des are having a conversation. She stops and turns to face him, but with his eyes cast downward, he barrels right into her.

Layna catches her balance as she tries to steady Blake. "Are you okay?"

"Oh, yeah, totally fine," he replies, panting heavily.

She returns a skeptical look, and he keeps his eyes on hers, not daring to survey the tight space around them.

"It's nothing. I'll get over it," he assures her in a tight voice. "We've battled evil and almost died a couple times in the last few days. I should be able to handle a dark, caved-in hallway."

"Okay," she responds, offering a reassuring smile.

She turns back around to follow Des, but she holds her hand out behind her in invitation. He grabs it harder than she expected, and within a minute she can no longer feel the tips of her fingers. They catch up to Des just as he stops and turns to face them, and as Layna looks past him, she realizes why. There is a wall behind him. It's a dead end.

She can hear Blake cursing under his breath as his grip on her hand tightens. She winces but does not pull her hand away.

"Alright, you two," Des begins with a smile, "hope you enjoyed the impromptu tour. Sometimes it's difficult to port around in here because it's a bit of a maze and getting your destination just right could be difficult. Don't want you two to end up in a wall, now, do we?"

Blake makes a guttural sound in reply.

"Kidding, kidding. Can't happen, remember? Matter can't occupy the same space and all that. So then, about getting around in the tunnels while we stay here—"

"We're *staying* here?" Blake exclaims. "Don't we get to sleep in some fancy castle or hotel or something? Aren't 'Orders' supposed to be like super-rich and influential and stuff? Why are we even an Order if we have to live like moles tunneling through creepy, old, buried cities, huh? I mean, is it just me, or is there a serious lack of oxygen down here? *Is* there oxygen?" His voice rises in pitch with each word, and Layna can tell he is flirting with hysteria.

"You alright, kid?" Des asks as the smile disappears from his face.

"He's claustrophobic," Layna whispers.

Des winces and replies, "Aye, that's right. Sorry 'bout that. I should have ported you both directly to the arena. Just thought you might like to see a wee bit of our history. We *are* staying here, but not to worry, there's plenty of oxygen. A while ago, they built in quite the elaborate ventilation system throughout the tunnels and in each chamber so we could start using it again on the semi-regular. The arena chambers where we'll be spending most of our time are massive, just like the ones in the Citadel. The main arena is right on the other side of this wall, and the other recruits are probably already waiting for us in the homeplane where we'll have orientation. So, let's get our bums in there, eh?"

CHAPTER

Much to Blake's immediate relief, the three of them now stand in a cavernous space at least double the size of the Caledon High football field. 'Arena' is definitely the appropriate title for this place, as it conjures images in Layna's mind of the gladiator arenas of ancient Rome.

"Guess there's no electricity down here, huh?" Blake grumbles, as their eyes adjust to the firelight emanating from forty or so torches mounted along walls between more enormous columns.

"Who needs electricity when we got all the light we need right here?" Des chirps, patting his own chest. "Would be nice right now in the homeplane, I suppose, but the torches do the trick when we need them. Most of our time in Oneiropolis will likely be spent within the Ouroboros. It'll maximize our training to stay in OB time."

"OB time?" Layna repeats.

"Ouroboros time, versus home time. You know, the time lag. Get about five times more…er, time. We're only doing orientation in the homeplane because some Activates aren't entirely comfortable yet with physical projection into the dreamplane."

Layna nods distractedly, only half-listening as she surveys the grand surroundings flickering in the torchlight. More richly colored frescos like the ones in the Consulate Chamber cover nearly every inch of wall space. These are even more detailed than the others, with most of them depicting what appear to be battles between Naut and umbrae. In some images, the subjects sport leather skins and long, flowing hair. In others, they wear simple, white linens with their hair pulled into braids, and in others still, the subjects are decked out in rudimentary armor. It's clear that the images scattered across this arena span many millennia. Layna's skin prickles with an eager thrill as she marvels at the breadth of history in just this single chamber. The discovery of this room alone would be an archaeologist's dream come true.

On each end of the oval chamber are large, stone balconies similar to the ones in the Citadel. Beneath the balcony on the opposite end of the arena from where Layna stands, she sees some fifty people milling about. Their fellow recruits, apparently. It's the first time she has ever really thought about how many Nauts exist on Earth. Until yesterday, the Order still seemed somewhat theoretical to her, and it comes as a bit of a shock to see that there are so many of just the *newbies* gathered here.

"Ah, finally, you have arrived!" a heavily accented woman's voice rings out.

Everyone in the room turns to appraise the late newcomers as Des announces, "One Guide and two recruits from Region Six, and we're sorry for being late."

"Des, did she just speak English or French?" Layna whispers out of the corner of her mouth.

"English with a French accent," Des whispers in reply. "She probably assumes you haven't ascended yet and can't understand. You'll be able to tell when she speaks in French, trust me."

The petite woman who announced them joins a dark, burly man as they disappear and instantly reappear in front of Layna, Blake, and Des. She looks at Des, assessing him, and addresses him directly. "Region Six? You would be Desmond Hart?"

Layna notices at once that the woman has switched back to her native tongue. She hears French with her ears but English in her mind. Almost like having the subtitles on during a foreign film. "Sick!" she exclaims under her breath.

The woman glances at Layna in confusion as Des stifles a laugh and replies, "Aye, I would be. And you are?"

"Selene, I am a Guide from Region Two," she says coolly, stretching out a hand. Layna can't help but envy the self-assured way she carries her tiny self, like a prima ballerina. Her sandy-blonde hair is cropped short, which suits her high cheekbones and full lips. If not for those sole feminine features, she could probably be mistaken for a teenage boy.

Des takes her outstretched hand and shakes it once. But Selene doesn't release her grip, yanking him closer as she seethes, "And for *some* reason, you have been chosen as my second-in-command to train the recently Ascended, despite my understanding that these two are your first trainees, yes?"

She doesn't wait for a response, leaving Des scratching his beard in confusion as she turns to Layna and Blake to continue the introductions, now in her charming, accented English. "So...you two will be Layna and James, er, or Blake, I hear is your preference?" She offers her hand to each of them in turn, but Layna didn't miss the contempt in her voice when she said their names. She shakes Selene's hand with all the confidence of a child feeding a slab of meat to a hungry tiger.

"This is Enzokuhle," Selene adds, indicating to the foreboding giant to her left. His deep, brown eyes glance at them in greeting, and his beefy arms remain crossed over his chest. The word *soldier* springs to Layna's mind as she looks at his stiff posture and clean-shaven face. "Enzo is a Guide from Region Three and will be the lead trainer of the Activate group. Enzo and I are in charge of this training program."

Des nods, and then asks warily, "And why is it you seem to know so much about us?"

"Word travels," she responds curtly as she turns on her heel, following Enzo back toward the group.

Des glances at Layna and Blake, thumbing at the woman's back with a dumbfounded shrug. As they follow Selene and Enzo toward the rest of the group, Des leans over to Blake and whispers, "Bloody feisty for such a wee thing, isn't she?"

Blake keeps his eyes trained on his feet, but Layna sees the barest glimmer of the smile he tries to hide. She thinks Des sees it too, because he walks ahead of them and begins imitating Selene's lady-strut behind her.

"I can see you, you crétin," Selene announces without turning around.

Des stops in his tracks as Blake stifles a laugh.

"Ah, so you're a seer," Des remarks, shooting Layna and Blake a mortified grimace. "Nice divination power you got there, love."

"Yes, it is. And please spare me your uncouth terms of endearment," Selene returns. Then to the rest of the group, "Attention, please! We finally are to begin orientation now that *all* have arrived. I would like recruits to gather please with their region. We must create a manifest of us who are present." For the Activates' sake, she and Enzo repeat the instructions in several other languages, and everyone scrambles into groups.

Other than an elfin Asian girl who can't be older than fourteen, Layna and Blake appear to be the youngest in the crowd, and Layna feels suddenly out of place. It reminds her of the time Suzanne convinced her and Kat to sneak into a college party last year, from which they all immediately fled after being greeted by a guy whose only piece of clothing was the underwear he wore proudly on his head. Until a second later when he pulled it off so he could have something to throw up in. It was always one of their favorite stories to tell, but the humor she once found in the memory is swept away in a nauseating wave of anguish. She fastens her arms across her stomach and moves closer to Blake and Des as they join the other four Nauts holding up six fingers.

"When we get to your group, I ask you please each to state your name, Guide's name, and whether or not you have reached ascendance. Region One, please begin."

Beginning with the young Asian girl, who announces her name to be Jae Lyn, every Naut in each region introduces themselves in turn. Layna listens in awe as each language is translated seamlessly in her mind, and Selene and Enzo scribble notes onto parchment as they walk down the line. After Region Three, Selene instructs Region Five to begin. Confused, Layna leans forward and whispers to Des, "What about Region Four?"

Des gives her a shrug, but a chunky bear of a man standing behind Layna leans forward to respond to her question. Even at a whisper, the depth of the young man's voice seems to reverberate in her bones as he says, "There's no one left from Region Four. No recruits, that is."

Layna, Des, and Blake all turn to look at him. "What do you mean there are no recruits left?" Layna asks, fearing the answer.

"I mean the Activate attack, of course. The recruits from Region Four were wiped out by the umbrae, and some of their families were too. I mean, there were only a few Activates from there. Not the most populated region. Like, mostly Antarctica, I think. But I heard they got it bad in Regions Two and Three, too. Guess communication broke down a little there between the Consulate and the rest of the Order, and word didn't get out until it was too late for some folks. All just happened so fast. No one was prepared for Erebus to be able to take control of so many umbrae all at once like that. Never been anything like it. Like a damn massacre, y'know?"

"Alright, mate, we get it," Des blurts, glancing anxiously at Layna. She turns away from the bear-man, unable to contain her dismay, as he starts spewing apologies.

She knew Lady Anora was sugar-coating it, but she'd hoped so badly that her instincts were wrong. Now the truth is right there in front of her, in the empty space between Regions Three and Five. How many would be standing there if she hadn't been a coward and gone with her telesthetic impulse when it first gripped her? How old were they? As young as Jae Lyn?

"Region Six," Selene bellows in front of them. Layna listens numbly as Blake rattles off the requested information, and then she follows it with her own. Although she only sees it out of the corner of her eye, she swears several of the recruits turn abruptly to look at them when they announce themselves. But by the time the bear-man behind her introduces himself as Molimo, they have all turned away. She's about to chalk it up to paranoia when she finds a set of eyes that have not turned away with the others—a short, slender girl from Region Two, all severe lines and sharp edges. Her black hair is pulled into a tight, neat braid that parallels the grim set to her mouth. But it's the cold fury in her violet eyes that sends a shudder down Layna's spine.

Then the truth clicks uncomfortably into place. The contemptuous greeting, Selene's comment about word traveling, the bad communication in Regions Two and Three. Thaddeus and Nuru's regions. Layna was right. Lady Anora must have used her influence as Senecta to bring them help that belonged to other regions, and those regions didn't get warned in time. Maybe some of these recruits even lost family members or training partners because of it. Layna has never wished so badly to be someplace else, to be *someone* else.

The last person in their group finishes speaking and, the manifest being complete, Selene directs them to break into two groups— Activates and Ascended. "Those who have ascended will be with me and my second-in-command…Desmond Hart," Selene announces in English, being sure to lace his name with disdain. "You will be the First Class, and for training, we will be your Guides. For you who have not ascended, you will be with Enzo and Phoebe, his second-in-command, who will be arriving tomorrow. Once you have completed ascendance, you are to be the Second Class. I am understanding that for how long you have been in training, this will happen very soon. If we did not think this, you would not be here, as you will not be of use until you have ascended."

The majority of the recruits follow Enzo toward a group of several older Nauts who have appeared, and Enzo begins assigning these Activates to each one. Only eleven of the recruits remain with Selene and Des in First Class, including Layna and Blake. And much to her added disappointment, the girl with the piercing, violet eyes is one of them. Molimo is the only other one from their region who has ascended. Though their ranks had impressed her only minutes ago, now reconsidering the fact that they're about to enter a war with the cosmic entity of darkness…eleven is a sobering number. She certainly *hopes* there is a formidable army of full-fledged Nauts out there. Otherwise, this is all completely hopeless.

"Listen up, all of you," Selene barks in her native French so that both groups can hear her. The older Nauts whisper to their assigned

Activates in unison, and Layna realizes they are there to act as interpreters. "We do not have much time to learn how to stop this impossible threat. We cannot know what to expect from Erebus, particularly after the control we saw it wield in the attack, using the umbrae like puppets. But we know Erebus sensed a weakness in our defense. And right now, Erebus is *not* wrong. So forget all about your cushy little lives before this. You are Nauts now, and nothing you were before matters here. We are going to push you, and you are going to be ready. You do not—*we* do not—have a choice. When the time comes, you will be prepared to join our brothers and sisters to fight, and you will be prepared to give your lives in that fight. I say it now, and I will say it again. Because that is the least of what it will take to win our world back from the clutches of darkness. Understand?"

Selene pauses in the wake of an uncomfortable silence in which even the interpreters appear to have given up part-way through their translation.

Des claps his hands together and steps forward with an uneasy laugh. "Well, that was…educational." Selene seems about to interrupt, but he continues on, "I'm Des, I'll be assisting Selene, and I'm quite sure you all have been training for a while now, yeah? You all got Guides? So we all know that we're in a wee bit of trouble here. But you also know what it means to be a Naut. It means we all come from the same energy. From the Ouroboros. It means we are bound as family, and we are all in this fight together. I'm sure that Selene and Enzo have prepared a brilliant program for you lot, and I promise you that we will prepare you as best we can so that you'll have no doubt in your abilities. Sure, Earth may have a weakness, but that doesn't mean *we* are weak.

29

We're Nauts, we were put on Earth to fight for it, after all. Have faith in that, at least. Now, just my humble opinion, but maybe we could skip the rest of the pep talks and get on with the training bit?"

Selene's stare could easily turn him to stone, but he refuses to meet her eyes. Instead, he pins his gaze on Layna, unblinking. She can sense his intense discomfort as the awkward silence lingers. The way Selene's delicate fists are clenched at her sides, Layna thinks she might actually throw a punch at Des' face.

Well, great. Way to smooth things over with the scary ballerina, Des.

Eventually, Selene peels her eyes away from him, muttering something too quietly for Layna's mind to translate, and readdresses the group. "Each day we will train for sixteen hours, home time, and—"

"*What*? Are you nuts, lady?" a voice exclaims from behind Layna, as others in the group break out in uneasy chatter. Layna turns to find the voice belongs to a plump, pimply redhead, his arms crossed defiantly over his protruding gut.

"Silence!" Selene roars. "*You*…which one are you?" she asks of the redhead.

"Harkin," he replies.

"Harkin, what? Do you not have a last name?"

"Sure do."

"What…*is*…it?" Selene hisses through her teeth.

"Harkin," he replies with a dry smile.

Selene narrows her eyes, then she straightens and nods to herself. "Listen to me now, all of you, no one will interrupt while I am speaking. You are to do exactly as I say without question. With. Out. *Question*. Understand?"

Everyone in the group, save for Harkin, nods emphatically in response.

"Now, thanks to your new brother, Harkin, we will all be skipping breakfast tomorrow," Selene declares.

No one tries arguing with Selene, but Layna joins the others in casting Harkin the dirtiest look she can muster. He ignores them, but Layna can see his puffed-up chest deflate just a little.

"Since you in First Class have all ascended and the rest of you soon will," Selene continues explaining, "you will be needing less sleep each night to be of good energy in the day. It is how we Nauts work. We heal fast and sleep little. Given that we do not know our timeline, we must take advantage of this and spend as much time in training as possible. Therefore, we will train for sixteen hours a day, not including meal breaks, while you're *awake*. We expect you all to continue your training in your dreams with conscious projection while your bodies rest.

"After we eat, we will give you some time to settle into the bunkers, which I will assign in the mess hall. After this, we begin fitness testing to see where you stand on using the powers against an opponent. Tomorrow we start with the advanced oneironautics. Hopefully, we will be able to train on new weaponry in a few days' time. Now, please follow me to the mess hall."

Layna idly pushes the spiced couscous around on her plate. She doesn't remember the last time she ate a proper meal. But despite the pleasant aroma of the couscous, buttery vegetables, and roasted lamb, her stomach is too busy crumpling itself into a little ball of self-loathing to be concerned with hunger pangs. Everything about her current situation makes her feel restless. The darting eyes and accusatory glances. The deadened quiet between her, Blake, and Des—the only people who could be a source of comfort in this place. And this *place*. This ancient, glorious, buried city of her ancestors. She doesn't deserve to be here with the rest of them. She doesn't deserve to be a Naut.

Selene and the other Guides led the recruits in porting through a series of winding tunnels to another big chamber, where they now eat dinner. It seems to be the remnants of a once grand banquet hall, lit again by torchlight. Even though one end of the hall has collapsed into a crumble, there would still be enough room to hold several hundred people across the stretches of long, wooden tables lined in rows. Currently, the fifty or so recruits are spread out along the tables with a smattering of Guides and interpreters, all grouped loosely in their respective regions. But Layna, Blake, and Des sit apart from the others from Region Six.

Layna shifts uncomfortably on the wooden bench next to Blake as she eyes the four recruits at the other end of the table. She has never been an outcast before. At least she's outcast with two others, as opposed to Harkin who sits all the way toward the collapsed end of the hall by himself. Not even his training partner has joined him. She feels a brief bubbling of pity that fizzles as she watches him start snapping his fingers at one of the 'servers' to get her attention. It doesn't surprise Layna in the least that he's *that* kind of guy.

The servers are an unexplained phenomenon themselves. Several Nauts, some wearing white aprons smeared with grease stains, appear here and there out of thin air juggling platters of steaming food. On each table, they place various dishes—cheese croquettes, Greek salad, lamb and chicken skewers, fried pork chops, grilled sardines and oyster mushrooms, hearty chickpea soup, and a plethora of dips like hummus and tzatziki. Back and forth they come and go, appearing with arms full, unloading, vanishing, and reappearing with more.

It suddenly occurs to Layna that they can't possibly have a kitchen down here where they're cooking all this food. Surely there can't be proper ventilation or gas hook-ups this far down and without alerting humanity to their presence beneath the city above.

"Where is all this food coming from?" Layna quietly asks Des, who sits across from her staring at his pork chop and looking forlorn beneath his shaggy, blond hair.

He perks up at her question and replies, "The Order actually owns a number of restaurants up top. Enough that when 'mistaken' orders are placed and prepared with nowhere to go, no one notices that instead of going in the trash, they disappear underground. Though this is probably the largest gathering of Nauts we've had to cater for in quite some time."

"So I'm guessing there's also no plumbing down here then?" Blake asks sourly.

"Well, actually, we've had the luck of being able to extend the plumbing of a few Naut residences from the surface. Enough at least for some dodgy showers and toilets that, until now, I'm fairly certain have been used only by Nauts in rather desperate circumstances."

"Perfect," Blake mutters into his chickpea soup, scrunching his nose in disgust.

"Hey, guys," comes a deep baritone over Layna's shoulder. "Heard you talkin' about the accommodations down here. Mind if I join you for a little?" It's Molimo, the bear-man who told them about Region Four. He has left the other three Activates from their region who now gape at him from the far end of the table. Layna glares up at him, suspecting he has come to poke fun at them or something. But her guarded expression melts as she sees the genuine lopsided grin on the guy's full-moon face. He looks to be around twenty, with big, curious, brown eyes and long, black hair hanging in a loose braid down his back. He exudes a generous warmth that Layna can feel seep into her weary heart like medicine. Des offers him a friendly handshake in greeting as Molimo plops down on the bench next to him.

"I'm Molimo," he says, smothering Des' hand with both of his beefy ones and shaking it with hearty exuberance. "That dude down there is my training partner, Zain, and the other two are Ellen and Kiran from Canada."

The three others from Region Six give hesitant waves from the end of the table as their names are invoked, which Layna, Blake, and Des return in kind.

"Nice to meet you, mate. I'm Des, and this is Layna and Blake."

"Likewise. Looks like we'll be spending lots of time together since we've all ascended. I know Zain won't be far behind. He's honestly better than me, not to mention two years older. I can't believe he didn't beat me," he says with an earthquake laugh.

"When did you complete ascendance?" Des asks.

"Oh, maybe three weeks ago now. Thought it would never happen. I've been in training...let's see...nearly fourteen months I guess."

"Fourteen months?" Layna and Blake both exclaim at once. Molimo looks surprised at their reaction, and Layna instantly regrets opening her mouth. She certainly doesn't want to put off the only person willing to talk to them by scoffing at his training record.

"Not bad," Des says lightly, shooting a censorious look at Layna and Blake. Molimo now eyes them with an amused curiosity that immediately has Layna questioning what his divination power must be. She better learn to watch her thoughts around these people.

"Yeah, my Guide says it's about average," Molimo finally replies. "But it still felt like forever."

"Always does, brother," Des replies. "So you're from the West Coast, eh? Maven's territory?"

"Sure am, born and raised on the Barona Reservation in California."

"Oh, hey, that's pretty sick," Blake remarks.

"It was," Molimo replies with a melancholy chuckle. "I'll have to tell you guys about it when we have more time. Once I get started, it's hard to shut me up."

Layna can tell it's more than time constraints that stop him. Since he's a little older, he's likely one of the recruits who escaped the tragedy of having his family convinced he's dead, but the prospect of never returning home is itself enough to want to distance yourself from the memory of all you've ever known.

"So you said all this food comes from restaurants up there?" Molimo asks, changing the subject as he shovels almost an entire skewer of grilled chicken and vegetables into his mouth.

Before Des can reply, they are interrupted by a small chirruping sound. Layna leans around Blake's shoulder to see the young Asian girl, Jae Lyn, standing some feet away on the other side of him. She'd approached so quietly they hadn't even noticed her presence.

"Hello," she says with a little wave of her hand. "You are the Americans?"

"We are," Layna says with a smile.

Jae Lyn settles down next to Molimo, who positively dwarfs her in size. "I have been working hard on my American English. My sister and I planned to visit America before I was activated. I would love very much to hear more about it."

"You've done very well," Des replies. "And not just with your English, but bloody hell, you must be the youngest Activate I've ever seen."

Jae Lyn smiles shyly down at her hands. "I am told that I am the fourth youngest in history. It humbles me to be part of the Order, with all of you. I am not yet fifteen."

"That's incredible, little sister," Molimo says, looking down at her fondly.

Jae Lyn beams up at him, but her smile fades as a shadow falls across her. Layna turns to see Selene's petite yet somehow intimidating figure standing over them.

"Region Six," she says, snapping her fingers at the three activates at the other end of the table to get their attention as she eyes the list in her hand. "Molimo, Zain, Kiran, and Blake will be in bunker twenty-eight. Layna and Ellen will be in bunker thirteen with Aysel and Zahra, the two ladies from Region Two. Desmond, you will be with the rest of the Guides in the South Wing."

Ellen shoots her training partner, Kiran, a frustrated look, and Layna glances apprehensively toward the table where the recruits from Region Two sit, already knowing what she will find.

Yep, God totally hates me. I'm going to get shanked in my sleep.

There are only two girl recruits sitting with Region Two. And one of them is violet-eyes.

Selene moves off without another word and ports over to Harkin, who has just lit a cigarette. She grabs it from his mouth and crushes it beneath her foot as she turns on her heel and walks away. Harkin stares after her, raising his arms in bewildered frustration.

"What an unpleasant woman," Des says under his breath.

"Hmm...not as much inside," Molimo murmurs as he stares after her.

"Oy, you're an empath?" Des exclaims.

"Yep, sure am."

"An empath?" Layna asks. "Is that what it sounds like?"

"Aye, a kind of telepath, except instead of thoughts, Molimo picks up on the mental or emotional states of other people," Des explains.

"It's *all* emotion, dude," Molimo says with a laugh. "Emotions everywhere. Been trying hard to get it under some kind of control."

"That must have been a bloody hard one to go through activation with."

"Tell me about it. You try getting through a party with that ability surrounded by a bunch of, um…" He looks down at Jae Lyn, and continues, "*Impassioned*, drunk college students. Dropped out of college pretty quick once that started."

Suddenly, in retrospect, Layna's ability doesn't seem like the worst thing in the world.

"I do not know yet my divination ability, but I am excited to find out," Jae Lyn says with an enthusiastic grin.

A double clap echoes across the hall, and everyone falls silent. Selene stands at the end of the chamber with Enzo awaiting everyone's attention. "In five minutes, please finish eating. We then will begin your fitness tests back in the arena."

"Fitness tests," Molimo says with a shudder. "Never was too fond of those. Always been a husky dude."

"Don't worry, mate," Des says, clapping him on the back. "Naut fitness tests are a bit more fun."

Late that night, Layna settles grudgingly into the bunker with Aysel, Zahra, and Ellen. Apparently, violet-eyes is Aysel, who is eighteen years old and from Turkey. Zahra, her training partner and three years her elder, is from Pakistan. Layna only learned these details because Ellen from Canada struck up a conversation with the two girls. They all ignored Layna when she arrived, and she ignored them right back. She tries to block out their friendly babbling as she pulls her t-shirt and pajama pants out of her bag, before shoving it with unnecessary roughness under the only remaining bunk.

The bunkers are all clustered around the arena and were clearly designed for utility and not comfort. Their bunker can't be more than one hundred square feet, with two sets of bunk beds, an oil lamp sitting atop a small, wooden table, and zero room for activities. The walls and flooring are cold, jagged rock, and the bunk beds are each made up with a single white pillow and a scratchy, wool blanket the color of horse turds.

Whatever branding consultant from hell designed this sleep-away camp definitely got a promotion.

Layna changes quietly in the corner as the girls stumble through their respective introductions. Since Ellen and Zahra haven't ascended, their mental interpreters haven't 'come online', as Des put it, but Aysel makes a solid attempt at speaking English to Ellen and translating to Arabic for Zahra. Layna could easily help with the translating if they'd just ask. She keeps tabs on the words being lost in translation as Aysel prattles on about how English was her favorite subject in school. Zahra knows only a few words, since she was not permitted a formal education at home. Though only a few years older than the rest of them, she's been married for six years. Her family thinks she was taken, but they won't look for her.

As much as she doesn't want to admit it, Layna can't help but be fascinated by these girls who have been living such vastly different lives from her own. Questions slip forward on her tongue, but she holds it. She isn't here to make friends. No one could replace the ones she's

K.A. Vanderhoef

lost. The pit in her stomach grows deeper and darker as she crawls under the itchy covers of her bed, facing the wall.

Never before has she wished so badly for her phone. It feels almost like a phantom limb, and she repeatedly reaches for it under her pillow where she used to store it at night. What she wouldn't give to temporarily escape reality as she used to do by scrolling through Instagram or sending out some Snaps. Instead, she just lies there and thinks about the fitness tests they took earlier.

The testing for First Class felt mostly like a review of what Des taught them in North Carolina, and Layna found it satiating to flex her oneironautics muscles, so to speak. They were tested on speed and agility when projecting into the Ouroboros, porting on cue, and the accuracy and power of their lucetelum. No one in First Class seemed to struggle too much, except for Harkin, that is. Selene used him as the guinea pig, having each of the other ten Nauts take turns battling him in the Ouroboros. Harkin's movements were slow and labored, as was his breathing. Layna lost track of how many times he was knocked back into the homeplane. At least it gave everyone a chance to settle the score over him losing them breakfast.

Blake was a sight. He knocked Harkin out three times in the same amount of minutes. There was a fire inside him, and Harkin was an easy target. Layna hated seeing the pain in his eyes and the hunger of his fury, but it didn't prevent her from being impressed with his skill. And it seemed she wasn't the only one. Despite herself, for a brief instant Selene actually seemed pleasantly surprised at both Layna and Blake's performances. Likely she heard they had only been training a short time and expected the worst.

40

But this is just another thing adding to Layna's anxieties. From the brief interactions she's had with other recruits, it seems everyone has been training much longer than she and Blake. How are they going to be as prepared as the others when the time comes to really fight? Even if they caught on to the basics quickly, they have not been trained as soldiers. They are still just two clueless teenagers from New Jersey.

After the fitness tests were over, Des left them to go to the South Wing with the other Guides. The parting was difficult. Despite the lingering tension between the three of them, Layna couldn't help but feel abandoned when he disappeared from their sides, and the space he left behind quickly filled with dread.

Layna accompanied Blake to his bunker in an attempt to prolong her last remaining comfort. Blake was not happy about the cramped sleeping quarters, sweating and rambling on as the four boys picked out their bunks. But she left him in good hands with Molimo, who had already begun to distract him with friendly conversation. It took all of her willpower to port away from Blake to bunker thirteen.

The other girls finally fall silent and settle into their beds as Layna wonders about what tomorrow's training will bring. She doesn't remember closing her eyes or falling asleep, exhaustion hitting her like a bullet. She only realizes she'd been sleeping when she wakes with a start sometime later. The light from the oil lamp is low and her nerves are on edge. She searches the darkness to try to get a sense of what jolted her out of sleep. Something is tugging at her, almost like the sensation in her belly that precedes porting. But this is involuntary, and new. And personal.

It's Blake.

Something feels wrong.

She throws her bare feet over the side of her bed and onto the cold, stone floor, grabbing Hunter's pocketknife from her bag as she tries to focus. She feels him out there and concentrates her telesthesia on pinpointing his location.

The mess hall.

Layna ports to the center of the hall and strains her eyes in the dark, but she sees nothing. Then she projects into the Ouroboros and the space becomes ablaze with the familiar indigo light she associates with Blake. She spots him huddled in a corner at the far end of the hall where it has crumbled into ruin, his knees tucked up under his folded arms. *He's okay*, she thinks with a sigh of relief.

He looks up at her with a vacant expression.

He's not okay.

She stands there in clumsy silence, unsure whether she should let him be alone. But then he unravels his arms and pats the ground next to him. She strides across the hall and sits cross-legged by his side, waiting for him to speak as he idly turns his broken eyeglasses over in his hands.

"For some reason being in the dreamplane actually *helps* with my claustrophobia now," he finally mutters. "Just feels...freeing."

"I guess that makes sense. Maybe it reminds you that you'll never actually be trapped ever again. You can always escape wherever you are."

Blake nods in response. "Yeah...that would be it." He lifts his head to look at her, but his eyes linger on her arm, his eyebrows pinching with concern. With his finger, he traces the fine, dark line running perpendicular to her bicep. The scar from where the shadowspear grazed her on the bridge. His light touch sends sparks skittering across her skin.

"I didn't see this before…you got hit?"

"Barely. It's fine," Layna mumbles, pulling the sleeve of her t-shirt down further, as if that could cover a dark spot in her aura. She doesn't want to think about that moment, or any of the moments leading up to that one. Or any of the moments that came after. Or anything.

Blake looks back down at the glasses in his hands, and when he doesn't say anything further, Layna gently asks, "Do you want to talk?"

He takes a deep breath and doesn't respond right away. When he does, his voice comes out as a pained croak. "I can't stop thinking about my parents. Worrying about them. I can't help but feel like I shouldn't have come here, and I know that's selfish considering everything that's going on. But they're my *parents*, and I just left them there to deal with that…that lie. I should have fought harder to stay with them."

"I know," she says, as she tries to prevent her own black hole of remorse from swallowing her. "It's hard to know what we're supposed to do."

"No, you don't get it," he retorts.

The bitterness in his voice hits her like a slap in the face. But as he looks up at her, his eyes instantly soften. "I'm sorry. I didn't mean for it to come out like that. It's just…you don't know about my family."

Layna hesitates, unsure whether it's an invitation. "Well…I'm willing to listen. If you want me to."

Blake's eyes linger on hers, and she can almost sense the deeply buried sorrow rising from the depths of his soul to the iridescent, blue shallows of his eyes. He holds up his broken glasses and looks at them with a longing that seems misplaced. "Remember I told you these weren't mine? I just wear them because they remind me...because they were my brother's," he finally whispers, forcing the words out.

He holds his hands over his face, as though it will act as a barrier between himself and the truth that starts pouring from his lips.

"My brother, Billy. He was the greatest person I've ever known. Five years older than me, but not too old to be my friend. He just had this way of always making things feel alright, you know? And he was always watching over me, real protective. It'd get annoying sometimes because I was like this adventurous, rebellious little kid. My parents were never really strict with either of us, but *he'd* never let me get into any kind of trouble. He was just...I don't know. Better. Better than anyone else."

"What...what happened to him?" Layna stammers.

Blake swallows hard as he drops his hands into his lap. "It wasn't just night terrors I used to get. I used to sleepwalk too. When I was younger, I had this recurring nightmare of this creepy, old doorway, and something was trying to pull me through it. All the time, same thing, over and over. And one night, someone left the front door to the house unlocked. I was having the nightmare, and I walked right out the door in my sleep. Right out into the busy road in front of our house. I woke up when my body hit the pavement. I can still remember that screeching sound, and how confused I felt. Like I woke up from one nightmare right into a worse one. A real one. Because Billy, he heard the door open. He ran out after me and was trying to get me out of the street. I guess I must've been struggling against him, but he managed to knock me out of the way of the car."

Blake tilts his head back against the wall and closes his eyes as a few silent tears streak down his upturned face. He struggles to continue for a moment, trying to find his voice.

"Once I realized what happened, I just crawled over and grabbed him. The car didn't even stop after it hit him. That stupid red sports car. I still see it every time I close my eyes."

Layna clamps a hand over her mouth as everything falls into place with agonizing clarity. She's puzzled over Blake's curiosities since she met him, but she never expected the pieces to come together in a truth so tragic. The red sports car in the collection of sketches she had seen scattered across the floor of his bedroom. The melancholy that lingered in their home like a spirit. The way he reacted when she asked about his family, when she risked her life trying to save him from falling off the balcony in North Carolina. And his parents...his poor parents. Blake was all they had left. They had brutally lost one child, and now they were made to believe their only other child had been killed before their eyes.

"I remember screaming for help," Blake continues, his voice distant now. "He was still awake, looking up at me like he knew it was the last time he'd see me. I kept asking him not to leave, but he couldn't even talk. He was too broken inside, ribs were crushed. My parents came running out of the house just when he stopped breathing. And...I just felt like everything inside of me was dying right along with him."

45

"Oh, Blake…" Layna doesn't remember grabbing his hand, but she is gripping it tightly between both of hers. Her eyes are wet with tears, but she has no words she can give him. No solace or wisdom to impart. His grief is his to carry, but it has filled her, so unexpectedly bare and raw, and she wishes so badly that she could lift that burden from him somehow.

"He was fifteen when he died. I had a really hard time with that this year, you know? He never got to see sixteen, and I do…because of him. Because he died for me. It just felt so unfair. So sometime a little after my sixteenth birthday, I fished these out of my drawer and put them on, just like that," he says, holding up the black-rimmed glasses again. "I felt…I don't know, like maybe in a way it was kind of giving him the chance to see sixteen with me. Like we were experiencing it together. Sounds dumb I guess."

"Not even a little," she whispers. He rolls his head to look at her for what feels like an eternity, his eyes soft and vulnerable and sad. Then without a word, he leans forward and plants a gentle kiss on her cheek.

It's so quick and unexpected that Layna almost misses it. But she is certain it happened because it leaves behind a light tingle of electricity where his lips touched her skin. She absently raises a hand to her cheek as he bends forward and buries his face in his hands.

Layna drapes her arms around his shoulders, and he leans into her. After a breathless moment embraced in stillness, Blake sinks toward the floor, his head coming to rest on Layna's lap as he remains curled up beside her. She freezes with her hand hovering above him, surprised by his unguarded closeness. Hesitantly, she lays her hand on

46

his head and begins tenderly stroking his hair, burying her fingers in the soft, dark waves. Blake sighs in comfort as his eyes close, and she feels him slowly relaxing against her, his breath growing deep and steady.

Assuming he's fallen asleep, Layna allows the world to melt away as she gives herself a few quiet minutes to unabashedly absorb him. The heavy realness of him. The somewhat pleasant, musty scent of his deodorant, sweat, and tears. The gentle, indigo glow of his aura against copper skin. The depth of his pain and emotion lingering in the air. Her eyes trace his jawline, rove over his long eyelashes and the crook in his nose, and linger on the corner of his mouth.

"I know we didn't have a choice." His voice suddenly interrupts the stillness and causes her insides to leap, as if she's been caught amid some mortifying act. "I know the Consulate didn't have a choice in making us all come here," he continues in a more composed whisper, without opening his eyes. "This is so much bigger than us. I just have to try to keep it all in perspective."

"Maybe when all of this is over, we can go back to our parents, and Lucien will be able to take it all away. Maybe we don't have to stay dead," Layna replies, her voice pleading, willing it to be true.

Blake opens his eyes, but he doesn't respond. Layna thinks about how Lady Anora gave her that ray of hope in the kitchen before they left North Carolina—that they might someday go back home to their families—and she wonders whether there was any truth to it or if it was only designed to comfort. She thinks of how difficult it was for Des to tell them the plan. The way he couldn't look at Blake, couldn't even finish speaking. Because, of course…

"Des knows about your brother, doesn't he?" she asks. "He saw it by reading your objects when he was scouting us."

"Yeah. Des knows," Blake replies with a sigh as he sits back up.

Layna feels a cold emptiness where he'd lain against her, and mournfully observes the space between them.

"It was the glasses, actually. When Des shared his readings with me on the train, for a split second, I felt what Billy felt that night. And even though it was only a flash, it wasn't all pain and fear like I always thought. Mostly, I felt...I don't know, love, and even pride. For me. At the end, that's what he was feeling. And this sort of calmness, knowing I was safe. That he'd saved me. It's almost like Des muted the bad stuff so I could feel that. So I could have that."

A fleeting smile appears on his lips as he gives an awed shake of his head.

"I know he tried explaining to us what it was like but, damn, Layna. He feels *all* of it. It wasn't just that night with Billy, but like every time I touched or wore the glasses after. I seriously don't know how he deals with it. He's got so many people's baggage up in there. He never brought it up or asked me to talk about it or anything. But just the fact that he knew...it helped. Like it didn't have to be all mine anymore, you know?"

"Yeah," Layna replies with a nod of agreement. She noticed this too with her memories of Mount Hope. Knowing that Des knew what she experienced there. There is a strange sort of unburdening and comfort that Des' readings provide.

"I guess we should get back to our bunkers and try to get some sleep," Blake says with a reluctant shrug. "I have a feeling tomorrow is going to be rough."

"I have a feeling you're right."

Layna has no desire to move, feeling much more comfortable sitting next to him on the cold, stone floor of the mess hall than in her bunk with those girls. But she lets him help her up, and they port to the corridor outside Layna's bunker, in front of the wall marked with a bright yellow XIII.

"If I'm not at training in the morning, I've probably been shanked. Avenge me," Layna pleads with mock sincerity.

Blake gives her a sympathetic smile. "Screw them, Layna. They clearly don't know what really happened. You saved a lot of people. You can't blame yourself for not saving *everyone*. Try not to let them get to you, okay?"

Layna gives a heavy nod that feels like a lie. She turns toward the wall and prepares to project back to the homeplane on the other side, but Blake places a hand on her shoulder and turns her back toward him.

"Layna...I've never been able to tell anyone before. About that night. What I really remembered. Not even our family counselor. It felt good to talk to you about it. So, um...thanks for listening."

"I'm glad you could talk to me. I'll always be here if you need me." She hesitates and then offers him a hug, which he gratefully accepts with a sigh into her hair. The moment lingers, the electricity between them intensifying, until a sudden fluttering of panic in Layna's gut forces her to break the building tension.

"That is…you know, until we all die in the apocalypse," she adds in a sarcastic monotone.

Smooth, Layna. Real smooth.

Blake pulls away, and she's relieved to see her lighthearted morbidity at least put a smile on his face. Assured that their friendship remains undamaged, the panic subsides, and she returns the smile. She can't afford to mess up the only remaining good thing in her life. No more quiet moments in hallways.

"Good night, Layna."

"Good night, Blake."

CHAPTER

A horrific, blaring sound jolts Layna from her sleep and she bolts up, slamming her head into the bunk above her. She clutches her forehead, grunting in pain as her vision explodes with stars.

"Is that an *air horn*?" she exclaims groggily before she remembers to keep her mouth shut around her present company. She turns to find a disturbing sight across from her.

Aysel sits at the edge of the bottom bunk, fully dressed and hands clenched in her lap. Her eyes glint in the eerie glow of the flickering oil lamp, and they are locked on Layna. It's clear she has been sitting there since well before their discourteous alarm blasted through the corridor, just...watching.

Okay, that's it. Not spending one more night in this room with spooky ninja chick.

The air horn sounds again from the corridor, followed by Selene's flowery voice, "Wake up! Up, up, up, recruits! Report to the arena. Training will begin in ten minutes." Then Selene ports away and Layna hears the air horn blast in some distant corridor of the North Wing.

Ellen and Zahra climb down from the top bunks as Layna pulls her duffel bag from under her bed. She inconspicuously shoves the pocketknife back in the side pocket after having slept with it under her pillow last night. Just in case. She throws on yoga pants and a fresh grey t-shirt, wishing she had time for a shower but putting on an extra layer of deodorant instead.

Layna has no watch, but her body senses it's still at least a couple of hours until sunrise. She prays that this apparent new ability to function with less sleep will kick in soon, because at the moment her whole body tingles with numb deprivation. It can't have been more than a few hours since Blake left her outside bunker thirteen. She absently raises a hand to the phantom of his lips on her cheek, and a secret smile pulls at the corners of her mouth in the dark. But she wipes the smile off her face the second it appears, out of place here in this room in this city in this country in this new life.

She pulls her hoodie back on and slips on her running sneakers before porting to the girls' bathroom they were introduced to last night, if you can even call it that. More like a hole dug in the wall with some barely sufficient plumbing and absolutely zero privacy. She heads to the least crowded of the three grimy sinks and waits her turn to wet her toothbrush beneath the trickle of water coming from the faucet. The pipes above them groan in protest, but none of the girls speak as they shuffle quickly through their morning routines, the room laden with a mixture of exhaustion and apprehension. After brushing the knots out of her long, golden hair and tying it up into a ponytail, Layna returns her belongings to bunker thirteen and then ports to the arena.

Most of the boys are already there when the girls start arriving. *Do boys even brush their teeth?* Layna searches their faces for the one she needs and finds him at the other end of the arena doing stretches with Molimo and Zain. Blake glances up at the same time she locates him and offers a quick smile as he waves her over.

Molimo's training partner, Zain, is leading the other two through a series of squat jacks when she reaches them. Surprisingly, he pauses to wave to Layna in friendly greeting. A night in the boys' bunker seems to have warmed Zain up to them, unlike Layna's experience in the girls' bunker. Typical.

"Glad to see I don't have to avenge you," Blake says breathlessly between squat jacks.

"Not yet anyway," Layna replies with a laugh.

"Want to join us?" Zain asks, as he switches them to a series of lunges. "Who knows what they're going to have us do today. Thought it may help to warm up a little."

Zain is probably about four years older than Layna, tall with mahogany skin and an athletic build, and he is attractive in a way that last-summer Layna would have totally swooned over. But, like secret smiles in the dark, swooning of any kind seems very out of place here. "Sure," Layna replies with a friendly grin. "That's a smart move."

She turns toward Blake and finds him frowning at her, though he quickly neutralizes his expression as she comes to stand next to him.

She joins them in doing lunges as she contemplates why Blake's scowl has sparked a gratified little fire in her belly.

As Zain starts them on toe-touches, another air horn blast echoes off the walls of the arena and everyone instantly falls still. Selene stands on the balcony overhead with Enzo, Des, and another woman Layna didn't see yesterday. She is stunning in an understated sort of way, full-figured with long waves of chestnut hair and olive skin.

"Attention! Activates, this is Phoebe," Selene announces, her voice softening around the name as she glances at the woman on her right. The Activates' Naut interpreters begin whispering to their assignees as Selene continues. "She will be assisting Enzo in your training as Desmond and I focus on the Ascended in First Class. Today and each day going forward, Phoebe and Enzo will work to get each of you to reach ascendance. You will be at this end of the arena today. First Class will be on the other side where we are to start training in advanced lucetelum techniques. But first, ten laps around the arena. Go," she finishes with another blast of her air horn.

There are some agonized groans as everyone moves in tandem to the perimeter and breaks into a brisk jog. The four Guides port down from the balcony to lead the charge. Enzo breaks out in front and begins chanting a military cadence in another language, which is echoed by Selene and Phoebe who run side-by-side just behind him. Translated in Layna's mind, the words don't flow quite as well. But she finds if she doesn't focus on understanding the words, they remain untranslated and melodic. She settles gratefully into the rhythm of it as Des slows his pace and drops back toward her and Blake.

"Oy, how was your first night in the bunkers?" Des chirps, as he falls into stride with them. His tone is lighthearted, but Layna can tell by the way he looks at them that between Blake's claustrophobia, Aysel's scorn, and the events of the last couple of days, he has probably been worried since he left them last night.

"Well, I successfully avoided a mental breakdown, and Layna successfully avoided getting shanked, so I guess we'll take the win," Blake replies with a quick grin.

His smile is an olive branch. Apparently talking through things with Layna last night helped him resolve the bitterness he was feeling toward Des.

Des seems surprised at Blake's geniality, and then he brightens with relief. He claps Blake on the back, and just like that, everything between the three of them shifts back into place. Layna knows it won't be quite so easy to absolve Lady Anora of her part in the whole false memory scheme, considering she helped to orchestrate it. But she desperately *wants* to forgive her. After being forced to leave one family behind, the least the universe could do is grant her some peace with this new one.

The recruits run the remaining laps in relative silence as Enzo switches seamlessly from one cadence to another. Molimo has fallen behind, but Zain sticks beside him and offers words of encouragement that seem to keep Molimo's spirits up. Harkin brings up the rear, every now and then stopping to cough like he's hacking up a lung.

The two groups then separate as instructed to opposite ends of the arena, and Layna finds herself in the Ouroboros, spread in a line with the ten others of First Class before the golden glow of Des and the indigo glow of Selene.

"You all have displayed adequate use and accuracy of the lucetelum," Selene begins. "So now we are going to work on advanced techniques, starting with the lucy-bomb."

Layna recalls the way Des used this technique on the ship to save her mom and Jim. The way he exploded like a stun grenade, casting all the remaining umbrae back to the netherworld at once. She feels the prickling of a thrill, ever so slight, like she felt back in North Carolina when she was starting to learn her abilities.

Selene and Des take turns interrupting each other on the proper way to explain and conjure a lucy-bomb. Layna's take-away from their bickering is that it is essentially like shaking up a bottle of Coke and then removing the cap. A stand-off between body and mind. In your mind, you're meant to pour all of your will into releasing your lucetelum the same way you would normally but maintain clenched fists and bowed posture, letting the momentum build, and forcing your body to hold in the power until you can't possibly contain it any longer.

The practice following this is just as messy as the instruction. Suffice it to say, none of their bombs are stable. Sparks of lucetelum escape hands and torsos, even legs and feet, and hit the others nearby. Des and Selene keep spreading them out further, but it does little good with the range of the lucetelum.

Layna finds it almost laughable to be expected to concentrate on building a damn bomb inside yourself while getting repeatedly electrocuted. Each spark is strong enough to elicit frequent yelps of pain, and one spark from Molimo is even powerful enough to knock

Aysel out to the homeplane. Layna sends him a mental high-five for that one, and she can tell he sensed it when he glances at her with the ghost of a smile and little shake of his head.

Molimo and Aysel are both nyx like Blake, along with two girls from Region Five—Bolivia and Argentina specifically—and a Russian boy from Region One. The remaining four of First Class are hemera, including Harkin, who is practicing the closest to Layna and sparks with every cough. At least that's the only thing coming out of his mouth now—no more wisecracks.

After nearly a full workday's worth of practice in OB time, none of them have had even a modicum of success. Selene finally interrupts them with a double clap. "Quite enough of *that* for now," she derides. "You will have a short break and then we will try working on the speed of oneironautics. Some of you were slow in and out and around the Ouroboros yesterday." She aims a pointed look at Harkin. "We need to work on that. To do this, we will have you engage in a few rounds of…tag. This is Desmond's suggestion, and from what he has explained to me, I can agree it is *one* way to work on this skill. But none of you should think of this as a game. Desmond, please?"

"Righto, so we're going to be playing—I mean, er—*engaging* in ringolevio, or jail tag. Hemera versus nyx. The goal is to try to capture all the players from the other team in your chosen jail by porting them there. Porting both yourself and another person will take concentration, and that person is free to port away from you before you are able to take them. They could bloody well take you with *them* instead. So speed and concentration are vital. You can free your teammates by porting them out of jail.

57

"I encourage you to work with your teammates to devise strategies for finding the other team's jail and freeing teammates, otherwise these rounds will go on forever with all of you lollygagging about. First team to capture all players from the other team wins the round. I know none of you are familiar with the tunnels but practicing your intent to port to places you haven't been is an important flex of the oneironautics muscles. Got it?"

"But our teams aren't even," Harkin points out. "Hemera needs one more."

"Right you are, mate," Des mumbles. He looks around at Selene.

She rolls her eyes at him. "I will go ask Phoebe and Enzo to lend us a more advanced Activate." She returns a minute later with Zain.

"Oh, hey, dude!" Molimo says excitedly. "You're so going down."

Zain responds with a wily smile as he makes his way over to Layna. "Looks like I'm on your team today," he says with a wink.

Layna can hear Blake crack his knuckles from twenty feet away.

This is going to be interesting.

It's just after ten a.m. when Aysel successfully captures Zain, the last free hemera, in the third round of the game. It was a stand-off, with only the two of them remaining. It's the second win for the nyx, after the hemera easily won the first round. Zain and Layna had devised a buddy-system strategy that caught the nyx team off-guard, but in round two, the nyx team was ready for it and planned a sneak attack. Round three took the longest, with strikes and counterstrikes and several jailbreaks. Layna was captured by Aysel just before Zain, much to Aysel's wicked delight. She'd made an attempt to capture Layna in the first round, but Layna was faster at porting, and they ended up in the hemera jail instead. It did nothing to improve Aysel's attitude toward her.

Harkin was surprisingly less useless than Layna thought he would be. Turns out when he's not being repeatedly attacked by ten other Nauts, he is decently fast and actually rather clever. He devised the strategy for the third round and ended up freeing three of them from jail at once, extending the game at least another hour.

Just once, Layna captured Blake. Most of the time they danced around each other, mirror images, seeming to anticipate the moves of the other. When she did finally wrap her arms around him in the last round, he didn't even try to stop it. He just gave her a cheeky grin as she ported them both to the empty hemera jail. They clung to each other in the vibrating stillness, bathed in each other's light, until Harkin popped back into the periphery weaving a tapestry of frustrated curses.

Layna surprised herself by enjoying the game, even though, according to Selene, it wasn't intended to be fun. It was a welcome distraction, and it felt good to work as a team with the others, despite the fact that Zain was the only one cooperating with any degree of warmth toward Layna. He reminded her of Cameron, her old boyfriend from her recently deceased past life. It was a weird reminder, and she felt at once endeared to him and saddened by his presence. He had the same affable spirit, and he even had the same dimple in his left cheek.

She found herself wondering how Cam was doing. And whether he and Natalie were still together. They were fleeting musings only, a detached bubbling on the surface of a deep, murky sea of memory that she dare not dive into. Not with what lies behind her, not with what lies ahead.

The challenge of porting to unfamiliar places was also a subtle, supernatural thrill. Some part of her—not her human senses, but the part from the Ouroboros—inherently knew how to navigate the dimension in order to appear where she wanted both within the Ouroboros and in the homeplane. As she navigated, it was almost as if her brain was mapping where she'd been. In her mind's eye, she could see the labyrinth of corridors and chambers she had explored, searching for the nyx jail and escaping capture. And she gets the sense they haven't even covered a quarter of the vast underground city.

"That was a modest show of skill," Selene says flatly, as they all gather once again in the arena. "You may have your lunch break in the mess hall. The other recruits are already there. You have about forty-five minutes, and then we will start the fitness program."

"Wasn't *that* a fitness program?" Harkin mumbles to Molimo, sure not to let Selene hear him this time. "This chick is a few French fries short of a Happy Meal."

Molimo humors him with a quiet chuckle as First Class begins to disperse.

"Get it? *French* fries," Harkin adds with a snort, as he elbows Molimo and they turn to gather their discarded sweatshirts.

Des heads toward Layna and Blake, his olive-green eyes gleaming in the torchlight as he leans close to whisper, "You kiddos fancy a bit of a treat? Was thinking it would be okay if we port to the surface for a quick bite."

"Yes!" Blake exclaims. "That would be sick. I need fresh air."

"You guys are goin' up top?"

The question belongs to Harkin, who, of course, eavesdropping. He and Molimo now look hopefully at Des.

"Er...well, *we* were going to, yes. Don't think it'd be quite as surreptitious if five of us went up though."

"Come on, man," Harkin pleads.

"We'll be super quick, and we won't tell anyone," Molimo adds. "I need sunlight."

"Well...okay. Twenty minutes, I guess. Hands on," he instructs, pointing to his shoulders. Layna and Blake place their hands on his left and Molimo and Harkin scramble to place theirs on his right. Layna anticipates the smell of fresh air, a breeze on her face, the sounds of a bustling city. But after the tugging and whooshing sensation of porting subsides, the world comes back into focus to the sound of a toilet flushing and the smell of stale bleach and urine.

The five of them are crammed into a single bathroom stall. Layna is squished sideways between Des' back and the door. Harkin is atop the toilet bowl, and his foot slips into it with a splash. "Ugh! What the hell, man?"

"Sorry. Couldn't very well port all of us right in the bloody open with all the locals and tourists around."

"Where are we?" Molimo asks.

"Public toilets in the Plaka. Everyone out."

K.A. Vanderhoef

Layna manages to slide her hand toward the door handle and the five of them tumble out of the bathroom stall. Two men stare at them wide-eyed before making a hasty exit through the door.

Blake looks from Layna to the three other guys who just poured out of the stall with them. "Yeah, they're totally going to call the cops on us."

"Dude, you're a Naut. Cops are a non-issue," Harkin says with a playful punch to Blake's shoulder.

"Careful with that attitude there, mate," Des interjects. "Don't want to end up on *DARC*'s radar down the line. If we survive all this, that is."

"Who the hell is Darc?"

"Disciplinary Action and Reparations Council. Sometimes Nauts get a little too, er, free with their freedom. Or, you know, they put personal or national interests ahead of the interests of the world, and DARC needs to step in. We are here for the good of humanity, after all, not our own fancies and follies."

"What possible discipline could DARC take against a Naut?" Harkin argues. "Put us in Naut jail? Not like they can take away our abilities."

"Actually, they can. They can have an Augur put a block on you. Astral imprisonment. Essentially, it's like putting a lock on the door to the Ouroboros. Usually for some specified period of time while you do humanity service, but with repeat offenses, you could be banned for life. Back when Lucien was part of the Council, they even had a few cases that warranted memory wipes. Some people...they just don't know how to stop being human."

"Damn…that escalated quickly," Harkin mumbles, as he pushes at the bathroom door and they all walk out into the bright sunshine and muggy heat of Athens.

Layna's world explodes in sights, scents, and sounds, and she tries to soak everything in. They're really here. In *Greece*. Having been underground, part of her had doubted they were in another country at all.

The air is distinctly crisp, lined with the subtle perfumes of jasmine and clove, garlic and oregano. They walk out onto a long and vibrant pedestrian walkway buzzing with people and lined to the brim with market stalls, storefronts, and restaurants. The street echoes with a harmony of languages and laughter, bird calls, drifting musical riffs, and the gentle clattering of dishes and glassware.

Being amidst it all is a beautiful reminder that the Earth hasn't stopped turning, and time hasn't stood still in the outside world just because Layna's world came to an end. This is what she sacrificed everything for. This is what's worth fighting for. Keep the Earth turning, keep these streets teeming with life.

An elderly man with a deeply tanned face and a bright smile approaches them with a colorful collection of balloons and offers a red one to Layna. The man's face is so earnest that she hates to refuse the offering. She turns to Des, and he sighs, shoving his hand in his pocket and handing the man a collection of coins. The man looks at the money in his palm and smiles even more broadly. He offers Des a second yellow balloon before backing away with a wave of his hand. Des passes his balloon off to the first child they walk by, but Layna hangs onto hers. There's a simple sort of pleasure in holding tightly to the string of a balloon, knowing you're the only thing grounding it to this world.

They walk past merchants selling an endless assortment of wares, from touristy t-shirts, dresses, and trinkets, to gelato, fresh fruit and produce, to handmade pottery, artisan crafts, and antiques. The restaurants boast outdoor seating at charming, little tables with red-and-white checkered tablecloths, and some restaurants spray gentle mists of water toward passersby, enticing them to dine with rejuvenation.

Layna spots a stray black cat lounging languidly in the sun, and for a moment her heart is drawn back home to Moxie. Her mom once told her that whenever Layna would go stay overnight at a friend's house, Moxie would parade around the house meowing for hours before she would drop her little melancholy self onto Layna's bed to await her return. Is she still waiting now? Or does she think that her favorite human has abandoned her? After all, that's exactly what Layna did. It breaks her heart to think of it, to think of any of it, so she buries it along with everything else.

Des stops in front of a restaurant called Mythos. "This is our stop. Grab a table and I'll run back to the kitchen and get some plates to share," he instructs.

"See if they have any hotdogs!" Harkin shouts at Des' retreating figure before lighting a cigarette and sucking on it gratefully.

"You're in *Greece*, dude. Maybe try a Greek salad or something," Blake suggests.

"That's rabbit food. I need some meat and carbs if we're going to be doing some fitness program now. I haven't exercised properly in...well, ever."

They all take seats around an empty table and Layna ties her balloon to her chair. "Where are you from, Harkin?" she asks, more out of genuine intrigue than just an attempt at pale conversation. It just occurred to her that he seems distinctly American, but he's not with them in Region Six.

"Originally, Washington State. But been in Iceland seven years now. My mom moved us there when I was twelve because she got some fancy research position."

"What region is that?" Blake asks.

"Region Two."

"Oh, same as Aysel," Blake remarks.

"Yeah, whatever. Haven't talked to any of them. Don't seem like they want much to do with me."

Layna can tell he's trying to be flippant, but he doesn't quite pull it off. "What about your training partner?"

"Scouts haven't found me a partner yet. Been training with my Guide for almost a year by myself. It's all good though. Always been good at being by myself."

Layna can't imagine having to go through all this without a partner, and she makes a mental note to try to be nicer to him. Des returns, arms full with plates of food, followed by a server with several more. Layna takes a generous helping of the Greek salad, some grape leaves, pita, and crushed olives, and something Des calls saganaki, which is apparently fried cheese but tastes like fried heaven. Des hands

Harkin his own gyro, which Harkin begrudgingly accepts in lieu of his hotdog.

"This is awesome," Molimo says, smiling at the sights around them. "Thanks for taking us, Des. I needed this. On my read, I think we all did."

His mouth full of chicken souvlaki, Des gives a wordless salute and attempts to return the smile without losing his food.

"Man, I've never been so hungry in my life," Harkin says between bites. "Selene is going to starve us all to death. We've spent like a whole day's worth of time in the Ouroboros already today and no food breaks!"

"Well, your stomach doesn't exactly run on OB time," Des replies. "Digestion and other bodily functions slow in the Ouroboros, or, more precisely, they stay on home time. So we can go for long periods in the Ouroboros without needing to eat."

"Speak for yourself, man," Harkin replies, taking a giant bite of gyro in protest.

Another cat, this one orange, comes to weave between Layna's legs. "Aw, hi, little one," she says, stroking the cat's head.

"You know, some Nauts believe that cats can sense the Ouroboros outside of dreams," Des remarks as he helps himself to the grape leaves. "They tend to have an affinity toward Nauts."

Blake looks under the table at the cat, who has plopped itself at Layna's feet. "I think this one just has an affinity for crazy cat ladies," he says with a smile.

Layna feigns insult and throws a French fry at him. He starts laughing, but it's interrupted by a loud yowl as the cat goes running off down the street.

Layna huffs and turns to Blake. "Look, you insulted the poor—"

"Wait, stop," Des says, suddenly tense. He rises from the chair and they all stare at him for an instant suspended in time. Layna's balloon pops over her head and everyone jumps out of their seats. A finger of chilly fear runs up Layna's spine and explodes across her skin.

Something is watching.

"Everyone project into the Ouroboros, *now*," Des commands.

Harkin looks around at all the people. "But everyone will—"

"Just do it!" Then, turning toward the host in the doorway, Des yells, "Mac!"

The man named Mac nods and closes his eyes.

They all cross simultaneously into the Ouroboros, where they are greeted with a hair-raising sight. Amidst the thronging crowds of grey, slow-moving figures, at least twenty humans are eclipsed in the shadowy darkness of an umbra.

Layna and the others raise their hands in defense and stand back-to-back with each other in a circle. Mac has crossed over after them and remains alert and ready to fire from the doorway of the restaurant. Layna's palms begin sweating in anticipation of her lucetelum, and her heart threatens to beat out of her chest. She's never seen so many umbrae gathered together, not even on the cruise ship, and she has a feeling the experience is not new only to her.

The umbrae have them completely surrounded in their own orderly circle, all of the eclipsed humans turned inward to face their group of five. But they remain at a distance, motionless, not one of them advancing. No vortex appears, no shadowspear is launched. The umbrae just continue to stand there, watching them through the dark, pitted eye sockets of their human counterparts.

"What are they *doing?*" Blake whispers, his voice unsteady.

"Don't know, but none of you are staying here to fight," Des sputters. "There are too many. Go back and get help. Mac and I will hold them off."

Yeah right, Des. "Don't be ridic—"

"Look!" Molimo breathes, pointing to one of them. The shadow is dissipating fast. Not just around that one, around all of them, simultaneously. They are retreating...voluntarily.

"What the..." Des murmurs. In seconds, the world around them is all shimmering grey innocence, with no trace of an umbra. "Let's get back."

The four of them place their hands on Des' shoulders, and he returns them to the arena. Harkin collapses to his knees, and he sucks in deep breaths between expletives.

Blake glances at Layna, his eyes searching hers to be sure she's okay. She nods and moves a step closer to him. "That was beyond disturbing," she says to the whole group as she tries to rub the goosebumps from her arms. "You okay, Harkin?"

Expletive. "Sure." Expletive, expletive. "I'm fine."

"I'm so sorry I put you lot in that position," Des says darkly. "I wouldn't have suggested it if...I mean, with the way things have been, I didn't think..."

"It's not your fault, dude," Molimo says, his big, brown eyes filled with empathetic concern. He places a meaty hand on Des' shoulder and pats it gently. "Don't beat yourself up so much."

"Agreed," Blake adds. "And what do you mean the way things have been lately? Something new?"

"Aye, well...since the attack two days ago, the umbrae have...disappeared."

"How d'ya mean?" Harkin asks from the floor.

"Just that. There have been *no* umbrae encounters since the attack. Not anywhere, until this. They've bloody *vanished* from the Ouroboros. It's unheard of."

"What does it mean?" Layna asks, though she thinks she already knows the answer.

"Most of us think it's the calm before the storm. When we expel them, they're weakened and can't return to influence their human counterpart for days, sometimes weeks or even months if it's a very weak umbra or strong Naut. It's like they're saving their strength, reserving themselves...for the breach."

They lapse into an apprehensive silence as recruits gradually begin returning from the mess hall, the chatter of a dozen different languages echoing across the arena.

"Well, obviously I've got to go inform the Consulate about this," Des finally mutters. "And unfortunately, this probably means no more surface time."

"Glad I got one last cig," Harkin says despondently. "Thanks."

"Wait, Des," Layna says before he can port away. "What did that guy do? The one you yelled to. Mac, was it?"

69

"Aye, Mac. He's the owner of Mythos. He has a manipulative divination ability like Lucien."

"Manipulative?" Blake questions, prompting a flabbergasted look from Harkin.

"You guys haven't studied the types of divination abilities yet?"

"Manipulative," Des confirms, disregarding Harkin's interjection. "Most Naut divination is in the typical realm of extra-sensory perception. Whether past, present, or future, you're just seeing or sensing stuff. And then some, like the Augurs who work for DARC, have defensive divination abilities. But the blokes with manipulative abilities can *alter* perception. Mac is an illusor. He just entered his dream-state right quick and sent out some brain waves to those in the vicinity so that they perceived us exiting the restaurant normally rather than disappearing. He's quite good in a pinch."

"Well, shit. You know what else is good in a pinch?" Blake remarks. "The whole 'Limits' thing you explained to us back in North Carolina, where we're supposedly able to sense the umbrae when they're close by. So why did like twenty eclipsed not set off the radar for *any* of us?"

"Yeah, and why didn't my telesthesia alert me to anything like last time?" Layna asks.

"It's a fair point," Des says with a frustrated shake of his head. "I can only assume it has something to do with the fact that Erebus was using these umbrae to observe through their counterparts, not to attack like last time. But this behavior is as new to me as it is to you. The fact that umbrae are being *used* for anything at all is just bloody outrageous. Remember, until days ago, all the umbrae could do was influence their

70

counterpart in carrying out the Chaos that was already in their minds. I reckon the Consulate won't have anything but guesswork either."

"That's reassuring," Harkin scoffs, "given that they're the ones supposed to know everything."

"Well, let's not lose all faith just yet," Des replies. "The more information they have, the better. So you all sit tight, and tell Selene I've gone to see the Consulate and to start the fitness program without me. Wish me luck."

"Luck," Harkin mumbles as Des disappears. Layna and the others look down at him, and he looks up at them with an exaggerated sigh. "Guys, we're so screwed."

71

CHAPTER

The sweltering Grecian sun shines through the pines, and the light dances across Layna's skin as the towering trees sway in the breeze. She closes her eyes, tilting her head up toward the sky and allowing the warmth of day and the smell of the sea to wash over her. Blake materializes at her side, and without a word, they walk uphill through the familiar pinewoods of Lycabettus Hill toward their spot near the summit.

Since they arrived in Oneiropolis twelve days ago, these pinewoods have become Layna and Blake's private refuge. After the umbrae incident in the Plaka, the city is off-limits to recruits. Initially, all surface time was prohibited, but a mere four days of irritable teenage tantrums got the all-powerful Consulate to change their minds and grant some limited surface time in designated areas.

The pinewoods of Lycabettus Hill have no crowds, really hardly any people at all, especially up near the summit. Tourists use either the cable cars or designated trails to reach the top. Blake and Layna's spot on the grassy ledge at the foot of St. George's church would be difficult to reach without porting, given the vertical drop of the cliff face below them and the foundational wall of the church above. Regardless, since the first day, none of the recruits, nor any Nauts anywhere, have seen or sensed a single umbra. They remain in the netherworld, gathering strength. Waiting.

Layna ports to the ledge and takes a moment to soak in the view. She can just see over the tree line to the spectacular sight of Athens spread out before her. Lycabettus Hill is the tallest point in the city. And as they learned from Des, the hill lies over the Citadel of Oneiropolis below, which once was the tallest building in its city. The land has simply grown over it—a fact that has escaped the detection of ambitious archaeologists and the general public thanks to some advanced augury tactics.

A blanket of green sweeps down the hill toward the city that encircles it. The city is like the dreamscape of a child, an untidy patchwork of sun-kissed structures in pearl and cream and peach stretching out to the sparkling Aegean Sea. And to the southwest, in the middle of it all, is another patch of green boasting the sheer limestone cliffs of the Acropolis with the Parthenon perched atop. No matter how many times Layna has seen it all, this vantage point of the city always fills her with awe and a renewed determination to keep on fighting through the intense training in the tunnels below.

Blake sits next to her, setting down two plates of food he snagged from the mess hall as Layna unfolds the crude map of Oneiropolis. The map is their own creation, starting out as a rudimentary outline of the major structures of Oneiropolis one day over lunch, and has become their little shared lunchtime project. Though they are sure maps of their underground city exist somewhere, creating this one is a welcome distraction from the usual crushing responsibility and impending doom. They leave all that down in the tunnels when it's just the two of them up here on the hilltop, looking out over the city and working side by side in comfortable silence.

"I need another piece," Layna says, as she takes a messy bite of her gyro and spills tzatziki sauce down the front of her purple tank top. "Oh, crap."

"Can't take you anywhere," Blake teases, as he rips a piece of paper out of his sketchbook. Layna hastily rubs a napkin on her shirt and then tapes the new piece of paper to the top corner of the map. She closes her eyes, reimagining the dimensions and location of the new tunnel she discovered during oneironautics training that morning. Her sketches are nowhere near as artistic and detailed as Blake's, but the dichotomy gives the map an endearing sort of quality.

It's grown quickly, thanks to the increasing intensity of their training. They've moved on from jail tag to timed travel courses that Selene and Des have designed throughout the underground maze of tunnels, which the recruits practice in both their waking and dreaming hours. The map now reveals the Citadel at the center, with tunnels—formerly streets—shooting off in all directions. The arena is located to the southwest of the Citadel, just beneath the Acropolis. The mess hall is to the east of the arena, the recruits' bunkers are to the north, and the Guides' bunkers are to the south. In addition, they've mapped at least a dozen other massive halls and around fifty smaller spaces, which they've assumed were meant to be residences back in the day.

The church above offers little shade at this hour, and the sun beats down on them as they work. Layna already has a deep tan from their lunches on the hill, and Blake's copper skin has turned to a light, toasty bronze. Their time in Athens has flown by in a blur of activity, but it's also hard to believe they've only been here for two weeks. With much of their days spent in OB time, it feels more like several months. As a Naut training for the apocalypse, it seems time has truly lost its meaning.

As she glances at Blake now, Layna notices how much he's already changed since she met him. He has grown taller and sprouted muscles in his back, arms, and chest. She can see them moving under his characteristic black t-shirt as he leans forward to sketch another tunnel at the top right corner of the map. She thinks of that day in the school hallway when she first saw him, not even a full month ago in home time. The scrawny and insecure boy who tried to block out the world with his giant, red headphones. Even the way he carries himself is different. It's a confidence, she thinks, that comes with knowing your purpose in life. A sucky purpose, but a purpose all the same. How quickly both their lives have changed since that day.

Layna has registered new strength in her own body too. Yesterday, after taking another mediocre shower under the trickling stream in the girls' bathroom, she stood in front of the single, cracked, full-length mirror. Several of the girls managed to convince Phoebe to confiscate it from an abandoned apartment building above. As Layna brushed her hair in the dim light, she noticed muscles in her arm that weren't there before. She carefully peeled back the towel wrapped around her and was shocked to see the same transformation in the muscles of her stomach, back, and legs. It was no wonder, the way Selene was working them.

The combat fitness program she designed with Enzo is some Frankenstein monster of cross-fit boot camp torture. All recruits participate in that part of the program together after lunch. The Guides port equipment—dumbbells, kettlebells, ropes—from one of the storage rooms to the arena for the first part focusing on calisthenics and aerobic training. The second part takes place in a smaller chamber to the west of the arena that the recruits call 'The Rig' since it's where the rigs are set up for the pull-up bars, posts for racking weights, and barbells and plates and rowing machines.

Each day, combat fitness is slightly different, and each morning, it's a different part of Layna that wants to die. Each night, she falls asleep within seconds, and before she knows it, she's in deep sleep and consciously projecting back in the arena with a gaggle of other recruits. Sometimes they do the travel courses, sometimes lucetelum practice. Occasionally, if enough members of First Class are around, they slip in another game of jail tag. But one thing none of them have done in their dreams is sense any umbrae within the Limits around Oneiropolis. Their continued absence gnaws at Layna with each passing day.

"Blake?" she murmurs.

He looks up at her with a smile, and she doesn't want to say anything that will make it go away. It's a rare bird, difficult to capture and impossible to keep.

"What's up?" he asks.

"We've been here for almost two weeks," she says, as she remorsefully watches the smile fade from his face.

"And not a word from the Consulate," he mutters.

Layna nods. "I just thought they would have figured out what the full Prophecy meant by now, or at least found a way to make weapons. It seemed like Selene and Des thought we wouldn't even have this long to prepare. There can't be much time left."

"I know," Blake agrees. "And have you seen the way the Guides look at each other? It's like they've all lost hope. And how hard Selene has been pushing us to learn the multiluce…it's like she thinks that's the only thing between us and death."

Layna and Blake, along with Harkin, Aysel, Molimo, and Zahra each managed to produce lucy-bombs last week, though none as powerful as the one Des produced on the ship. They've now been grouped together to practice the multiluce, which seems to Layna to be about one hundred times harder. It's basically a group bomb—an expulsion of lucetelum from a collective of Nauts. It requires not just working together physically, but also 'aligning your minds' as Des would say, or 'becoming one mind' as Selene explained. Next level stuff.

Zahra was put in First Class with them, along with Zain, when they both ascended on the second day of training. As of today, sixteen other recruits ascended and have been moved into Second Class.

They're now being led by Phoebe—who turns out to be possibly the most patient person Layna has ever known—while Enzo continues to work with the remaining Activates. The rate of ascendance would be impressive under any circumstances. But there are still nineteen Activates training under Enzo, and Selene is now splitting her time between First Class and the remaining Activates to move them along.

"Guess we should prepare for death then," Layna mumbles. "I think we're the problem."

"How do you figure?"

"Aysel and Zahra still obviously hold a grudge against us for whatever happened in the Activate attack. Or against me, at least." Layna reluctantly spent one more wakeful night in the bunker with them until the third day when Jae Lyn mentioned she had a spare bunk in her room. Layna switched without telling Selene or her bunkmates, but so far there are no complaints. Likely her former bunkmates are as pleased by the transition as Layna is.

Instead of the pressing awkwardness, Layna now ends her days with Jae Lyn's beautiful stories about growing up in Wuzhen, China, a water town on the Yangtze River that sounds nothing short of magical. In return, Jae Lyn wants to hear every last detail about Caledon, New Jersey, which must sound horribly mundane in comparison. At first, it was painful for Layna to speak about home, but as the nights wore on, she found it therapeutic to trade little bits of their past lives from opposite sides of the world.

"That's on them, then," Blake replies. "If anything, they should be grateful. You're the reason they're alive."

"They're alive, but we don't know what happened to them or who they might have lost. If you had been on your own in the attack, wouldn't you hate the person who got extra help from the Consulate? I think I would."

Blake's hand stops moving across the paper as he seems to consider it, but he doesn't respond.

"Maybe we should just tell Des to put us in the other lucetelum group," Layna suggests.

"*Zain's* group," Blake mutters under his breath.

"What?" Layna asks, incredulous.

"Nothing. Let's give it a couple more days, see if we can get a multiluce. I'd hate to start from scratch with a new group. And we'd have to wait for all of them to produce bombs first."

"Alright," Layna concedes, as she tries to concentrate on the map. But she can't ignore the tension between them. At first, Layna found Blake's prickly jealousy endearing, but now that Zain is in First Class and spends more time with them, it's just grown infuriating. Who could possibly find time for jealousy at a time like this?

At noon, Layna and Blake grudgingly port back to the arena for their hell-inspired combat fitness. But it's late afternoon when they head to their next, even more dreaded session of the day: mental training. Or as Des prefers to call it, Armageddon meditation. It's the last session before dinner, which gives them an hour of recuperation before their lengthy evening training in the *Aetherem*, ancient martial arts techniques used by Nauts in battling the umbrae.

They were introduced to the Aetherem as the origin of many other martial arts, with the greatest parallel to Tai Chi, a later, human iteration of the ancient methods based on the flux of light and dark—yin and yang. Both methods share the goal of maximizing the flow of the energy force, which ancient China labeled *chi*. It almost seems like Tai Chi is what the Aetherem might look like if you were watching humans do it through the OB time lag.

All the recruits join in on that training too, but unlike combat fitness, they practice it within the Ouroboros. It's Layna's favorite part of their training, learning to move the way she has seen Des do when battling the umbrae. And it comes almost as naturally as oneironautics did in the beginning, like her body already knows the movements and she's simply remembering them.

The Aetherem is also the only session that Selene and Phoebe teach together, both of them being Aetherem masters. There is something beautifully primal about the movements they teach. And although Selene is generally exhausting in her rigidity, she seems to become a different person when she's around Phoebe. Layna even caught her smiling once. Watching the two of them perform the Aetherem in the Ouroboros is like watching an ancient firefly ballet.

Armageddon meditation, however, is far from beautiful. It wasn't part of the original training program, but Des was able to convince the Consulate that it could be the difference between life and death for many. It's something he's trained in himself to deal with the emotional weight of his divination power. He started with First Class as a trial run, but he's pressed to have them institute a similar training for all Nauts, since they are all susceptible to the same new vulnerability. Now that Nauts are capable of being eclipsed, it exposes their inner darkness as a weakness. Des is working to train First Class in subduing their dark thoughts and emotions, not entirely, but just enough to prevent them from being *consumed* by darkness, even for an instant. Because an instant is all it will take.

While Selene initially considered it a 'spurious waste of time', she and the others aren't as intimately familiar with Erebus' new ability to eclipse Nauts. All have heard it is now possible, but none know the truth about Darcie. None know the personal cost like Des, who lives every day in the shadow of her death.

At first, it was just your basic meditation training, clearing your mind and deep breathing and such. Then, a few days in, Des raised the stakes. Just as he did with Blake on the train, he began sharing readings with each Naut that he got from their personal items. He focused on memories he thought would invoke dark thoughts. Not everyone reacted quite as well as Blake did the first time. When Des first attempted it with Harkin, he got punched square in the jaw. Harkin did not look sorry. But sometime over the course of the next week, it actually started to work. They were learning to control their emotional and physical reactions to the stimuli, to steady their heart rate, slow their breathing, and refocus their thoughts. Selene, sometimes joined by Phoebe, has even taken to sitting in on sessions over the past few days, wearing an inadequate mask of indifference to cover her obvious curiosity.

Though they all started getting better, the training itself wasn't getting any easier. Layna has re-experienced her time at Mount Hope, has repeatedly watched Joe die in Trent Park, and has relived her own near-death experiences with the umbrae in the alley and on the cruise ship. Thankfully, Des has yet to make her relive what happened with her friends on the bridge. And once that time comes, Layna is sure she won't be able to handle it. She won't be able to control the guilt and grief that lingers just beneath the surface of her mind.

As the members of First Class arrive, Des announces to the room, "Oy, listen up! We're going to do things a bit different today." He paces in front of them, looking much scruffier than he did upon their arrival, his green eyes tired and haunted. It has not escaped Layna's notice what Des himself is sacrificing by putting all thirteen of them through the traumas of their past. Reading their objects and sharing his readings with them over and over. For their safety, he is doing something he's always worked to avoid to maintain his own sanity.

"I was hoping this problem would solve itself, but seeing as nothing appears to be improving on its own, I've got to step in," Des grumbles, massaging the bridge of his nose. "If there's bad blood between some of you, which there is, it ends today. I don't care whether you think it's warranted or not. What I care about is that you get over it. Right now. It's doing nothing but putting you all in danger. We are *Nauts* for mercy's sake. We are a team whose roots go far deeper than the anger and resentment you're feeling. And frankly, you're driving me bloody mad. So today we're going to get this out in the open and move on. Alright?"

All thirteen recruits remain silent as Des walks around the room and begins placing them in pairs. Layna finds herself standing across from Aysel while Blake is on the other side of the chamber standing across from Zain. Des pairs himself up last, with Selene, who stands across from him looking skeptical and annoyed.

"Alright," Des barks, "antagonize one another."

There are a few confused looks exchanged around the room before Selene's voice rings out, loud and clear. "You are an arrogant, pig-headed man!" The insult is intended for Des, and he seems to have been expecting it.

"Aye, fair enough!" Des shouts with an affirmative nod. "And you are an intolerable, uptight priss!"

Layna realizes that this is the exercise Des has intended for them. Her face falls from curiosity into dread as she slowly shifts her gaze from the pair at the front of the room to Aysel's stone-cold stare across from her.

As the room erupts with heated accusations and declarations, Des leaves his post and begins circling the room, spurring them on. "Get angry, let it out!" he yells. Layna can't hear what Blake and Zain are saying, but she sees Zain hold up his hands in defense as Blake lays into him about something. Next to her, Harkin and a boy named Elior are going at it.

"You aren't trying hard enough and you're going to end up getting us killed. Do you think this is all a big joke or something?" Elior asks in Hebrew.

"I know perfectly well what a big, stinking pile of shit we're in, man. I'm a Naut too, in case you hadn't noticed from up there in your ivory tower," Harkin scoffs. "You think you know everything just because you read a bunch of history books. Sorry to tell you, but there ain't nothing in your books that's going to save us."

Layna and Aysel still have not said one word to each other. Layna opens and closes her mouth, but she can think of nothing to say.

83

The truth is, she has nothing personal against Aysel. What is she supposed to say? 'Please can you stop hating me?'

Before she can think of anything, Aysel finally opens her mouth and roars something in Arabic.

Layna has become so accustomed to her eerily composed and mysteriously quiet demeanor that her sudden intensity forces her back a step. Her outburst seems to surprise the rest of the room too, and they all simultaneously fall quiet.

Then, Layna's brain reluctantly translates Aysel's words. *It is your fault my father is dead.*

She did lose someone in the Activate attack. Her father was killed, and she blames Layna, maybe rightfully so. The image of Jim flashes through Layna's mind as she feels a coldness seeping into her heart. How she wishes she hadn't been right.

"Thaddeus is *my* representative, and if he was focused on looking out for his region like he was supposed to, my father might still be alive!" Aysel shouts, moving toward Layna. "Thaddeus was gone to protect *you*, and by the time Meira organized a response, my father was already dead. Because of you!" she finishes with a hard shove to Layna's chest.

"Hey!" Blake shouts from across the room as he takes a step toward them. "It wasn't Layna he was helping, it was me. And if it wasn't for Layna, you would probably *all* be dead. She's the only reason we had any warning at all."

"Blake, don't," Layna murmurs. "Aysel, I am so sorry about your father. I never would have—"

"*No.* You do not get to apologize to me," Aysel sneers. "Just because you are Lady Anora's, and it was you who saw it happening, does not mean you should get help that should have been mine."

"I know. You're right," Layna replies, holding her hands up in surrender. "I didn't ask for any kind of special treatment. I swear I don't know why it worked out that way. If I could go back…" Layna trails off. Nothing she could say could bring back this girl's father. And if she *could* go back and keep Thaddeus in Region Two and Nuru in Region Three, would she? Would she really have risked the safety of her own family for a stranger's family because it's what was right?

"She's telling the truth, Aysel," Des says softly next to them. "Layna didn't even know who Thaddeus was when he showed up. If you're going to be mad at someone, which you have a right to be, then be mad at the Consulate. Whatever happened, it was their decision where to send themselves, not Layna's. It was their failure of an organized response—or rather, our failure as an Order to respond to this threat—that caused the loss of life."

"That means nothing coming from you," Aysel mutters. "You are her Guide, no?" Her voice is still tinged with anger and accusation, but the rage has gone out of it. She just wants someone to blame for all the pain she's feeling. Layna does too, and she knows just where to place it.

"No, forget that," she interjects. "There's no point being mad at the Consulate either. I don't blame you for resenting me. But you, me, the Consulate, we're all on the same side, and there is just one thing to blame. *Erebus.* Erebus took your father from you, and it took my friend from me. The Order was unprepared for that attack because we didn't know how strong Erebus already was. But if Erebus can turn us against each other like this, it only gets stronger. It weakens us. It wins. Right now, we all just need to focus on destroying any chance Erebus has to cause more pain and death. And when this is over and we've won, you can go back to hating me all you want."

Aysel stands there and eyes Layna indignantly, but she doesn't say anything further. Neither does anyone else in the room, but Layna can sense a subtle change. She can feel the barriers between them all breaking down. Even if her plea has not reached Aysel, she hopes it has at least made the others less skeptical of her and Blake, and each other. She looks to Des, whose face betrays just the hint of a smile as he walks back toward the front of the room.

"That's enough of that for now," he says brightly. "Everyone feel free to take a seat across from your partner. This time, instead of antagonizing each other to invoke anger, I'd like you all to try to invoke a fear response by focusing your conversation on the coming war. You will work to control your fear as you do this, and help your partner control theirs. Let's begin."

Layna sits with Blake on the floor of his bunker as they await his three bunkmates and Des to show up for divination practice. Although they don't officially have any training scheduled after ten p.m., they're all supposed to engage in practice on their weakest skill before bed. Divination is not meant to be one of these, and Layna and Blake initially spent extra time studying the Aetherem, as they were months behind the other recruits in learning those moves. But now they save Aetherem practice for their dreams after Des suggested they focus on divination, given how it came in so useful during the last attack.

Even though Layna was told it would happen, she still can't believe how little sleep she actually needs each night, especially since she's spending all her deep sleep to continue her training. Nevertheless, she feels just as refreshed on three or four hours as she used to on eight.

Des appears in the bunker and sits across from Layna and Blake, clearing his throat. "Sorry about that bit before," he says, glancing up at them. "I just couldn't take it anymore. I knew Aysel blamed Layna for her father's death, and Zahra for her sister's injury. I knew the others resented all three of us for what they believe happened. It just needed to be out in the open, in an organic way. You get me?"

Layna nods. "Yeah, it was smart, Des. Besides, they kind of had a right to be mad."

"Well, that's the other part I wanted to—"

Des is interrupted as Molimo appears and takes a cumbersome seat on the floor. He is followed soon by Zain, and then Kiran who is accompanied by Ellen. This is a first. Kiran and Zain usually join their informal divination practice only because they bunk there, but neither one has a developed divination ability yet. Kiran usually remains silent up in his top bunk, listening to Des but not partaking in the conversation. Now, he and his training partner, Ellen, both offer Des brief smiles before porting to the edge of the top bunk to await his instruction.

"Alright, brilliant, everyone is here," Des says with a delighted grin. "Let's begin."

Then, as exactly no one expected, Harkin appears in the midst of their increasingly cramped bunker.

"Bloody hell, look who it is," Des says, his grin widening. "I'm going to have to move this to one of the chambers if anyone else shows up."

"Hey…" Harkin says, looking awkwardly around the room. "Think I could join the divination practice tonight? I've had enough extra fitness training to last me a lifetime."

"Well, look at that," Des says, with a theatrical glance at his watch. "Only took you two weeks to get over yourself and ask for help."

Harkin offers an uncharacteristic smile and snickers lightheartedly. "Yeah right, let's see what you think you know about my divination ability and then we'll see who helps who."

"Oh, so you've come here to help *us*? How magnanimous of you. What's your big, fancy power then?"

"I am a precog," Harkin crows. "An alter-precog."

"Bugger off, you're not serious," Des replies, sounding genuinely impressed.

"Serious as a freaking heart attack."

"Why haven't I picked up on that in any of my readings, then?" Des asks.

"Well, that'd be why I'm here. Haven't really gotten the greatest grip on it yet. I mean…okay, I have no idea what I'm doing, man."

Des chuckles and looks at Blake and Layna. "Harkin claims to have one of only two abilities that sees into the future. Blake's being the other one, of course. And as an alter, he can see others' futures, rather than his own, which is the more usual form of precognition."

"Yo, Blake is a mancer?" Harkin asks in surprise. "I don't think I knew that."

"Oneiromancer, yeah. Pretty sure I've mentioned it, mate," Des says impatiently.

"Oh. Sometimes I don't listen when you talk," Harkin says with a shrug. "Must be the accent."

"So how does yours work for you, Harkin?" Molimo interrupts before they can devolve into bickering.

Harkin shrugs again. "I mean, it seems like I've got to be touching the person in order to see anything. And it's only hours or so into the future, far as I can tell. It's actually only happened twice, and I wasn't even trying, or expecting it."

"It happens when you're thinking about that person, not yourself as you relate to that person," Des explains. With a laugh, he adds, "And since you're hardly ever not thinking about yourself, it hasn't happened very often."

"You got that right," Harkin says with a smirk. "Ain't nobody more important to me than me."

Blake snorts and buries his face in his hands as he breaks into exhausted laughter. Layna watches him in amusement as he tries to stop, clearing his throat and straightening up. "Sorry, Harkin, it's just...do you have any idea you're training to probably die in the apocalypse for the sake of all of humanity right now?"

89

It seems Blake's delirium is contagious, and a state of collective, feverish laughter ensues. The kind that breaks down walls, settles fear, stirs hope. Layna only now realizes how long it's been since she's laughed, and it's clearly something they all desperately needed. Maybe the world isn't doomed. Maybe they will all survive this. In this moment, it actually feels possible.

"Alright, alright," Des says finally, as he smothers his grin and raises his hands. "For Harkin and Ellen's sake, I'll briefly review what we've learned so far, and then we can—"

Des is cut off by yet another intrusion. "Oh, sod off!" he exclaims, throwing his hands up in defeat. But they all turn to find the large, muscular figure of Enzo towering over them. The tiny room is so crowded now that Enzo has to grab the sides of the bunks to keep from toppling over onto the group packed onto the floor. Des looks at Enzo expectantly, eyebrows raised and lips pursed as he waits for him to speak.

"The presence of all Nauts is requested in the Consulate Chamber," Enzo announces in his native Zulu. He nods to Des, confirming what he is wordlessly asking, and then he vanishes.

"Alright, you heard the man. To the Citadel, all of you," Des says, as he too disappears.

CHAPTER

They all reappear in the Ouroboros, and the Consulate members are present in the chamber, bustling about in their gold and blue robes, gathering objects and speaking in hushed whispers with one another. Layna spots Lady Anora, who appears to be doling out instructions to the others, the Dream Book glowing like a sunset in her arms. Layna hasn't seen her since the last time she was in the Consulate Chamber on the first day in Oneiropolis, and the difference in the woman is striking. Before, Lady Anora was somehow both delicate and strong, but this woman standing before them looks so frail that a harsh wind could shatter her. Her once radiant, golden-brown skin is sallow, and her grey eyes are glazed with exhaustion.

Emotions war for supremacy inside Layna's mind at seeing the state of her mentor—concern and betrayal, admiration and anger. But it's a remarkably deep-seated affection that prevails over all else. It seems Lady Anora senses it, and she looks up sharply, instantly finding Layna, Blake, and Des among all the arriving recruits. Her eyes soften, and there is a wordless exchange between the four of them. A sort of tenderness and yearning. Yearning to return to North Carolina and pretend that no trust was ever broken, that their lives are not in imminent danger, that the universe is not about to come to an end. To play The Beatles and cook dinner together and sit on the back porch overlooking the ocean. To still believe the world is made of magic.

When all the recruits appear to have joined them, Lady Anora steps away from the other members of the Consulate. Without ceremony or introduction, she makes the announcement. "My fellow Nauts. Brothers and sisters. We have found a way to weaponize the Order."

Layna exchanges an exhilarated look with Blake as the recruits break out in shouts and cheers, but Lady Anora raises her hands to cut off the celebration.

"We have limited time. Another chance will not arise for several months, at which point, in all likelihood, we will have missed our opportunity. Furthermore, every Naut must individually go through the ritual to receive their weapon. All Nauts have been called to the Citadel. If you do not participate tonight, you will not have a weapon to fight Erebus."

She doesn't wait for questions or reactions, returning to the basin with the other Consulate members. The Ouroboros fills with a chorus of soft popping sounds as the veteran Nauts begin to pour into the Citadel from around the globe.

"Des, how do they all know to come?" Layna whispers.

"See that lanky bloke across from Lady Anora? That's Siraj, representative of Region Three from Algeria. He's a powerful sender telepath. He can't hear thoughts, rather he can send them to other Nauts. He just made an announcement in the minds of the whole Order simultaneously. Just heard it myself a minute ago. They must've decided to spare the recruits since it's a bit off-putting if you're not expecting it."

"On the ship…that's how Nuru knew there was an attack in Region Three."

"Aye, that was Raj calling for backup. He'd also alerted all Guides that there may be an impending attack on their Activates after what you saw during your impulse. The Guides were meant to follow up with their Consulate members if it seemed the attacks were actually transpiring so Raj could alert the whole Order. Unfortunately, it was just much bigger and faster than any of us could have anticipated, and we lost our opportunity at a coordinated defense. In truth, Layna, they should have taken your warning more seriously. Perhaps next time, they will."

Layna looks up at him, her eyes widening at the implication. "Damn, Des…you better hope there's not a next time. I don't think I can handle that kind of responsibility ever again."

Des pats her on the shoulder, and they turn their attention back to the basin, where the Consulate has dropped each of their pendants to form the undulating white fire. The twelve members clasp hands and begin softly chanting, the harmony of a dozen distinct dialects blending together like a symphony.

Soon, the massive chamber is filled to the brim with thousands of glowing Nauts from all over the world. They pack themselves into the dozens of balconies overhead and pour out into the smaller chambers of the Citadel. The sight is both breathtaking and humbling, and for the first time, Layna is filled with a profound sense of pride. These are her people now, the defenders of Earth, and there is so much power in this space that she can feel it vibrating inside her blood and her bones.

The chanting at the center of the chamber changes in cadence as several of the Consulate members pick up small, stone mortars and dump the contents into the fire one by one. Lady Anora then picks up two objects from the ground—a blade and an empty mortar. She doesn't even wince or cease in chanting as she slices her hand open with the blade and drains a small stream of blood into the mortar. She then passes the objects to Maven, her Region Six nyx partner with the electric-blue hair, who Layna learned a little about from Molimo.

Maven is a scry, her specific divination ability being the use of maps to locate other Nauts or events. Molimo met her only once, just after the Activate attack. He told Layna she was one of the most fascinating people he's ever read—layers upon layers of emotional turbulence packed neatly into a cool exterior, like 'a Russian nesting doll you'd definitely want to grab a beer with'.

Maven repeats Lady Anora's action, and the blade and mortar go around to all twelve members, not one of them so much as flinching as the blade punctures their skin. Layna does plenty of flinching for them though. She's always been a bit squeamish at the sight of blood.

The objects are handed back to Lady Anora, the mortar now filled with the blood of the Augurs. Lady Anora grasps the handle of the blade and thrusts it into the center of the white flame in the basin with her uninjured hand. The Consulate begins another chant, deeper and more urgent than the last, as Lady Anora slowly pours the collected blood over the blade, coating it as completely as she can. The blade and the surrounding flames both begin to glow a pulsating crimson.

As the Consulate's chant stops abruptly, Lady Anora stiffens, dropping the empty mortar from her other hand. It goes clattering across the stone floor, echoing off the walls in the sudden silence. Lady Anora lets out a small gasp, and next to Layna, Des takes a step toward the basin, but Enzo puts an arm out to stop him. Des glares at the larger man but yields, his hands balled into fists at his sides.

The red flame in the basin swells until, without warning, it explodes in a brilliant wave of heat that surges through the room, knocking Nauts off their feet. Blake catches Layna as she topples backward into him, and she manages to keep her footing. She meets his eyes and sees her own cautious thrill reflected there. She can almost sense the rise in his pulse and the coursing of adrenaline through his veins. *Everything* is riding on this.

They turn back toward the basin to find that Lady Anora is the only Consulate member who remains standing. The others rise to their feet as the blade in Lady Anora's hand begins changing—elongating—as tendrils of blood-red fire work their way from the blade up her forearm. Her face is contorted in pain, but she doesn't move.

Layna's sense of exhilaration becomes mired in fear as she watches the fire spread. Is it going to consume her mentor? What if this ritual requires Lady Anora to sacrifice her life? Layna knows that she would do it without a second thought if it meant giving the Nauts a fighting chance.

Layna looks frantically at Des, whose eyes are locked onto Lady Anora in horror.

"We have to do something," Blake whispers anxiously from behind Layna.

Layna's mind races for a solution, but she knows there is nothing the two of them could do. The Consulate would never allow them to interfere. But apparently, Des isn't thinking through things quite so rationally. He shoves Enzo aside and rushes toward the basin. He barely gets a few feet before Enzo grabs him from behind, pinning his arms roughly behind him, ready to tackle him to the ground.

"Wait!" Layna yells. "Des, look!"

The tendrils of fire have stopped spreading up Lady Anora's arm. Instead, they spread outward, forming what appears to be an elaborate handle. Lady Anora releases her grip, and the small, pulsating, red blade she originally held clatters into the basin. But the new weapon remains attached to her. She swings her arm out away from the fire, and the weapon changes in color to match her aura. It's a beautiful thing, made of shimmering, golden light that looks almost solid against the grey of the Ouroboros. An elegant hilt resembling two intertwining snakes coils up her forearm, and the long, narrow blade extends several feet from her body.

"This," Lady Anora begins breathlessly, but triumphantly, "is an aetherblade. From what we understand of it, it is quite powerful, harnessing the capability to destroy both shadow and light. It can be conjured and wielded only by Nauts, thanks to the balance of light and dark within us. The blade is an extension of our very Aether, and once you conjure it, it will be as much a part of you as your own limbs. From this day on, so long as you are in the Ouroboros, you will be able to call upon it.

"We must work quickly, now. The Dream Book uses the word 'nychthemeron' for this ritual, which means we will have a full day and night. Each Naut must conjure their aetherblade before the second sunrise. After the Consulate, we will proceed by region with the veteran Nauts first, and finally with our newly ascended Nauts. Activates, I am very sorry, but you are not yet capable of conjuring an aetherblade."

The nineteen Activates start throwing a bit of a fit as Lady Anora's words are translated to them. Guides lead the despondent bunch away from the chamber as Lady Anora lowers her weapon and closes her eyes in concentration. The aetherblade makes a soft, sizzling sound, and after a few seconds, it begins to fade and then disappears.

"Each Naut will approach the basin and take hold of the conduit-blade," she continues, opening her eyes. "It will burn, but it is a passing pain that will cease the second the process is complete. Do not drop it. You must wait until your aetherblade has fully formed because you will not have a second chance. As you saw, it takes but a minute or so. However, that is a minute times thousands for each Naut to go through the ritual, so I recommend passing some of the time in the homeplane as we will be here for several days in OB time. Once you conjure your weapon, see one of the Consulate members to instruct you on sheathing it as I just did. We have no time to lose. Region One, please come

97

forward and be ready once the Consulate has completed our conjurings."

And so it begins. Despite Lady Anora's recommendation, the Nauts largely remain in the chamber, even those who have already conjured their weapons. It's clear everyone is aware they are witnessing one of the most monumental events in all of Naut history. Many leave to take sleep breaks, but they return by way of conscious projection. There is a subtle difference in their auras when they do, a tell-tale sign of conscious projection that Layna only notices now as she is physically projecting at the same time. It gives the conscious projector a more ghostly appearance. Less solid. Like the sparklers she used to light on the Fourth of July that always left an ethereal trail across her vision.

After a few hours in OB time, Selene and Enzo suggest that the recruits return to the homeplane for the night, since they will be the last to conjure their weapons. Layna makes a feeble attempt at sleep in her bunker with Jae Lyn, who shocked everyone two days ago by becoming the youngest Activate ever to complete ascendance. But it proves nearly impossible for either of them to shut down their brains or their mouths about what is happening a few tunnels away in the chamber. They can't even get into a deep enough sleep to return to the chamber in their dreams. So after a few solid power naps, they both give up and head back, finding most of the recruits have done the same.

Nauts stay not only for the thrill of it all, but also to provide some much-needed moral support. Though it was somewhat subdued for the Consulate, as each Naut takes the conduit-blade, it is clear just how painful the conjuring truly is. A number of veteran Nauts nearly drop it within the first few seconds. They see it through perhaps thanks only to the cheers of support from their comrades spread across the floor and up the walls of the chamber.

As Region Six is finally wrapping up, Layna sits nearby in a circle with Des and their lucetelum training group as they engage in anxious banter to pass the time.

"It's true," Harkin argues. "Hemera are almost always extroverts and nyx are introverts, just the way it is. They both have tell-tale characteristics. I could have labeled every one of you in the homeplane without ever having seen your auras."

"You cannot just group everyone together, Harkin," Aysel retorts in her rich, native Arabic. "That is discriminatory. Just because I am nyx does not mean that you know me." Next to her, Zahra nods enthusiastically in agreement.

"You just don't like it because you don't like the idea that you're not unique, that you're just as predictable as everyone else. But let's see how well I know you. You got crazy emotions goin' on in there, but you know how to hide it. You're a recluse, prefer being on your own. And you definitely have a creative streak, like singing or painting or writing or some such whatever. And you'd rather people see you as mysterious than let them know any actual true thing about you, ever. Closed-book type. Am I right or what?" he asks the group with a smirk. "How 'bout you other nyx. Blake? Molimo?"

Blake just offers an uncomfortable smile, but Molimo nods, looking impressed. "I mean, I used to be a pretty shy guy until my divination power kicked in and everyone's emotions took over my life. But now that you mention it, there could be a pattern there."

99

"Damn right. And how about the hemera?" Harkin continues. "They're always real open and have like a kind of magnetism about them. Center-of-attention kind of peeps. They suck at lying because it makes them uncomfortable. They're always needing affection, ain't good at being independent, they need a squad, y'know? Layna, Zahra, Zain? How am I doin'?"

Layna doesn't think she likes this simple categorization of her personality any more than Aysel does. But she can't deny that it hits home a little. She exchanges a look with Zain, and they simultaneously give each other a shrug.

"Yes, Harkin, you are very wise," Zahra says with a playful smirk. "Oh! Well, look at that. I guess I *am* quite comfortable with lying."

Harkin crosses his arms in protest as everyone else breaks out in laughter. "It's an interesting theory, Harkin," Des says with a warm grin. "But it's a bit of an oversimplified categorization. People are both more *and* less complicated than you give them credit for."

"Yeah, how's that work?" Harkin says indignantly. "What's that even mean?"

"I think it means that on the surface, we all have so many intricacies and nuances that cannot possibly be put into simple-minded, little categories," Zahra interjects. "But deep down, every one of us is exactly the same—same energy. Same dream-dust."

"Dream-dust, I like that," Des says with a laugh. "May steal that one from you, Z."

"You are welcome to it, Desmond," Zahra says, her cheeks blushing ruby as she examines her hands folded in her lap.

"Yes. Harkin, you do not know what you speak about," Aysel adds with a dismissive wave of her hand.

"Listen, girly, I'm your elder, I've seen more of this world than you have," Harkin retorts. "And *oh*, that's right. I'm also a precog."

"Please," Aysel says with a snicker. "You are only one year older than I, and you lived in an insular research institution most your life. You have not seen *any* of the world. And you do not even know how to use your divination power, so do not pretend that gives you an advantage over the rest of us."

"Now, now. Don't be jealous just because you're a dyad. I didn't make you that way."

Aysel tenses and punches him hard in the arm, suddenly done playing around.

"Jesus, woman," Harkin mutters, rubbing his shoulder as cheers explode around them. Layna turns away from their argument to watch the Naut at the basin who is struggling to complete the last moments of his conjuring. He is shaking from head to toe and shouting German obscenities as beads of sweat roll down his temples. Layna joins in as the cheering gets louder and the hue of the blade begins to cool. The Naut finally drops the conduit-blade and stumbles backward to admire his handiwork. A bulky longsword the color and depth of sapphires.

Each aetherblade is a variation on the last. The size, style, and shape vary for each conjurer. Layna can't prevent the irrational butterflies of anticipation born in her gut as she wonders what she will conjure.

As the applause dies down and the next person in line steps up to the basin, Layna turns back to the group to find Aysel fuming in

101

silence as Harkin and Molimo compare life on a reservation to life in an Icelandic research facility. Layna thought Harkin was joking when he called Aysel a dyad, but she wonders if he must have been right. Aysel doesn't have a divination power yet, but that's not that uncommon. Maybe there is a way to tell if you are unlikely to develop one.

Aysel notices Layna watching her and narrows her eyes in disdain. She rises and disappears without a word. Layna deflates, sighing in defeat. Yet another setback after she thought she'd made progress with Aysel earlier.

Zahra catches Layna's eye and gives her a little half-smile and shake of her head. At least she seems to have forgiven them for what happened. Layna returns a grateful smile as cheering erupts around them again. Layna applauds the latest conjuring at the same time she notices a Naut port across the chamber to a large, metal chest. He has been frantically scribbling notes onto glowing parchment, and he now pulls out several more sheets before porting right back to continue his scribbling. Layna recognizes him as the same guy who was taking notes during their meeting with the Consulate when they first arrived. This time, there are two others with him.

"Des, who are those guys?" she asks.

Des follows her gaze to the frantic scribblers. "Oh, them? They're the scribes," Des answers. "Nauts with the divination ability of psychography. In addition to being able to read Kosmoli like the rest of us, scribes also have the ability to write it. Well, imitate it at least. It's their responsibility to document Earth's Naut history as a secondary source of the Dream Book. Poor blokes also have to make copies of our history from the Book as it's written, which is quite a bit harder than you'd imagine. Even though our whole history fits into the Dream Book, copied it takes up volumes and volumes of text, enough to fill most of the Records Chamber, actually."

"Does that include the mysteries too?" Blake asks.

"No, not even the scholars can transcribe the mysteries. It's been tried, but it just can't be duplicated in writing."

"Why is that?" Zain asks.

"I don't know…it's a mystery," Des answers with a wink.

Zain laughs at his bad pun as Layna asks, "Who are the scholars?"

"The best scribes usually go on to become scholars, those who dedicate their lives to understanding Kosmoli on a deeper level so that they can study the mysteries. It's pretty common for scholars to become Consulate members someday. For some reason, they have a better chance of achieving augury on their divination power than others. You can say being a scribe puts you on the fast track to the Consulate."

"Sounds like something I would never want to do," Harkin says disdainfully. "All that reading and writing, blech. Who would want to live their lives like that? No wonder they're all scrawny and pruney."

Layna shakes her head at him. "No one liked you much in school, did they?" she jokes.

"Actually, they loved me. I'm a hemera like you, remember? Hemera are likable," he says with a toothy grin.

Layna laughs and retorts, "You must be the exception to that rule." But as frustrating as he may be, Harkin *is* likable for some reason, once you get to know him.

103

Layna notices that Molimo is no longer joining in the conversation, his eyes trained on the floor in front of him. "Molimo, you okay?" she asks over the revival of applause.

When he looks up at her, she is surprised to see a tortured look in his eyes. "I don't think I can do it," he says in a low voice.

Of all the recruits, Layna certainly hadn't expected Molimo to be one to chicken out. "It'll be okay, Molimo. I'm nervous too, but it only lasts a minute or so, and then it's over."

He shakes his head. "It's not the process I'm worried about..."

"You don't want to use it, do you?" Des says softly, glancing up at him with understanding.

Molimo nods. "I just don't think I'll be able to do it when the time comes."

"Why the hell not?" Harkin demands.

"Don't you know what we'll be doing with those?" Molimo murmurs. "We're going to be killing *people.* That's what Lady Anora meant when she said they're weapons that destroy both shadow and light."

Harkin looks stunned, and Layna feels shame welling up inside of her. She already knew this. She sees Blake cringe and knows he too had set aside what Des told them about the weapons before they came to Athens. It's all they've hoped for these past weeks, and in her angst and excitement to have a weapon to fight Erebus, Layna lost sight of what it would mean.

"What are you talkin' about?" Harkin asks.

"He's talking about the incidental effects of the weapon," Des explains with a heaving sigh. "Light and shadow can't exist without the other, as you know. These weapons will *destroy* an umbra, not simply expel it back to the netherworld as our lucetelum do. If we destroy an umbra..."

"We destroy its human counterpart. We *kill* them," Harkin concludes.

Des gives him a solemn nod.

"Uh, incidental, my ass, man!" Harkin retorts, his knuckles cracking as his fists clench in his lap. "And when, exactly, was the Consulate planning on telling us?"

"The veteran Nauts are familiar with the concept. We were meant to tell you all tomorrow during training with the weaponry."

"And they expect us to just be okay with this?" Zain adds hotly.

"No." Selene speaks up for the first time in hours. Layna almost forgot she was there, sitting a little ways away from the rest of the group with Phoebe by her side. Selene conjured a blue sabre early on in the marathon ritual, with a curved, single-edged blade coming to a pointed tip at about two feet in length. Phoebe went shortly after her and conjured two golden daggers with intricate handles, one appearing in each hand as she completed the process.

"No one is okay with this," Selene continues. "We do what we must. We fight not only for the good of this world but the good of all worlds. All life. If Erebus is able to destroy the light of the Earth, it is said to be the end of everything. None of us wants to kill. It is against our nature even to think of ending the lives we are meant to protect. But we must remember what we fight for."

They all fall silent, and then suddenly it's Des' turn at the basin. Layna and Blake follow him to the front of the crowd. They cheer him on with the rest of the recruits and all of Region Six as he grabs the conduit-blade. He handles it with little difficulty, even flashing them a pained grin as his arm shakes with effort. His aetherblade is an unwieldy weapon, two inches broad, double-edged, and nearly four feet in length with a simple, down-sloping cross hilt. Once it transforms into its vibrant, gold hue, he heads right back to Layna and Blake to show off the new goods.

"Was it awful?" Blake asks, scrunching up his nose in anticipation of the answer.

"Nah, it was a breeze," Des says with a wink. "Just keep your mind on the end-game and remember what you're getting out of it. An honest-to-goodness claymore, this," he murmurs, holding his aetherblade with two hands and eyeing it in delighted reverence. "Just like my ancestors used—human ancestry, that is. This thing is bloody fantastic." The adrenaline of the moment seems to have erased from his mind the sobering conversation that took place just minutes ago. Layna takes a deep breath and prays she can do the same. *For the good of the worlds*, she reminds herself.

When it's time for the newly ascended Nauts to conjure their weapons, the recruits stand gathered around the basin. Jae Lyn is the first recruit from Region One to step up. As fragile as a gold leaf in the midst of the towering Consulate circle. As soon as she grasps the conduit-blade, she cries out in stunned agony. Layna cheers her on with the others, but she sees her bunkmate's arm begin quivering almost instantly, and she knows Jae Lyn is not going to make it through this.

Layna glances up at Lady Anora, who has remained awake and vigilant in overseeing the whole ritual thus far. Lady Anora nods to

Layna ever so slightly, and without hesitating, Layna ports to Jae Lyn's side, grabbing her arm to steady her.

Jae Lyn looks up at her in surprise, her eyes brimming with tears and her face contorted in pain. She clenches her jaw in an attempt at a smile as her whole body begins to quake. Layna smiles back as two veteran Nauts from Region One port to Jae Lyn's other side to help steady her. They say something to her in Chinese that Layna doesn't quite catch, and Jae Lyn nods with determination, standing a little taller.

From the surrounding circle, Blake and Zahra begin to chant Jae Lyn's name. All the recruits join in, followed by all those in Region One, and then everyone who remains in the chamber, until a chorus of thousands of voices sings her name.

Finally, Jae Lyn pulls her hand away from the fire with a slim and delicate short sword and a look of triumph on her face. "A longquan," she murmurs. "It's perfect."

The room breaks out in exuberant applause at the accomplishment of their youngest Naut. Jae Lyn turns and leaps toward Layna, wrapping her arms around her. "Thank you, Layna."

"Easy, Jae Lyn," Phoebe says with a laugh from behind them. "You've got a powerful weapon there. You don't want to take Layna's eye out, do you?" Jae Lyn gives her a sparkling laugh before running off to her Region One representative to learn to sheathe her blade.

The ritual proceeds without incident through each recruit's region. Harkin curses all the way through his conjuring. Layna doesn't think she's ever seen anyone turn such a bright color red before. But he gets a sturdy broadsword out of it and seems pleased enough when he collapses against a column to admire it. Aysel receives twin ninja blades she holds in each hand, as straight and austere as the rest of her. Molimo conjures an aetherblade resembling a tomahawk, and even he allows himself a moment of pride.

Finally, it's Layna's turn. She has been waiting for days now in OB time, and she is ready to get this over with. But as she walks forward and sees the pulsating, red conduit-blade at the bottom of the basin, her heart begins racing, and a lump forms in her throat. She looks up at Blake and Des, who stand nearby, ready to come to her aid if need be. She is determined that need not be. Her eyes latch onto Blake's glowing, blue eyes, as they always do now when she is looking for strength.

She takes a deep breath and wipes her sweaty palms on her leggings before reaching into the basin. She feels nothing as she takes the blade firmly in her grasp. But the blade quickly heats up and her hand begins to prickle, and then a white-hot yet invisible flame surges up her arm.

This is wrong. Something is wrong. I'm going to die here with everyone watching.

Every one of her senses tells her to drop the blade, to run, that she is being set on fire and she must escape. She can't even feel what once was her arm. In its place is just blazing agony. She can only hope that the blade is still in her grasp. She keeps her eyes on Blake as she hears the cheering of the crowd erupt through the ringing in her ears. Then the fire explodes through her body, spreading from her arm into her chest, her abdomen, her legs. She squeezes her eyes shut against the scorching burn tearing through her insides, reaching into every part of her.

But somewhere far away, she hears Des shout, "Layna, use your training!"

It registers somewhere inside her scrambled mind, and she focuses on the outline of her body, encouraging her muscles to relax and bringing her thoughts back into focus. *This is supposed to be happening. You're not going to die. You're growing a weapon out of your damn self. It's just pain, and it will end soon.*

She takes steadying breaths, trying to focus on the feeling of air flowing in and out of her lungs. She merges with the pain, analyzing it, examining it rationally. It's unique, almost beautiful in a way. The fire courses through every vein and artery that runs through her body. She can feel it pulsating along with the blood being pumped by her heart. Her heart...she is actually aware of her valves opening and closing, the fiery blood flowing from her atria to her ventricles. She senses the power forming in her hand, and her pain becomes secondary as she sees in her mind's eye the beautiful extension of herself that she is creating out of sheer will.

Finally, her veins cool down almost instantly, and the throbbing subsides. She looks down at her hand just as her weapon turns from red to gold, and she drops the conduit-blade back in the basin. She looks up to find Lady Anora standing a few feet away, apparently having ported down from her Consulate throne sometime during Layna's conjuring, her face now melting with relief. Layna smiles brightly at her and examines the weapon in her hand, exhaling a generous sigh of satisfaction.

109

It's exquisite. A slim, double-bladed sword that extends almost the full length of her body like an elegant staff. The two blades on either end branch out in a straight line from the hilt in her hand, from which two delicate strands of light coil up around her forearm. She holds it perpendicular to her body and makes figure-eight motions with her wrist, reveling in the way the two blades cut effortlessly through the air on either side of her.

"That's definitely the coolest one I've seen yet," Blake says, as he walks up behind her. "For a second, I thought you were conjuring a crossbow or something."

A euphoric laugh escapes her lips, much against her will, as she turns to him.

"Wish me luck," he says, giving her a nervous smile.

"Use Des' training," she says, as she reaches out to give his hand a reassuring squeeze. "It helps."

"You know, you kind of amaze me," Blake says softly, before turning away from her and walking toward the basin.

Weapon in hand, she falls back beside Des, who smiles and gives her a congratulatory hug before his gaze returns to Blake approaching the basin. "Come on, kid," he murmurs to himself, his eyebrows knitting with worry.

"He'll be okay," Layna says to convince them both. She sort of wishes Blake had gone first. She doesn't like knowing what he's about to go through.

Blake reaches in and grasps the blade without hesitation, and then he stands there, unblinking, unflinching. If she didn't know him so well, she might believe he feels nothing at all. But she sees the muscles in his jaw clenching and unclenching, his eyes laser-focused on the floor, and the whiteness of his knuckles holding the blade. She knows he is doing all he can to maintain his composure, and it makes his struggle seem almost effortless.

After about half a minute, he closes his eyes, and Layna knows he's reached the melting-your-insides portion of the conjuring. She tries to ignore the knowledge of how much he is suffering, quietly admiring his steadiness, how oblivious he is to his own inner strength. A minute seems like an eternity as she remembers the scorching fire in her veins. Finally, the blade turns midnight blue, and he removes it from the fire. It's an ancient-looking shortsword, straight on one side and curved on the other. Lady Anora gives him an approving nod as the cheers of the crowd die down and he turns back toward Layna and Des with a relieved grin.

"Man, did that suck. But this thing is awesome," he laughs. "I feel like an Arabian pirate."

They all laugh a little too enthusiastically, the euphoria and adrenaline having not worn off. It doesn't wear off as they both go to Lady Anora to learn to sheathe the weapons, which, like the conjuring, is simply a matter of will. It doesn't wear off as the remaining Nauts complete the ritual, and as Lady Anora announces the day's weapons training schedule. Layna doesn't know if this unnatural feeling of elation will ever go away, like it's now a part of her as much the blade itself.

Before dismissing everyone, Lady Anora quietly scans the chamber with a look of deep appreciation. "We did it. With forty-two minutes to spare until the second sunrise," she announces with a laugh.

111

"Thank you. For your steadfast devotion to each other and to our common purpose. Together, we have just taken a significant step toward defending our world, and all the worlds, from the darkness that threatens our existence. Y'all do our ancestors proud," she finishes with a warm smile.

The chamber breaks out in applause, and then Nauts begin a chant in a hundred languages that spread through the room. The meaning soon comes to Layna, and she looks around at thousands of powerful, glowing beings as she joins in elatedly, "In the darkness, we are the light! With our blades, we cast out the night!"

CHAPTER

Though many of the recruits went to catch some sleep before weapons training began, Layna never felt less tired in her entire life. Blake suggested they go watch the sunrise, making the somewhat morbid point that the world may not have many sunrises left. So instead of heading to the bunkers, she and Blake head to their spot on the hill. They reappear on their grassy ledge just as night is greeting day. Above, the deep, blue sky still boasts twinkling starlight, but the horizon is aflame with the russet-orange glow of the coming sunrise.

The air is refreshingly crisp for this time of year, and Layna tugs up the hood of her sweatshirt. The movement has her registering yet another change in her body. Now that she's back in the homeplane, the difference is even more noticeable. The presence of her aetherblade. There is a feeling of fortified strength in her bones, not just in her right arm but throughout her body. She can distinctly feel its presence, the extra weight tugging on her like some kind of eerie phantom limb. Eerie, but even more so, it is a comfort to know it's still a part of her and always will remain a source of protection.

Layna starts to lower herself onto the grass when Blake disappears from her side. She spins around and then hears a whistle from above. She looks up to find Blake grinning down at her from the highest point he could reach—the roof of the bell tower next to St. George's Church at the top of Lycabettus. His feet dangle over the edge, and he pats the spot next to him. Layna laughs and follows him to the tower. It feels a little like being on top of the world, and she fights the urge to shout toward the sea and claim her dominion like Jack Dawson in *Titanic*.

"So, that was absolute insanity," Blake says, as Layna sits down beside him.

"The craziest."

As usual, sitting side-by-side, Layna becomes instantly aware of the microcosm of space between them, his closeness tugging at her with some magic form of electromagnetism. Feeling giddy and just a bit reckless, she leans into him, and he spares no hesitation as he drapes an arm around her and pulls her in closer. She sighs with content as she watches the fiery light of the sun peek over the horizon and spread across the Parthenon and ruins of the Acropolis. For a second, she imagines life as consisting of just this single, perfect moment. It delights her, but unexpectedly, it leaves an emptiness in her heart that she wasn't expecting.

I want more than just this moment.

She lifts her face to Blake, and he looks down at her, a warm smile playing around the edges of his lips and filling the pools of his eyes. Her heart begins pounding, and before she can ruin it with rationalization, she closes the last inch of space between them and softly plants her lips on his. She gasps as her body is rocked with an intense jolt of electricity, and Blake pulls back in surprise.

"Woah," he breathes. "That was…woah. You alright?"

But Layna is speechless, and all she can think is, *more*. So, in answer, she wraps a hand around the back of his neck and pulls him toward her, his delighted smile flashing briefly before her lips consume his. His mouth tastes sweet, and she kisses him greedily as she runs her fingers through his dark waves of hair. He caresses her face with the tips of his fingers, sending another wave of sparks skittering across her skin. She feels as though she may break apart, like a meteor shower as it enters the atmosphere, a thousand explosions of light where once was only darkness.

It's not her first kiss. The kisses she had with boys at school were hesitant, sloppy things, though certainly not without their pleasantries. But *this*. There's something else here, something new and exciting and…*magic*.

She should have guessed, with the way his touch has always electrified her skin, her senses, that kissing him would be a different kind of experience. But she knows now that she's had it, nothing will ever compare. How could it? Kisses with other boys were just that, the human part of her physically connecting with another human. She and Blake, they are Nauts, and she can feel the power of their shared energy igniting between them.

115

Her hood falls back, and Blake tangles his hands in her golden hair as he sighs heavily, moving his mouth to her cheek, then toward her neck. Tender kisses under her jawline, behind her ear, edging toward her collarbone. The sparks in Layna's body burn brighter. She doesn't want it to end. All she wants is just to sit here atop the world, beneath this sunrise, with this boy, and kiss him and kiss him for the rest of forever.

Forever, she thinks. Forever won't be very long if Erebus has its way with their world. She yearns for ignorance, wishing she could still believe she is just an ordinary girl, kissing an ordinary boy, and that they could spend together whatever remained of their ordinary lives without the knowledge that it was about to come to an end.

So, just for now, that's what Layna pretends to be. Blissfully ordinary. Until she hears voices coming from the church below. And the world, with all its flaws and fears, forces its way back into her heart.

With difficulty, she gathers what self-control she can and pulls away from Blake. An inch.

Good, now another.

Blake looks down toward the voices and then back at her with longing. He strokes a strand of hair out of her face, his gaze so intense that the world almost falls away again. But he pulls back just as two recruits from Region Five emerge from the grand, front entrance of the white-washed chapel to their left.

The two girls are speaking jovially to one another in Spanish, but they look up toward the sunrise and see Layna and Blake, smiling and waving in greeting. "Sun is up, time for weapons training!" one of them calls.

Layna nods a thank you before the two girls disappear. Layna and Blake stand up on the roof, and Layna stretches in silence. With reality settling back in, she starts to feel a creeping awkwardness.

We just made out...Yep. I just made out with Blake.

A steady heat rises in her cheeks as she steals a fleeting glance at him. She catches his eye for just a second and they both break into nervous laughter.

"Come on," he says, grinning uncontrollably as he takes her by the hand, and they port back into the dark tunnels of Oneiropolis.

Sunlight changes back to starlight as Layna and the other recruits fly through days' worth of weapons training in and out of the Ouroboros. A number of veteran Nauts also chose to train in the arena with them rather than taking part in the trainings being conducted in their regions. Those in the arena receive instruction from Jacque and Aalok, who are both masters of Aetherem.

Jacque was apparently an experienced sword fighter in his heyday but is now an overweight, loud-mouthed Parisian squeezed proudly into tight shorts and a tank top. Aalok is a guru of Kalari, an Indian martial art and one of the oldest martial arts in existence aside from the Aetherem. Like with Tai Chi, there are similarities between Kalari and the Aetherem, except that Kalari incorporates the use of weapons and hand-to-hand combat. The combination of Jacque's

117

ostentatious instruction and Aalok's sober, meditative approach makes for an interesting day of yin and yang.

Though Lady Anora told them that an aetherblade would be drawn reflexively if a Naut were in danger, they began with the practice of drawing their weapons in the Ouroboros to familiarize themselves with the sensation. Without the presence of any threat, it took a slightly higher level of concentration to draw the weapon than it did to merely sheathe it. Layna felt it might be akin to the initial efforts of wiggling your toes after being temporarily paralyzed.

Despite the difficulty, the arena was soon filled with the sizzling sounds of aetherblades flickering back into existence. As Thaddeus eagerly explained to them, this photoacoustic effect is caused by the extremely high frequency at which pure Aether enters the dreamplane, heating the air and creating an audible reaction. The blades even give off a little heat in the first second or two before dropping to match the temperature of the Naut wielding it.

To prevent injury, their instructors decided to begin the swordplay training with fake weapons, which were promptly ported to the arena from all over the globe. Layna had to tie two fencing swords together, pommel to pommel, in order to even remotely get the correct feel of her double-bladed sword. They largely remained in the Ouroboros as Jacque focused on basic footwork and how to correctly hold and swing their blades, and Aalok built on their training in the Aetherem to incorporate Kalari skill in weaponry.

As evening fell and everyone was getting the hang of their weapons, Des gently reminded the present Consulate members that detached umbrae can morph their appendages into deadly weapons of their own. So, on the Consulate's instruction, Jacque and Aalok moved on to training in dueling techniques with partners. Since no one was sure exactly what level of threat it would take for a blade to be drawn reflexively, they moved to the homeplane for dueling practice.

"En garde," Jacque shouts for the millionth time. Layna puts her right foot forward and left back, bending her knees as she was instructed. She holds the makeshift sword with both hands out in front of her, diagonal to her body.

"On my mark, partner one will advance and thrust. Partner two will parry left and counter." Then Jacque yells, "Now!"

Blake lunges forward toward Layna and thrusts his weapon. Layna slides her right foot back to meet her left and swings her blade across her body to the left to block Blake's sword.

Now counter.

She flips her right hand over her left and brings the pointy back end of her double-bladed sword forward as she lunges toward Blake. The fake sword strikes him in the gut and he plays injured, dropping to the mat in a dramatic fashion.

On either side of them, Zain and Molimo and Harkin and Elior break into laughter at Blake's theatrical death. "Dude, stop losing to her, you're embarrassing us," Harkin adds between guffaws.

Barely containing a smile, Blake closes his eyes, and with his fabricated dying breath, utters his last words, "That's…sexist." This only makes the boys laugh harder.

Layna smiles and shakes her head. "Get up, you idiot," she says lightly.

But when Blake jumps back up, his smile falters as he looks past Layna. She turns to find Selene standing directly behind her with a scowl on her face and her arms crossed over her chest.

"You think this is a joke?" she hisses.

"I'm sorry," Blake murmurs. "I just—"

"You stay here," Selene interrupts. "Layna, you come with me." She grabs Layna by the crook of the arm and drags her across the arena, right toward Aysel.

"Zahra, please go partner up with Blake," Selene commands, as she situates Layna on the mat across from Aysel. Zahra looks back at Layna with a wince of apology.

In the flickering torchlight, Layna sees a wicked smile spread across Aysel's face as Jacque shouts from the balcony, "Again!"

Layna hastily unzips her sweatshirt and tosses it aside, bringing her weapon in front of her. Aysel sidesteps to the left and Layna matches her step by moving to the right. From their time training in the Aetherem, Layna knows she is no match for ninja-girl. There's a reason Layna got that impression of her right from the start. In Turkey, Aysel trained in Ninjutsu as well as Syokan, a Turkish martial art. Before coming to Oneiropolis, all Layna had by way of background was a couple of self-defense courses in the gym classes at Caledon High. She can only hope that Aysel hasn't gotten the hang of her twin blades yet.

Jacque shouts an instruction that Layna barely registers, and Aysel lunges hungrily, jabbing with the replica blade in her left hand. Layna parries right and swings her own blade toward Aysel's head. Aysel ducks effortlessly out of its path, and though they are supposed to end there, Aysel spins toward Layna and clocks her in the eye with her right elbow.

Layna's vision explodes with stars as her head goes reeling backward. Aysel follows the blow by immediately spinning into a crouch and sweeping her leg under Layna's already unsteady feet. As she hits the mat, Layna hears the double clap from Selene, the signal to begin again.

"Remember recruits, this is training in swordplay, *not* hand-to-hand," she hears Selene shout.

Gee, thanks for the help, Layna thinks, as she tenderly touches the blossom of pain over her right eye and gets to her feet. She repositions her mock double-blade out in front of her body.

They move around each other in a circle. Aysel does not take her eyes off Layna, taking her time and waiting for the opportune moment to strike. Though they are on equal footing, Layna still feels like the prey being hunted. She is on the defense, anticipating the ways in which Aysel will attack. She needs to get her head in the game, remember the ancient wisdom of the Aetherem. You don't resist your opponent's force. You yield to overcome it. Advice easier said than done. Aysel is almost half a foot shorter than she. That's her advantage, and she needs to use it.

Layna swings one end of her sword down toward Aysel, but Aysel blocks it by forming an X above her head with her two blades. She closes the X around Layna's weapon and twists, pulling Layna forward and pinning all three blades on the ground beneath her grip. Before Layna can get back in control, Aysel balances on her hands and kicks out with her feet, both of which land hard in Layna's side.

Layna releases her weapon and doubles over, both the wind and any remaining patience thoroughly knocked out of her. With a grunt of frustration, she moves with instinct and without thought. She pushes off one foot from her crouched position, spinning sideways into the air and porting mid-leap—an Aetherem move she learned days ago. But instead of reappearing at a spot a safe distance away, Layna comes down on Aysel from above. Her legs wrap around Aysel's neck as she reappears, and using the momentum from her spinning leap, she twists Aysel down to the mat.

Aysel's eyes are wide with surprise as they latch onto Layna's. She struggles against the hold, attempting a defensive move to free herself, but instead causing Layna to tighten her grip as she rolls to her side for more leverage. Aysel starts scratching at Layna's legs in desperation, and it is only then, as Layna sees Selene making her way over to them, that her thoughts catch up with her actions.

What the hell am I doing? Horrified with herself, she releases Aysel and shoves herself away on all fours. Aysel rolls away from her, grabbing her throat as she starts coughing.

"Aysel, I am so sorry," Layna cries.

Aysel looks back at her with furious hatred, and Layna dreads having to tell Des she destroyed all their hard-earned progress with the group. But that simple feeling of dread suddenly blurs and blooms into a chilling telesthetic impulse. She's learned enough from Des to maintain her awareness when her telesthesia sweeps across her mind. So she is the only one in the room aware of the change that has occurred.

The switch is sudden, instant, and undetectable. Layna doesn't even have time to shout a warning.

A dark, tortured scream escapes from Aysel's lips as she runs at Layna. Layna wastes no time and projects into the Ouroboros. Aysel now stands across from her, frozen in the homeplane, her grey figure shrouded in the dark shadow of an umbra.

She is eclipsed.

Layna raises her hands to expel the umbra before it can launch a shadowspear. *At least while she's eclipsed, she can't possibly—*

Aysel projects into the Ouroboros.

—oh, well shit.

She looks like a full moon on a foggy night, both light and dark, glow and gloom, swirling in violent energy around her body. Both Aysel and the umbra, at once, *physically* in the Ouroboros.

Impossible. If matter can't occupy the same space…

While Layna stands in awe, Aysel fires a dark-tinged lucetelum at her. The biting pain knocks her back into the homeplane where she lands on her back. Before she can catch her breath, Aysel reappears over her and wraps her hands around Layna's throat. Layna has time only to see the surprised faces of Jacque and Selene before she projects back into the Ouroboros, further away this time. Aysel follows her in again, her indigo aura fading toward black and her eyes like obsidian marbles.

"Aysel, no!" Layna shouts as, unsolicited, she feels her true aetherblade form fluidly in her hand. But Aysel ignores her and takes a menacing step forward as her own glowing blades form in each balled fist.

Before either of them can make a move, Aysel is hit with bolts of both blue and gold lucetelum from over Layna's shoulder, and she is thrown into the homeplane. Layna spins around to find Selene in the Ouroboros with them, and further back across the sea of grey figures, Lady Anora. Selene looks shaken and crosses over after Aysel.

"Are you alright, Layna?" Lady Anora asks after porting to her side and quickly inspecting her. She pauses as her gaze lands on Layna's midriff. Layna looks down to see the same peculiarity. A flaw in her light where Aysel's lucetelum hit her. Not a dark mark like if she was hit with a shadowspear. Just...a smudge.

Lady Anora's grey eyes grow with concern as they lock onto Layna's, and Layna can tell the woman is trying to assess her with her invisible third eye as well.

"I'm alright, promise," Layna says.

Lady Anora nods and they both project back to the homeplane after the others. Aysel is on her knees on the ground with her head in her hands as Selene crouches over her.

"How is that possible?" Selene demands of Lady Anora when she sees her reappear with Layna. "And in the protection of Oneiropolis!"

"How is what possible? What just happened?" Des yells, as he shoves his way through the crowd already forming around them, with Blake and Zahra at his heels.

"I was...I was eclipsed!" Aysel cries. "I was, I felt it!"

Des and Blake both look at Layna in alarm as the room breaks out in nervous chatter. Layna knows from the frequent conversations on the topic that most Nauts still cling to the belief that the stories they've heard can't actually be true. That Erebus cannot possibly have gained enough power to eclipse Nauts. That it is impossible—since Nauts don't have a reciprocal umbra of their own—for a random human's umbra to 'jump' to a Naut through the Ouroboros. There is no way to deny it now.

All around Aysel, Nauts begin firing questions at her. "How do you know?"

"What did it feel like?"

"Where did it come from?"

"What do you remember?"

Aysel is visibly overwhelmed, and her eyes dart across the faces around her until they land on Layna. Her distressed expression melts into determination, and she rises to her feet and steps toward Layna. Blake deftly moves between them, hands clenched at his sides and ready to fight. Aysel stops in her tracks, palms raised in front of her.

"Layna," she croaks, "I...I did not mean for that to happen." Her shoulders slump and she looks down at her feet. To Layna's dismay, she buries her face in her hands and begins to sob.

Phoebe ports to Selene's side, exchanging a nervous glance with her as she goes to comfort Aysel. Lady Anora walks through the crowd, breaking it up and trying to calm everyone down.

"Aysel, why don't you take the evening off, yes? You can go rest in the bunker," Selene suggests, as she places her hand on Aysel's shoulder.

Aysel blinks in surprise at Selene's sudden benevolence. She starts to head to the back wall of the arena to collect her things as Jacque and Aalok dismiss everyone for a ten-minute water break. But she hesitates as she walks past Layna, stopping by her side. Without lifting her eyes from the floor, she murmurs, "I cannot forgive what happened to my father that day, Layna. But I am not...not *them*. I am not a monster. And I do not wish you dead. I am ashamed by my actions."

"It's not your fault, Aysel. I've felt it before too..." Aysel looks up sharply as Layna continues, "Just for a second back when I was first being activated. It's a horrible feeling, being powerless."

"All the time he made us practice," Aysel says, looking toward Des, "I thought it was just wasting our time. But...to feel it. To feel it was erasing me...*replacing* me." A tremor courses visibly through her body, and she adds, "It will not happen again."

Layna nods, stunned by Aysel's chilling description. Her own memory of being eclipsed during activation flashes across her mind. In the front hall of Brandon Bardot's house, standing across from Suzanne but also next to her, full of fury and fear. It was an unsettling out-of-body experience, to be sure. But she doesn't remember feeling an *it*, the umbra, trying to replace her. Granted, she didn't know what umbrae were then. But what if this was different? What if projecting into the Ouroboros with it still clinging like a parasite somehow made it stronger?

Aysel gives her a subtle nod in return, then spins on her heel and walks away. Layna turns around to find Blake watching her, head tilted inquisitively.

"What?" she asks.

"Did you and the crazy ninja just become best friends?"

Layna tries rolling her eyes, which causes a sharp pain where Aysel elbowed her. "Yeah, when hell freezes over," she says, gingerly touching her injured brow. It's already starting to swell and will probably look super ugly by tomorrow.

Blake reaches up and removes her hand. He brushes his fingers gently across her eyebrow as Selene clears her throat with unnecessary force next to them. Blake drops his arm to his side as Layna turns to face Selene, her cheeks darkening a shade.

"Layna, please tell me," Selene commands, as Phoebe, Des, and Lady Anora appear behind her, waiting expectantly. "The Limits was silent. How did you know she was eclipsed? Where did it come from? And how...oh, you don't know, but *how* did she physically project into the Ouroboros with it still latched onto her?"

"It was my telesthesia. I have no idea where it came from, it was just suddenly there. It wasn't like with human eclipses lately—it wasn't Erebus controlling the umbra to manipulate Aysel. It felt more like the way they normally just influence a person's actions. Like it was hitching a ride, fueling her. Fueling her rage. I think she was able to project because she was still in control. Maybe that's what it wanted."

"Umbrae don't *want*," Selene says dismissively.

"Aysel said she felt it trying to replace her. Tell me that's not an intention."

"She said that?" Lady Anora asks. "Confounding indeed how both Aysel and umbra could occupy the same physical space in the Ouroboros...Perhaps it, in fact, *was* replacing her..." she murmurs, trailing off.

Blake and Layna share a horrified look.

"We must investigate this," Lady Anora announces. "Forgive me, darlin's."

127

She disappears as Selene turns back to Layna. "And one other thing," she snaps.

Oh, right, that, Layna thinks, remembering how she lost her cool with Aysel. She readies herself for Selene's lambasting.

"What you did to Aysel…well, while clearly not warranted, that was…quite advanced. Porting mid-air to a target that precisely. Impressive, for someone so highly inexperienced."

"Not the first time, either," Des says proudly behind Selene.

Selene rolls her eyes so dramatically that they practically disappear into the back of her skull. "Don't make me regret saying it, *king of idiots*."

Layna questions her brain's translation of the insult as Des retorts, "I'll try not to, princess." He winks at Layna over Selene's shoulder even though he knows full well that Selene can see it. As a seer, she can see three hundred and sixty degrees with her divinatory third eye. It's why she is one of the most highly respected new Aetherem masters.

Phoebe places a hand on Selene's shoulder, cooling whatever fiery comeback was forming on her lips. Instead, she sighs and refocuses on Layna. "Anyway, well done," she concludes before she and Phoebe disappear.

"Two for two with the ladies today, Layna," Blake murmurs next to her with the tilt of a smirk. Then he looks at her face and his eyebrows knit with concern. "We should get you some ice," he murmurs.

"Agreed," Des says, "and ask them to do a full checkup, just to be safe after…that."

Layna wants to ask them what they think happened, what it could mean, whether it could happen again. But she finds herself suddenly exhausted, and she allows Blake to guide her to the Medical Chamber as Jacque announces a two-minute warning to the returning recruits. "Let's be prepared to get back to work," he yells above the chatter. "Lots to do before the night is through!"

That night, Layna and Blake sit in the corner of Blake's bunker during divination practice as Layna ices her black eye. In the middle of the small room, Des is working with an increasingly frustrated Harkin on his precognition while Molimo acts as the willing test subject. The aetherblade training concluded a few hours ago. They were released a little earlier than intended given that, after Aysel was eclipsed, no one could concentrate worth a damn. That and the fact that most of them hadn't slept in the past who-even-knows-how-many hours.

The Consulate did several sweeps of the Limits around Oneiropolis after the incident, but they found no trace of the umbra that had somehow eclipsed Aysel. An umbra has never, in the history of Oneiropolis, been within its walls, its presence a portent that the relative peace they've enjoyed over these past weeks is coming to an end.

Layna and Blake scan through Blake's most recent sketchbook to be sure they aren't missing any important signs about the Prophecy. Layna uses her training to try to get a telesthetic impulse linked to one of the pictures. So far, she's gotten nothing except reminders of the last couple of weeks. A picture of Selene barking orders at them. A picture of a dead-end tunnel in Oneiropolis. A picture of Athens from atop the hill. But also, she's admittedly a little distracted.

She and Blake sit side-by-side, just close enough for a brush of an arm against an arm, a leg against a leg. Just enough to ignite the fire in the space between them without drawing unwanted attention from the others. It is at once torture and pleasure, satisfaction and frustration.

There are more sketches than Layna thought there would be given how little they've been sleeping. But since they arrived, Blake has developed some control over his oneiromancy. He's learned how to retrieve his flashes at will during that edge-of-sleep dream state they use to project physically into the Ouroboros.

Layna has improved on her telesthesia too, both learning how to maintain control during the unprompted impulses and learning to summon them. Although, specifics are still rough. Given her past ability to sense events in the netherworld and the current importance of precognition of upcoming events, Des has been working hard with the two of them, and now Harkin, to get them to where their abilities can be of use to the Consulate.

"Whether or not you can change what you see in a vision depends on how big the desired change is compared with your sphere of influence," Des is explaining to Harkin.

"What's my sphere of influence?"

"Well, it's like time and space. How much time you have before the event and where you are situated relative to the event. You know, like if you touch someone and get a vision of them accidentally stepping out into traffic. That's a fairly isolated incident that's within your sphere of influence if you stay with them until you can stop it. If you see a vision of a nuclear bomb dropping on that person's head, that's a complex event outside of your personal sphere of influence. You, Harkin, can't bloody well stop the bomb from falling. Though you may be able to at least get that poor bloke somewhere else."

"So...your answer is yes, I *can* change the future," Harkin bluntly concludes.

Des sighs. "It's not really changing the future, mate. The future is what it is. It's prophetic visions themselves that are subject to change. It's all probabilities. What precogs see is the most likely possible version of a future moment out of the infinite possible versions of that moment. So it's *practically* certain...but not quite. Just barely not certain enough so that someone with the prophetic means could theoretically alter the course enough that the outcome is different from their vision. Probabilities don't generally account for precognitive interference, since it's the viewing of the probabilities themselves that would invite the interference. You get me?"

"Uh...yeah, no."

As Des and Harkin continue discussing the finer details of precognition, Layna returns her concentration to the sketchbook with renewed awe for the ability. "Have you ever tried changing any of your visions?" she asks Blake.

He hesitates and then shrugs in response. "Never really been anything worth changing."

131

"What about flashes of my life, do you still get those? Can you even tell if it's happening, now that we're experiencing the same things?"

"Actually, yeah," he says, as he thumbs back through a few pages. "Like this one of you in the Records Chamber. I wasn't there during that travel course, remember?"

"Oh, right. So weird how I'm the subject. You'd think if you were seeing flashes of my life, you'd see it through my eyes, not like you were standing next to me." Then she breaks out in a grin. "Wait…have you ever seen *yourself* in one of your flashes of my life?"

Blake glances at the floor and mutters, "No, not really."

Layna raises a skeptical eyebrow at him. "What do you mean, 'not really'?"

"Well, I mean, I may have seen one or two. But, like, it was weird. I didn't draw them. It's weird to draw yourself. I don't think I could have gotten it right, you know?"

"Well, what was it you saw?" Layna probes further.

"Nothing much. One was the back of me during lucetelum training. I need a haircut."

Layna laughs, but she can tell he's purposely misdirecting. "What about the other one?"

"I don't remember. I think it was just my face."

"Well, what if it had a clue about the Prophecy?"

"It didn't."

"How do you know that?"

"It was just my face."

"Why are you being weird?"

"I'm not being weird. I just know it wasn't important."

"What was in the picture, Blake?"

"*Just me*, Layna."

"And what in the background?"

"Okay, damn! It was up on the bell tower, alright?" Blake yells as his ears begin to flush red.

Des, Harkin, and Molimo freeze mid-conversation and look over at them in surprise. Blake offers them an apology as realization hits Layna like a brick wall. She's not quite sure how to feel about this. She waits for the guys to pick up their conversation again and then turns to Blake and whispers as soundlessly as possible, "You saw me *kiss you?*"

Blake looks at her and winces. "Sort of?"

"You knew I was going to do that? You've...you've known that for like a *week?*" she continues in an increasingly aggravated whisper.

"Well, you know, it's all probabilities," Blake says with an apologetic grin.

"You...but...*I* didn't even know I was going to do that!" she hisses through her teeth. "That's totally...a...an invasion of privacy!"

Blake snorts with laughter, which infuriates Layna even more. For some reason she finds this absolutely mortifying, and even though she knows it was her decision in the moment, she can't help but feel like she's been played. Like he's just been smugly biding his time, corralling her into the location he saw in his flash and charming her into his arms. Her mind flicks through all the time she spent with Blake in the past week, now with the knowledge that all the while he knew where it was headed while she remained entirely in the dark. Her head starts to spin as the humiliation ignites a quiet spark of fury inside of her. She rocks forward and rises to her feet, but Blake grabs her by the arm.

"Wait," he pleads. "Layna, I'm sorry, don't be angry."

"I'm not angry. I just need to get some air that *you haven't breathed!*"

"No, wait, let me—"

Layna doesn't let him finish before she ports to the surface. The night air is cool on her face, and she sucks in a breath, releasing an aggravated cry at the sky above her. She pulls up the hood of her sweatshirt and starts pacing amidst the pinewoods, trying to regain her composure and sort out her feelings. There's a lot there to sort through, and she doesn't even break into the shallows before something else rises to the surface. And there in the fog of all her muddled thoughts and emotions emerges a sudden telesthetic impulse like a hurricane in her mind.

She immediately ports back to the bunker. Des, Molimo, and Harkin look up at her, but Blake isn't there.

"Where's Blake?" she asks.

"He left right after you did," Molimo says, looking at her with concern. "Layna, you feel panicked, what's wrong?"

"I'm having an impulse," she says, raising her hands to her head in aggravation. She tries to pull the impulse forward into awareness, to get to the eye of the hurricane in her mind where she can get a clear reading. "Something bad is happening and I can't fully...oh God, Des...just go to Raj and have him get everyone out of the bunkers, *now*. I need to find Blake."

Des opens his mouth to respond but she doesn't wait for it. If Blake disappeared from the bunker right after she did, it was probably to try to follow her. She ports to their spot on the hill and shouts his name. No response. Her thoughts are scrambled, clinging to the impulse as she also tries to sense where Blake is, the two subjects warring for her attention and neither coming in clearly. Whatever is happening, she can sense Blake in the middle of it.

She ports to the foot of St. George's, the white structure looming like a silent ghost in the dead of night. "Blake!" she cries.

Footsteps echo at the church entrance and she spins around to see a shadowed figure in the entrance. Her first thought is that it's a detached umbra, but she's in the homeplane so that can't be. He steps out into the dim moonlight and she sighs with relief as she makes out Blake's features. But the relief is fleeting. His face is frozen with alarm, and there is a smear of blood down the side of his head.

"Layna, run!" he yells, just as Layna sees another figure emerge behind him, the glimmer of a metal knife in his hand. She steps back in shock and bumps into something solid. A hand closes around her mouth, smothering her with a cloth. She breathes in something wet and foul and sharp, stinging her throat and lungs. The Earth starts to spin madly as nausea hits her like a tidal wave. She hears Blake shouting her name as the world falls into a still blackness and swallows her.

CHAPTER

She is roused by a groan escaping her own lips. Awareness creeps back, tethered to pain, and she longs to return to oblivion. Her brain threatens to burst from her skull, and a suffocating darkness surrounds her. As her cramped muscles jerk involuntarily, she realizes two things. The darkness is from a thick bag pulled over her head, and her hands are bound behind her back as she lies on the rough, loose gravel of the earth. A steady, brisk wind whips against the front of her, and she hears the cries of a night bird from somewhere nearby. Her mind is a fog, and she tries working her way back toward reality, toward the last thing she remembers. Blake with a knife to his back.

For a moment, all Layna can do is writhe against her binds, panic-stricken and unable to think. But Des' mental training kicks in on instinct and she steadies herself, finding the stillness in her mind and settling into it. Connecting with her breath, focusing her thoughts. The fog lingers. She's been drugged. *Come on, think. You can fix this. Step one, where are you?*

There is the sound of water carried on the wind. Not ocean waves. A distant, gentle lapping. A lake, maybe. She has no idea how long she's been out. She could be in a whole different country for all she knows. But then she hears the clanging of a church bell, once. One a.m. It sounds familiar. It sounds like the bells she's heard from their spot atop Lycabettus. She could be near Vouliagmeni Lake in Athens. One of the places they'd been permitted to visit with Des one evening early in training. If so, she is close enough to port back to Oneiropolis, even with the drugs in her system. She can port herself back and get someone to untie her once she's there. But first, she needs to figure out whether Blake was brought here with her.

"Blake?" she whispers. The sound of her own voice sears through her head.

No answer.

"*Blake*," she says a little louder. She hears a groan a few feet to her left and turns her head toward the sound, which only sends the world spinning out of control. She holds still and waits for it to pass.

"Layna?" she hears Blake mumble, followed by a retching sound.

"Yes, I'm here," she whispers. "Are you okay?"

"Well...my head is stuck inside a bag of puke, but I think so. Are you?"

"I'm okay. We've been drugged, but we need to try to port back to Oneiropolis. Think you're up to it?"

"Maybe, but...Layna, they did something back there," Blake responds groggily.

"What do you mean?"

"I think they might have set off some sort of detonation."

No. Please, no. Layna's heart freezes like ice in her chest. *The bunkers.* She felt the plot forming in her mind, though it had never become clear. Des couldn't have had much time to act on her warning. Minutes, maybe.

Steady. Breathe. "Okay...we'll just have to port above ground first to be safe, then. Our spot. Let's go," she says. She concentrates on Lycabettus and feels a weak tugging in her gut, but it fizzles. She shakes off the trepidation, collects herself, and tries again. She goes nowhere, almost as if something is physically pinning her to the spot.

"Layna, are you still here?" Blake asks.

"I...I can't leave. I can't port," she says, forcing down the lapping waves of panic.

"Neither can—"

Blake falls silent as they hear a single set of footsteps crunching across the earth toward them. The person comes to a stop just next to Layna, and she hears a man's scratchy voice saying something in Italian. He pauses, apparently waiting for a reply. The reply comes from behind them in the listless voice of a woman. The woman must have been here the whole time, listening to them.

The man snorts with laughter at whatever the woman has said, and Layna hears shuffling, followed by a thud. Then another thud and a loud grunt from Blake. With sickening clarity, she realizes that the man is kicking him.

"Stop! Stop it!" Layna cries, struggling against her binds with renewed desperation as her stomach threatens to heave up its contents.

Someone lifts her roughly by the back of the neck, setting her on her knees, and rips the bag off her head along with a chunk of her hair. From behind her, she hears the woman say, "Hello again, bambolina."

Again? Layna loses the battle with her stomach and vomits onto the ground in front of her. Her vision swims madly as her eyes adjust. Moonlight shining from above, the glow of artificial light coming from below. Layna's insides jolt as she looks down toward the light and realizes they are indeed near Vouliagmeni Lake. High atop the cliffs above it, a forty or fifty-foot drop to the water below.

Layna gags as the woman grabs the hood of her sweatshirt and drags her along the ground away from the edge of the cliff. She then shoves Layna to her knees again before circling around to crouch in front of her. Through the mess of hair hanging in her face, Layna examines the woman and the man standing in front of Blake. They both have long, black hair and dark eyes, with sharp noses and sharper chins. Maybe brother and sister, at least related. She's never seen either of them in her life.

Some twenty feet to Layna's left, two men stand in the dark, eyes trained on the ground. The younger one still wears a sunhat and brightly colored clothes with a camera slung around his neck. Tourist, by the look of it. The older one is dressed more discreetly, and something about him is familiar—not his looks, but something deeper. "Help us!" Layna cries.

It elicits no reaction from the two entranced men, but the woman backhands Layna hard across the face. She gasps in pain, swallowing the metallic taste of blood.

"Do not speak to them. I said hello!" the woman snarls. "Don't recognize me now? I know it is English you speak, I heard you."

"I don't know you. What do you want from us?" Layna spits maliciously, her courage spurred by the stinging pain in her cheek.

"We want answers," the man says, as he takes a step away from Blake. The bag over Blake's head makes it difficult for Layna to tell whether he is badly injured or even conscious. Other than the heaving of his chest, he lies still.

"You haven't asked any questions," Layna mutters through gritted teeth.

The man glares at her and then turns and kicks Blake in the side. Blake gasps and coughs, rolling as he tries pulling his legs in to protect his stomach.

"Alright, stop!" Layna cries. "Just ask me then! What? What do you want to know?"

The woman nods to the man and says something else in Italian. She turns back to Layna with a vacant expression. "Tell us how to find the gateway."

Layna's jaw falls slack as her mind races. Could these people be *Nauts*? No. If they were Nauts, she would be able to understand them when they speak Italian. And even if they were Nauts, only Blake, Layna, Des, and the Consulate know about the last stanza of the Phantom's Prophecy. It has to be a coincidence. "What gateway?" Layna asks, trying to sound genuinely ignorant.

"You know what gateway," the woman snaps. "Tell us or we kill him."

No, no, no. This can't be happening. Layna shakes her head and replies, "But...but I don't know what you're talking about!"

The woman nods toward the man, who pulls out his knife and yanks Blake upright, ripping the bag off his head. His temple and lip are bleeding, and he looks around wildly before his eyes adjust and he finds Layna. His eyes, which normally bring her peace, fill her with a crippling fear. She can't let anything happen to him.

"Final chance, bambolina," the woman sings menacingly.

"Okay, okay...Please, if you can just give me some context about what you're looking for, I'll tell you anything I know."

The woman offers an acerbic smile that sends shivers down Layna's spine. "Context, hmm? Well, let us see now, you are an Oneironaut. Yes? You and your wretched Order are trying to stop the inevitable darkness that will come to this forsaken world and spread across the Kosmos. Yes?"

Layna looks past her at Blake, whose eyes are filled with horror. The woman grabs Layna by the chin and forces her to look her in the eye.

"*Yes?*" she repeats.

"Y-Yes..." Layna responds. "Are you...Nauts?"

The woman throws her head back with a horrific cackle that ends as abruptly as it started, with not the slightest hint of humor in its wake. Something about it feels distinctly non-human. She doesn't answer Layna, but instead just repeats her demand. "Tell me how to find the gateway."

"I…but we don't *know* anything about a gateway," Layna utters, her voice trembling. "We only just joined the Order a few weeks ago. We don't know anything."

The woman sighs and cocks her head. "I think, no." At this, the man steps behind Blake and grabs him by the hair, positioning the knife at his exposed throat. Blake sucks in a breath but doesn't take his eyes from Layna.

"No! Don't do this, please. I'm telling you the truth, I swear," Layna cries. "No one knows what the Prophecy meant by it!"

"Prophecy?" the woman says, sounding intrigued and leaning in closer. "And what does this Prophecy say?"

Layna clamps her mouth shut. She's going to be sick again. The woman never said anything about the Prophecy. How could she be so careless? She wracks her brain to come up with a convincing lie as she keeps her eyes on Blake and the man who could end his life with a simple flick of the wrist.

Please, she pleads desperately to no one, *he's all I have left.*

Layna watches as the fear in Blake's eyes mellows and shifts to resolve. "Don't tell them anything, Layna, these people are not *human.*"

"Shut up!" the woman hisses at him before returning her focus to Layna. "Go on, bambolina," she coaxes.

"Layna, remember what's at stake. My life isn't worth this," Blake pleads in a feverish whisper.

The woman spins around on him. "One more word, you die, and we start *torturing* answers from her, yes?"

Blake looks steadily back at the woman, his jaw clenching and his eyes glinting with fury.

The woman turns back to Layna. "I would like nothing more than to finish what I started earlier and kill you. So...before I lose my temper...tell me what the Prophecy says, *subito.*"

Layna's eyes dart between the woman and Blake. He's right. These people are going to kill them both, in the end, whether they give them information or not. If umbrae are in control and somehow communicating through these people, telling them anything means giving information to Erebus that could be the key to destroying the universe. There is no bargain to be made. They are both going to die here tonight.

Forgive me, Blake.

"I don't know what it says. I never read it. Like I said, we're new to this."

The woman looks at her for what feels like an eternity without speaking, without blinking an eye. Then she smirks again and mutters, "Yes, I believe you."

She says something in Italian to the man, who releases Blake and steps away from him. Layna feels a hesitant bubbling of relief as the threat of Blake's imminent death subsides.

"I believe you told us everything you know," the woman continues, as she lifts Layna roughly to her feet. "So, alas, I have no more use for you. Goodbye, bambolina."

Layna's body tenses, but before she can resist, the woman shoves her toward the edge of the cliff.

"*No!* Layna!" Blake screams.

The sound reverberates in Layna's mind as adrenaline surges through her. Just before she loses the last bit of ground, she uses her momentum to push off with her legs, leaping out into the air and attempting to port again, to no avail. Blake's screams are drowned out by rushing wind in her ears, and as she falls, all she can hope is that she doesn't smash into any shallow rock below. Her stomach rises into her throat, forcing a scream to her lips that she swallows before it can escape. Instead, she sucks at the air just before she hits the water.

The impact nearly knocks the last stolen breath from her lungs, but at least she sinks into the lake without meeting any rocks. She tries to find the bottom with her feet to rebound toward the surface, but the water is deep. She thrashes and kicks, desperate, sinking.

Her thoughts scatter and land on the haunting image of Suzanne, drowned in that stupid green Camaro, her hand outstretched...

A flash of light floating in the water. A reflection of moonlight on metal.

Hunter's pocketknife.

It had been in the front pocket of her hoodie, and now it's sinking through the water right in front of her. Like Suzanne reached forward through time and space and death to place it there just for her.

Layna catches it on her foot and kicks it up, spinning in the water and just managing to grab it as it sinks into her bound hands. Her lungs begin burning as she opens the knife and slides it between her wrists. Back and forth across the twine that binds her. The twine isn't thick, and it takes only seconds before she is free and swimming desperately toward the surface, her whole body screaming for oxygen.

She isn't going to make it. She's sunk too far. Frantic, she makes a reflexive attempt at porting again. Whatever force was preventing her doing so has been lifted. But with her mind splintered in a thousand panic-stricken pieces, she merely projects into the Ouroboros where there is still no air. And there she is faced with a reality more horrifying than drowning alone in a deep, dark lake.

The black shadow of a detached umbra is there, floating in the water directly in front of her. Its arms elongate and sharpen into swords at the same instant that her aetherblade materializes in her hand. She thrusts her blade through the water toward the umbra as it simultaneously jabs its right arm toward her. Both meet their mark, and a shockwave explodes through the water as shadow and light collide.

The pain is unbearable. An icy fire where its blade meets her chest spreads rapidly into muscles, tendons, and veins. It both scorches and freezes her, and a hole of screaming agony splits her open from the inside, forcing her mouth open in shock.

Water rushes into her lungs and her body spasms as the umbra she pierced through the neck begins disintegrating in the water around her. Her body is rocked by another spasm, and then all is still.

Strange, to drown in the dreamplane. It cradles her in a silver pool, back to sleep in the dimension from which she came. Quiet. She feels a sort of peace settle over her as the lake becomes illuminated in gold and blue, and she serenely drifts off.

CHAPTER

S ea-glass eyes and auburn waves of hair. Suzanne is there,
looking down at Layna and lightly tapping her cheek. "Wakey,
wakey, Layney-daisy."

"Suzanne...?" Layna bolts up and wraps her arms around her
friend's neck with a stifled cry. "Suzanne! You're here! Oh my god, I
missed you so much."

"I know, I'm very miss-able. Now lay down before you hurt
yourself," Suzanne says, pushing her gently back down onto the stark,
white linens of a hospital cot.

"I'm so sorry, Suze," Layna cries.

"Sorry for what?"

Layna hesitates. Why does she feel so guilty when she looks at
her friend? Why was an apology the first thing on her lips? "I...I don't
remember."

"Well, then there's obvs nothing to forgive," Suzanne says with a playful roll of her eyes. Then she smiles. Not the flashy kind she'd give the boys at school, or the innocent one she'd give to gullible teachers and parents and store clerks. It's the one that was just for Layna and Kat. One that was born of sleepovers and secrets, adventures and stories, and making up after fights. Layna's heart aches with unfathomable depth to see it.

"You know I'll always be here when you need me, right?" Suzanne says, as she grabs hold of Layna's hands. "Just like you always were for me, even when that shit was totally hopeless."

"I don't deserve you," Layna replies with a smile.

"No one does," Suzanne laughs.

"But I do need you, though. I *really* do."

"Nah, you're going to be totally fine. I know it. You just have to come back."

"To Caledon?" Layna asks. "I…I don't know what you mean," Layna wheezes, clutching her throat as the ache in her chest strengthens, sharpens to a point.

"You have to come back, Layna," Suzanne says more urgently. But Layna can't seem to respond any longer. She can't even seem to breathe. Suzanne's face swims before her eyes, and as she tries to grab a hold of her, her friend disappears into a cold, inky darkness.

"Come back, Layna!" The desperation in the voice pains her. She needs to ease it. She has to get back. "Layna, *please*! Please don't leave me," the voice cries. But it's not Suzanne's voice.

Blake.

From somewhere far away, she pulls herself toward the sound. *I'm here. I won't leave you.*

"Breathe, Layna!" Another voice. *Des.*

As always, she follows her Guide's instruction. She tells herself to breathe. The pressure in her chest subsides, and there are seconds of sweet relief. But it is replaced with a horrible, biting pain around her clavicle, as though something is tearing through her flesh.

Visions of a beast with sharp teeth, chewing on her, eating her alive. For a while, she disappears into the pain, indistinguishable from it, fighting her way through it. Then, a tumult of sounds and sensations. She vaguely feels hands on her, pressing, turning, lifting. Piece by piece, she registers the rest of her body, her arms and legs prickling, her heart thumping heavily in her chest. It's a laborious process. It takes years, or hours, or minutes.

"I think she's coming around," she hears Des say.

She sucks in an agonizing breath and opens her eyes to a blur of activity. She blinks several times and focuses on the faces of Des and Lady Anora above her, and just behind them, Molimo, Zain, and Harkin. Molimo is beaming with relief as he claps Des on the back. But Des looks far from relieved, his face pinched with intensity as he looks from Layna to his watch, holding onto her wrist to check her pulse. He has a streak of dried blood in his hair and he is filthy.

Why are you covered in dirt, Des?

"Welcome back, darlin'," Lady Anora purrs, as she gently tucks a strand of hair behind Layna's ear. "You're alright now. You're safe."

Layna can't make sense of anything, and she wonders if she might be dreaming. She looks past the five sets of eyes in search of the one she needs to find. He is there, standing behind all of them with his hand clamped over his mouth. His eyes are bloodshot, and he makes no attempt to hide his tears.

Memories of the past hours flood Layna's mind as she sees the distress on Blake's face. Oneiropolis was attacked, they were kidnapped...the lake, the umbra. She was drowning. Dying. Now she's lying on the ground beneath the familiar torchlight of Oneiropolis. There is a raw throbbing beneath her left clavicle where the umbra pierced her, and her body shivers under a blanket from a dissipating coldness.

But she is alive. And so are her friends, and they're here, surrounding her, back in the place they've called home for the last several weeks. Maybe Oneiropolis wasn't attacked after all.

Blake. She mouths his name.

He responds as if he was waiting for the signal, shoving past the others to kneel at her side next to Lady Anora. He scoops her gently into his arms and she feels his body shake with a sob.

"I'm sorry. I'm so sorry," he whispers into her hair.

"Stop," she rasps, lifting a heavy hand and wrapping it around the back of his neck. Talking causes the deep ache in her ribs to sharpen to a point, searing her lungs. But she focuses on the feeling of Blake's arms wrapped around her. She was so cold, floating alone in the water. And now she's here with him.

"She's shivering," Blake says to Des.

"Harkin, can you find some more blankets?" Des asks, turning to the others. "And Molimo and Zain, will you try to get us another IV drip?" Layna looks up to find that she is attached to a nearly empty bag of the same luminescent fluid that had fed into Des' arm after he was injured on the cruise ship.

"You got it," Zain says, and they all disappear.

"Layna, I want to try to sit you up a little further," Des says gently. "Just tell me if you get dizzy or uncomfortable."

She lets Des and Lady Anora lift her, as Blake shifts behind her so she can rest against his chest. That's when she realizes that she's in the arena. There is debris lining the north end where part of the wall used to be, and it looks like most of the recruits have hunkered down here. Layna's heart sinks as she sees that several of them sit or lie wounded on blankets, as others rush around and attend to them.

"I'm just going to pop back home and make you some special tea that should help both ease the pain in your lungs and promote healing of your injury," Lady Anora says. "We Nauts are exceptionally quick healers, but this should accelerate the process."

Layna nods as she is again struck by Lady Anora's weathered appearance. The weight of the Kosmos drags heavily on her, the leader of the only Order standing between Erebus and its destruction. Before she leaves, she plants a light kiss on Layna's forehead and pats Blake's cheek with a relieved smile.

"What happened, Des?" Layna croaks.

"Someone planted a bomb in the bunkers. I went to find Raj straight away like you said, and he made the announcement. Most everyone got right out of the bunkers soon as they heard him. Enzo and I went to look for the rest just as the detonation went off, and then it was lights out for me," he says, reaching absently to the spot of dried blood on his head. "Lady Anora found me with Maven's help, and we set about finding you two."

The thought of Des brushing so close to death makes Layna's stomach tie up in knots, and she doesn't want to ask the follow-up question she knows must be next. But Blake beats her to it.

"How many recruits did we lose?"

"A few," comes Des' quiet reply.

"Who?" Layna adds reluctantly, "First Class?"

"Elior," he murmurs, swallowing heavily as he cracks an ice pack from the med kit and places it across the swollen wound on Blake's head. "Saskia from Second Class, and...seven Activates. Not all Activates can hear Raj in their minds yet. It's harder for him to reach those who haven't ascended. The detonation was just outside their bunkers. There was nothing we could do."

Blake punches the ground next to them and curses under his breath.

Nine Nauts. It happened again. She's failed them again. Elior. He was eighteen, smart, dedicated. She trained side by side with him. And the others she didn't even have the chance to get to know.

The boys return, along with Selene, and they help Des get Layna hooked up to a second glowing IV drip.

"What is it?" Layna says softly.

"It's ethereal plasma," Des replies.

"Where does it come from?" Blake asks.

"Well, you know how people make a decision in life to be organ donors? It's kind of like that, but with Nauts."

"This stuff comes from dead Nauts?" Harkin asks, as he eyes the bag of liquid in his hand.

Des shoots him a disapproving look. It goes unnoticed as Harkin begins prodding at the liquid. Des waits. Finally, Harkin perceives the silence and looks up, his face hardening with characteristic recalcitrance.

"You really need to work on your tact, mate," Des mutters. "But yes. If they've gone on the donor list and we have the opportunity to prepare for it, we are able to extract some ethereal plasma from the body of a fallen Naut during the Rite of Return. It's used solely for this purpose—to prevent the spread of darkness in injured Nauts. It's a matter of honor, and most Nauts are more than happy to donate. Without it, I wouldn't still be here, and neither..." He trails off, glancing at Layna with a pained expression.

Layna nods, unable to convey her gratitude in such a simple gesture. She's alive because her Naut brothers and sisters checked a box before they died, so to speak. She thinks of the dark mark that still stretches down Des' spine, the way the darkness had started to spread across his back before he was treated, and an icy shiver runs through her body. Her wound could have easily been fatal, and yet here she is. She feels a burgeoning affection for all her Naut brethren and suddenly realizes she hasn't seen her bunkmate anywhere amidst the chaos of the arena.

She catches Selene's eye above her. "Jae Lyn?" she whispers, still finding it painful to speak.

"She is okay, bump on the head. She asked about you also," Selene says, pointing to the south end of the arena. Layna breathes a sigh of relief as she spots Jae Lyn sitting on a mattress holding an ice pack on her head as Phoebe shines a light in her eyes.

"Recover with all speed, Layna Emery," Selene says with unusual warmth, as she drapes the second blanket over Layna. Then, immediately hardening again, she turns to Harkin, Molimo, and Zain and commands, "You three, with me."

"Yes, ma'am," Harkin grumbles, as they follow her to help with the others.

Layna flinches as Des swabs the cut on her cheek where the woman hit her. He doesn't look her in the eye, and she can sense the torment in his heart. She knows what it must mean for him to have lost Elior, having read him so many times during Armageddon meditation.

If only she hadn't gotten wrapped up in her feelings for Blake, hadn't ported away from him and forced him to follow. Hadn't put him in danger in the first place. If only she had a clear head when this was happening. A minute even, and they may all still be alive. She can't let herself get carried away with her emotions anymore. She has to use Des' training at all times, even to subdue the good stuff. Even if it means pushing Blake away.

As if he read her thoughts, Blake holds her a little tighter as Lady Anora reappears with a thermos and takes a seat next to them. She hands Layna the top of the thermos filled with a viscous, pleasant-smelling liquid. "Breathe it in some first," Lady Anora instructs.

Layna does so several times and feels immediate warming relief spread through her throat and lungs. She takes a gulp of the liquid and soon feels it beginning to dull the pain.

"Whatever this is, it's amazing. Thank you," she says with a grateful smile.

"Glad to hear it, darlin'," Lady Anora murmurs, as she places a bucket of steaming water next to Layna and soaks a cloth in it. She begins tenderly washing the blood from Layna's wrists where the pocketknife sliced skin in Layna's frantic attempt to free herself. The warmth of the water and Lady Anora's gentle touch sends grateful shivers of comfort through Layna, and she fights the sudden, overwhelming urge to sleep.

"Blake, can you tell us what happened?" Des asks.

Blake takes a deep breath. "Well, for starters, you said the explosion was just outside the Activates' bunkers. That's because it was an Activate who planted the device. He obviously must have been eclipsed. After the woman got Layna, she met him around the side of the church. Jomei, I think his name was. She handed him a device—I could tell it was explosives. I tried shouting to him, but he disappeared. That's when the guy put that damp cloth over my mouth, chloroform or whatever, and I was out."

"So they got to two of ours tonight," Lady Anora sighs. "We thought it must have been an eclipsed Naut who planted the device. Oneiropolis is well protected, and only Nauts can sense its existence and walk its halls. Preventing worldlings from getting in has always meant preventing umbrae from getting in. But clearly our protections are no longer sufficient. The darkness has found us. However, though I'd prefer to take our injured to the local hospital where we have Naut assets on staff, we have fortified our defenses around the arena. This is the safest place for y'all to be."

"What do you mean 'two of ours'?" Layna asks.

"The older guy who was up there at the lake with us was another eclipsed Naut," Blake explains. "Like a minute after you…went into the water, he snapped out of it all of a sudden, yelling, and then he disappeared. Before I could even try porting again, Lady Anora and Harkin were there grabbing me, and we were all back here."

"Aye, that was Dritan who was eclipsed," Des replies. "He's a senior member of DARC, and he's why we couldn't find you."

"Couldn't find us?" Blake asks.

"You were missing for hours. Maven, she's a scry, and she should have been able to find you with her maps, but she…" He pauses to collect himself, massaging his eyes with his fingertips. "She kept saying you must have been in the bunkers, but I kept telling her you wouldn't have been. That Layna is the one who said to get everyone out. But she said it was like you'd both disappeared from the Earth. Like…your lights had gone out."

Dead, Layna thinks. *They thought we were dead for hours.* She grabs Des' hand, and he gives hers a reassuring squeeze.

"And that's because Dritan has some sort of defensive divination ability?" Blake asks.

"Yes, Dritan has a powerful psychic shield," Lady Anora clarifies. "Think of it like an EMP—an electro-magnetic pulse weapon—but against Naut energy. It can be used so that Nauts experience the equivalent of a power outage. They are unable to access the Tripartite Powers, and this is why Maven couldn't sense your light."

"And that's why Layna and I couldn't port back here."

Lady Anora nods once. "When Dritan was able to overpower the umbra's hold and expel it from his mind, the shield was lifted."

"And suddenly, there you both were, back on the map," Des adds. "Maven, Lady Anora, and I, plus the boys, ported to you straight away. Dritan had projected into the Ouroboros to fight the eclipsed couple. And Maven and I found Layna in the Ouroboros at the bottom of the lake, aetherblade in hand, and an umbra breaking apart in front of you."

"The umbra that eclipsed Dritan must have followed me into the water," Layna says. "Maybe making sure I didn't survive."

"You fought one of those things while you were drowning and your hands were tied behind your back?" Blake asks Layna in wonder.

Layna shakes her head and then winces at the icy pain it causes in her wound. *'Fought' is a major overstatement. More like dying with a bit of finesse.*

"Just luck," she replies.

And maybe a little help from the beyond. She pictures the pocketknife that must now be lying at the bottom of Vouliagmeni Lake with the remnants of an umbra. Then, the implication of that fact hits her.

The umbra didn't disappear, it *disintegrated.* She didn't just expel it back to the netherworld, she destroyed it. That's what her blade does. And that means...

"Des, the other man who was up there with Dritan..." She trails off, unable to speak the words.

"Aye, it was his umbra that eclipsed Dritan and followed you into the water. It appears when umbrae detach into the Ouroboros, they still need to stay in somewhat close proximity to their counterparts. I'm sorry, Layna, but…he's gone. You did what you had to do, love."

Layna has to fight down a shuddering swell of nausea. Lady Anora is saying something to her, but she is lost in a single earthquake thought, and it's all she can hear.

I killed a person.

It may have been self-defense with the umbra, but that man, he didn't know what was happening to him. She saw that when she looked at him, called to him for help. One minute he was enjoying his vacation and the next he was conscripted to some evil purpose that cost him his life. At her hands. Why couldn't she have had the wherewithal to use her lucetelum instead? She looks down at her murderous hands and can't stop the tears falling down her cheeks. Blake gently wipes them away and pulls her closer.

"He was in some sort of trance," he murmurs. "Like when his umbra detached, it's like he went offline or something. And the couple that took us, I swear we were *not* interacting with humans. The way they talked, their expressions, their movements, even. It was like…an imitation."

At the mention of the couple, the connection Layna couldn't make before suddenly becomes clear. The way the woman acted, what she said. "It was the same umbra," she whispers, half to herself, then looking up at the others. "That woman, it was *her* umbra that eclipsed Aysel."

Des and Lady Anora look at her in surprise. "What makes you think that?" Des asks.

"Things she said. She knew me, said she wanted to kill me, to finish what she started earlier," Layna explains. "I think the umbrae have been scouting us, like the ones in the Plaka. I bet there were more times we didn't even know about. And then yesterday, somehow one found us down here. That's how they knew where to plant the bomb."

"Shit, she's right," Blake says with a nod. "And they knew other stuff too, Des. They were trying to get more information. About the gateway, what we know."

"What? No, no," Des responds with an emphatic shake of his head. "Sorry, but none of that is possible. Firstly, how could the woman recognize you if it was only her detached umbra you interacted with yesterday? Umbrae don't...*recognize* people. They don't speak through people, and they don't 'know' things. If you spoke with that woman, you were speaking to a human being. And no human could possibly know about the gateway. They must have meant something else, or maybe you misunderstood."

"I'm telling you, Des, it wasn't a misunderstanding," Blake urges. "This was an interrogation. They didn't just ask about the gateway, they called us Oneironauts, they talked about the darkness coming to consume the Kosmos."

"Oh my," Lady Anora murmurs to herself.

Des runs a hand through his hair, contemplative. "Alright, so maybe not a misunderstanding. But...I mean, there's no way a human would know that stuff. So, in my mind, it can mean only one of two things. It could mean that Erebus is now strong enough not only to control the umbrae from the Shadow Universe like puppets, but to cross into the Ouroboros itself and completely take over eclipsed human minds. But if the Ouroboros is no longer closed to Erebus, what's stopping it from destroying us all right now? It can't possibly have that much power here yet or the end would have already come."

The thought that she may have been interacting with Erebus itself sends a ghostly shiver across Layna's skin, and she pulls the blankets closer around her. "And the second possibility?" she urges.

"Option two, well, continuing on the belief that it's still only the umbrae who have limited access to the Ouroboros by way of the human ego…it could be the *umbrae* are able to take over the minds of their counterparts. But that would have to mean that all this time, the umbrae were not being controlled by Erebus after all. It would mean that they are themselves becoming…sentient," Des finishes without conviction.

"But you said that wasn't possible," Blake counters. "That they werc…what did you call them? Empty reflections of us. Mindless extensions of Erebus."

"Well, yes," Lady Anora responds. "Just as all life on the aetherworlds are extensions of Aether, the shadows of life on the netherworlds are extensions of Erebus, this remains true. But the scholars are now convinced that our original assumption was wrong. That Erebus could not gain *control* over the umbrae to carry out its desired actions any more than Aether could control humans, or a tree, for that matter. A tree is a mindless extension of Aether in that it is life that is not sentient. But it is still separate and distinguishable from Aether such that it could not be manipulated as if it were the limb of a body.

"However, here is the sticking point. When Layna was relaying her impulse about the Activate attack, she used a word that has nagged at me. She said Erebus was *directing* the umbrae. But one cannot direct that which is not sentient. Just as that tree could not be controlled, neither could it be directed. You could not direct a tree to give you shade. It may happen to do so as it sways with the breeze, but it's not subject to your bidding. The Activate attack was no tree swaying in the breeze. It was more akin to soldiers carrying out an order. And such a thing requires sentience on the part of the soldier, not just the general."

"It fits with what I remember from that impulse," Layna says. "That's what it felt like...an army."

"You really think it's possible?" Des asks, searching Lady Anora's eyes.

"One of the scholars proposed a similar theory to us a few nights ago. It could perhaps be the common denominator to a lot of the umbrae anomalies. Their ability to detach from their counterpart into the Ouroboros, for example. The scholars have thus far found nothing in the mysteries to sufficiently explain it. But we know that all sentient ethereal beings have access to the dreamplane as though peering through a window. The same rules would not necessarily apply to sentient *nethereal* beings. After all, they are not made of the same matter, they do not follow the same laws of physics, they are not *life* in the way we are able to conceptualize it. But perhaps sentience allows them to not only access the Ouroboros but to detach and *physically* enter it as only we have ever been able to do.

"And then, what happened tonight. Eclipsing Dritan specifically and getting him to put up his shield, as though they somehow knew it would prevent Layna and Blake from porting. And apparently remembering Layna from a prior encounter. Through sentience, they may have discovered how to commandeer their alternate's ego entirely, for a time. In so doing, they could be learning how to think and feel and remember. In other words, they could be learning how to...*be human.*"

"It's bloody madness..." Des mumbles in disbelief. Layna can't even comprehend the implications of such an evolution or what it means for the universe, and she is too exhausted to try.

"I suppose the scholars don't have any theories on *how* it would be possible that they've become sentient," Blake remarks.

"Not just yet, I'm afraid."

"Either way," Des says with an exhausted sigh, "it still doesn't explain how the umbrae or Erebus would have learned of the Phantom's Prophecy and that it mentions a gateway."

"They didn't know about the Prophecy," Layna says remorsefully as she recalls her blunder. "When they were interrogating us, I said we don't know what the Prophecy means by gateway. The way she reacted...the fact that there is a Prophecy was new to her. I'm sorry, it just slipped out. We didn't tell them anything else, not what it said. Not even when they..." She looks up at Blake, reassuring herself that he is still with her, as she recalls what she was willing to sacrifice to keep what they know a secret.

"Oh, Layna," Lady Anora murmurs, looking back and forth between her and Blake. "Neither of you have any reason to be sorry. What you did tonight...You two are Nauts, through and through. And I don't need my third eye to tell me that. The umbrae got no information of any import, and yet they know there is a gateway. Which means Erebus knows, and it is looking. We must find it first."

K.A. Vanderhoef

Des clicks the first aid kit closed. "I should try to see where else I can be of service," he says, patting Layna on the leg before setting off to attend to the other injured Nauts. Lady Anora stares after him as he goes, an uncharacteristic heaviness settling in her expression as she fiddles absently with the Consulate medallion hanging around her neck.

"Are you okay, Lady Anora?" Blake says softly.

Pulled from whatever dark thoughts were attempting to consume her, Lady Anora turns to Blake with a pained smile. "Yes, darlin', thank you. It's just, when he went back into the tunnels and that detonation went off..."

Layna reaches for her hand. "He's okay," she soothes.

"Yes," Lady Anora replies with a relieved sigh. "I don't know what I'd have done if he wasn't."

"You really love him, huh?" Blake remarks.

Lady Anora's eyes grow distant as she watches Des checking the vitals of another recruit across the arena. "Like the son I couldn't have," she murmurs.

"Couldn't?" Blake blurts, before immediately following the question with a grimace of embarrassment.

Lady Anora looks back and forth between Layna and Blake without responding. "You two should try to get some rest." She stands up and plants a kiss on Blake's forehead before disappearing.

Blake looks down at Layna with a sigh, shaking his head in self-admonition. Layna offers him a reassuring smile as he tugs the blanket up around her shoulders.

162

Lady Anora's tea has dulled the pain around Layna's chest, and her body longs for a long, deep sleep. It must be close to sunrise at this point. She can't even remember how many hours they've gone without sleep, particularly with the days spent in OB time during the weapon conjuring and training. However long it's been, it's too long, even for Nauts. But instead of drifting off, she watches everyone going to and fro with medical supplies, food and water, mattresses and blankets, as she lies there in Blake's arms feeling useless.

She thinks about Elior and the others they lost. She thinks about the man with the camera and the sunhat, tormenting herself by trying to guess his name and where he was from. What his life was like before she took it.

"Layna, can you do me a favor?" Blake whispers, interrupting her dark ruminations.

She looks up at him hovering over her. His beautiful, bloodshot eyes, the butterfly bandage over the cut on his forehead. His long eyelashes and soft lips.

"Please don't scare me like that ever again," he says with a smile, brushing a thumb across her cheek.

She returns the smile as she thinks how nice it would be to kiss him again. But she buries the desire as soon as it emerges, recalling her promise to herself. *No distractions. Distractions means people die.*

"I don't intend to," she answers. Though, it's a silly thing to say, considering the whole universe may be coming to an end shortly. "We should probably try to sleep, huh?"

Blake nods and carefully removes himself from behind her, just as Harkin, Molimo, and Zain reappear with a mattress. They all help

163

Layna onto it, covering her with the blankets and shoving a couple pillows under her head.

"What about all of you?" Layna asks.

"Ah, we're good," Zain replies with a grin. "Most of the mattresses got roasted or buried, so we're saving them for the wounded. Besides, real men sleep on stone, right, boys?"

They all nod enthusiastically.

"Well, thank you," Layna laughs. "Oh, and thank you!" she exclaims, realizing she owes them a much bigger apology. "You guys saved our lives."

Harkin shrugs. "Hey, you saved us first getting us out of those bunkers. Guess that's what fellow Nauts are for, right? Besides, it was Des who brought you back."

"Brought me back?"

"Yeah, you know...from like, the dead. After you drowned and all."

"Cut it out, Harkin," Blake snaps.

"What'd I say?" Harkin asks innocently.

"She's okay now, let's just focus on that, alright?"

From the dead. Even though Layna knew she'd had a brush with death, it didn't really hit her that she maybe momentarily *did* die. In a way, death had seemed like a relief. It was peace. No more responsibility, no more guilt or pain or anger. But there are things she isn't willing to leave behind just yet. Somewhere between North Carolina and the bottom of that lake, she started living for more than just revenge.

The others settle down around them, and Layna closes her eyes, sleep tugging on her like gravity. But in her mind, the events of the night and their discussion about the umbrae replay on an endless loop. Des returns, speaking quietly with Selene, Phoebe, and Enzo as they discuss what sounds like funeral arrangements for the fallen Nauts. She hears the rasp of Aysel's voice as she whispers with Harkin and Zain a few feet away, and she listens to the deep reverberation of Molimo's snores. Blake doesn't lie down but remains sitting beside her, watching over her like a sentinel. There, surrounded by them all, she finally lets go and falls into a deadened slumber.

Layna wakes hours later, eyes bursting open, and she sucks in the air like she's drowning again. She sits up slowly, her body stiff and her wound aching with a bitter cold. She pulls back her sweatshirt to inspect her chest and finds a faint, elastic-like scar stretching down from her right clavicle. It looks like an old, healed injury, barely even noticeable in the homeplane, but she knows what it must look like in the Ouroboros. A solar eclipse in her aura.

She swallows two of the painkillers from the bottle Des left and looks around to see some Nauts up and whispering to each other, but mostly everyone is still asleep. Des and the other Guides are gone somewhere, other than Enzo who sits among the sleeping Activates looking forlorn. Blake settled down next to Layna at some point as she slept, and he doesn't stir. She feels the need to get up and walk and breathe in solitude, but she knows they're supposed to stay in the area of the arena. She compromises and ports into the tunnel just outside the south end of the arena.

It's pitch black in the tunnel, and in the darkness, she senses the chill of the lake creeping back to try and claim her. She projects into the Ouroboros and feels instantly comforted as the tunnel fills with her own warm glow. The mark on her chest is ugly. Veins of darkness branch from the three-inch slice at the center. It *had* been spreading before they gave her the plasma. She looks over her shoulder at her back, and there is a smaller stretch of dark there too where the blade went through the other side of her.

She paces slowly back and forth, stretching both her sore muscles and tired mind. She channels her telesthesia to check for any unusual activity, something she needs to make sure she starts doing more often. She senses nothing out of the ordinary. It feels as though the umbrae have retreated again.

She hears a soft pop, and indigo light ignites and mixes with her own as she walks into something solid. Blake grasps her arms and gently pulls her back. "Layna, what are you doing out here?" He puts on an air of calm, but his voice is unsteady.

"I'm sorry, I didn't want to wake you. I just needed to stretch my legs. Feels better to move around a bit."

"That's good, but try not to overdo it. You should probably be resting. Did you take the meds that Des left?"

"Yes, doc," she says, unable to prevent the smile that comes to her lips. "I honestly thought I would feel worse than I do. I guess Lady Anora wasn't exaggerating when she said Nauts are fast healers. How are *you* feeling?" She reaches toward the cut on his forehead but stops short and drops her hand back to her side.

"Oh, I'm fine. Des checked me out. Mostly just some bruised ribs. Right now, it's my empty stomach bothering me the most. Hold on for a sec." He disappears for literally a second and reappears with his backpack in hand. He goes to sit against the wall as he unzips it and pulls out two wrapped lamb gyros and his sketchpad.

"Hungry? Had a few reserves in here," he says with a smile that doesn't reach his eyes the way it once did.

"I'm *starving*, actually. I guess dying really warms the appetite," Layna jokes.

The smile disappears from Blake's face as he looks away.

"I'm sorry, too soon," she adds with a grimace.

"It's okay. I just don't like thinking about it," he says, as he lightly brushes his knuckles across her cheek. His fingers linger near her mouth, and he leans toward her. His lips an inch from hers, Layna forces herself to turn away. She made a promise.

"I can't, Blake," she murmurs.

Blake drops his hand and stares at the ground. "Listen, I'm sorry about the picture. Let me just show you something." He opens his sketchpad and pulls a folded sheet of paper out of the back pocket.

Layna had nearly forgotten what they were even arguing about before all this. "Don't worry about it, seriously it's..." She trails off as she looks at the drawing. It's a picture of both of them, sitting against the bell tower and intertwined so that their edges blur. Lips against lips, his hand on her cheek and hers in his hair.

K.A. Vanderhoef

"I can't really explain it, but when I saw this in my flash, it wasn't your experience or mine. It was *both* of ours. Honestly...it was like the strongest flash I've ever had."

Layna glances up at him, and though she can't be sure in the glow of their respective light, she is fairly certain he's blushing. "Huh...that's new," she murmurs as she focuses once again on the sketch. The image conjures emotions that she doesn't want to feel right now, so she pushes them, and the picture, away.

"Yeah, but see, this is what I saw. So I didn't know what was going to happen, really. Whether you'd kiss me, or I'd kiss you, or what. If you hadn't done it just then, I was going to. I was this close," he says, indicating with his thumb and forefinger. "You just beat me to it, that's all. Please don't be mad."

"I'm not mad, I promise. I just...can't do it again."

She considers explaining further but decides against it. If she tells him why, she knows he'll just try to make her feel better, try to convince her she did all she could. But she doesn't want to hear it. She knows she could have done more, could have saved them all. Better just to let him think she doesn't want to. But she catches the wounded look in his eyes before he turns away, and it nearly breaks her resolve.

He nods in understanding and places the drawing back in the pocket of the sketchpad. As he does, a folded sheet of paper falls out of the back. Layna picks it up and holds it out to him, but something about it tugs at her sixth sense.

She unfolds it to see the image of a large, stone arch, in the center of which is a deep, eerie blackness. Layna can see the pitted impressions where Blake pressed his pencil hard into the paper as he

168

drew the void. In front of the arch is a young boy facing toward the darkness with his hand outstretched in front of him. "Blake, what is this a drawing of?"

"Oh, that," he mutters, holding out his hand for it. "That's nothing, it wasn't from a normal flash. Just something I draw sometimes."

"It's not nothing..." Layna urges, the impulse getting stronger as she examines it.

"Yeah, no, it's just a stupid memory. Remember that recurring nightmare I told you about that made me sleepwalk as a kid? The one I was having when Billy...Anyway, this is what I used to see. With everything that's happened, it sort of popped back up out of my subconscious, and I felt the urge to draw it out. It always used to help to put it on paper, but not this time. After I drew it, I couldn't even look at it." He holds out his hand again, but Layna doesn't relinquish the sketch.

"Just give me a sec..." She clears her mind and concentrates on the image, and the impulse hits her almost instantly. It takes her breath away, but she is now more prepared to absorb the force of it. She breathes deeply to maintain her awareness, pushing through the eye of the storm to the part of her consciousness that is traveling far away from the darkness of the tunnel. Part of her is aware of her lips moving, speaking what she is sensing. And then the impulse has passed, and she knows the true significance of the picture. And so does Blake. He is staring at her, horror-struck, and they both lean in to find the date on the picture.

It's going to be too late.

169

There's a soft pop as Des appears before them. "Oy, what the bloody hell do you two..." He stops as he sees their faces. "What? What is it?"

"Des..." Layna breathes. "We need to see the Consulate right away. We found the gateway."

PART II

"You will never do anything in this world without courage. It is the greatest quality of the mind next to honor."

- Aristotle

CHAPTER

Thank you for your votes. By unanimous consent, we shall now hear from our witnesses, Layna Emery and James Blakely Knox, on the matter they wish to bring before us."

Once again, Layna and Blake find themselves before the intimidating, glowing figures of the Consulate. This time, Layna is sitting, as Des insisted on bringing in a chair for her so she wouldn't exert herself. But she is about to leap from it any second out of sheer exasperation. She doesn't understand why they have to keep sticking to these archaic rules when it's something this important. She could have just come out and said what she needed to say, without all the stupid formalities.

"Like I said when I came in, we found the gateway," she cries.

"Yes, and you stated that you wish to present a drawing?" Lady Anora's voice is steady, but Layna can see her apprehension in the way she sits at the edge of her throne, hands clenched tightly in her lap.

Layna nudges Blake with her elbow and he pulls the folded sketch out of his pocket and stands there holding it awkwardly out in front of him.

"I ask the Consulate that we accept this drawing as part of the tangible record as to which our witnesses wish to speak," Lady Anora announces. After a full infuriating minute of waiting to see if any Consulate members are going to flip their medallions, Lady Anora declares, "By unanimous consent, we shall accept the drawing as tangible record in this matter."

The Consulate members all port down to the basin and Lady Anora takes the paper from Blake with an apology in her eyes. It is passed around to each member, and when it is handed back to Lady Anora, all twelve return to their regal perches.

"Please continue with your account," Lady Anora instructs, as she settles back into her seat with Blake's sketch in hand.

"I drew that from one of my flashes. From my oneiromancy, I mean," Blake explains. "I've actually been seeing it since I was a kid, so I didn't think anything of it."

"And just now, I got a really strong telesthetic impulse when I held it," Layna adds. "That's a picture of the moment that the gateway will open."

"This archway depicted here, you believe this is the gateway of the Phantom's Prophecy?" Lady Anora asks, as she continues to inspect the drawing.

173

K.A. Vanderhoef

"No…not the archway," Layna says hesitantly, "…the boy."

Lady Anora looks up sharply. She examines Layna, her eyes growing more concerned with each passing second. "The gateway…is a child," Lady Anora confirms.

From the deadened silence that follows, Layna gets the impression that this is absolutely not good news.

"Please tell us what you experienced in your impulse, Layna," Lady Anora urges.

"Well, I didn't see the boy as he's drawn in this picture. Because I can only sense what's happening now. But I know it was *this* boy. He was sitting and playing outside, looked like a normal little kid, maybe four or five years old. Then the vision changed. I was still looking at him but this time from the Ouroboros, and his aura was blinding. I saw a solar eclipse once. This boy's aura was just like that. At the very center was darkness, but all around him was a bright, white light, way brighter than the dull, white aura of other humans. And it…well, it *hummed.* With energy. It felt powerful."

Lady Anora presses a fist to her lips as Layna recounts what she saw. Even after Layna has finished speaking, Lady Anora stares intently at the ground, lost in contemplation. After a minute of silence, she murmurs, "Thank you, Layna. I would like to open the circle to questions for the witnesses."

With her words still echoing across the chamber, one of the hemera Consulate members rises to his feet. "Witness, was this boy's anomalous aura the only thing that led you to believe he is the gateway?" He is a stern-looking, old man, tall and slender with a long nose, thinning, white hair, and a cultivated Australian accent.

"No, I mean, what I saw was part of it, but my impulses are more than just visions of something. It's hard to explain, but I can also sense things—"

"I know how telesthesia works," the man interrupts. "What did you sense?"

Layna glares at him and replies, "When I looked at the boy, I sensed...Erebus. Kind of like before the Activate attack. But this time I felt it searching. And I felt that I'd found what it was searching for. Like a strong urge to hide the boy, to protect him. Because there's something else that still needs to happen before Erebus can sense him too. Like...I don't know how else to say this, but something that will *open* him. His mind."

Thaddeus stands. "If I may, Lucien, I think we know to what the witness speaks."

At the mention of the Australian man's name, Blake recoils as if someone has slapped him. This is Lucien, the Consulate member whose power of oneirokinesis stole their lives from them. They said he was a good man, and Layna knows now is not the time to be making enemies of her superiors. But she can't prevent the immediate sense of loathing that bubbles up inside of her.

"We have discussed at length the disappearance of the umbrae from Earth this preceding fortnight," Thaddeus continues. "We believe this is a matter of the umbrae preserving themselves. But, whether in intention or only effect, our world now grows heavy with light. I proposed this may be accelerating us toward the spark—the phantom's spark that will break the balance as foretold by the Prophecy. I believe

175

what Layna senses coming is that very spark. Once that spark is ignited, the gateway will open in the mind of this boy…this *anomaly*."

"Yes," Maven agrees, rising to her feet next to Lady Anora. "Moreover, Layna said he is around five years old, just the age that a child typically develops their dream-ego, giving them the ability to consciously observe the Ouroboros through dreams. Perhaps once *this* child develops his dream-ego, it will not only give him access to the Ouroboros but will unlock the Ouroboros to Erebus once more."

A number of Consulate members nod in agreement, but one hefty man stands in protest. "We're wasting time. It doesn't matter what Erebus is or isn't waiting for," he says in Russian. "*We* do not need to wait for anything. If it is the gateway and we've truly discovered it, it must be destroyed immediately."

"*What?*" Layna exclaims. "Destroy it? It's a *him,* not an *it,* first of all. And second, he's…he's just a little boy! You can't just kill him."

"I'm sorry, witness, but you seem to have lost sight of what we are discussing," the Russian man retorts. "The existence of this gateway means the destruction of *the universes*. Sacrificing one human life hardly seems to matter, even if it is a child. It must be found and terminated. I ask that we put this to a vote at once."

The Asian woman seated beside him stands next. "I agree with Urie," she declares in Mandarin. "This is what the Prophecy directs. We have no choice but to destroy this gateway."

"Wait, wait," Layna pleads. "I know what's at stake, but I also know that we are not *supposed* to kill him. He has to live. And besides, the Prophecy says to close the gateway, not destroy it."

"We have no idea what the Prophecy means by closing the gateway," Urie argues. "Ying Yue is right. This is what the Prophecy asks of us. We've run out of time to ask questions. We don't know how much longer we have until this boy develops his dream-ego. It could be any moment now. We *must* act."

"That's not true!" Blake practically shouts. Urie looks affronted, but Blake quickly continues, "It won't be any moment. We do know how long we have. I drew that picture four nights ago, and it's always six days from my flash that whatever it is happens in real life. We still have two days to figure it—"

"May I remind you that it is now late morning? Meaning we have begun the fifth day, and we could have no more than twenty-four hours," Urie replies.

"Home time, yes. That gives us plenty of time to at least have a conversation about it here in the Ouroboros," Raj says in Arabic, standing abruptly. "We should take advantage of this information, try to find an alternative before we resort to destroying this child when we have reason to believe that would be detrimental."

"Your 'reason to believe' is rather weak, though, Siraj," Lucien retorts.

"I disagree," Nuru adds in his brusque Kenyan-English. "I believe Layna's telesthesia is quite strong. And it should be given deference, regardless of her age. But, Layna, can you tell us why you believe it's worth the risk?"

Layna opens her mouth and then closes it. She's thrown by the way he asked for her opinion, like she's an equal. And it's a totally legitimate question, one she can't answer with *because I say so*. All she

177

knows is the second she saw the boy and felt the significance of his life—his *life*, not his death—that he had to be protected at all costs. Why should they trust what she's telling them when she has nothing to back it up but intuition?

She takes a deep breath and tries to channel Kat's passionate confidence. "Because I know that killing him will mean the end. His survival is necessary for ours, I felt that. And I know that might mean nothing to all of you, but I can only tell you what I know. It's just…a very strong instinct."

"I'm sorry, witness, I do believe you think you are telling us the truth," Lucien proclaims, "but if he survives long enough to allow the gateway to open in his mind, it truly will be the end. Of everything. Forgive me for not putting the fate of the Kosmos in the instincts of one young girl."

Blake sucks in a breath next to Layna to retort, but Lady Anora raises her hand, and all the Consulate members take their seats in silence. "I will remind the Consulate that Layna's instincts have protected us on two separate occasions and saved the lives of many young Nauts," she says softly. "Though I am unable to read instinct, I trust that hers are true. That being said, Layna, I am doubtful that we will be able to find an alternative solution in the amount of time we have left. Should this be our only option in the end, we have no choice but to take the risk. And should we happen to find an alternative, I don't know that it would be a better one."

"Any option is better than this one," Layna asserts. "Please, we have to at least *try* to find out what the Prophecy meant by closing the gateway, whether it meant for us to kill him or something else. And if you don't find an answer by the end of the day today, I'll take you to the boy myself."

Layna knows that it's an empty promise, but in the moment, she throws all her will into believing its truth for the sake of prying minds. It's totally possible that at least one of these Consulate members is a receiver telepath, able to hear her thoughts.

Lady Anora gives her a hesitant look and replies, "Very well. I will put this to an initial vote, and please keep in mind that the more time we spend coming to an agreement, the less time we have to find an answer. Please place your votes as to whether we should give ourselves until midnight tonight as opposed to immediate destruction of the gateway."

Urie, Ying Yue, Lucien, and a light-haired hemera from Region Five all walk to the basin to flip their medallions to black.

"Thank you for your votes. We do not have unanimous consent. At this time, I will dismiss our witnesses as we return to discussion in an attempt to come to a unanimous decision."

After Des finishes inspecting Layna's wounds to be sure there has been no further spread, she ports to the secluded nook in a small chamber off the arena with an oil lamp, bucket of water, and a rough sponge. She longs for a real shower, even the pitiful, trickling ones she's had here for the past couple of weeks. But the bathrooms were destroyed in the bombing, so a sponge bath is the best she can do for now. But as she tries to wash away the fear and guilt and pain of the past day, she closes her eyes and imagines she's back at home in Caledon, standing under the hot stream of her shower. Her mom downstairs cooking breakfast. Her homework waiting for her on her desk. Her phone buzzing with texts from her friends. It was beautiful, once. Her life. Perfect in its simplicity.

She carefully pulls on her comfiest grey t-shirt and blue leggings, and she tries fixing her hair to cover the black eye from the fight with Aysel and the cut from where the woman hit her. Glancing at the compact mirror she borrowed from Phoebe, she almost breaks into tears. She looks like some horror movie extra. She has never looked more unlike herself, even the depths of her eyes have changed. Darkened. She can barely see their golden flecks that once glinted like a reflection of the sun in even the lowest light.

She slips into her sneakers and ports to the mess hall for a sort of brunch. It's nearly when they would normally be taking a lunch break anyway. Schedules are off-kilter since training was canceled for the first half of the day. The recruits, along with many veteran Nauts, spent the morning helping in the arena and damaged bunkers, clearing debris and finding belongings.

First Class sit together at a long table, as they usually do at breakfast and dinner. But Layna can't sit still. She paces down the length of the table, concentrating on trying to discern the Consulate's imminent decision. If they decide to destroy the boy, she needs to get the hell out of here and get him to safety. She can only hope that none of the Consulate members could read her true intentions. She tried her best to block her thoughts, but even Lady Anora, who doesn't read thoughts, can sense truth. The thought of Lady Anora using her power against Layna causes her stomach to tie up in knots. But who is really betraying whom? Could she really turn against Lady Anora and the Consulate? Not to mention Blake and Des, who have no idea what she plans to do.

Blake's restless eyes follow Layna's pacing as he scoops a spoonful of yogurt and berries into his mouth. Des clears his throat in an exaggerated manner, and Layna pauses to look at him.

"There's no point driving yourself mad," he whispers. "And you're wasting valuable recovery energy. They don't typically come to a consensus about something like this immediately. Besides, Lady Anora will call you back the second they've made a decision. I'm sure of it."

That's what I'm worried about, Des.

"Decision about what?" Harkin says through a mouthful of custard pastry.

"None of your bloody business, that's what," Des answers, trying to sound lighthearted.

Harkin rolls his eyes and turns to Molimo, "Hey, Molly, use your telepathy feels. What do you think they're talkin' about?"

"Don't call me that," Molimo grumbles.

It's the first time Layna has ever seen Molimo act irritated toward anyone, let alone Harkin. He's always made a point to be extra patient with Harkin for some reason. Maybe he's picking up Layna's feelings of angst. Or maybe they're just his own. After last night's attack, it seems to have become painfully obvious to all recruits that they are nearing the end. Half of them look like they're ready to jump to action at any moment. The other half looks like they're ready to jump off a cliff. Only Layna, Blake, Des, and the Consulate know they only have until tomorrow.

"Alright, jeez. If none of you will talk to me, I'll just go eat with the ladies," Harkin whines. He picks up his plate and goes to sit across from Aysel and Zahra instead.

Layna ignores him as she continues her pacing, and Blake continues watching her. Layna glances at the cheap, digital watch Des bought for her on their fourth day here, when surface time was still prohibited and the timelessness of being underground was driving her mad. It's only been an hour and a half since they left the chamber. This day is going to drag on forever.

Instead of their afternoon fitness program, the recruits head to the arena for an entirely different and far more upsetting purpose. They are laying to rest the nine Nauts lost in the bombing. A group of veteran Nauts, including the remaining Activate interpreters, are crowded around Enzo in the middle of the chamber as the recruits arrive. He looks awful, his dark eyes red and irritated, and an uncharacteristic shadow of black stubble budding across his head and jaw.

"Listen up, recruits," he announces in his native Zulu. "Though the Consulate usually performs the Rite of Return, they are apparently involved in a more important matter at the moment." Even though he always manages to be diplomatic, Layna still doesn't miss the undertone of contempt. "Since seven of our nine fallen Nauts were under my guidance, I have offered to perform it myself," he concludes.

As Layna moves in closer, her heart clenches, and she grabs hold of Blake's hand. The bodies of the nine young Nauts are laid out on white cloth side by side along the floor behind Enzo. They are dressed in simple, white gowns, their eyes closed, and hands clasped over their stomachs. Their wounds have all been cleaned, but you can't clean away missing limbs, and their absence on several of the young Nauts is haunting.

Layna thinks about Joe's body in Trent Park, the deep red spreading across his white t-shirt. Suzanne's eyes staring lifelessly into the murky water that claimed her. The final looks of terror on their faces torment her, but the faces of these Nauts are different. They are peaceful. She remembers the peace she felt as she drifted, dying in the cradle of the Ouroboros. She hopes these Nauts felt that same sense of calm at the end. But more likely, their deaths were too quick for them to feel anything at all.

Layna has no idea what to expect as Enzo directs the recruits to form a circle around the bodies as the veteran Nauts fall back. He picks up what appears to be a small branch from the ground and uses a match to set it aflame. The branch sparks to life and burns like a fuse. "Please kneel beside one of your fallen brothers and sisters and place both your hands upon them," Enzo instructs.

They move in unison toward the bodies until each one is surrounded by a small group of Nauts. Layna kneels beside Elior, offering a silent goodbye of her own to the smart boy she barely got to know. As soon as all their hands are in place, Layna senses the tug almost immediately and instinctively knows what to do. They are pulling the fallen into the Ouroboros to be laid to rest there. Enzo throws the burning piece of tinder into the air at the same time that everyone simultaneously projects. Here in the Ouroboros, the tinder hovers in the air above them as it falls slowly to the earth, now a brilliant, white flame like the fire in the Consulate basin.

To Layna's surprise, the auras of the fallen Nauts have dimmed significantly but have not entirely gone out. The light is feeble, cracking in places like it is disintegrating. Even as she observes this, she notices light seeping out from her own hands where they lie upon Elior's shoulder. The same thing is happening all around her. The light from their hands causes the nine bodies to glow brighter and brighter until they outshine the living Nauts holding onto them.

Layna squints through the blaze at Blake sitting across from her. His face remains awestruck as he watches the light of the fallen break apart and float up into the air like a million embers of a dying fire caught in a whirlwind. At the same time, Layna notices a misty darkness leaching away from the bodies and drifting around the knees of the living Nauts. The darkness fades into nothing, but the light continues to spiral up and up, until there are nine radiant columns, some golden and some indigo, rising from the center of each circle of Nauts.

Though Layna has never witnessed this ritual before, it triggers something inside of her. A deeply embedded, visceral response and emotional association with the sight of it. She becomes vaguely aware of the tears streaming down her cheeks as she watches the spectacle.

She's not sure how long they sit there watching the breathtaking transition of energy, but after some time, the air calms and settles. She looks back down to find there is nothing but a white sheet where Elior once lay. Nine white sheets lying among the thirty-nine remaining recruits. Enzo lifts his eyes toward the ceiling far above, and whispers, "With honor and peace, we return your light." He gives the Naut salute, and each Naut repeats his words and his gesture before they all stand and port back to the homeplane.

Many of the recruits are crying, some being held or supported by others. Most of the veteran Nauts disappear after offering somber salutes to Enzo. He comes to stand before the recruits and remaining interpreters, Des on one side and Selene and Phoebe on the other. He clears his throat, collecting himself before addressing the group.

"I know you all feel overwhelmed…I know you are afraid and wondering how we expect you to fight something this big. You have not had the time to acclimate to this life, and we are forcing you into a battle that none of us are prepared for…" He pauses, seeming to struggle with the weight of it all.

Next to him, Phoebe reaches for Selene's hand. Selene grips it tightly and turns to look at her as though there is nothing and no one else in the world. Layna's heart aches for them. To be willing to sacrifice your own life to save the lives of countless others is courage. But having to accept that same sacrifice by the one you love is cruel.

"These men and women, these…boys and girls, they were pure, they were good. They were us," Enzo continues. "We will not allow them to have died in vain. Soon this will all be over, and we will either be victorious, or we will have left this world with honor and courage, having done all in our power to protect it and all life in the Kosmos. Yes, as Nauts, this is our sacred duty. And no, we have not allowed you a choice in that. But as the four of us have come to know you all during this time, I can say with confidence, and with pride, that I do not think one of you would choose to leave, if given the choice. Take a moment to look inside yourselves, and you will know this is true. Take back your will, make the conscious choice right now whether to stay or leave."

Layna doesn't even have to think about it, and she knows none of the others do either. As angry as she was with the Consulate for forcing them to come here the way they did, she knew as soon as they arrived in Athens that this is where she must be. She made the decision then to stay and fight. What Enzo has given them is the knowledge that they already have made that choice. That they are here of their own free will, and not because they were told to be. It fills Layna with even more trepidation over the idea that she might have to make another choice. A harder choice, to abandon her comrades if the Consulate makes the wrong decision today. She is mostly certain that leaving would be what's right, what's necessary, to protect them all. But it doesn't lessen the burden.

Enzo scans their faces as a sad smile forms on his lips. "You have all worked incredibly hard. I'm honored to stand beside you."

"As am I," Selene says.

"And I," Phoebe echoes.

"Aye, me as well," Des declares.

"We can take a ten-minute break, and then I think we should return here to pick up with the weapons training," Selene instructs. "But remember that we are to remain within Oneiropolis for the time being. No porting above ground."

Everyone nods, and then they scatter about for their brief respite. Layna heads toward the far south end of the arena and sits back against the cold, stone wall. She watches the flickering light of one of the torches above her head and tries to concentrate on what's happening with the Consulate. Blake sits down beside her, and she tenses. Even his closeness is distracting.

Concentrate. Just concentrate.

"Picking up on anything?" he asks, his voice both hesitant and hopeful.

"Nothing yet," Layna replies without taking her eyes off the torch above her.

Blake reaches for her hand, but she lifts it away to tuck her hair behind her ear. His hand lingers there for an instant before he drops it and bounces to his feet.

"I think I'll go for a walk," he mutters as he saunters away.

Layna follows him with her eyes before squeezing them shut and fighting the urge to run after him. The thought of going through the next twenty-four hours without him by her side scares her more than the idea of going through it at all. But she thinks about those nine sheets of white and remains steadfast in her decision.

She performs her telesthetic sweep of the Consulate. Nothing from them. Outside, nothing from the umbrae. She focuses again on the boy, still in the same location she found him during her impulse, but she does sense something that startles her. It's not quite an impulse, but more of an urge to go to him, like he is calling out to her. She looks at her watch. Still a few minutes until they have to return to practice. She knows she's not supposed to leave Oneiropolis, but she can be quick. They'll never know, especially if she stays in the Ouroboros. She needs to see him, just for a minute.

It's the farthest she's ever ported on her own, but the pull on her is strong, and she knows she will be able to reach him. She concentrates on where she wants to go, and in a flash, she is standing in Egypt, just outside the boy's house. She remains in the Ouroboros and sees the grey figure of a woman in mid-step coming out of the house, followed by the boy, glowing with his brilliant, white light around the dark core of his center. Layna walks closer to them as the woman turns away from her. But instead of following, the boy turns toward Layna. Though she can't clearly see his face through the glare of light, impossibly, she senses his gaze on her.

"Can you see me?" She crouches down so that she is eye level with him and stretches out her hand. Layna watches in shock as the boy lifts his arm from his side. It glides slowly through the air until his hand is outstretched in front of him, meeting hers in the air.

He is reaching out for *her*. He can actually see her across dimensions.

Layna lets out a surprised laugh as she spreads her fingers out against his. Though she can feel only the barrier of the Ouroboros, she observes him in awe as he begins tracing her hand with his index finger.

The woman has turned around and must be calling to him, because he slowly turns away from Layna to follow her. She watches him for another minute, mesmerized by his light and the impossibility of what she just witnessed, before returning to the arena.

Of course, no one has noticed her brief absence, as she's not been gone more than thirty seconds in the homeplane. Her hands are shaking with adrenaline, and she knows it was stupid to leave. But she got what she went for. Confirmation that she must protect him at all costs. Even if it means turning against the Order. There's no longer a choice to be made.

Her thoughts are interrupted by Selene's double clap, and the Nauts start making their way back toward the center of the arena. Layna scans the room, instinctively looking for Blake, and sees him walking in from the other direction flanked by Harkin and Aysel. She watches as he says something that makes Harkin throw his head back with a great guffaw. A smile involuntarily plays at the corners of Layna's mouth as she watches them, until Blake looks at Aysel and *she* actually smiles at him. Blake smiles back. Layna's smile disappears entirely.

Well, that didn't take long.

Everyone breaks up loosely into groups with Jacque and Aalok returning for instruction. Blake takes a step toward Layna, but then he seems to think better of it and pairs off with Harkin. Seeing Layna without a partner, Jae Lyn crosses the arena with a hopeful grin on her face.

"Hi, roomie," she says in English, using the Americanized term Layna taught her. Before Layna can respond, Jae Lyn throws her arms around Layna's waist, and she has to smother a yelp of pain. "I am so glad you are okay. You scared me a little!" Jae Lyn scolds, now in her native Mandarin.

Layna laughs and rests her head atop Jae Lyn's. "I scared me too! I'm sorry I didn't come find you at brunch."

"That is alright. You seemed very restless, so I decided not to bother you."

"You never bother me."

"I shall miss our little bunker," Jae Lyn says, her bottom lip curving into a pout. "It had to say goodbye to this world."

"Well, you're still my roomie," Layna replies with a smile. "Maybe when all this is over you can come visit me in Caledon and we can be roommates again for a little while."

Jae Lyn's face lights up with glee. "I would love that very much!"

"And I can come see you in Wuzhen, too," Layna adds, hoping with all her heart that she does one day get to see Jae Lyn's magical hometown. That both their hometowns won't soon cease to exist along with the rest of everything. Jae Lyn gives her an emphatic nod of approval.

"In the meantime, let's duel," Layna says with mock solemnity.

The recruits pick right back up where they left off yesterday, and it feels good to be doing something productive again. Though Jae Lyn's twelve-inch dagger is no match for Layna's double-bladed sword, Jae Lyn has much better control over her weapon than Layna has over hers. Plus Layna is repeatedly instructed by Des to take it easy. So Jae Lyn mostly flits around her like a hummingbird, advancing, defending, and countering in swift and fluid motion as Layna practices fairly stationary defense.

After hours of practice, Selene gives the signal to break. Most of the Nauts disappear in search of food, but some mill about, conversing in anxious whispers. Some just sit down, cradling themselves or staring off into space.

Layna watches Blake with Harkin, Aysel, and Zahra, the only ones who appear to be even remotely enjoying each other's company. She can't believe how Blake is acting. Just because she hurt his pride a little doesn't mean he can immediately go flirt with the one girl who hates her. A more rational part of her brain tells her that he's just trying to respect her space, but the emotional part kind of wants to smack him in the face. Then her whole brain admonishes her for caring one way or another.

This is exactly what you're supposed to be trying to avoid, you idiot.

She focuses once again on performing her telesthetic sweep, so far sensing nothing out of the ordinary. She absently watches Jae Lyn walking back across the arena with two cups of water for her and Layna, looking tired but pleased with herself. Enzo passes across Layna's half-focused gaze to stand beside Des nearby. She can't believe it's possible, but he looks even worse than he did this morning before the Rite of Return. She continues her sweep as she overhears Enzo ask Des, "What do you think the Consulate is doing?"

"I'm not sure," Des replies. "Probably trying to figure out how the umbrae planted that bomb."

"Yes, perhaps," he mumbles. But then something in his voice changes as he adds, "Or do you think it has something to do with the Prophecy?"

The impulse hits Layna at the same time Des falters in confusion, replying, "Well, sure, Enzo...all of this does, doesn't it? The Prophecy—"

"Des, no!" Layna screams, as the impulse relinquishes control. "He's *eclipsed*!"

Layna scrambles to her feet as the arena abruptly falls silent. Without a second of hesitation, Enzo and several other Nauts disappear at once. Everyone else jumps to their feet, and Jae Lyn stops dead in

191

her tracks halfway to Layna. Layna locks eyes with her for a breathless moment, and then Enzo reappears, grabbing Jae Lyn from behind and projecting both of them back into the Ouroboros.

The two cups of water Jae Lyn was holding fall toward the ground, but Layna is in the Ouroboros before they can land. There she finds the eight Nauts who projected—Enzo, along with all nyx from Second Class—waiting with their aetherblades drawn. Their indigo auras are mixed with shadowy blackness. They're all eclipsed.

CHAPTER

L ayna hears the popping of other Nauts joining her in the
Ouroboros as she spots Jae Lyn in Enzo's grasp. Layna takes
a hurdling step toward her as Jae Lyn's golden aetherblade
flickers feebly into being at her side. But then Layna notices the point
of a blue aetherblade—Enzo's serrated sword—protruding from the
front of Jae Lyn's stomach. The look of dismayed betrayal on Jae Lyn's
face is already melting into a lifeless glaze as Enzo pulls the blade from
her back and tosses her aside like she's nothing.

"*No!*" Layna screams as she rushes blindly at him.

"It wasn't her!" Enzo roars to the others. The seven other
eclipsed Nauts all turn toward Layna, raising their weapons in front of
them. Layna stumbles to a stop. Her aetherblade surges to life in her
hand as Des, Selene, Phoebe, and Blake come to stand on her left.
Aysel, Zahra, and Harkin fall in line to her right, followed by Molimo

and Zain. The other recruits who'd remained in the arena for break begin appearing in the Ouroboros, all blades drawn.

"Enzo!" Selene pleads. "Please, Enzo, it's us. You need to snap out of it!" she shrieks.

"Find it," Enzo commands the others, ignoring Selene's cries. As one, the eclipsed Nauts advance at them, and Layna finds herself no longer facing a practice duel, but a real one.

"Anwar, stop!" Layna yells at the boy coming at her. "We're on the same team! You have to fight it!"

He swings his weapon toward her head, and she ducks just in time.

"Fine!" she shouts, as she takes a halfhearted swipe at his legs. He shifts sideways and the blade shears the fibers of his pant leg. He then twists around and jabs toward Layna's torso with his spear-like aetherblade. But Layna ports out of the way of his attack and reappears right behind him, shooting him in the back with a lucetelum. He gets knocked out to the homeplane but is back in front of her before she can blink. Unlike with Aysel, the lucetelum isn't enough to expel the umbra that controls him.

They're getting stronger.

Anwar thrusts toward her chest but she blocks him and leaps backward out of the range of his spear. She allows herself a quick glance in search of Blake, but all around her is a chaotic clashing of blades and flying lucetelum. Nauts port in and around the Ouroboros, trying to stay one step ahead of each other. Anwar disappears from in front of her and she spins around just as he reappears behind her. She stumbles backward and falls, holding her weapon out to shield herself as he brings his down on her.

She blocks it once, and then again. She needs to get back on her feet. As he raises his arm a third time, an indigo lucetelum hits him in the chest and he is momentarily thrown back to the homeplane again.

Layna spins around to find Blake moving toward her with an eclipsed Naut right on his heels. She aims her hands just above his shoulder and shoots the Naut directly in the head, knocking her out of the Ouroboros. At the same time, Anwar reappears in front of her. Blake takes a final leap, porting in mid-air and reappearing between them as he slides on his knees and blocks Anwar's blade with his own.

It gives Layna just enough time to leap to her feet, and she and Blake stand side by side and shoot at Anwar together. This time, he doesn't return from the homeplane.

"*Them*!" Enzo yells. Layna turns to find that his aura has already darkened significantly in the minutes since they first projected into the Ouroboros. Then she notices he is pointing directly at her and Blake. They share a terrified glance as the remaining eclipsed Nauts disappear from their respective battles and reorganize themselves in a circle around the two of them.

"To Layna and Blake!" Des shouts, and he and the others appear in still a tighter circle between them and the eclipsed Nauts.

All Nauts raise their weapons together, and the cracking of light on light tears through the Ouroboros. One of the eclipsed Nauts knocks Harkin to the ground and comes at Layna, but Aysel lands a lucetelum to the girl's chest.

"We need a multiluce!" Des instructs, and he and Selene move closer to Layna and Blake. Harkin, Molimo, and Aysel follow suit. It's a hell of a time to attempt something that they've never gotten to work properly. But it seems like it might be their only hope for escaping this before they all kill each other.

The seven of them each place a hand on the shoulder of the person next to them while the others try to keep the eclipsed Nauts at bay with their aetherblades. Layna closes her eyes to the chaos of battle, relinquishing her control and trusting the surrounding circle of Nauts to protect them as she reaches out with her mind. It's different than in training, all her senses sharpened, her intention laser-focused on the task at hand.

Time stands still, and there it is, vibrating beneath her fingertips. The individual energies of each of the seven physically connected Nauts. She can feel the misalignment, just like Des and Selene explained. They all come from the same energy, and it is only their physical separateness that has caused a break in the continuity of power. The multiluce is simply the closing of an open circuit. Now that Layna finally senses the truth of it, it's as easy as flipping a switch. There is the sensation of something clicking into place as their energies align, and then the current is flowing through her—the lucetelum of seven Nauts building among them until they can no longer contain it.

Layna's eyes burst open just as she hears Phoebe's anguished cry. And the suspended flash of an image she sees before the blast is Enzo's look of rage as he descends on Selene, and the glimmer of one of Phoebe's two golden daggers as it slides between his ribs. Then, an explosion of blinding energy crackles through the air with a sonic boom, and they are all flying backward, simultaneously thrown into the homeplane by the shock wave.

Layna lands on her back a dozen feet from where she was standing, the dark wound in her chest exploding with renewed, icy pain. She rolls up as she tries to catch her breath and prepares to continue the fight. But all the Nauts remain where they landed. Blake lets out a sigh of relief beside her as some of the Nauts who'd been eclipsed begin to sit up slowly in confusion.

"Enzo?" Selene asks, as she bounces to her feet and moves cautiously toward him.

Enzo doesn't move. Phoebe drops to her knees, covering her mouth with her hands.

"Enzo!" Des yells, and he and Selene port to him, turning him over. He looks up at them, his expression pained and his grey shirt turning maroon. "What happened?" he mumbles, his voice weak.

"You were eclipsed," Selene croaks, and cries of shock echo through the recovering Nauts. Des lifts Enzo's shirt to inspect his wound, then presses down on it to staunch the flow of blood as he looks up mournfully at Selene and Phoebe.

Enzo's confusion turns to horror as he latches on to Selene's words. "Did I hurt you? Did I hurt *anyone?*"

Dread throttles Layna's heart in its vice-grip. "Oh God, Jae Lyn," she cries. She returns to the Ouroboros and sees the tiny, crumpled figure lying face-down across the arena. "No...please, no."

Jae Lyn's golden light has dimmed to a faint glow, and Layna ports to her side as Nauts begin appearing behind her. She drops down and rolls Jae Lyn onto her back.

The front of her body is covered in blood from where it pooled beneath her, her eyes cold and unseeing. Layna raises a hand to her mouth as she stifles a sob. She says her name, but there is no response, and she watches as cracks begin to form in Jae Lyn's aura. Enzo appears and collapses next to Jae Lyn as the other three Guides materialize behind him.

"She's gone," Molimo whispers from behind Layna. "I…can't feel her anymore."

"No, she cannot be," Enzo moans, clutching his ribs. "I would not do this…I could not have done this."

"It was not you doing it," Selene says softly behind him. "Enzo…we need to get you to the hospital, please."

"No. I will stay here for her return," Enzo murmurs, dropping to his side as he coughs up blood onto the ground. The breeze from his movement sends little sparks of light from Jae Lyn's body scattering into the air. "Perhaps…I will return with her."

"No, you will not," Phoebe pleads as she kneels next to him. "Enzo, I am so sorry. Please…we need to get you help."

"I can feel it, Phoebe. The peace. It is okay…" He closes his eyes. Phoebe and Selene grab each of his hands, and they all watch in silence as his light slowly fades.

Phoebe begins sobbing, and Selene takes her into her arms and softly kisses her brow. "It is not your fault, my love."

Enzo's indigo aura begins scattering with Jae Lyn's gold, mixing together in the air above them.

"What's happening?" Layna cries.

"When we're killed in the Ouroboros, the return happens spontaneously," Des replies in a choked whisper. "We should help them along."

The Nauts gather round Enzo and Jae Lyn, either placing their hands on their bodies or reaching toward them as their own auras pour toward the beautiful, heartbreaking tunnels of light. It swirls above until there is nothing left. The Nauts raise their heads together, saluting as they whisper, "With honor and peace, we return your light."

Phoebe remains next to where Enzo's body lay, a blank expression on her face. Selene stays with her as the others all cross back into the homeplane.

They all stand in tense silence as the remaining recruits who had gone elsewhere for the break begin to reappear in the arena.

"Are you two okay?" Des asks Layna and Blake.

Jae Lyn isn't, Layna thinks, as she closes her eyes and the tears well up again. She feels Des pull her into a hug and she lets herself cry into his shoulder. "None of us felt them, Des. The umbrae. My telesthesia only picked up on it when Enzo was asking you questions. But there were eight of them right here with us..."

"Aye," Des sighs, releasing her. "They're more in control of themselves, it would appear. What we sense when an umbra is present is the Chaos of its energy. It seems, in sentience, they've learned to quiet the Chaos inside their...their minds."

"Why did they go after Jae Lyn like that?" Blake asks. "And then us? And how did they all get in here with the extra protection the Consulate said they added around the arena?"

199

"I'm not sure. But I'm going to go interrupt the Consulate gathering, and to be safe, I'd like to separate you two from everyone until we figure out what that was about." He looks around and finds Molimo. "Molimo, if you could take everyone to the mess hall and try to settle them down, I'll send one of the medics to look at everyone, alright?"

"You got it, boss," Molimo says with a sniffle, his eyes wet and bloodshot.

Des takes Layna and Blake by their shoulders, leading them away from the others and says in a lower voice, "I can't help but imagine this must have something to do with what you told the Consulate this morning."

Layna can't help but imagine the same.

"Let's get someone to take a look at the two of you while I go see the Consulate, eh?"

Layna and Blake wait in a small, unfamiliar room occupied only by the stone bench they sit upon and the older Naut staring at them. The medic who saw to them left several minutes ago, but the man who remained behind with them is not a medic. He must be some kind of Naut bodyguard or something, because he just stands there watching them. Layna is unsure if he's there to keep them in or keep others out, and she makes a few attempts to engage him in conversation. He ignores her completely until the third time she tries, when he shoots her a disinterested look and moves to stand just outside the doorway, facing the dimly lit hall.

Rude.

They've already been in here for nearly an hour. Neither one of them has spoken much, lost in their own thoughts and unanswered questions. Layna's mind goes in circles. Why did Enzo target Jae Lyn? Did she die only because they thought she was the one who'd found the gateway? How would they know *anyone* found the gateway? Why would they have killed her and not questioned her? And how did that many umbrae get into Oneiropolis and go unnoticed in the first place?

As the incessant questions tumble around in her mind, Layna becomes increasingly impatient. They were whisked away so quickly, and she wasn't able to see how their friends were doing, or properly mourn Jae Lyn with them. It feels like she is already betraying the memory of her friend. And what could Des possibly be talking about with the Consulate for this long? He told them when he left them that he would be back in a few minutes. Did he forget they were in here?

Just as she thinks it, Des appears in front of them.

"Finally!" Blake whines. "Where have you been? What's happening with everyone else?"

Des doesn't respond right away, and his hesitation makes Layna even more anxious. She's familiar with this hesitancy. It's the way she would sometimes falter while trying to come up with a mom-friendly recitation of events. While she was trying to come up with a lie.

"Sorry, they wouldn't see me right away, they were deep into…the other issue," he says, glancing toward the guard who is now leaning backward as though trying to eavesdrop. "I went to go check on the others for a little while before the Consulate took me in. They're doing alright, physically. Emotionally…I can't say. Particularly the poor buggers who were eclipsed. That kind of thing obviously messes with a person a bit. I should get back to them, but I just wanted to come tell you to sit tight for a few more minutes. The Consulate will see you soon."

His response is so formal and cold. Now Layna is certain he is hiding something.

"But what did they say? About what happened with the Nauts?" Blake asks.

"Well…" Another hesitation. "They said it's telling that it was all nyx who were eclipsed. Because of their closer 'proximity' to the netherworld, they think it's possible that they're more susceptible to control than the hemera. I guess it makes sense…Darcie was a nyx. So was Jomei, and so are Aysel and Dritan."

"Yeah, so Aysel is a nyx. But so am I, and so is Molimo," Blake says a little defensively. "But none of us were eclipsed with the others today."

"Right, but didn't you notice? All the nyx who were eclipsed today were from Second Class. They didn't go through Armageddon meditation. I think Phoebe was helping them with it a bit, but nothing as rigorous as what I put you lot through."

"Yeah, plus everyone is pretty vulnerable right now after the bombing," Layna adds. "I know it was affecting Enzo pretty bad…"

"That's certainly true," Des agrees with a sigh. "He was a right good bloke. I can't imagine…ending that way."

"I know…" Layna replies with a shudder. What lower circle of hell could there be than being turned into a weapon to kill your own friends?

"I best get back to the others," Des says. "They're probably going a bit mad by now."

He doesn't say goodbye or even meet their eyes before disappearing. Layna exchanges a look with Blake. "There's something he's not telling us," she says.

"Tell me about it. Des is a worse liar than you are."

Layna has a sinking suspicion that Des was avoiding telling her the Consulate has decided to destroy the boy. She does a telesthetic sweep and feels nothing, again, and then she realizes with a sudden, sinking clarity that the Consulate probably has a block on themselves. One of the twelve members must have a defensive divination ability they use to obstruct prying minds from their privileged communications.

What if they've already done it? What if the boy is already dead? Would she have felt it? She frantically sweeps outwards in search of him, using the Limits to enhance her telesthesia. She only starts breathing again the second she locates him out there. Still in the same place, still alive and safe for now.

"What are you looking for?" Blake whispers.

She opens her eyes to find he is watching her. She struggles momentarily with whether or not to tell him anything about her plan. What if he tells the Consulate? What if he tries to stop her? *No, it's Blake. He wouldn't. I have to believe he wouldn't.*

She looks toward the guard, who has lost interest in them again and leans his head back against the wall with his eyes closed. It's now or never.

"Blake, I need you to come with me now," she urges in a whisper.

"Wait, what? Come where? We can't go anywhere with that dude right there," he whispers back.

"He's not looking, and we'll stay under a minute. It'll be the blink of an eye in the homeplane."

"Stay where? Where are we going?"

"Just trust me," she says, as she holds out her hand.

Blake takes her hand without hesitation. "I do."

She ports them both to the inside of a small room in Hijazah, Egypt, being sure to reappear in the Ouroboros. The boy sits in front of an open toy chest and looks up as soon as they appear. Layna was prepared for the brilliance of his light, but Blake recoils and shields his eyes.

"What *is* that?" he exclaims.

"It's him. It's the boy," Layna replies, unable to keep the veneration from her voice.

"You've got to be kidding me." Blake removes his hand and squints toward the light.

The boy has been moving toward them since they appeared. He comes to a stop just in front of Blake, his head turned up to him.

"Wait, what?" Blake says, looking over his shoulder for some other object of the boy's attention. "Can...can he see me?"

"Wild, right?" Layna says with the tilt of a smile.

She kneels down to face the boy, and he slowly raises his hand out to her as he did last time. She holds her palm out toward him and he again begins to trace the outline of her hand as Blake watches in astonishment.

"No way," Blake breathes, raising his hand next to Layna's. The boy moves to trace Blake's fingers next. Blake laughs. A real, deep laugh, his cares and fears temporarily forgotten. It's something Layna hasn't heard since they left North Carolina, and only now does she realize how much she's missed it.

Layna watches Blake and the boy in contented silence for another minute before she realizes they've already been here too long. "We should get back before he notices we're gone," she sighs.

"Yeah, you're right," Blake agrees, his smile fading.

Layna waves at the boy then places her hand on Blake's shoulder and ports them back. The guard stands in the room staring at the bench when they reappear in front of it.

"Hey!" he shouts. "Where did you two just go? You were told to wait here until the Consulate asked for you."

"We just had to use the bathroom," Layna says. "Or would you have preferred we pee in the corner?"

"I'd have preferred you'd asked permission. Stay put now, you hear? That's an order," he commands, not waiting for a response as he returns to his post in the doorway.

Blake and Layna take a seat on the bench again as Blake lets out an exaggerated breath. "Okay...mind officially blown. Can't wait to hear what the Consulate has to say about this one."

"We're not necessarily going to tell them."

Blake looks at her in surprise. "What do you mean?"

Layna glances once again toward the guard and then leans into Blake and whispers, "If they decide on destroying him, I'm not waiting around to try to convince them not to. I'm going to leave the Order. I can't let them kill that boy, Blake. If that's their decision, I need to get to him and hide him right away. Protect him. Stop them, whatever I need to do."

"But Layna...Lady Anora and the others...they're *Augurs*. I'm sure they'll make the right decision, whatever that is."

"I'm not so sure. The right decision is to let him live. I know they think destroying him will end the threat, but it won't. Or at least, it would create a bigger threat. I'm not totally sure of the details."

"But then isn't it sort of a lose-lose?" Blake asks. "If they let him live, then Erebus can enter through his mind and wins. If they kill him, somehow Erebus still wins?"

"I don't know," Layna whimpers, putting her head in her hands. "And that's why I don't expect to convince the Consulate."

Blake nods, his troubled eyes trained on the floor as he runs a hand through his hair.

He really does need a haircut.

As the inconsequential thought crosses her mind, Layna realizes she's made a mistake. She should never have put this on Blake. It was selfish of her to show him the boy, to tell him about her plan. This doesn't have to be his burden to carry. His presence through the past weeks has been the only thing keeping her sane, but she needs to let him go. And Des, Lady Anora, all the friends she's made here. This is something she has to handle on her own, without putting the people she cares about in unnecessary danger alongside her.

"I'm sorry, Blake, I know this seems totally crazy. But I didn't tell you this so you'll join me and turn your back on the Consulate and everyone. I guess I just told you because…I wanted you to know. That I'm not a traitor, if it comes to it."

To her surprise, Blake actually starts softly laughing.

Irritated, she starts to retort, "Hey, I don't see—"

"Layna, come on," Blake whispers as he looks up at her. "Do you really think after what we've been through together that I would ever *not* stand with you, whoever or whatever you stand against?"

Layna stares back at him, at a loss. "I don't know, I just think…"

"Hey, I don't know what's going to happen in the next twenty-four hours so…I think I need you to understand something." He takes her face gently in his hands, his eyes burying themselves in hers. "What Enzo said about us choosing to be here…that was all well and good, but I'm not here because the Consulate told me to be, and I'm not here because I'm choosing to fulfill my destiny as a Naut. I'm here because here is where you are. So whatever you do, wherever you go, whether you want me to be or not, I'm with you. I'm yours."

Then his lips are on hers, and there is no part of Layna that attempts to avoid it this time. She wonders how she ever had the strength to do so. She tastes the comfort of him, the familiarity and the rightness of this, of *them*. It fills every atom of her body until there is nothing left but him and her and the fireworks.

And the guard clearing his throat.

They both jump at the sound and he looks at them with a sheepish grin. "Erm...sorry. The Consulate will see you now."

"Thanks a lot, man," Blake says at an uncomfortable volume. He looks at Layna and takes a deep breath. "Ready?"

"Ready," she says, as she tries composing herself with the hope that the flush in her cheeks will subside before they reach the Consulate.

Standing now beneath the twelve glowing figures, Layna tries in vain to catch Lady Anora's gaze. But Lady Anora keeps her eyes trained on her hands clasped in her lap, and Layna feels the seeping chill of abandonment, almost as if an invisible tether between them has suddenly snapped.

They're going to kill him.

She feels a tugging in her gut. Toward the boy. But she is suddenly filled with doubt as she realizes the stupidity of her plan. What if they *want* her to go to him? To lead them to him like she said she'd do? She could go to him now and run. But this is the Consulate. Could she really outrun and outsmart them? Are they listening to her thoughts even now? And could she really ask Blake to come with her?

Lady Anora rises from her seat and Layna's mind falls still as she holds her breath and prepares for the worst.

"Well, it's time...that you both know the truth," Lady Anora announces in a small, tight voice, "which I'm afraid carries both good news and bad. The good news is that we did reach a unanimous decision not to destroy the boy. This is because we believe we have found the solution on how to close the gateway as dictated in the final stanza of the Phantom's Prophecy."

The breath escapes from Layna in a delighted, panting laugh as she clutches her chest with relief. *They're not going to kill the boy. I don't need to leave. I don't need to betray everyone.*

She glances up at Blake with a relieved grin, but it fades as she sees the look on his face. Layna follows his gaze back to Lady Anora, whose eyes are finally fixated on them. Layna wants to stop time, run it backward, anything to keep from hearing whatever has caused the anguished look in Lady Anora's eyes. But time marches on, and Lady Anora sucks in a breath to speak. "The bad news is…it's you."

Layna's stomach clenches with dread. "I don't understand," she stammers. "What do you mean?"

"I'm afraid," Lady Anora replies, "that I haven't been entirely honest with the two of you. When Desmond found you, he told you he was scouting you because we believed you were being activated. This is partially true, though Desmond was no ordinary Scout. He was part of an advanced task force assigned by this Consulate with investigating…anomalies. You were his assignment.

"Around the end of March, one of our Region Six Scouts felt an enormous surge of aggregated power in Caledon, New Jersey. The surge caused what he referred to as a sort of 'bend in the Ouroboros'. At this point, we had already witnessed a number of anomalies in the balance, which we worried were harbingers of the Phantom's Prophecy. We thought perhaps an entire group had just been activated in New Jersey, which would have been unprecedented. But when the Scout located the source of the bend and saw it was only you two generating that power, Desmond was assigned. Then, when the umbrae detached in your presence, Desmond thought it may be possible due to this 'bend', and he made the decision to bring you directly to me."

Lucien clears his throat with impatience and Lady Anora gives him a piteous look, swallowing hard before continuing.

"There is a reason you progressed so swiftly through the phases of Naut achievement, why you achieved ascendance and have now practically attained augury. Many Nauts do not even know what their divination power is until years into training, let alone have a practical mastery over it as you two do. You are beyond just being naturals at the Tripartite Powers. You already knew them. What I'm trying to say is, while you are Nauts, you are not just a hemera and a nyx. You are *Hemera* and *Nyx*."

Layna stares at her in bewilderment as Blake sputters, "I don't get it. What's the difference?"

"You are Hemera and Nyx returned to us. The reawakening of their energies. The very first Nauts who existed on this planet, and the only ones who received their powers directly from the Oneiroi."

They are wrong. How can they have gotten this so wrong?

"You think we're them, reincarnated?" Layna trills.

"We know you are. I could feel the ancient and powerful nature of your energies the first time I laid eyes on you in my kitchen. We determined for the time being to train, observe, and protect you. This is why we took slight extra precaution with you during the Activate attack. And the attack itself confirmed that your presence here threatens

Erebus' ability to breach our world. We believe that when you had your First Walk, Erebus must have also sensed the surge of power as you entered the Ouroboros and sought to find and eliminate you before you accessed the full range of your abilities."

"But if that's true, why didn't more umbrae target us when they found us during the Activate attack? Or any time after that? When they kidnapped us? We were right there, in their hands," Layna argues.

"In the Activate attack, you had not yet achieved ascendance, and you were hundreds of miles apart. When you were kidnapped, you remained in the homeplane where they could not sense your energies. It was when you fought side by side in the Ouroboros during the arena attack that they saw the truth of who you are. Of your powerful twin energies.

"When you discovered the final stanza of the Phantom's Prophecy, it further validated my suspicion. As did Layna's telesthetic sense of the netherworld, and Blake dreaming of the gateway since childhood. I think, perhaps, a part of you may have even felt this truth yourselves. I know you two share an unusual connection, and that you've never felt quite at home in your own skin. Out of place in this world…in this time."

Layna opens her mouth but doesn't have a response. Of course she's always felt out of place, but don't all girls her age feel that way? And the connection with Blake, sure, it's confused her since the day they met. Since the second her telesthesia compelled her to go to his defense in the hallways of Caledon High. The strange energy that courses through her body when their eyes meet, when they touch.

211

When they kiss. She's never had an explanation for any of it. She just assumed it was all part of the territory of being a Naut.

"I thought you said all new Activates would probably read the Prophecy with the third stanza," Blake points out.

"We've tested nearly all the recruits since they've arrived. And Oneironautica did deem it time to reveal the Prophecy to just four. All read it the same way it's always been. Two stanzas only."

"Okay, but wait," Blake says, holding up his hands in protest. "Even assuming you're right about us being…reincarnated. How could Layna and I be any kind of threat to Erebus? It's like this cosmic entity and we…we're just *teenagers*. I mean, I barely made it through sophomore year of high school. We don't know what we're doing!"

"The answer lies in the words of the Prophecy as it appeared only to you and Layna," Lady Anora replies. "According to our history, just before they perished, the Oneiroi told Hemera and Nyx that the words of the Prophecy that had stood for eons, over the comings and goings of many aetherworlds, would come to pass during the life of humanity's Earth. Hemera and Nyx begged them to find a way to stop it, but the Oneiroi insisted there would be no Nauts powerful enough, as Hemera and Nyx were the last two Nauts who would be granted their power by the Oneiroi.

"Though the Dream Book makes no specific mention of it, we believe Hemera and Nyx themselves set something in motion upon their death. The historical account of their Rite of Return contains an extended ritual that has been and remains indecipherable to our scholars. However, we now believe it was intended to preserve their energies in the Ouroboros so that they could reawaken on this world at a predetermined tipping point.

"Our guess is that it was Hemera and Nyx who added the final stanza to the Prophecy before they died. As Nauts, they would not have been capable of writing in the Dream Book in the same way it writes itself. But they were somehow able to get a message within those pages that only their future incarnates would be able to read. And to ensure that you would one day read the Prophecy for yourselves, Hemera and Nyx included in our Tenets a decree that each new Naut must read the Prophecy as a rite of passage. Layna, I'm sure you remember the way the Book called to you when you arrived at my house, and Blake, how it appeared to you through your dreams. It recognized your energies."

"But...we read the Prophecy already," Layna replies. "We didn't understand it. It hasn't gotten us any closer to knowing how to stop Erebus."

"Actually, it has," Lady Anora murmurs. She looks around at the other Consulate members as though seeking comfort or escape, but they all keep their eyes on Blake and Layna.

Lady Anora takes a deep breath and continues.

"The answer is in the last two lines. 'Unless day joins night, and night joins day, as one to close the Gateway'. You see, in the beginning, we didn't live in secret, and Hemera and Nyx had the power to reveal themselves to worldlings in dreams. Because of the light and dark coloring of their auras, they came to be known as the Goddess of Day and the God of Night. The last lines of the Prophecy refer to them...to you. We've suspected that you two were the key to stopping Erebus, but once you discovered what the gateway actually is, the full meaning of the Prophecy became clear."

Lady Anora looks back and forth between them, her eyes glimmering with sorrow. And with sudden clarity, Layna knows what's coming. Her knees nearly buckle with the weight of it. She instinctively reaches out a hand to Blake, and he grabs ahold of it tightly.

"We believe, my darlin' ones, that you have been reawakened on Earth for one singular purpose. In order to prevent the complete annihilation of our universe, the Goddess of Day and God of Night must exit this world and enter the boy's mind—must enter the gateway and close it from within. And I'm afraid...it will be a one-way trip."

CHAPTER

11

Time seems to have stopped. Layna's ears ring with the last words spoken as she tries to grasp the reality of them. *I'm going to die. I'm going to die soon.*

She's thought about her own death a number of times since they arrived here, even knocked at its door only yesterday. But there was always the hope of survival. No longer is the hope of her own survival tied to the survival of the universe. Now they are opposing outcomes. She must die for the universe to live. And then another truth hits her.

Blake has to die too.

She looks into his eyes and they stare back into hers, reflecting the same fear. The same denial of truth.

"Layna, I didn't want to believe you about the boy," Lady Anora's quavering voice interrupts. "But I could see the truth of what you told us as you spoke. That for our survival, he must live. That killing him was not what Hemera and Nyx intended, and we must trust that this was the only option. Fighting Erebus through the boy's mind will be targeted, centralized. And with your help, we may actually stand a chance of stopping it from breaking through."

"Our *help*?" Blake sputters. "You mean our *lives*. At least call it what it is. You're sending us on a suicide mission. And what if I say no? What if I won't let you just send her to die?" His grip on Layna's hand tightens as he says it, as if it will stop time and keep her from moving one moment closer to death.

Lady Anora responds without meeting his eyes. "Blake, I understand how you must feel—"

"No, you don't! Don't say that. How could you possibly understand how I feel?"

"Because whether you believe me or not, my darlin', I have come to care deeply for you both. And asking this of you breaks my heart more than you could know. I've considered all the alternatives imaginable, in hope that we could perhaps fight Erebus off without you. But these were fleeting dreams only. Because I know that it's impossible. Without you, everything—light, dark, life, creation, reality itself—will begin to end tomorrow."

Blake doesn't respond, his brazen anger replaced with an unblinking sort of vacancy. He must feel the same sense of inevitability that has settled inside of Layna. Who are they to say no to this? This is their fate, one they apparently designed for themselves millennia ago. They made the choice already in ages past, to give their lives in trying to prevent the prophesied fate of the universes. These lives…they never belonged to Layna or to Blake. They belonged to the Kosmos. To all the life that their death could preserve.

But still, there is fear. Fear of failing, yes. Layna is hardly able to comprehend the magnitude of such a failure. But more so, more present at this moment, is the selfish fear of succeeding. Of the universes continuing, of the world still turning, without them in it. Of ceasing to exist. She tries to drown her fear in shame for her egocentric concerns. Tries to put it in the context of what is at stake. But the fear won't subside. Her survival instincts are still telling her to run. But she won't run from this. She looks up at Lady Anora and takes a deep breath to steady herself.

"What do we need to do?"

Rather than responding, Lady Anora reaches back toward her seat and lowers herself into it, her face stricken. But Layna can sense the rest of the Consulate relax, and only now does she realize the level of tension that was in the chamber. She wonders what they would have done if she and Blake had said no, or just disappeared. Were they expecting it? Would they have *forced* them to do what was necessary? Controlled their minds somehow? She can't explore those possibilities. She needs to continue to think of these people as her allies. If she allows herself to dwell on the fact that they are sentencing her and Blake to death, she may fight back, and she can't risk that. She will accept her fate and do everything she can to change Blake's. That is all that's left.

"Layna?"

The sound of her name pulls her out of a light, dreamless sleep. She hasn't been dreaming at all lately. For a fleeting, ignorant moment before fully waking, she wonders if, as a Naut, she will ever have normal dreams again.

No. I'll never dream again, because tomorrow I'll be dead.

Part of her wants to fall back into the nothingness, but she feels an arm around her tighten and she opens her eyes. She fell asleep in Blake's arms, her head on his chest and her arm gripped tightly across his stomach. After they left the Consulate, they ported straight back to their newly assigned bunker in the undamaged South Wing, where they collapsed together on the bottom bunk without a word.

The Consulate will be addressing the entire Order in the arena tonight to reveal their plan. For their part, Layna and Blake have been forbidden from discussing the specifics of their role with anyone but the Consulate, including Des. Des was informed of the nature of their energies, but as Lucien put it, nothing good would come of him being "distracted by the truth of your fate."

The truth of their fate…The words seemed hollow coming from Lucien's lips. Certainly, their fate was no distraction to him and the others. It was simply a solution.

Yet before dismissing them, each member of the Consulate stepped down to the basin and one by one knelt before Layna and Blake in an ironic and unexpected show of veneration directed at their apparently former selves. Layna couldn't have imagined a more uncomfortable way to end the worst moment of her life. And to top it off, the only one who did not step down was Lady Anora, her eyes following them out with a hollow gaze as they left the circle.

"Layna?" Blake says again gently.

"I'm awake," she whispers, turning her head up to face him. He has one arm bent beneath his head and the other wrapped around her shoulders. If not for the lines on his brow and the dark marks under his eyes, he would look almost relaxed.

"Des just came in. He thought we were both asleep. Didn't say anything but he left us some food," he says, as he inclines his head toward the small nightstand where the food sits piled high on two plates. "Are you hungry?"

Layna hasn't eaten since the sandwiches they had this morning in the tunnel, and it's well past dinner time now. But she has no appetite and no interest in moving from the bed. "Not really. You should go ahead though," she responds, as she props herself up on her elbow to move out of the way. But Blake holds her there, their faces inches apart.

"I'm not hungry, either. And I don't want to sleep anymore," he whispers, his voice thick. He pushes a lock of golden hair away from her face and tucks it behind her ear. But he doesn't remove his hand. Instead, he begins slowly tracing her jawline with his fingers, and then her cheeks, leaving behind a trail of tingling electricity that seems to spread to every part of her body. Her heart is a wild drumbeat, and she's sure he can feel it. But she no longer cares.

His thumb gently brushes across her lower lip, reawakening all the human senses she'd been neglecting. Each breath they take sounds like thunder in her ears, and even in the dim candlelight, she can make out all of the details of his face, his blue eyes so piercing that they nearly glow as they do in the Ouroboros. He draws her body to his and buries his hands in her hair. Every part of her that is touching him seems to ignite into flame, and she melts into him.

He closes the last inch of space between them, kissing her as if it's their final seconds on Earth. The feeble walls she'd tried to build around her heart crumble, and she kisses him back hungrily, without care for pretenses or distractions. She wants as much of this as she can get before she dies.

But Blake stops abruptly, pulling several unbearable inches away from her. He raises a hand to her cheek to wipe away the tears that have begun streaming down her face. He gazes at her, his eyes tormented. "I'm sorry, Layna...I shouldn't have—"

"Blake, *no*," Layna chokes as an uncontrollable sob escapes her. "That's not...I just..." Blake pulls her to him as the fear, anger, shame, and despair come pouring out of her. It was reckless for her to open her heart like this, even for a second, given all that she knew it was trying to contain.

An instant is all it will take. She hears Des in her mind and thinks of the eclipsed Nauts in the arena. *Come on, Layna, keep it together. Just a little longer.* She reels herself in, breathing through the darkness, focusing her thoughts. Fear is just another state of mind, and beyond the fear is peace.

It's not hard, she realizes, to accept that you're going to die. What's hard to accept is the time you wasted. All the stupid things she thought were so important, the things she worried about, the experiences she avoided, the preparations for a future she would not live to see. It didn't mean anything. It almost feels as though life—*real* life—didn't start until the day she met Blake. Such a shame that the beginning was really the beginning of the end. A shame that her family and friends never got the chance to know who she really was beneath all the masks. But then, she never got the chance to really know herself either. And now she never will.

She wishes she could go back for just a day to say goodbye to her mom and Kat and Jim. She could tell them that her death has a purpose. That it's for them, for her family and her friends, old and new. For all the people who she never got the chance to know. It's for the billions of people on Earth and all the beings across the Kosmos who she was born to protect. If her life didn't mean anything, at least her death will. She takes comfort in that.

"What are you thinking?" Blake murmurs as he strokes her hair.

She doesn't think telling him that she's trying to accept death will comfort him in the least. She tries to offer hope instead. "Maybe they're wrong about what's going to happen to us. They've been wrong about other things."

"Maybe..." Blake offers. But the word is empty, and it reminds Layna of the way he was looking at Lady Anora when she told them they'd found an answer. Like, somehow, he knew it was going to be a death sentence before she even spoke.

"Blake...did you know?"

She feels him sigh beneath her, and she straightens up to look at him.

"I never thought it'd be anything like this," he says softly. "But...yeah, I've suspected for days now that something was going to happen to me."

"What do you...why?" Layna demands. "You saw something in your flashes?"

"I saw...nothing," he says with a shudder. "Darkness. Every time I've tried using my oneiromancy in the last few days, I've gotten nothing but this suffocating blackness. So I figured it must mean I was going to die. When that couple took us, I thought maybe that was it. When we were fighting the eclipsed Nauts in the arena, I thought that was it. I was almost...hoping for it. I didn't want it to be related to, you know...the end of the world. To other people dying. To you dying."

Layna forces down the lump in her throat and gives a feeble shake of her head. "It...it could mean something else. Why didn't you tell me?"

He reaches for her face again but hesitates and then drops his hand to her shoulder. "There were more important things for you to focus on, I know that. I know how hard you've been trying to use your telesthesia to protect everyone. I didn't want you to waste your energy trying to figure it out. Not like we could do anything about it."

"*You* are important to me, and what happens to you is important to me. Blake—"

She is interrupted as someone else's voice abruptly starts speaking inside her mind, and she and Blake both bolt up at once. *All Nauts report to the Oneiropolis arena immediately.*

"Holy crap, how does anyone ever get used to that!" Blake shouts, grabbing the sides of his head.

"It even kind of *sounded* like Raj...but also me," Layna says. She shakes out her arms to try to rid herself of the crawling sensation from the intrusion.

Then Molimo appears in the center of their bunker. "Hey, guys, sorry, Des sent me for you, though I'm sure you just heard that too. The Consulate is…uh…" He squints at them in the dark. "Hey, woah, is everything okay? Feels seriously intense in here."

"Sure, we're fine," Layna says, trying her best to sound normal. "We heard the announcement, which was super creepy."

"Yeah, it was…" Molimo mumbles, still looking concerned. Then his brow unfurrows and his eyes go wide with fear. "Wait, Layna…" he breathes. "Blake? What's with the…Why do you feel like…?"

Layna doesn't need him to say anything more to know the emotions he must have gathered from their subconscious minds. He's going to find out in a minute that the end may be coming for them all tomorrow anyway. She'll just chalk it up to regular fear of death instead of the certainty of it. Not like they told him anything they weren't supposed to. She can't be held accountable for what her subconscious says or doesn't say to telepaths.

"Blake saw something in his dreams…it's going to be tomorrow," Layna offers in half-truth, as she stands to face him. "The Consulate is going to tell everyone about it now."

Molimo swallows hard and nods. "You…you both seem to already feel how it's going to end for you, though."

"Yeah," Blake says with a sigh. "Guess that's the not-so-fun part about seeing the future. Don't say anything to anyone, okay?"

Molimo looks back and forth between them with a forlorn expression. He takes a step toward Layna and wraps her in a bear hug that forces the breath from her lungs, which once again begin

223

screaming in protest. As soon as Blake emerges from the bunk, Molimo reaches out and envelops him into his enormous grasp. After a minute of this, Layna begins to wonder if maybe she'll die from affectionate suffocation before she gets her chance to save the universe. But just before she can consider tapping out, he releases them.

He holds them by their shoulders in front of him, and his eyes glisten. "Does the Consulate know how it's going to happen? Do we...stand a chance of winning?" he asks hopefully.

"They don't know exactly what will happen, but I'd say we stand as good a chance as we could have hoped for," Blake says with a smile for Molimo's benefit.

"Okay, little brother," Molimo replies, trying to return the smile. But it turns into somewhat of a grimace as he once again grabs them both in an even tighter hug.

Layna's eyes begin watering from her aching ribs, as Blake wheezes, "We should probably get going, Molimo."

"Yeah, okay," he says with a sigh as he releases them. Layna takes a deep breath, and together the three of them port to the arena to await the Consulate's remarks.

The entire Order already appears to be waiting in the Ouroboros when they arrive. Tense, clipped whispers fill in the remaining space between the thousands of glowing bodies. It feels so different from the last time they were all together for the aetherblade conjuring. This time, she knows they can all sense it. The darkness is coming.

Layna, Blake, and Molimo find the other members of First Class, but there is no sign of the Guides. The popping sound of several Nauts entering the Ouroboros at once signals the Consulate's arrival, and the whispering ceases at once. The whole arena salutes the twelve members standing in a glimmering row along the south balcony. Lady Anora is at its center, scanning the crowd below.

As she finds Layna and Blake, she closes her eyes and clutches the stone ledge of the balcony, as though she was hoping not to find them there. Despite the role that Lady Anora has played in sealing her demise, Layna's heart still aches to see her in pain. Though there may be a sense of betrayal somewhere in all the darkness Layna has buried, something about having only hours left on this planet makes forgiveness an easy task. After all, it wasn't Lady Anora's decision to send them to their deaths. It was theirs—hers and Blake's. Though from a different body in a different time, apparently them, nonetheless. She must keep reminding herself of that, despite how difficult the idea is for her to fully grasp.

Layna watches as Thaddeus casually slips his hand over Lady Anora's for an instant before tucking it back beneath his golden robe. It seems to give her strength, and she raises her hands above her head to get everyone's attention. It's a useless exercise as all eyes in the room are already trained on the balcony in breathless anticipation.

Lady Anora looks into the crowd and then down at her feet. "Not one of us ever asked for this life."

Though it is softly spoken, the acoustics of the chamber carry the declaration to the thousands of waiting ears. There is a pause that lingers to lengths of discomfort, but not a single Naut breaks the enraptured silence.

"It may often seem like a tiring, thankless, burdensome struggle, our lives," she says, louder now, her eyes connecting with the Nauts below. "For many millennia, we have carried the weight of not only our world, but our universe, on our collective shoulders. We, the Nauts of Earth, the Nauts of humanity, were forged with a foretelling of failure. The Oneiroi left us with the burden of knowing that with their death, the darkness would come to consume the Kosmos during the life of Earth. An ancient school of thought instilled in us the belief that it would be Earth itself that would let the darkness in.

"As an Order, we have existed in an eternal struggle against this destiny. Individually, we have struggled against our nature to be free, to be flawed, to be...quite simply, *human.* Yes, humanity is flawed. It has allowed darkness to take root here, to spread and grow. But have no doubt, the part of us that is human is the best part of ourselves. It is the part of us that is hope, that is courage and conviction. It is the part of us that is love. Love for each other, for the world that has borne us through the millennia to this very moment, and for the precious life on all aetherworlds across the Kosmos. Though it is as Nauts that we must fight Erebus, it is our humanity that will persevere. It is our humanity that will save us."

Her eyes land heavy on Layna and Blake as she continues.

"A very long time ago, two ordinary human beings were transformed and given the power to protect our world from darkness.

And where the Oneiroi gave up on us and gave in to fate, Hemera and Nyx did not. It is thanks to their faith in humanity, their determination and sacrifice, that we may have found a way to defeat the darkness—"

Lady Anora is interrupted by a loud cheer that Layna knows is unmistakably Harkin. He is quickly joined by others around the arena until it is filled with a deafening chorus of cheers and applause.

Lady Anora once again raises her hands for quiet before continuing. "Make no mistake, brothers and sisters, this fight will not be easy. Lives, both human and Naut, will be lost. But the fight is no longer *impossible*, so long as we work together in the brief time we have left. With the help of our scholars, our texts, and some of our youngest Nauts, we have now identified a gateway that will open a portal to the Shadow Universe and allow Erebus to enter this world, and thereby, the whole Kosmos. And we know this will occur before tomorrow's end."

Hushed murmurs of fear erupt around the room, but Lady Anora doesn't pause for quiet.

"We discovered that this gateway will come into existence inside the mind of a very unusual boy. Erebus will be able to sense the portal the instant it opens, so there will be not a moment to spare. Every one of us will have a role to play, and each role will be critical to our success. And we *will* succeed. Hemera and Nyx believed in us. I believe in us. My fellow Nauts, let our fate be shaped not by the foretelling of failure imparted by the Oneiroi, but by the heart and soul of humankind."

Another round of cheers erupts as Lady Anora steps back to allow Lucien to go over the details of the plan. As the noise dies down,

Lucien moves to the front and clears his throat. Just the sound of it makes Layna's skin crawl.

"The plan I am about to tell you is straightforward," he announces. "The specifics will be developed and then provided by us and your squadron leaders. The basics of our plan thus far are as follows. First, protect the boy. For reasons we don't yet understand, we cannot simply destroy him and thereby destroy the gateway. He *must* live.

"Second, there are two Nauts among you who have a…unique ability. They possess the power to close the gateway inside the boy's mind before Erebus can use him to enter our world. They will only be able to do so the moment the gateway is opened, at the same moment that Erebus will also have access to it. So we have a microscopic window of opportunity.

"Third, we anticipate large-scale umbrae attacks in tandem with or in anticipation of the breach. I warn you not to underestimate the umbrae, as they are now more deadly and unpredictable than ever before. More information on this will be provided to you by your squadron leaders. But everyone's primary objective is ensuring our two Nauts make it into that gateway. Ultimately, their success is all that matters. You will each do whatever it takes, and I mean *whatever it takes*, to ensure that they are able to complete their mission. Layna Emery and James Blakely Knox, please join us up here so that everyone can identify their objective," Lucien says, as he holds his hands out on either side of him.

Layna's stomach explodes in irrational butterflies as she feels her cheeks flush red. *Get over yourself, Layna. This isn't Caledon*

High. You're in the freaking army barracks of the apocalypse for God's sake. She glances at an equally flushed Blake, and they port together to the balcony. Layna keeps her eyes on her hands instead of the thousands of glowing figures below her until she can get her racing heart under control.

"*Them?*" a voice yells from the front of the crowd. "What are they, twelve? *They're* our secret weapon?"

Layna looks up sharply, her face now flushing from more than embarrassment. She searches the sea of faces for the speaker, but instead, she finds Harkin making his way through the crowd and shoving veteran Nauts out of the way with callous indifference. He grabs a middle-aged Naut by the shirt collar and shouts in his face, "You got a problem with that, you dickless wonder?"

The look of affronted surprise on the man's face sends Layna into an adrenaline-induced fit of laughter that she immediately smothers with her hand.

"Hey…hey, you there," Lucien barks. Then, looking at the other Consulate members for help, he asks, "What's that kid's name?"

"His name is Harkin," Blake responds with a satisfied smirk.

"Harkin what?"

"Harkin."

"Harkin Harkin? Oh, *never mind.*" Lucien clears his throat impatiently, and then yells out again, "Excuse me, Mr. Harkin, please desist and let Riley go."

Harkin shoves the man away from him and glares at Lucien. "Desisting," he mutters.

"Now listen, I know it's difficult to believe that two juvenile, inexperienced Nauts could hold the key to our success."

Layna's fists clench at her sides. *How about I take my key and shove it right up your—*

"But believe it or don't, it is the truth. So take a good look at these two and remember your objective," Lucien continues. "Now I believe the Nauts we have chosen as squadron leaders should be returning from their own instruction shortly."

Almost on cue, Nauts begin appearing at the back of the arena. Among them, of course, is Des. Just the sight of him being there in the room gives Layna courage and relaxes her mind. But she also feels a subtle constricting around her heart as she realizes how much she will miss him.

"Ah, and here they are. We will now break you all into squadrons, some of whom will be preparing here and some in the Citadel. Regions One through Three, please head to the north of the arena. Four through Six, stay on this end," Lucien concludes, turning then to Layna and Blake. "You two will be accompanying us briefly to the Records Chamber for recon."

"I must remain here to oversee preparations," Lady Anora says softly to the rest of the Consulate. "Let's please have one representative from each region with me and one of each with Lucien in the Records Chamber," she commands.

The Consulate splits up and half begin disappearing from the balcony as Urie leans forward and whispers something in Lucien's ear. Lucien looks out toward the crowd and nods.

"Mr. Harkin!" he bellows.

Harkin grudgingly turns around, and Lucien beckons him to join them. Layna looks at Blake in disbelief. How can they actually consider punishing Harkin at a time like this for something so stupid?

"You're also going to come with us," Lucien mutters when Harkin pops up on the balcony beside them.

Harkin just shrugs in response, but Layna steps between them. "He didn't do anything wrong."

Lucien raises his eyebrows. "I'm well aware of that, Ms. Emery."

"Then why are you making him come with you?"

"Since Lord Alden passed, we haven't had an alter-precog in our company. Though I imagine this young man's skills are still quite underdeveloped, Urie has pointed out that we might be able to use his ability to our advantage."

"Oh…" Layna replies feebly. Before she can say anything else, Lucien disappears, expecting them all to follow.

"Looks like you guys aren't the only important ones," Harkin crows from behind Layna. She spins around to retort but finds him smiling. "Thanks for coming to my rescue anyway. My hero," he laughs, giving her a friendly wink before disappearing.

In the Ouroboros, Lucien has one of Maven's glowing maps spread out over the large, wooden table at the center of the room. It's the eighth one he's pulled out since they've been in the Records

Chamber, and Layna can sense his growing frustration. Maven stands at the table with them, while four other Consulate members pour over documents on the other side of the room.

Urie and Raj are deep in conversation across from Thaddeus' nyx counterpart, Meira. Where Thaddeus is all soft and rosy, Meira is a steely and slick woman with short, black hair, sharp eyebrows, and a no-nonsense attitude. She sits in contemplative silence as she listens to the Naut next to her, an elderly woman from Region Five who introduced herself as Luz from Argentina.

They all speak in low, feverish voices. Every now and then, Layna catches words like "first wave," "attack," and "retreat." They must be far out of their element, transitioning from gatekeepers to army generals in a matter of weeks. Simply for the sake of understanding, Layna finds herself wishing she'd paid more attention in World History at school. She has no idea how battles are fought and won. She's never even been able to sit through a war movie.

"Let's try again," Lucien says impatiently. "Maven, if you will."

As she has done already seven times, Maven raises one hand over the map in front of her and places the other hand on Harkin's shoulder. In turn, Harkin places his hands on Layna and Blake's shoulders and squeezes his eyes closed in concentration. Maven explained that this was a method of gathering useful intel that she and Lord Alden used often before he died.

Though Maven can only use her scrying ability to locate the energies of Nauts or anti-energies of umbrae in the present moment, when she joined with Lord Alden, they were able to combine their abilities to do what she refers to as 'psychic recon'. Together, they would locate near-future umbrae incidents that Lord Alden, as a precog, would see in his visions. Using the intel they gathered, they were better able to prepare for the incidents, and potentially save more lives. Except the process is not working quite so well with Harkin given his total lack of experience.

Maven has already attempted psychic recon with the few veteran Nauts in the past weeks, but the limited glimpses of their own futures proved unhelpful. Harkin is the only alter-precog currently in the Order. Besides the one guy who supposedly sees three minutes into any person's future just by looking at them.

Their aims now are to try and determine exactly when and where Erebus will enter the gateway so they can plan a ground reconnaissance and devise a strategy. They all naturally presumed it would happen somewhere around Hijazah, Egypt, since that is where the boy lives. It was the first map they tried. But when Harkin finally got the briefest glimpse of a vision, all Maven could tell was that it did not align with any energy signatures on that map. And so it went for the next six maps. Layna is starting to wonder if it's worth scouring the whole world while they have so little time to spare.

But now, as they all hover over the eighth map, Harkin's hand flinches on Layna's shoulder. Simultaneously, Maven's hand begins to twitch and move over the glowing parchment.

Finally. They're getting something.

Then Harkin shouts so loud that everyone around the table jumps in surprise. He is silent and still for a blink, and then he jolts as though he's received an electric shock and releases his hold on Layna and Blake.

Lucien curses under his breath as Harkin's eyes burst open. He stumbles backward into a pile of maps and charts, sending them scattering to the floor. His eyes are wide with fear and his pupils are so fully dilated that his irises look black. Though he's looking at them, he doesn't seem to really see them.

"Harkin?" Layna stammers.

"Hey, Harkin! Dude!" Blake shouts, as he steps toward him and begins tapping him lightly on the cheek.

Harkin takes a dazed swipe at Blake, who jumps back in surprise as Harkin's gaze finally settles on them. Layna watches as his pupils retract and return to normal. "Christ..." he breathes. "Jesus Christ. What the *hell* was that?"

"That was you almost getting us the information we need," Lucien grumbles with callous indifference.

"Not almost," Maven whispers.

They all turn to look at her, and she is holding a quivering hand above a portion of the map in front of her. "I got it," she says, her face pale as a sheet.

Lucien brightens and walks around the table to stand next to her. But Layna and Blake turn back toward Harkin. His breathing is laborious, and he rests his glistening brow in his hands.

"What did you see?" Blake asks gently.

"Bad stuff, man. Bad, bad stuff."

Layna and Blake glance at each other. This is their future he's talking about.

"I mean, it was flashes, ya know? Just glimpses." His eyes fill with unexpected sympathy as he looks at them. "You were running,

234

and we were all around you. Then a bunch of—I never seen 'em before—the detached umbrae. Scary as all hell. They were…they were ripping someone apart. I mean, like, limb from limb. Then…*shit*, man. It was this disgusting, shriveled nightmare-of-a-thing floating in the air. Then just screaming, flashes of light, sharp teeth comin' at my damn face. And that was it. Game over."

Layna tries to swallow the lump lodged in her throat, and she notices that Maven and Lucien have stopped talking and turned to listen.

"What do you mean by game over?" Lucien asks.

"What does it *mean*? It means I think we're all going to freakin' die, man. That's what."

"Well, what did you think, this was going to be a school field trip?" Lucien snaps. "The umbrae are going to fight. Nauts are going to die. It is war. It doesn't mean we will lose. We have *them*," he says, gesturing to Layna and Blake.

Go figure that it'd be Lucien's dispassionate conviction that seals Layna's grasp of what is expected of them, and finally the panic sets in. The wild realization of how unprepared she and Blake are for what lies ahead. They've been told they'll be able to close the gateway. But no one is going to bother explaining how, exactly, they're to go about that minor task? So, they're just supposed to *wing it,* on the spot, in their 'microscopic window of opportunity' in the middle of Armageddon?

"Um, that's nice," Layna trills, "but we don't even know what we're supposed to do once we're…in there. If we can even figure out how to get in there!"

"You will know," Lucien replies.

"But *how*?" Blake demands.

Lucien turns to face both of them fully, clasping his hands together behind his back. "Because you are Hemera and Nyx," he proclaims, as though it is the simplest explanation in the world. "And you will remember. We have faith in you."

At this point, Layna doesn't give a single shit about his faith.

Harkin whirls on Layna and Blake, looking them up and down in wild-eyed confusion, and then turns back to Lucien. "What…in the effin' hell…does that even *mean*?"

Lucien ignores Harkin and turns toward the others. "Listen, everyone. We've identified our potential ground zero. It appears that Erebus will try to use the gateway to enter our world by way of Jerusalem."

"Jerusalem? No, the precog must be mistaken," Urie says with a shake of his head.

"The precog has a name," Harkin grumbles.

"There are no mistakes in psychic recon, Urie," Maven snaps in exasperation. "I'm certain this is it. I've never seen so many Naut energies…and umbrae. All in one place." She visibly shudders as she glances back down at the map on the table.

"But the boy is in Egypt," Meira argues in Hebrew. "Erebus needs the boy to enter our world, does it not?"

"I guess we should assume that somehow the umbrae will get the boy to Jerusalem," Lucien replies. "Unfortunately, we don't have time to try to guess at umbrae capabilities. Without Lord Alden, our ability to perform psychic recon is quite limited. Perhaps we should plan with the intel we have managed to retrieve, which is that the gateway will likely be breached in Jerusalem. And as for timing, Harkin, what time of day do you think it was in your vision?"

"Not sure, seemed kind of dark. Like maybe dawn or dusk?" Harkin replies, looking to Blake.

"Yeah," Blake agrees, shutting his eyes in concentration. "In my flash, it didn't feel like nighttime, so maybe dawn."

"Alright, let's just plan for dawn," Lucien declares. "Assuming we spend most of our time preparing in the Ouroboros, a conservative estimate would give us about twenty hours left in OB time. Now that we have a time and location, let us determine how we are going to fight this thing."

"Wait…" Layna hesitates. "We have more intel than that. Blake and I sort of…visited the boy." Lucien shoots her a scolding look, but she continues anyway. Now is not the time for reprimands, and he knows it. "What we noticed is that he can actually *see* us in the Ouroboros. Maybe it means he can also project into the Ouroboros, or at least that we can port him across it. It'd explain how he'd get so far so quickly, because right now he's definitely still in Egypt. So…we could use that, right? And also, Blake and I have seen up close what the detached umbrae are capable of, but also what they're *not* capable of…"

"Right!" Blake blurts, suddenly animated. "We're thinking defensively because that's pretty much how Nauts have always fought the umbrae. We're trying to figure out what they're going to do and plan around that. But these visions aren't definite, right? It's probabilities. We can change them."

"They're as close to definite as you could come without absolute certainty," Lucien remarks. "We may have been able to prevent individual umbra incidents in the past, but it is statistically impossible to change the outcome of what Harkin, and you, for that matter, saw in your prophetic visions. Our sphere of influence is not big enough. The scale of it…it's unstoppable."

"Well, I don't know crap about statistics, but I'm not saying we try to stop it. Just shape it to our advantage. Alter the course. Do something unexpected. We need to think offense, you know, like tactical warfare. We take advantage of their weaknesses and play to our strengths. I mean, we're probably going to be crazy outnumbered, right? There's obviously no way we're going to win by straight up force on force, but if all we need to do is get me and Layna into that gateway, there's no need to waste Naut lives trying to do that. We know what the gateway is, we know where the gateway is, and we know generally around the time it's going to open. That already gives us *all* the advantage of time and surprise. We just need to use our forces as strategically as we can to buy us more than a microscopic window of time and keep casualties, human and Naut, at a minimum. We aren't going to play by their rules, we're going to change the game. Force them to play by ours."

Blake looks up and comes to an abrupt halt, having begun pacing the room. All eyes are on him, all mouths stunned into silence. Layna suddenly feels like maybe she doesn't know him quite as well as she thought, and a chasm opens inside her as she realizes that there is still so much…*Blake* left for her to discover. All of his memories, all of his experiences and thoughts and dreams, how is it possible for all of that to just come to an end? It can't. She won't let it.

Blake looks around at everyone and then says with a shrug, "I used to be really into Call of Duty."

"And if the rest of us are not using force on force to fight the umbrae, what are we to be doing during this operation?" Luz asks in Spanish, directing her question at Blake.

"Creating a diversion," Blake offers. "Erebus and the umbrae don't know what or where the gateway is going to be. Somehow, they just know that there is going to be one at some point, right? And they've been scouting us, following our activity to try to find it. So even though they can't sense when all of us are down here in Oneiropolis because of the augury defenses, they *would* be able to tell if a large group of us congregates somewhere else, right? So if a whole bunch of Nauts all port to, say, the Parthenon, wouldn't they assume that we've found the gateway and come to us?"

"Based on their recent activities, I'd say that's a fair assumption," Meira says.

"Well, alright then," Raj says with a quick nod of approval. "Let's get started."

CHAPTER

F ear has become a living thing. Real, tangible. Brushing up
against her like a shark in shallow water.

The world is going to end. We're going to fail. Everyone is
going to die.

Layna can't keep the thought of failure from surfacing in her
mind, over and over. Drilling its way deeper inside of her and
threatening to break her apart before they can execute their plan. It
won't be long now.

It's not that it's a bad plan. But it isn't perfect. And everyone is
going to die.

After Lucien and the others returned from the Records Chamber
and announced details of the plan, the entire Order spent the last twenty
hours or so practicing it to perfection in the Ouroboros. As dawn
approached, all the squadrons who'd spread to various chambers of
Oneiropolis reappeared in the arena for final preparations.

Layna and Blake were placed in Omega Squad, the last and smallest unit, under Des' command. While the Consulate initially assigned several of themselves and some of their most powerful veteran Nauts to make up Omega, Blake declined with a simple, "Thanks, but no thanks."

Lucien was appalled, but Layna knew exactly what Blake was thinking. "We already have a squad," she added. "We need our own training group with us. We've practiced with them every day and we already know how to work as a team." The Consulate was opposed to the idea, but when Des insisted these Nauts were the only ones who would suffice, they relented.

So, Molimo, Zain, Aysel, Zahra, and Harkin joined them in Omega. Des also requested Selene, and though she'd been assigned to lead Kappa, she just informed the Consulate in her usual blunt way to find someone else. And, of course, she conditioned her conscription to Omega on the addition of Phoebe, who has not spoken to anyone but Selene since Enzo's return. Selene has kept close to her side, offering soft words of encouragement that have appeared to keep her going. The Consulate's compromise was that several of the strongest Consulate members would join them when the time comes to ensure maximum protection.

Knowing when that time will be is now left almost entirely up to Layna, given her unusual telesthetic connections to the boy, Erebus, and their reciprocal netherworld. She has been performing telesthetic sweeps constantly since they left the Records Chamber. It has become almost like a computer program running in the background of her mind. Thaddeus and Maven spent an hour or so helping her to focus her concentration specifically on what they'd called the boy's 'dream-ego' to get a more accurate reading on the moment his mind will open to Erebus. It was difficult at first, but she's been able to see it more clearly with each sweep, like a fuzzy picture slowly coming into focus.

The arena has been a chaotic cacophony of sounds since the drills began, with the incessant yelling of orders, screams of frustration, crackling of lucetelum, and echoing pops as Nauts ported here and there in their attempt to learn the maneuvers. But now that the drills are over, there is an eerie absence of noise that has Layna wishing for its return. She remains in the Ouroboros with everyone else, sitting with her back against the undamaged south wall of the arena, surrounded by her friends in Omega. But there is no lighthearted banter this time. And the deadened silence only acts as a reminder that there is nothing left standing between them and the end of the world.

Yet dawn has come and gone, and still they wait. The entire Order, lingering in the dreamplane like restless spirits. The Consulate seems convinced that Harkin and Blake actually saw sundown in their prophetic visions, but Layna knows they don't have that long.

After his final debrief with the other squadron leaders, Des shuffles back across the arena, head down and hands stuffed into his pockets. Layna and Blake still haven't had a chance to talk to him other than shouting responses back to his commands during drills, but Layna hasn't missed the rueful glances.

Sure, it might be somewhat awkward to find out that two people you thought you knew are actually your reincarnated ancestors. But she wishes they could all just move past it. They need him now more than ever, even though he can't know why. No one but the Consulate knows that their mission is a one-way trip. It's probably better that way. Goodbyes would be too painful.

As Des nears them, he inclines his head toward an unoccupied area away from the others. Layna and Blake follow him until he stops abruptly and turns around to face them. He clears his throat and mumbles, "Layna, Blake...I need to apologize. You've all the right in the world to tell me to sod off, but if you can just hear me out..."

He pauses to await their reply without meeting their eyes, and Layna nearly laughs at how uncharacteristically stiff and formal he is being.

When they don't tell him to sod off, he continues. "I know I've failed as your Guide, and I've violated your trust. When I was first assigned to scout you, I thought it was going to be a quick, simple thing. Get in, find out some stuff, get out. I knew you were...well, anomalies, so they said. But when they asked me to be your Guide and you advanced as quickly as you did, I swear to you, I didn't know a bloody thing. Thought maybe Activates were advancing faster because the apocalypse was coming or some such rubbish. I didn't know it's because you were...or are..." He trails off, unable to complete the thought.

"Des, dude, it's still just us," Blake assures him with a clap on the shoulder. "The same two people you've trained and read like a hundred times. I mean, you probably know us better than anyone else could, including the Consulate. I'm still the kid who taught you slap-boxing in the surf. And what real music is. She's still the girl who tried to intimidate you with a baseball bat back in Jersey. *We* haven't changed just because the Consulate decided who we are, or were, or whatever."

Layna watches the tension melt from Des' golden, glowing face as he gives Blake a wistful smile. "Right you are, I suppose. Thanks, kid. But…it's important that you know something. Seether is literally what they listen to in hell. Also, I was only *pretending* not to know slap-boxing for your benefit."

"Sure you were, buddy," Blake laughs.

Des' grin widens for an instant before he grows serious again. "But truly, I want you to know that although I was technically working on the Consulate's task force, the second I became your Guide, that role took precedence for me, despite my whinging. It's the proudest thing I've ever done, guiding you two. No matter how many ulcers it's earned me. At least with you both being our secret weapon and all, it means the entire Order's got my back in protecting you now. Maybe I can finally relax a little, eh?"

"Right," Layna says with a tight smile and a sinking feeling.

It might be easier not having to say goodbye, but it also doesn't feel right. Not with Des. He deserves a proper goodbye, to make sure he knows he couldn't have changed their fate. Make sure he knows how much he has meant to them. She'll have to settle for offering him the forgiveness he didn't need to ask for.

"You've been the best Guide any Naut could have hoped for, Des," she says, wrapping her arms around his waist. "We couldn't have gotten through any of this without you. So you have nothing to apologize for, but you're forgiven anyway."

"What she said. Totally forgiven, idiot," Blake adds with a grin.

"You're an idiot," Des says fondly, as he pulls Blake into the embrace. "Glad I got stuck with you two, I suppose. Been a bloody wild ride so far." He draws back to look at them and clears his throat. "And thanks for, you know…bringing me back to life."

It is then that Layna's mask slips. Her smile falters as Des' words ring hollow in the face of what they're about to do to him. They brought him back to life just to destroy him again? If he survives this, Layna is sure he'll carry the weight of their death around with him forever. It's cruel, what the Consulate has done in assigning him to guide them, even if they didn't know it would end this way.

She forces a smile back on her face, but Des seems to have noticed the shift. He studies her for a moment and then glances at Blake. Layna can tell Blake is also working hard to repress his guilt. She can only hope Des doesn't see it too.

"Best get back to the group," Des suggests.

Layna and Blake steal an uneasy glance at each other as they turn to follow him. Layna can't stand the thought of leaving Des this way. There has to be something they can do.

DARC.

Layna comes to an abrupt halt as she remembers. Des said they've had to wipe memories before. So it is possible. Lucien used to work for DARC, he must know the Augurs capable of doing it. It might be cruel to steal someone's memories, but she's seen how Des tortured himself for not being able to prevent Darcie's death. It would be no less cruel than what he would otherwise put himself through. She resolves to find Lucien and speak to him before she enters that gateway and exits this world forever. She'll make it her dying wish, so he'll have to listen.

Blake and Des are walking side by side ahead of her, and she breaks into a jog to catch up. As she nears them, she watches Des raise his arm as though he's about to lay it across Blake's shoulders, but his hand lingers in the air. Just a single moment of hesitation, but Layna knows his intent. His hand comes to rest on Blake's shirt. The same shirt he was wearing in the Consulate Chamber when they learned the truth.

Layna holds her hand out in useless protest as Blake shouts, "Des, no!" He shrugs out from under his grasp as he too senses Des' intentions. But Des was quick. He's read the object he knew would give him the truth he glimpsed in their eyes. The truth he knew they wouldn't give on their own. He reels backward, his face ashen, and looks at them both in alarm.

"What...*no*," he whispers.

"Des, it's alright...it's...what we're meant for," Layna coaxes.

Blake reaches toward him, but Des spins around to face the balcony above them. "Anora!" he roars.

Lady Anora flinches in surprise, but she finds Des below her and sees the truth in his eyes. The ghosts of many suppressed emotions flicker across her face, but she remains silent and stoic above him.

"How could you do this? How could you let this happen?" Des cries. "There has to be another way!"

Hundreds of heads have turned to face them in the wake of Des' sudden outburst. Lady Anora ports to Des' side and places a hand on his arm, but he brushes it off.

"You weren't going to tell me. You *lied* to me," he continues, his voice breaking with hurt and disbelief. "I'm their Guide. It's my responsibility to protect them, and you would just send them off to be *sacrificed?*" He screams the last word at her, and it echoes across the silence of the chamber.

Lucien materializes on the ground beside Lady Anora, glaring hard at Des. "Get a hold of yourself," he snaps, glancing around at the onlooking Nauts. "Have you really deluded yourself into believing you were ever an actual Guide? You were a spy, a perpetuated falsehood, and your utility as such has come to an end."

The last word barely leaves his mouth before Des lunges for Lucien with a tortured cry that tears Layna's heart in two. In a swift, fluid movement, Lady Anora dives between them and ports all three of them away before Des' hands can meet the exposed flesh of Lucien's neck.

"What the hell was he going on about?" a voice barks from behind Layna and Blake.

They turn to face Harkin and the rest of Omega standing around him, all of them waiting for some explanation.

"It's not a big deal," Blake tries assuring them. "The Consulate suspects that once we enter the gateway through the boy's mind, we, uh...might not be able to get back out."

"Meaning what, exactly? You'll be stuck in some little kid's head?" Harkin asks.

Layna opens her mouth to respond, but something else comes out in a choked whisper, "It's happening."

K.A. Vanderhoef

Blake spins around to face her, his eyes seeking confirmation in hers. The telesthetic impulse surfaces from Layna's subconscious. The boy is nodding off, and his mind is shifting. No longer a matter of hours but minutes now.

Time to save the universe. Time to die.

"It's happening!" she yells, this time so the Consulate members standing on the balcony can hear her. The whole arena collectively stops moving. Stops breathing. There seems to be endless seconds of dead quiet as everyone waits for Lady Anora's command. Seconds to realize she and Lucien aren't there.

Raj shuts his eyes, reaching out to their minds to call them back as Thaddeus steps forward to take temporary command. "Alpha through Epsilon, move into position!"

"Let's go light 'em up!" someone shouts, and with a collective whoop and a blink, hundreds of Nauts disappear from the arena. They've gone up to the Parthenon directly overhead for the first planned diversion, as the rest of the Order remains in the arena and awaits their turn to fight. Layna does as she's been instructed and focuses on the Acropolis above her, while also staying with the boy in the backseat of a car headed for Luxor. She relays to the others what's happening at the Acropolis as it unfolds in her mind.

The Nauts linger in the Ouroboros above, taking positions among the enormous marble columns of the Parthenon. Layna detects the slow movements of the early-rising tourists milling about the Acropolis in the homeplane. She can feel the steady calm of their hearts, contrasted with the frantic heartbeats of the Nauts hidden in

248

their presence. She senses the fear of the thousands of Nauts still with her in the arena.

She senses everything, all at once. The amount of information she is trying to process feels like it is physically weighing down her brain, crushing it inside her skull. She clamps her hands around her temples and works to block out those in the arena to focus on the frontlines, her brothers and sisters in the most immediate danger. She feels the familial connection to them now more than ever.

There's a light touch of a hand on her back, but Layna steps out of it and closes her eyes to her own surroundings. Something else is emerging in her mind. Something from the netherworld. The Nauts above have captured the attention of the darkness, like the collective turning of billions of faceless heads in their direction. A shudder runs through Layna as she hears herself say, "They're coming." She knows that Raj is making this announcement to all Naut minds, including those up at the Parthenon. She senses the wave of fear roll across them.

Then, the tourists begin to turn.

One by one, the humans are eclipsed. The first shadowspear is launched, and on cue, all the Nauts at the Parthenon disappear simultaneously before it can meet its target. They reappear outside the circle of eclipsed and light them up with lucetelum before disappearing again in perfect choreography. This time, Alpha reappears atop the columns of the Parthenon, providing cover from above to the others who now port around the eclipsed so fast that they are a blur of movement and light. The eclipsed are no match for their speed, and shadowspears fly through empty space as umbrae are expelled back to their netherworld.

But for each umbra expelled by the lucetelum, several more humans turn. And as the umbrae run out of human bodies at the Parthenon, Layna's mind shifts to find a swarm of towering, detached umbrae speeding up the hill and away from their human counterparts in the city below. Shadows seeping across the terrain faster than any human could move. The Parthenon will soon be overrun. *They think this is it. They're taking the bait.*

Layna feels a moment of vindication until she watches as one of the Nauts standing on a column is hit with a shadowspear and goes toppling from the building, landing hard on the ground. She can sense the darkness consume him, can sense his consciousness slip away.

"The first Naut has fallen," she reports to the others in a choked whisper.

The umbrae, now mostly unbound by the bodies of their counterparts, race across the Parthenon, their arms lengthening into deadly blades, seeking Naut blood.

"Operation Starfall!" Layna shouts.

As planned, before any umbra can slice through the Nauts on the ground, they port into the sky at once. High above where Alpha stand atop the columns, they shoot lucetelum at the umbrae on the ground as they fall toward the earth. A second before they would hit the ground, they port into the air again. The umbrae may be able to move with greater speed outside the bodies of the humans, but they have not yet learned how to defy gravity.

Only Epsilon, the strongest veteran unit currently in action, returns to the ground and draws their aetherblades. They use the Aetherem to try and stay ahead of the umbrae, coming to blows only in defense. They are not there to destroy the umbrae if they can help it. They are there to distract them, and they need to stay alive as long as possible to continue to do so.

But the Nauts are outnumbered now and they begin to fall, the umbrae slicing clean through them like hot knives through butter. Detached umbrae crawl up the columns to Alpha, who frantically shoot at the formidable shadows to keep them on the ground. Some of Alpha Squadron make it into the air with the others. Many don't.

They all knew they would be outnumbered. This is what they planned for. But Layna can barely stand to watch as the squads are slaughtered while she remains safely hidden in Oneiropolis. She's overcome by a strong urge to get up there to help them, but she has no choice but to stick to the role she was assigned. At least for now. Her time will come.

"They're really outnumbered now. More umbrae coming," Layna hears herself saying.

It's followed by a command, this time from Lady Anora, who must have returned to the arena with Des and Lucien. "Zeta through Kappa, to Rome!"

Layna keeps her eyes shut in concentration, now expanding her mind to include the Nauts appearing in and around the Colosseum of Rome. They remain tightly in their squadrons, save for several smaller units of fifty centered around a young Nyx male and Hemera female couple. Decoys for Erebus. After the fight with the eclipsed Nauts in the arena, they know it will be seeking out Layna and Blake.

Layna and Raj continue to work in tandem, announcing commands as needed, and soon the Colosseum is overrun with umbrae.

251

As Layna announces that they are also outnumbered, Lady Anora shouts, "Lambda through Omicron, to Damascus!" Then as umbrae begin to appear there in droves, she cries, "Pi through Tau, to Lima!" And finally, "Upsilon through Psi, to Xi'an!"

Layna's head threatens to burst open as she maintains her focus on the entire Order now scattered across the globe while keeping part of her mind trained on the boy. She barely manages to maintain a single thread of focus on him as he arrives with his mother at Karnak Temple in Luxor. "Not long now," she yells through clenched teeth.

She is vaguely aware of having fallen to her knees, both her hands still clenched tightly to her head as if that will help hold it together. And there is now an incessant tugging in her gut as her body attempts to port to the boy's side. All at once, everything inside her is screaming to get to him, like a primal instinct buried deep in her subconscious. *Soon. I'll be with you soon.*

A few minutes is all they're allowing themselves. Raj and Lucien will go to the boy and attempt to port him back to Oneiropolis, the safest place for Layna and Blake to try to enter the gateway the moment it opens. If they are unable to port the boy, Layna and Blake will go directly to him and try to find somewhere secluded to make their attempt. Either way, they don't want to risk unnecessary exposure to Erebus ahead of the endgame. But the longer they wait, the more Nauts die.

Epsilon has been practically wiped out. Kappa is falling fast. The Nauts are now outnumbered everywhere, as thousands of umbrae pour toward their locations in each city. The evasive tactics are the only things keeping the Nauts alive now. And the umbrae seem to loom larger than ever, moving faster and more deftly as they attack the Nauts with unprecedented skill and forethought.

Layna watches as a group of five umbrae appear in Damascus, surrounding a single Naut. They move so fast that she doesn't have time to port before they've taken hold of her limbs and head. Her scream cuts short as they simultaneously spin outward and rip her to pieces.

Bile rises in Layna's throat. She doesn't want to watch this anymore. She can't. She scans the five cities across the world where the Nauts battle and senses only loss. Her fellow Nauts are dying, the humans she is meant to protect are dying. And here she sits and watches.

Just as she thinks she can't take it any longer, a large group of the umbrae at the Parthenon stop. They stop moving, stop advancing. The Nauts who were fighting them exchange glances with each other, keeping their blades and hands raised. But then the umbrae slowly begin to shrink. No...not shrink. They begin to *seep*. Into the ground below them. They disappear from the surface of the earth, seeping down, down...toward whatever lies beneath.

We do. We lie beneath.

Layna's eyes burst open to find Lady Anora's glowing figure kneeling in front of her, with Blake and Des at her sides. Maven, Raj, Nuru, and Lucien are there with Omega, and they are now the only Nauts left in the arena. After being in five places at once with all of the Nauts and the screams and the pain, the emptiness of the space strikes Layna with a finality like death.

Lady Anora reads Layna in the split second before Layna is able to form words to announce what she saw. "We need to move," Lady Anora declares, as Blake and Des grab hold of Layna's hands to help her stand.

"They're coming," Layna whispers.

"What do you mean they're coming? *Here*?" Raj asks.

Layna lifts her aching eyes, up and up, one hundred feet to the ceiling above. "They're coming," she repeats. The others all follow her gaze and see the oozing mists of darkness clotting one by one across the ceiling, a hundred at least. Like the gathering of storm clouds.

"What the hell is that?" Harkin cries.

"Let's not wait to find out," Zain responds, stepping toward Layna and Blake. "We need to get them out of here and go to the boy."

"It could draw too much attention and destroy our window of opportunity if we all go," Lady Anora counters, glancing at the shadows that are now seeping down the walls all around the arena. "Raj and Lucien, take them with you. Everyone else, let's buy them as much time as we can. We'll head to the Citadel, see how long it takes the umbrae to make their way through our maze of tunnels."

There is a sizzling in the air as all aetherblades are drawn. Raj steps forward and places a hand on Blake's shoulder. But as Lucien moves away from the others to join them, Layna tightens her grip on Des and Blake's hands. "We're not going without Des," she argues, staring Lucien down.

"Fine, we don't have time for this. I will stay here," Lucien says in exasperation. "Raj, get the announcement out when it's time, and we will come to you."

The umbrae are pooling on the ground all around them, reshaping into their full form. They all need to get out of here, now. Layna glances past Lucien at the friends they're leaving behind. If this plan works, she and Blake are never going to see any of them again. All Layna can hope now is that her friends go on to live out their lives when this is over. "Please be careful," she whispers to all of them.

Her gaze settles on Lady Anora last, whose grey eyes swim with tormented sorrow. As Layna's mind latches onto the boy's position, she pushes a final thought to the forefront of her mind, hoping Lady Anora will sense the truth of it.

We won't let you down.

Layna, Blake, Des, and Raj reappear at a spot in the Ouroboros nearly a thousand miles away from Oneiropolis. Layna is momentarily blinded by the boy's light, but as her eyes adjust, she sees they are standing in a courtyard, just inside the pylon that serves as Karnak Temple's towering main entrance. In the homeplane, the boy's mother is offering trinkets to tourists entering the temple. Behind her, the boy is resting on a blanket set against one of the columns, and he has fallen asleep. Layna can sense his dreams blossoming. Any second, his dream-ego will spark into existence, and his mind will open to Erebus.

They need to get him to seclusion, away from the tourists who may become a threat if they begin to turn. There is an archway across from them leading deeper into the temple, and a smaller archway to their right with a crude, wooden barrier set across the entrance. "Over there," Layna says, pointing right. "Looks like it's blocked off."

"Go," Raj instructs, as he ports to the tops of the columns to provide cover if the need arises.

Des lingers, grabbing Layna and Blake by the shoulders. "Listen to me," he demands, his voice breaking around the words. "Don't give up. You two are stronger than any of us. The Consulate has been wrong before, they have to be wrong about this. You can make it back out somehow. Please, just…find a way to come back, alright?"

They both wordlessly nod their promise, and Des pulls them into a brief, final hug before they turn away from their Guide and port to the boy's side. Remaining in the Ouroboros, they crouch beside him, laying their hands on his arms through the swirling, grey barrier. The plan is to try to port him across the Ouroboros to their secluded spot in the homeplane. It would be an impossibility with any ordinary human. Layna prays her instincts about the boy are right.

"One, two…" Blake begins counting.

Layna holds their intention in her mind, and on three, they flicker into the homeplane together and almost instantly reappear behind the archway to the right. They find themselves alone in a smaller court lined with crumbling statues of Egyptian gods, still crouched over the boy on the ground between them. *It worked.*

Layna says a quick thank you to the universe for at least letting them get step one right. But her gratitude is snuffed out by an unfamiliar and unsettling sensation. A sort of rumbling deep inside her own mind, growing stronger, like a volcano about to erupt. Nothing like her usual telesthetic impulses—hotter, heavier. Deadly.

Next to her, the boy stirs, the volcano erupts, and Layna jolts as something invisible collides with her very being, with the space between her atoms. Waves of oppressive energy rolling off of the boy, slamming into her subconscious, and for a moment it feels like drowning. Blake grabs her hand, and she clings to him, but they are both sinking, shrinking. And then, all falls still, and Layna and Blake collapse on all fours. Panting, they look up into each other's eyes with dread and understanding. The gateway has opened.

Layna gently shakes the boy awake, and he sits up, rubbing his eyes in confusion. As planned, she and Blake flicker briefly into the Ouroboros and back to show him who they are. "It's still us," Layna says, holding up her hand in front of her as she did in the Ouroboros when she first saw him.

The boy smiles and places his hand on hers. "Hafathah," he whispers, pointing to Layna and Blake in turn. *Guardian angels*, Layna's mind translates.

Layna locks her fingers with his for a second and gives them a light squeeze. "Please try to stay still." On instinct, she and Blake each hold one hand on the boy's head and clasp their other hands together. The boy's inquisitive, brown eyes peer up at them, but he doesn't try to move away.

Just like projecting into the Ouroboros. Just crossing into another dimension. Inside another person's mind. No biggie.

Not seconds after Layna and Blake close their eyes, a loud clap of thunder rolls across the sky above them. Layna looks up to see the sky changing, churning with ominous darkness. From somewhere in the temple, a blood-curdling scream pierces the air.

Erebus is coming.

Layna's telesthesia forces upon her a rapid succession of horrifying images from Athens, Rome, Damascus, Lima, and Xi'an. The sky above each city blackens with a caliginous mist, blocking out the sun, and people begin screaming. Athens—tourists jumping from the Acropolis to their deaths. Humans turning on each other. Lima—a man beating a woman to death with his hands. Xi'an—a shrieking woman tears out her own eyes before setting her nails on her throat.

And it's not only the humans. In each city, Nauts begin to turn on one another. The umbrae are now eclipsing them right there in the Ouroboros, and a scattering of Nauts begin slicing each other apart with their aetherblades.

"Oh my god," Layna moans. "Blake, we have to hurry!"

"Layna," he replies, squeezing her hand tighter, "we can do this. I'll see you in there."

He shuts his eyes again, and Layna uses her training to suppress the horrifying images in her mind as lightning strikes somewhere outside the temple. People are screaming, and the boy's wide, terrified eyes dart between them, but he doesn't run. Layna follows Blake's lead and closes her eyes, forcing the world to fall away, concentrating only on the boy.

She starts to feel like she is in two places at once. She is sitting on the ground in Karnak Temple, but she is also alone in nothingness, a bright, white space with no discernible floors or doors or ceilings. She can't even tell which way is up or down. But she feels her right hand clasping onto something. In the white space, she looks down to see her hand is still in Blake's. He materializes beside her, piece by piece, like a mirage forming on a barren horizon.

Her other hand reaches into the white emptiness, disappearing at the fingertips. Then suddenly, the boy is there too. His dream-ego, looking up at them just as he is doing in Karnak Temple. She latches onto the empty place with all of her senses, like trying to stay with a dream as you emerge from sleep. It grows clearer, and the temple falls away. Layna's heart leaps. *We're doing it. We're—*

A sharp pain explodes across the back of her skull and her body slams into the dusty ground of Karnak Temple. She blinks the world back into focus and finds the boy's mother towering over her, an inhuman madness in her eyes and a wooden plank in her hand. Next to Layna, Blake backs away from another eclipsed man.

At the mouth of the archway, Des blinks into the homeplane, his eyes frantic as he tries to get to them. But Raj materializes behind him, his face contorted in uncharacteristic fury as he grabs Des by the shoulders and pulls him back into the Ouroboros.

Layna's heart flutters with panic as she realizes Raj is eclipsed, which means he might not have been able to get the announcement to Omega. Help might not be coming, her friends could be dying, and Des may be in the Ouroboros fighting the umbrae on his own.

The boy's mother lets out an animalistic scream and dives at Layna, who ports out of the way and reappears behind her. She wraps her arms around the woman's neck in a chokehold, and though the woman struggles against her, Layna holds fast as they drop to their knees together. She releases the woman just as she seems to go unconscious in her arms, praying she used the method correctly and

259

didn't inflict any permanent damage. But before she can get back on her feet, she is tackled to the ground by two more eclipsed men.

We're wasting time. We need to get out of here.

She rolls to her side and reaches for the boy, intent on trying to port him back to the Citadel in Oneiropolis where at least they will have their squad to help. If the umbrae haven't gotten to them yet. But the boy is no longer sitting where she left him. Amid the commotion, he has wandered off. Layna locates him just in time to see him disappear through the archway toward the main courtyard, walking as though in a trance.

"Wait! Come back!" she cries, as one of the men grabs her by the hair. His rosy cheeks, laugh lines, and t-shirt boasting the adage 'love is love' tell her she need not fear him. But his eyes are wild, his fist lands hard against her jaw, and she reminds herself she is no longer dealing with human beings.

With the adrenaline coursing through her, she barely registers pain from the blow. The man's bald-headed partner pins her arms behind her back, but she ports behind him and kicks him in the groin. As he falls forward, Layna leaps off his back and into the air, delivering a roundhouse kick to the other man's rosy cheek. The man crumples in a semi-conscious heap, and Layna turns to see Blake take out the bald-headed man with the wooden plank that the boy's mother carried.

"Blake, the boy!"

Blake's eyes are wild as he looks up at her. He drops the plank, and they turn toward the archway only to find themselves face to face with a line of five eclipsed.

An involuntary cry escapes from Layna as she sees their faces. They are each frozen in the same contorted, horrifically inhuman expression. Their eyes swell from their sockets, black irises vibrating in pools of red, the blood vessels broken by the force of a scream that doesn't escape in this dimension. A scream that has forced their mouths open so wide that their jaws are broken, unhinged. These are the faces of madness...of Chaos. Of the umbrae coming to claim the bodies they now think belong to them. And Layna knows that the humans these people once were are not coming back this time.

As Layna and Blake prepare to port past them after the boy, all five eclipsed drop to the ground, suddenly dead weight. Des materializes on his knees between them and the fallen humans. His breathing is hitched and ragged from the battle raging in the Ouroboros. From using his aetherblade to kill umbrae and human at once.

"I'm sorry! Raj was eclipsed," he wheezes, rising to his feet. "Brought him back and got the others. Come on!"

In the instant before she ports, Layna sees the boy's mother sit up with a shriek, and, grabbing a pen from her satchel, she stabs herself in the neck without a second's hesitation. Blood spatters across the beige-colored earth as Layna disappears.

The main courtyard is complete anarchy. All around them, people are attacking one another with their bare hands, their faces contorted in the same frozen state of madness Layna saw on the others. Outside the entrance, a bolt of lightning strikes a falafel cart, and the umbrella erupts in flames, setting the vendor's clothes on fire. His tortured scream tears through the air between deafening claps of thunder.

261

Layna's eyes dart across the pandemonium in search of the boy, and she spots him. Zahra drags herself across the ground after him, both of her legs mangled. She reaches out for him but is kicked in the head by an eclipsed, falling just as Maven materializes next to the boy only to be tackled by several others. The boy continues forward. His arm is outstretched in front of him toward the stone archway that leads deeper into the temple. An archway that is swirling black with mists of darkness.

"*No!*" Blake cries, his eyes wide with horror as he watches the unfolding of the very vision that has haunted his nightmares since he was a child.

The three of them port to the boy at once, but just as they reach for him, he disappears into the mist and they grasp only air. The darkness is dispelled the moment he enters it, leaving the entrance to the temple clear. Layna stares at the other two, frozen with disbelief.

"Ouroboros!" Des cries. They all project into the Ouroboros to see if they can locate him, but in this dimension too, he is nowhere in sight.

"Where is he? I can't sense him anymore!" Layna cries. She spins around helplessly as she tries to tamp down the panic so she can perform a more expansive telesthetic sweep.

Now in the Ouroboros, Layna witnesses the underbelly of the madness that they saw unfolding in the homeplane. Members of Omega are struggling for their lives, wildly outnumbered by the umbrae. The temple is crawling with them. Literally. Detached umbrae taking the shape of enormous spiders and scorpions have begun crawling over the walls from outside the temple, a relentless horde.

Zain and Molimo are back to back, fighting off three of the spiders with their aetherblades, while Aysel and Harkin crouch atop stone columns and try to provide cover with their lucetelum. Aysel ducks out of the way of a shadowspear and topples off the column, only to reappear on another one nearby to continue her barrage from above. Selene, Phoebe, and Lady Anora fight off a line of humanoid umbrae who are currently trying to get to Layna and Blake, while Nuru and Lucien port around them, firing off powerful lucetelum.

It's all pointless. The boy is gone. Erebus has him, and Layna and Blake have failed. But Layna's eyes land on Harkin and she remembers…his premonition in the Records Chamber. Though she can't feel him anymore, she knows where the boy must be. The most likely of all possible outcomes. They may have failed to alter the vision of the future, but they haven't failed entirely. Not yet.

"Des!" she cries. "We need to go to Jerusalem!"

Des nods and searches the chaos beyond her. "Anora!" he yells. "Jerusalem!"

"Nuru, get as many as you can," Lady Anora commands. "Everyone else, to Layna and Blake!"

She ports to their side with Selene and Phoebe, and one by one, they each abandon their respective battles and appear in a tight circle around Layna and Blake. Aysel and Harkin port to them from the tops of the columns, but as Zain and Molimo turn away from their foes to join them, Zain is hit from behind by a shadowspear and stumbles to his knees.

"No!" Layna screams, darting forward toward him.

263

Arms hold her back, but Molimo spins around and doubles back. "Zain! I got you, dude!" He scoops him up from under the arms and ports them both toward the others. As Blake helps prop Zain up with Molimo, all the umbrae scattered across the courtyard stop moving. There is a moment of breathless stillness as each featureless face turns toward them.

"Time to go!" Blake shouts.

The umbrae rush at them from all directions in a shadowed blur just as Maven returns from the homeplane, without Zahra, and latches onto Lady Anora as they all disappear.

CHAPTER

The world spins as Layna tries to regain her orientation after traveling so far. They're still in the Ouroboros, now presumably in Jerusalem. Layna begins running with the others before her body has its bearings, and she stumbles forward into Des. She stops short and is pushed from behind by Lucien. Blake grabs her elbow with his free hand as he continues to support Zain with his other arm, who barely seems able to put one foot in front of the other. His face is ashen, his features pinched with pain.

"Everyone just keep moving," Lucien shouts. "Layna, try to get a reading on the boy!"

The crackling of lucetelum fills Layna's ears, and she realizes that Omega is already fending off both eclipsed and detached umbrae lining the streets of Jerusalem. Above them, the sky is a moaning cyclone of sinister blackness, an unearthly storm raging in the Ouroboros and spitting lethal bolts of lightning in every direction.

Layna feels all the hairs on her body prickle just as a bolt of lightning somehow crosses dimensions and strikes a building in the homeplane. She watches in awe as slow-moving flames begin to lick up the side of the building. The shadowed flood has arrived, and Earth is opening to Erebus. Up ahead, umbrae begin pooling up from the ground, forming a barrier between them and their path.

"Right!" Lady Anora shouts from up ahead, and they all turn right down an alleyway. They don't have a destination in mind, not until Layna pinpoints the boy's location. All they can do is keep moving.

There's a popping like firecrackers as Nuru rejoins them with Thaddeus, Meira, and a couple dozen Nauts. Then Urie and Ying Yue and about twenty more Nauts form a thicker perimeter around Omega.

And then, there is Raj in their minds. *All Nauts to Jerusalem for Operation Endgame.*

No point in keeping up diversions now. They've lost their advantage and they've run out of time. All they can do is use every last ounce of remaining force to get Layna and Blake to the boy and hope it's not too late. How did they ever believe they could outfight this swarm?

The second after Layna hears the announcement in her mind, Raj is there with them looking bloodied and beaten. "Desmond, I am sorry!" he calls as he runs alongside them.

"Forgotten, brother!" Des answers.

"Left!" Lady Anora yells. Their ranks swell to a hundred as they turn another corner and Layna tries focusing her mind to get a location on the boy, but there is only darkness.

"The whole city is in shadow," Layna cries. "I can't sense him at all!"

They pour out into a vast, open square and everyone slows to a halt. An army of detached umbrae are spread before them, hundreds of them, lying in wait. The shrouded, grey figures of dead humans are scattered across the square, their dim, white lights extinguished. But the fallen humans can't be the counterparts of the gathered umbrae, otherwise these umbrae would be dead too. The detached umbrae don't even need to be in proximity to their counterparts anymore. They only need them to not die.

The gathering of Nauts continues to swell around them, a troop of several hundred now and growing. Those on the outermost of the circle draw their aetherblades and prepare to fight.

Before anyone can react, all umbrae in the square disappear at once. There is a split second of confusion before their tactic becomes clear. One by one, the light of the Nauts around the edge of their troop dims as it is mixed with darkness. It spreads inward toward the center of the circle like a disease.

"Omega, use your training! Don't let the darkness in!" Des commands, as he and Lady Anora move in closer to Layna and Blake. The rest of Omega follows suit, forming a tight inner circle of light within the spreading shadow.

Layna does her best to subdue the darkness in her mind, focusing on the task at hand, drawing courage from the friends who surround her. *Beyond the fear is peace. Go beyond the fear.*

Veteran Nauts struggle against the darkness, but it's little use. Erebus has only gained in power, and they've had no training to prepare for this invasion of their minds. Even some of the Consulate members begin to turn. "Fight it!" Des cries as he sees Maven go dark next to him. "Stay in the light!"

Blake grabs Layna by the shoulders and turns her toward him. "Look at me," he pleads, his voice strained. Layna's heart stops as she notices little, dark tendrils snaking out from his temples down to his neck.

"Blake, no!" she cries.

"Just look at me," he says more calmly.

She obeys, looking into his eyes, their sapphire glow nearly consumed by black already. Once again, it is only them, alone and separate from the chaos that surrounds them.

"Now tell me you're going to survive. Say it, and mean it," he whispers.

She forces herself not to look away, placing a hand against his cheek as she utters the lie like the life of the world depends on its truth. "I am going to survive this, Blake."

Nearly the second the words fall from her lips, Layna can see the shimmer returning to his eyes, the tendrils of darkness dissipating. She feels a momentary sense of relief, but the sizzling sound of a collective drawing of aetherblades jolts her back to reality. The eclipsed Nauts now all face inward toward their small squad of eleven and the other few remaining Consulate members who have not turned. And just like that, they stand not among a sea of protectors but of enemies.

Yet the close gathering of so many umbrae presents an opportunity. Layna sees Des put his hand on Blake's shoulder just as Blake reaches forward toward Molimo, and Layna reaches for Lady

Anora. Within the blink of an eye, Omega is clasped together, and Layna feels the flip of the switch, the aligning of their energies. Before any eclipsed Naut can strike, a multiluce explodes from the center cohort, throwing them and all the surrounding Nauts into the homeplane and sending their umbrae parasites back to the netherworld.

They are all ripped from each other as they fly through the air. But the second Layna and Blake land, Lady Anora is already diving toward them. She grabs hold and projects them back into the Ouroboros and away from the swarm.

Layna tumbles onto her stomach and lets out a tremulous cry as she stares at the ground, now some sixty feet below her. They've landed atop a wall barely wider than the height of a man, overlooking the square where they just stood. Layna can see the blast radius of their multiluce at the center where there are only the grey figures of Nauts who were knocked out to the homeplane and have not returned. But there are too many Nauts still eclipsed, and the square remains a churning mixture of light and dark as more Nauts from other parts of the world arrive. Some are immediately eclipsed by the umbrae also pouring into the square from all corners of the city and beyond. Some are instantly killed. Most swing their aetherblades with the deadly combination of fury and skill, now intent on taking down as many umbrae with them as possible.

Layna scrambles to her feet with Blake and Lady Anora. They are the only three atop the wall, and the umbrae seem not to have noticed their escape just yet.

"Des!" Blake cries, eyes wide as he gapes at the bloody battle below. He looks prepared to port back down, but Lady Anora grabs his arm. Before she can issue a warning, Des appears on the wall to their left, along with Aysel, Molimo, and Harkin. Then Lucien, Selene, and Phoebe show up to their right. To Layna's great relief, all their auras glow, pure and bright around them. But as she looks back down at the square, she realizes they may be the only ones continuing on.

Des notices the look on Blake's face and offers a reassuring nod. "I'm not going anywhere, kid."

"None of us are," Phoebe adds, as a loud crack of thunder splits across the sky. "We'll stay with you as long as we are able."

"Yeah...so what now?" Molimo asks, the quiver in his voice betraying his steady demeanor. Layna realizes Zain is no longer with him, and she glances down at the square and back up at Molimo. He answers her unasked question as his eyes fill with sorrow. Layna takes a deep breath and shuts down the rising tide of fear for her friends' lives. She has to stay focused. Zahra and Zain could still be alive, and she has to continue to believe that.

"Harkin," Lucien barks, "do you think you can—"

A bright flash of light erupts between them and Lucien goes flying backward and disappears into the homeplane. They all spin around to find three Consulate members—Meira, Urie, and Maven—on the wall with them, all three of them eclipsed with aetherblades drawn.

Lady Anora shoves Layna and Blake behind her and pummels the Consulate members with a steady barrage of lucetelum. The lucetelum rebound off the aetherblades, which the eclipsed Consulate members hold out in front of them like shields. Lucien reappears beside Lady Anora and adds his light to hers. As Layna also tries to take aim, she is knocked down from behind and lands on her stomach. She looks over her shoulder to see Aysel on top of her.

"Aysel, what the hell?" Layna yells. She tries to shove her off, but without a word, Aysel wraps her arms and legs around Layna and rolls them both sideways, right over the edge of the wall.

The sound of Layna's own shocked scream is muffled by the rushing wind in her ears, but both come to an abrupt halt as Aysel ports them from the air and they land together at the far end of the wall. Layna can now see why Aysel tackled her. Umbrae in their insectoid form have begun climbing the walls at alarming speed, and Omega has scattered. But Des and Blake are nowhere to be seen, and neither are Harkin and Molimo. Layna forces herself to look down at the ground below. But the storm of Chaos raging overhead has spread outward toward the horizon, and it is nearly too dark to see. *They're not down there. They're still alive.* She knows somehow that if Blake were dead, she would have felt it.

She jumps to her feet just as a scorpion umbra appears in front of her and Aysel, swinging the point of its enormous, deadly tail down on them.

Layna instinctively raises her arm, and the air around her sizzles as her weapon comes to her aid. The reverberation of the violent meeting of light and shadow nearly knocks her off the wall, but her blade takes the brunt of the blow, and she remains on her feet. She wraps her other hand around the hilt at the middle and dives sideways as she slices through the umbra's first four insectoid legs. Then she leaps up, spinning her weapon around and piercing the scorpion right through the center of its body with the other end. The umbra shrinks in on itself, convulses once, and disintegrates, its remains disappearing into the whipping winds of the storm. Layna's mind flashes to the man in brightly colored clothes and a sunhat, but she shakes the memory away. *Deal with it later.*

"Thank you," Aysel breathes.

"Ditto, for before," Layna replies, as they both turn back to see Selene and Phoebe fighting two humanoid umbrae, and just beyond them, Lucien is battling Meira as Lady Anora fights Urie and Maven. Lady Anora still has not drawn her weapon, and Layna knows she won't. Not against them.

One of the umbrae breaks through Selene and Phoebe's defense, and Layna and Aysel raise their hands and fire at once. But the umbrae are nearly unstoppable now, and the lucetelum does little damage. They are forced to split and dive off the wall to avoid being skewered, and they both reappear just behind the umbra. Aysel bends down and stabs her twin blades straight through both its calves as Layna spins, swinging her weapon at the same time that it falls to its knees, and slicing its head off in a clean sweep.

As it disintegrates in front of her, Layna hears a scream behind her that chills her to the core. *Lady Anora.* She spins around to find Lady Anora frozen, reaching toward Lucien. He stares down at his aetherblade where it is lodged in Meira's abdomen. Meira wears a look of shock, her own blade hovering at Lucien's throat.

Though Maven and Urie remain eclipsed, they stand motionless, staring toward Meira. Layna can see the strain in their eyes, in the trembling of their hands on their weapons. The Consulate members are the strongest of the Nauts, and Layna realizes they're still fighting in there. A part of them has not yet given in to the darkness.

Meira drops her arms to her sides as her aetherblade flickers and disappears. The shroud around her dissipates and her eyes return to the shining indigo of her aura.

"I'm sorry…" she whispers to Lucien as she staggers backward.

She disappears over the side of the wall as Lucien reaches helplessly toward her. He turns away, pain flashing like lightning in his eyes before he finds Layna and his face is set once again with determination. "Layna, you need to find him, *now*. You're the only one who can do it." He spins back around as an umbra descends upon him.

But I can't do it. He's gone.

Everyone believed in her, and her failure has condemned the universe. Layna drops to her knees as the weight of it all crushes her, and a tidal wave of darkness approaches the shores of her mind. And then, there it is. Erebus, trying to writhe its way into the desolation of her subconscious. But instead of trying to defend herself against it, she surrenders to it. Not to give up. Not to give in. But because she feels something else. *A location.* A telesthetic impulse breaks through the wave like a lighthouse in the night.

She can't find the boy because Erebus already has him. But she *can* find Erebus. Or rather…she can let Erebus find her.

Don't resist your opponent's force. Yield to overcome it.

The battle rages on around her as a new wave of umbrae appear on the wall. But Layna closes her eyes, trusting that the others will do what they can to protect her while she does what is necessary. She hears Lady Anora yelling her name as she feels the darkness take hold. She can sense the cold, dark tendrils spreading down her body. If she can just hang on a little longer, allow herself to go a little deeper, trace back to the source of the darkness that's set on consuming her...

Her eyes pop open with triumph just as Selene and Phoebe reach her. "Layna, snap out of it!" Selene cries, grabbing her by the shoulders.

"There!" Layna shouts, pointing at the domed building in the distance that she saw in her mind. "He's there!"

Selene follows Layna's direction and then announces to the others, "The Dome of the Rock!"

Selene, Phoebe, and Aysel are closest, and together they port with Layna toward the Dome. But the second they reappear, Maven materializes next to them. She grabs hold of Aysel by her braid and swings her blade down toward Aysel's neck with a bestial cry. In a flash of light, Phoebe and Selene are on top of her. Selene knocks Aysel aside as Phoebe blocks Maven's blade with her own. In the swift moves of the Aetherem, the three of them trade blows with deft precision, and Maven barely misses in a swipe at Phoebe's neck. In reply, Phoebe slices Maven's hand off.

Maven screams in agony as her aetherblade disappears along with her right hand, and Selene knocks her back out to the homeplane with a dark lucetelum. The second Maven is gone, Selene sheaths her blade and pulls Phoebe to her. "Okay?" she asks.

Phoebe only stares back at her, a look of astonishment frozen on her face.

"Phoebe?" Selene hesitates.

Phoebe swallows hard, and to Layna's horror, it causes a gush of blood to spill out of the indiscernible slice across her throat where Maven's razor-thin blade met her flesh.

She didn't miss after all.

Selene cries out as Phoebe grabs at her throat and tumbles forward into Selene's arms. Lucien and Lady Anora appear beside them as Selene tries desperately to stifle the flow of blood.

There is a mere second of hesitation before Lucien shouts, "Keep moving!"

He grabs Layna and nudges a shocked Aysel toward the building in front of them and tries to pull Selene to her feet.

"No, leave me be!" Selene shrieks. She replaces her trembling hands over the flood at Phoebe's neck, but Phoebe is no longer moving, and her amber eyes have already lost their light.

"Whatever it takes," Lucien reminds Selene, as he grabs her again.

Selene spins around and pins her fierce eyes on him, ready for a fight. Layna can see the tendrils of darkness snaking out from her temples. But as she spots Layna standing behind Lucien, she grabs the sides of her head with her blood-soaked hands and lets out a tortured cry. She allows herself one last glance back at Phoebe before following the others forward, her light still shining.

They stand outside a hexagonal-shaped structure topped with an elaborate, golden-plated dome that Layna can see clearly even through the grey haze of the Ouroboros. It's as if the barrier of the Ouroboros is growing weak around it. The front door of the building has been blasted outwards, and the inside reveals an impenetrable, chilling blackness.

As they sheathe their weapons and move toward it, a bolt of black lightning discharges from the inside of the Dome and strikes the earth in front of their feet, tossing them all through the air like ragdolls. Layna lands on her side and rolls up into a crouch. She tries to catch her breath as she hears a pop next to her and feels hands close around her arms. She yanks herself free, fearing that another eclipsed Naut has come for them, but she turns to find the comfort of glowing, blue eyes.

"Blake!" she cries, throwing her arms around him.

He holds her tightly and says in a choked whisper, "I'm sorry, they wouldn't let me get back to you."

Layna looks around and sees Des, Molimo, and Harkin helping the others to their feet, and however irrationally, she nearly cries with renewed hope. They've located the boy, Blake is beside her, and her friends are going to be here with them at the end. This isn't over yet.

"How did you know to come here?" she asks.

"I felt you out here...like something invisible pulling me toward you," Blake answers.

Layna has no time to question this, as Lady Anora announces, "We need to get inside the Dome. Everyone stay close and stay aware...We don't know what we're going to find in there."

They all regroup around Layna and Blake, and together they port inside the Dome. There is a roar like the sound of a passing freight train and a vicious wind whips at their bodies. Layna holds her arms in front of her face as she tries to remain standing. Though from the outside it seemed there was only an eerily silent blackness, they now stand in the eye of a wild cyclone that somehow rages inside the ancient building without breaking it apart.

"There, on the Foundation Stone!" Lucien shouts above the clamor, pointing ahead of them.

At the center of the room, directly under the domed top, is the vision of evil itself. It hovers in mid-air within a pulsating cloud of darkness at the center of the storm. A horrific, shriveled body the size of a child and the color of charcoal, dripping a black, tar-like substance onto the stone beneath it. Its eye sockets are empty and its mouth, like the eclipsed at Karnak Temple, is open unnaturally wide in a silent scream.

Layna knows exactly what she is seeing, because now that she is here with them, she can sense it with every fiber of her being. "Oh god...it's the boy *and* Erebus! We need to hurry!" she yells. The boy is in a dream, hiding from Erebus inside his mind. But he won't hold out for much longer before Erebus consumes him.

Behind them, a roar like the detonation of a bomb resounds as a large chunk of the ceiling is ripped away by the growing vortex, landing yards from where they stand. They all move together toward the Foundation Stone, but Lady Anora holds out her arms and stops abruptly in front of them. Layna sees it too. Charges of dark energy crackling and growing around the body.

"Take cover!" Lady Anora yells, just as another bolt of black lightning flies over their heads. Layna grabs hold of Blake and ports them both away as several more charges fill the air to the fading cries of her friends. She and Blake reappear behind one of the pillars that surround the stone, and then Harkin appears and squeezes in next to them.

"We need to get up there!" Layna shouts above the incessant roar. She peers around the side of the pillar to get an idea of how best to approach the stone. Instead, her eyes fall on the four glowing bodies lying around a crater in the floor. Fear seizes her heart as she makes out the figures of Lady Anora, Molimo, Selene, and Lucien. They can't just leave them out there.

"Harkin!" she yells behind her.

"On it!" he shouts, as he looks over her shoulder and then disappears. He reappears next to Molimo and Lucien and places a hand on each of them, porting them back to the pillar next to the one Layna and Blake hide behind. He turns to go back for Lady Anora and Selene, but Des and Aysel have beat him to it, escaping to their own hiding place as three more streaks of lightning tear up the ground near the entrance.

Layna pokes her head around the pillar again and sees that the body floating above the rock is changing. There is no longer anything remotely human about it, its face now a gaping hole, its body at once both larger and more shriveled. The tarlike substance dripping from it seems to be congealing to form numerous smaller bodies beneath it, elongated figures that slither outwards from the center of the stone. The closest one, only yards away from Layna, abruptly grows in girth at one end, as if it's about to explode from the inside. But instead, a hole opens in the engorged end, revealing several rows of razor-sharp teeth. It lets out a hair-raising screech that sears through Layna's mind like a hot poker.

She tears her eyes away from the monstrosity and spots Des behind a pillar at her two o-clock, signaling for her to stay put. A moment later, Aysel appears with a motionless Selene behind the pillar to the right of Harkin, Molimo, and Lucien, and Des appears with Lady Anora behind the column to Layna and Blake's left. Des gently props Lady Anora against the pillar. She is conscious, but she clutches onto her chest where Layna can see the edge of a fresh dark mark etched in her golden light.

"The multiluce!" Des shouts, turning toward them. "It's theoretically possible to hold the power of it around you, use it like a shield. Seconds only. I can help get you up there with it, and if anyone can wing it, it's—"

Another bolt of lightning tears into the ground right in front of Des, throwing him backward and out from behind the pillar.

"Des!" Layna and Blake scream at once. They port to his side and pull him back behind the pillar with Lady Anora just as another bolt hits where he'd landed.

He wipes the caked dirt from his face as he focuses again on Layna and Blake, swallowing hard before continuing. "We'll go up together, alright?"

His words are barely audible above the howl of the cyclone, but Layna and Blake both nod in unison. Layna looks down at Lady Anora, expecting that she will be joining them. But the dark mark has spread up Lady Anora's neck, and Layna is struck with the impossible realization that she could be dying. Lady Anora's eyes are frantic as they search Layna and Blake's faces. Her mouth forms around words unheard, but Layna knows what is being said.

279

Forgive me.

Blake grabs Lady Anora's hand as Layna chokes back tears. She urges her genuine feelings for Lady Anora to the forefront of her mind, tied to a hundred memories of support and laughter and kinship. Leaving her with the truth that Layna goes forward carrying nothing but love and gratitude for her. *Survive*, she pleads, keeping her eyes on Lady Anora's as she grabs Des and Blake by the hands.

Des places his other hand against Lady Anora's cheek, his eyes tormented. "I'll come right back for you," he cries.

She covers his hand with hers as a single tear falls from her eye. Harkin and Aysel are shouting behind them, but they have no more time, and the three of them port as one to the stone.

It doesn't take long to figure out what Harkin and Aysel were trying to tell them. The snake-like creatures Layna saw have multiplied tenfold and are now hurtling themselves over the wall around the stone and toward the pillars. In front of them, the body floats even higher, their heads level with its torso. It is now bigger than a human adult, with a long, muscular tail where its legs used to be.

"Multiluce! Don't let it go!" Des cries as he grips their hands, and the three of them run toward the body. As Layna feels the energy building around them, she also senses Erebus, sensing them. And before Layna and Blake can reach toward the hovering figure, a circle of dark energy grows around it, exploding outwards and knocking all three of them off the stone.

Layna's arm crunches beneath her, and she feels like her whole body has caught fire from the explosion. She heaves herself up, ready to douse the flames that consume her, but there are none visible to the eye. She locates Des first, lying motionless on his back in the midst of the cyclone. Blake is on his hands and knees on the other side of the stone. There is no time—she and Blake have to reach the gateway. They will have to try to hold onto the multiluce themselves.

Please, please don't be dead, Des.

She ports to Blake, keeping her head down as she helps him to his feet. It causes a shooting pain in her forearm, and somewhere in the back of her mind she knows that it's broken, but it doesn't matter anymore.

"Quick, try again!" she shouts. She hears Aysel shriek in pain and looks past Blake to see Harkin slice through a shadow snake that has clamped onto Aysel's leg. Another launches itself at a barely conscious Molimo and latches onto his shoulder.

Layna forces herself to turn away from their fight and toward her own. The snakes have surrounded her and Blake, and several leap toward them at once. Layna sees the rows of sharp teeth flying at her as Blake ports them out of the way. But he isn't fast enough, and she feels a searing pain tear across the side of her face as the teeth rip through flesh. She gasps through the pain and opens one eye, the other shut beneath a hot stream of blood. She wipes the blood away with one hand as the other grips onto Blake's.

"Now!" she shouts, and the multiluce forms seamlessly between them. Just before it explodes outward, they reel it in like a protective shield and dive together toward the hovering body. Layna's hands land on something solid, and then everything is gone.

CHAPTER

The first thing Layna registers is the absence of sound. In the audible space where the cyclone just raged, there is nothing but its echo. A ringing deep inside her skull.

Then, fuzzy at first, the ringing sensation transforms into voices. The sound of singing.

No, not singing, exactly. Chanting. She opens her eyes to find she is sitting before a softly undulating white flame, just like the one in the Consulate Chamber. And when she then notices the crowd of glowing bodies standing in a circle around her, she realizes that's where she must be.

But the air is fresh and crisp, and her golden hair dances freely across her face in a soft breeze. She's not in the Consulate Chamber, but at the summit of a great mount. The limestone slab beneath her is identical to the one she just left. Everything else is gone—the building, the city, the war. Here, all is quiet and at peace. The night sky above boasts radiant starlight she never dreamed could exist in this lifetime.

And then, Blake comes into focus across from her. Or...definitely *not* Blake.

It's an older man with long, dark hair tied loosely down his back, and he wears a sparse garment over the lower half of a powerful body. This man doesn't even look like Blake, and she blinks at him, trying to understand why she would have thought it to begin with.

But then her eyes lock with his blue ones—deep and beckoning and so familiar—and with sudden clarity she realizes who this is. It isn't Blake, but in a way, it is.

This man is Nyx.

She looks down at herself, and it's not the body she knows as her own, but one she recognizes all the same. It's her as she was. As Hemera, in another lifetime. Surrounded by the Nauts of the Order she once helped to lead.

The chanting grows around them, and though she's never heard it spoken, she knows this is Kosmoli—the language of the Oneiroi. The instant she concentrates on the rich, melodious tones, she discerns their meaning.

Unify their energy, make them one. She with her and he with him, and she with him and he with her. Ancestor of old and descendant new, sacrifice for all the lives of two. Come back 'round when balance breaks, conquer darkness, begin anew. Unify their energy, make them one...

As it repeats, the auras of the hundreds of Nauts surrounding them on the mount begin to swirl and blend together, rising toward the sky. She spares a glimpse of awe at the tornado of light that builds around them, but with an inescapable magnetism, her eyes are pulled back to the man sitting across from her. She can see the same intensity in his eyes, the longing to reach out to her the way her hands are itching to reach for him.

Just as she thinks she can't hold herself apart from him for a single second more, the flame erupts between them and she is slammed backward by the force of it. And she is hit with…everything. *Everything*, all at once. A flood of a million images and memories and emotions pitch her from her body, and she is nothing but this. This utter chaos of mind.

Her hands deftly shaping clay pots—her hands fiddling with a combination on a school locker.

Bathing naked in a temperate stream—dressing for school.

Nyx's eyes finding hers as she picks wild berries on a cliff over the sea. Blake's eyes finding hers outside Trent Park next to a rotting park bench. Two beginnings in two different lives, mirror images of each other.

His fingers entwined in hers—her head on his shoulder. Lying together beneath an ancient sky of stars—sitting atop a hill in modern Athens. Blending now, all the same.

Holding each other as the Oneiroi who gave them their power take their last few shallow breaths of life. Breathtaking creatures of light and shadow, their serpentine bodies coiled around each other, enfolded in ethereal wings. Eyes gleaming with wisdom and sorrow as they utter their heartbreaking words of the end of Earth and the Kosmos.

The *Kosmos*. Never before could she comprehend, let alone *feel* the sheer vastness of it the way she does now. The unmistakable, overpowering sense of life, spread out across the gaping expanse of infinity, like a littering of precious diamonds held within the dark walls of a cave. The miraculous bloom of existence from the emptiness that preceded it, and which could succeed it if she fails now.

And in that moment, all her remaining fear melts into an aching resolve. A hunger, to wrap herself around those precious specks of light and protect them from all harm as though they are children born from her own womb. She will not let those worlds be swallowed by darkness. She will not let the life they hold fizzle, fade, and wink out of existence.

She sits up just as he does, their eyes locking onto each other once again with new recognition. A third beginning, a third parallel moment, the reunification of two lifetimes. And it is more than she can contain in this one fragile body.

Two lives she's lived, and two hearts she's had. And both hearts and both lives, and all she was and will be, at the core of it all, is him.

His eyes are wide and glistening, fixed on her. Searching her face as though his sight, his senses, are failing him. Failing to comprehend the depth of her.

They move as one, reaching for each other, hands grasping and pulling like gravity, and their bodies collide in an explosion that shatters the edges of self. No longer Blake and Layna, nor Hemera and Nyx. They are neither and they are both. One being, a single element of powerful energy. Floating now, rising into the sky, faster and faster, to the stars. They are everything, everywhere. Timeless, everlasting. And then...

They are nothing.

I'm trapped.

Layna instinctively reaches out her hands with the overwhelming sensation that she's been confined to some small space. It's dark. Eyes wide, she searches with her hands, but they only continue to meet open space around her. So why does she feel so restricted? Her brain feels cramped inside her skull, but there is also a cavernous emptiness inside, as though something has just been ripped out of her. Where was she just now? It was big, and powerful, and important.

"Blake?" she whispers. Her voice sounds both muted and amplified, as though her ears are stuffed with cotton.

She rises to her feet, hands outstretched, feeling out the darkness. And then a window appears. It sheds a dull glow across the room, just enough to cast shadows everywhere. The shadows seem to be moving, undulating in a unified rhythm. It must be just a trick of the eye. She becomes aware that she is standing in her living room, and the realization feels backward, or upside down. Wrong.

She calls out again for Blake and walks toward the foyer. He is there in the darkness, kneeling on the ground pulling objects from a backpack. Yes, that's right. She is supposed to be helping him set up the cameras. Why is she standing here like an idiot? She closes the distance between them, but as she draws near, his body morphs and elongates. It's not Blake, but just the shadow of a grandfather clock ticking idly against the wall.

But there is no grandfather clock in her foyer. She looks at the dining room to her right and up at the ceiling where a grand chandelier hangs and reflects the moonlight. She peers down a familiar dark hallway lined with a green carpet, and there she sees two shadows violently dancing around each other.

"Blake?" she cries, as she creeps forward after them. Her feet turn left down another hallway, leading her rather than her telling them where to go. She sees a door opening along a curved wall. A sliver of light escapes and shines across the two figures standing before it. One is an eclipsed man, and Layna staggers back, raising her hands to shoot. But then she realizes it's holding her mother, whose eyes gleam with fear in the light.

"Mom!" Layna screams as she leaps toward her. She isn't fast enough, and the eclipsed man shoves her mother through the door. Her mother's screams fade as she falls, sinking deep into the earth. The screams are joined by the cries of others, their fearful voices an ache inside Layna. The velvety cadence of a woman's voice, and a man's Scottish brogue, pleading, calling her name.

Layna launches herself through the door after the voices and falls endlessly through empty space until she lands on something soft. She bolts upright, swinging her legs over the side of the couch in her living room. She is panting, her mind groggy as she picks up the history textbook lying open on the floor. She must have fallen asleep while reading it.

It's dark. The digital clock on the end table flashes midnight, casting an eerie, red glow across the room. Wind howls through the woods behind her property, and she wonders if a tree has knocked out one of the power lines again.

Layna stands up and heads for the circuit breaker at the back of the house. But she stops at the entrance to the kitchen. Or rather, *something* stops her. She peers down in the darkness, trying to see what could be blocking her way. But there is nothing. As she lifts her gaze, she freezes, all the breath escaping from her lungs in an agonized cry. She drops to her knees, trying and failing to look away from the horror that her mind simply can't comprehend.

Kat and Suzanne float in the air, suspended as though in water. Their mouths are wide open in a scream that lingers beyond death. Their bloated eyes look straight through her, empty and hollow. The canary yellow of the kitchen walls start seeping red, streams of blood trickling to the floor. Pouring in from the windows. Layna feels a liquid warmth around her knees and finds the flood is rising fast.

She stands like she's moving through molasses and turns back toward the stairs. She wants nothing more than to run. Run far away as fast as she can. But her body won't let her. There is a heaviness to the air that weighs down her muscles and her lungs. She can barely take a breath. As she reaches the staircase, the heaviness recedes and she scrambles upward, tripping over herself as the bloody flood rises behind her.

She steals a glance over her shoulder and wishes she hadn't. The torrent of blood is filled with body parts, some of it illuminated with an unearthly glow of blue and gold. Heads float among the grisly pieces, their dead faces all looking up at her, judging her, accusing her.

Layna slips on the soaked stair and slides back down into the churning sea of bodies. She wants to scream, but there is nothing left inside of her. Weakness overcomes her as she grasps at the steps with one hand, pushing the dead faces away with the other. Then, throwing herself up the next step with every last ounce of strength, she tumbles from her bed.

She lies on the floor amid a sweat-soaked mess of sheets and blankets tangled around her limbs. She buries her face in her hands and begins sobbing as she realizes it was just a nightmare. A really horrible, realistic nightmare. Moonlight pours in through her closed window and she takes comfort in the dim light cast across her bedroom floor as she tries to steady her breathing.

There is a creak outside her door, and she turns toward the sound. The door handle jiggles.

"Mom?" Layna stammers. There is no response. She holds her breath as her heart picks up speed. She's being ridiculous, she knows that. It was just another stupid nightmare. "Mom, is that you?" she calls again.

A breath of hot air brushes her cheek and she looks back at her window. The curtains flutter lightly in the summer breeze. *How did it get open?*

She stands up to go close it but stops in her tracks, watching in horror as two ghostly, white arms reach in through her window. Hands grasping, searching. She bolts for the door, pulling desperately at the doorknob. But the door won't budge. Her whole body prickles with fear as she anticipates the clutching hands grabbing her from behind. She looks back over her shoulder and stops struggling. The ghostly arms are gone. The window is still closed. Was she hallucinating? It must be her meds making her see things. She's going to have to ask Dr. Nettles to reduce the dosage.

A flutter of movement near her dresser catches her eye. Hidden in the shadowed corner of her room, she makes out the darkened figure of a person.

Layna presses herself back against her bedroom door, a scream working its way up her throat as a woman steps out of the shadow and into the moonlight. The sight of her evokes a visceral response. Layna's mouth fills with bile and her whole body begins trembling as the woman whispers, "Hello again, bambolina."

The woman raises her arm, moonlight reflecting off the gun in her hand. Layna spins around to escape, but the sound of the gunshot tears through the air. Layna slumps to the ground as her legs give way beneath her.

The woman is gone. A fire is spreading inside Layna's belly, and she closes a hand over the bloom of warmth. Slippery to the touch, her blood is pooling around her. She lifts her other hand to find that she is holding the gun. But then it's not a gun at all. It's Hunter's pocketknife. She feels herself becoming smaller inside her own body, like she is melting away. Wax trapped inside the glass of a burning candle, softening at the edges and vaporizing into nothing.

She is vaguely aware of the door swinging open next to her, and then Blake is standing in front of her. Yelling, but she can't hear his words. Grabbing her by the shoulders, frantic and desperate to make her understand something. She just wants him to hold her now. Why is he shouting at her instead of holding her? Doesn't he see she's dying?

As she tries to comprehend his words through her fading senses, a shadow enters the room behind him. *Umbra.*

What is that? Why did she think it? The word sounds both foreign and familiar. And then it's gone from her mind.

The shadow raises an arm above Blake's head and Layna hears herself moan in warning. But it does no good. Blake turns just as the thing brings a long blade of darkness down on his neck. Layna can do nothing but watch as it slices clean through skin and muscle and bone. Blake's head tumbles neatly from his body and lands at her feet, his blue eyes looking up at her in perpetual shock.

A gurgling cry escapes her lips, the shadow figure stands there motionless above them, and the moment lingers, on and on and on.

His empty eyes, her empty soul.

Nothing exists for her outside of this horror. This moment of suspended animation, on the edge of bodily death, staring at the death of her heart, her hope, her everything.

Why hasn't she died?

Why hasn't the moment ended?

She has been here an eternity, staring into those empty eyes. It is agony. And it will never, ever end. This is her forever.

This is hell.

CHAPTER

Her mind is slipping. Not toward death, never toward death. But toward madness. She can't move, or speak, or remember…anything. Not who she is, or who he was, or where she came from, or where she was going, or how many days or months or years she's been here. Just this.

Him dead in front of her and the anguished screaming of her heart.

And then, the shift of a shadow. She must be imagining it. This is hell, and nothing ever changes in hell. Another subtle shift. It's the shadowed figure…that's what changed. A twitch, maybe. And then, inconceivably, it moves, kneeling down in front of her.

Euphoric with hope, she silently begs it for death, for it to end her misery. It reaches for her and grabs both of her shoulders.

Yes. Yes. End it. Give me peace.

But instead, it shakes her. Even more disturbing, though it has no mouth, it begins to speak.

"Layna, it isn't real! None of it is real! Please don't let go. Remember who you are…Remember why we're here!"

Layna doesn't dare blink for fear this will be just one of hell's little tricks. Should she move a single muscle, everything will return to the same endless misery. But what is the shadow trying to say? She repeats its words in her head…*It isn't real*. But what isn't real? She isn't even real.

The shadow in front of her starts to seep away into the air. Emerging from it, like the moon from behind a cloud, is him. The dead boy that once was her heart.

He's alive. Speaking to her. And she *knows* him.

Blake. She flings her arms around him and only after doing so realizes she can move again. She pulls away, inspecting his neck with trembling fingers, then searches her stomach. There is no scar on him, no gunshot wound in her, no blood.

She remembers who she is…where she is. She can't be sure how time works here, but it doesn't feel more than a few minutes since they left their friends at the Dome of the Rock. But the image of Blake's cold, dead eyes remains. And that feeling of unending anguish…

"You're okay," Blake soothes, stroking her hair. "It wasn't real."

"Blake," she chokes. "What was happening to me? I forgot. I almost forgot everything. And you…you were…"

"I know," he whispers, his eyes filled with the reflections of his own personal torment. "It was happening to me too…I almost lost it. He brought me back," he finishes, nodding his head sideways. Layna

293

looks to her left and notices the boy for the first time, standing there watching them.

"How did he...?" Layna trails off as she realizes where they are. "Why are we here?" she stammers.

"You know it?" Blake asks, his voice trembling. "This is my old street, the place where...where Billy died."

"No...it's the bridge," Layna replies, as she looks around in confusion. The bridge leading out of Caledon. The one over the canal that claimed Suzanne's life. The way toward Caledon disappears into a gently rotating halo of luminous, white light that bathes Layna with warmth. The other way leads to a stable vortex of icy, impenetrable darkness. And in front of the darkness, silently observing them, stands a man—if you can call it that.

"Blake..." she whispers thickly. "It's Erebus."

Blake whirls around to follow her gaze.

He looms larger than the detached umbrae, over ten feet in height and several feet across the chest. He wears a dark, fitted suit that stands in stark contrast to his translucent skin. Even from a distance, Layna can see the blackness of his veins running beneath his flesh. His eyes are enormous, black marbles and his lips a thin line of blood red.

He smiles then, showing off pearly white teeth in a mouth that seems far too large for his face. His slick, black hair is parted neatly down the side of his head. Polished, the caricature of a seasoned politician from hell.

"Hello," he offers, his voice a somber melody.

Layna and Blake rise to their feet and Layna shuffles the boy behind them as their aetherblades materialize at their sides.

"I am going to need that," Erebus says politely, pointing at the boy.

"Not a chance," Blake declares.

Erebus chuckles and takes an unhurried step toward them, darkness trailing behind him in a shadowy vapor. "Come now," he murmurs. "Why all the fuss? You don't want to die, do you? There is no reason for you to die," he finishes with another toothy smile.

"You can't have him, and you can't have our world," Layna spits. "Go back to your own universe and leave us alone."

Erebus laughs heartily this time. "Now how could you expect me to stay away when there is a whole other universe to be explored? *You*, for example. You human beings on the planet…Earth." He says it slowly, rolling the word around on his tongue like some foreign delicacy. "You are a fascinating species, one of my favorites, in fact," he remarks, as he looks down at his own rendition of the human body. "Fascinating, yet so very, very fragile. I only wish to get to know you better. Perhaps make some…improvements."

"You can't get to know us if we're all dead. You're killing everyone," Blake retorts. "You must realize that."

"I? I do not *kill*," Erebus replies innocently. "I *transform*. I am a creator, just like Aether. Didn't you know that? Didn't anyone tell you *my* story?"

Layna glances at Blake and he gives an almost imperceptible shake of his head. *Let him talk. Bide our time.* She can see Blake trying to formulate a plan, but they are infinitely out of their depth, and none of the promised epiphanies are coming to her.

"We both just wanted to explore, grow, create," Erebus reminisces. "Aether was like...how will you understand...like a sister to me. And yet we could not explore and create together. There was a repellant force between us. An impenetrable barrier. Light and Shadow, bound as one, yet destined to be always apart. It was the cruel and ironic truth of our eternal existence. So we tested fate, created the Oneiroi to bridge the barrier. Funny little creatures. They opened up new worlds to us, and we were freed. It was wonderful," he says, clapping his long, bony hands together and taking another step toward them. "But then," he sighs heavily, "they turned on us. Our own creations. Locked us away, cut us off from each other. Aether didn't even try to stop them. Now can you believe that?"

"The Oneiroi closed the Ouroboros to you because you were destroying the universes," Blake argues. "You were destroying your *own* universe. If we let you through and you spread across the Kosmos, you'd be destroying yourself too, you know?"

"No, no, dear boy. You misunderstand. See, my silly sister gave herself to her creations. She is in the aetherworlds, she is in all the ethereal beings in your universe. I, however, have preserved myself. So when I *transform* your Universe of Light into Shadow, she and all her creations, and all the shadows of her creations that exist in my universe, shall be no more. This is true. But I will remain. *Only* I will remain. And all of it will be mine to do with as I please."

Layna glances back at the boy for some kind of inspiration or insight. He is staring at Erebus with a discerning look that does not belong to a five-year-old boy. Maybe they should ask *him* what they're meant to do. Maybe somehow this dream-ego version of him knows.

"You should be thanking me for coming to your door," Erebus says impatiently. "Don't you see? Aether *condemned* you. Condemned you to this cursed thing that you must fight so hard to preserve. *Life*," he scoffs, as he continues to move closer. "Chaos is the natural state of things. It is inevitable. Your Kosmos—the orderliness of it—is an abomination. It is unnatural, weak, fragile, and so is the life it bears. Like you. You suffer because you are weak. You fight the darkness inside yourselves, and so you suffer. Aether may have created life, but I...I create *Chaos*. There is no weakness in Chaos. There is no suffering. And so, come the mists of Chaos to transform the Universe of Light into forces strong and eternal. Into *darkness*. And you shall suffer no more."

Without warning, he rushes at Layna and Blake, but they are ready for it. They simultaneously raise their hands and fire lucetelum at the approaching blur of shadow. They hit it, dead center, and it disappears. They are alone on the bridge again.

"That definitely can't be it," Layna whispers, as she whirls around in a circle, her aetherblade at the ready. "It's messing with us."

The air around them turns heavy as it begins to rain. The hairs on Layna's arms stand on end and lightning tears across a darkening sky. In a flash of light, Layna sees a ghostly figure in her peripheral vision and spins toward it, raising her blade. But she pauses mid-swing as she recognizes the apparition before her. *Hemera.*

Layna stands motionless as she tries to discern whether it is yet another phantom of her own mind or a trick by Erebus. She opens her mouth to shout for Blake, but then...

Light of my light.

Layna staggers backward in surprise. The words are there inside her mind, spoken in Kosmoḻi, as if it were her own thoughts. But she did not conjure them.

It is possible to save them both, Hemera continues.

What do you mean 'save them both'? Layna thinks.

When the bridge crumbles, the portals to both the Shadow Universe and the Light Universe must be sealed. One must go through each portal to close it from within. But only one must die. It is possible that he can live.

Layna hears the pleading of the voice in her mind, and it resonates across time, across their two bodies and their two hearts. Layna can save him—Blake, Nyx—he doesn't need to die.

How? Tell me how I can save him, Layna begs.

Hemera reaches a spectral hand toward Layna's cheek, a gentle breeze against her skin. *Simple. We must die. Ensure that we drive Erebus back through the dark portal. Then, we must follow it in, while he takes the boy and crosses back through the light portal. He is stronger than we are, and he may be able to return home with his mind and body intact.*

I promise I will save him. Thank you, light of my light, Layna responds with the same phrase, as natural in her mind as though she were the one who put it there. *But how do we drive it back?*

Thunder rumbles overhead and lighting strikes the water in the distance. Layna's eyes flicker toward the storm, and when she looks in front of her again, Hemera is gone.

She turns to find Blake gazing blankly in front of him, his eyes unfocused. She takes a step toward him and he looks up at her, his expression unreadable. She wants to question it, but the boy begins to scream.

They spin around to find he's collapsed to the ground, curled into a fetal position as his skin begins to turn a sickly grey. Layna and Blake sheathe their weapons and kneel down beside him.

"What do we do?" Blake cries as the rain starts to come down in sheets.

"I...I don't know!" Layna rests her hands on the boy. He is cold to her touch, and she starts to feel a tingling in her hands as her light seeps away from her and into his body.

"Your hands! He needs our light!"

Blake places his hands on the boy's head as the boy begins thrashing. A woman manifests on the blacktop next to them. It's the boy's mother, a deep hole in her neck where she lodged the pen.

The boy screams louder and thrashes harder beneath their hands as he cries out for his mother. But then his expression turns angry, his face contorting into something sinister, something inhuman. He screeches maliciously with a mouthful of sharp, jagged teeth. Layna doesn't let go but instead doubles the strength of the light she is releasing into his body. He gives them one final shriek before Erebus relinquishes control and the boy goes still. The image of his mother flickers and fades, and he opens his eyes. He looks at Blake and then Layna with that curiously astute gaze, and Layna considers again that he may know how to help them.

"Do you know how we can fight him?" she asks.

The boy continues to look at her, but he doesn't respond, and Layna realizes he probably doesn't understand English.

An arctic gust of air hits Layna's back as she's pelted with rain, and she turns to see Erebus take his humanoid form once again in front of the swirling blackness at the other end of the bridge. The dark portal seems to have moved significantly closer to them, and she looks to find that the light behind them has crept toward them as well. *The bridge is shrinking.*

"Why won't you let me have him?" Erebus whines.

Layna's aetherblade forms again in her hand as Blake's forms in his. *It's time.*

"Go wait for us by the light," Layna whispers to the boy. To her surprise, he follows her instruction and runs back toward the portal. Only afterward does she recognize that she somehow spoke to him in Kosmoli. And he understood.

"Ready?" she murmurs to Blake. He squeezes her hand in response, and she steels herself to block out her overpowering concern for his life. *He can live. You promised that he can live.* She forgets if it was she or Hemera who made the promise to the other. But right now, all that matters is its truth.

"Well, then you will die," Erebus seethes.

Lightning tears across the sky as Erebus begins to grow larger. His suit disintegrates, and the black veins under his translucent skin spread across his body as his legs congeal to form a long, powerful tail. He opens his mouth, and Layna can hear the cracking of bones as it stretches wider and wider, over a foot in diameter and still growing. Then it begins spewing darkness. The misty blackness curls around its body and forms long, tentacle-like appendages that solidify, raising its grotesque body high into the air above them.

The beast lifts one of its enormous limbs to pull itself toward them. It lands with such force that the whole bridge shudders. Several more tentacles reach for them, and Layna dives out of the way of one, slicing through another as she falls to her side. There is a flicker of hope as she sees that it can be hurt, that it can be cut down. But the limb instantly regenerates and comes at her again.

She tries to port out of the way but realizes that she is grounded. She can't port here. They are in an unfamiliar dimension, and she has no idea what laws of physics may apply. She can only assume that Erebus is likewise limited here inside the boy's mind. If it weren't, they would probably already be dead.

She ducks just as a tentacle swings over her head, and then another knocks her off her feet. It wraps around her legs and drags her across the asphalt before lifting her into the air toward its mouth, which is now big enough to swallow her whole.

Layna hangs upside down and tries wrenching herself free, but its grip tightens around her ankles, threatening to crush bone. She lifts her upper body and swings her blade with all her strength toward her feet. It slices through the monster's phantom flesh and she falls through the air for only a second before she's caught around the waist by another of its inexhaustible limbs.

At least she is right-side up now. She wipes the rain from her face as she looks around to find Blake. He is fighting back several grasping appendages, relentlessly attacking with his aetherblade and evading with the moves of the Aetherem. Layna raises her hands and adds a barrage of lucetelum toward the tentacles that reach for him. She doesn't let up until the one wrapped around her waist tightens and cuts off her air. Her eyes water as the pain in her bruised ribs becomes unbearable. She feels herself yanked forward as it brings her toward its mouth. She can't die yet. She needs to get Erebus and herself past the threshold to the Shadow Universe first.

Indigo light flashes across her vision, and then she is falling once again toward the pavement. She lands in Blake's arms and they topple to the ground as Erebus emits an earsplitting shriek. Not out of pain, Layna senses, but frustration. They may not be hurting it, but at least they seem to be more of a challenge than Erebus expected.

Layna no longer feels the pelting rain, and she looks up to find that they are sheltered beneath Erebus' monstrous, growing body. It has become so large that the bridge is groaning beneath its weight. The dark portal has crept up behind Erebus, and the light portal is nearly within its reach in front of it. The boy leans back against the impenetrable halo of light with his hands over his eyes as several tentacles reach for him.

"Blake!" Layna yells. They scramble to their feet, and as they run toward the boy, Layna feels an intense tugging in the center of her being. A tugging coming from beyond the boy—from the light behind him, as though it is reaching out to them. The tugging blossoms inside her, sucking the air from her lungs. And the memory that she needed, the one from another lifetime, is there again in her mind. She knows what they have to do. She grabs Blake by the shoulder and turns him toward her. There is recognition in his eyes.

"I feel it too!" he shouts.

Hand in hand, they turn to face Erebus together as waves of energy from the light swell and wash over them from behind. Like with the multiluce, Layna senses the realigning of their minds as she and Blake remember the mount, the stars, the ritual. They surrender to the memory of the unity as once again the edges of self blur and their entities merge—the barriers of matter and time and space dissolving as four become one. No longer individual selves, they are Hemera and Layna, Nyx and Blake, all of them and no one at all. They are pure, boundless energy.

One being, they channel the light from the portal. Wild power coursing through them, barreling directly into the beast's enormous center in percussive waves. It shrieks and recoils, taking several faltering steps backward, closer to the darkness behind it and away from the light. They advance in step with its retreat as the force surging through them seems to only grow stronger and clearer. They have never felt such power as this in any of their lives. They are all of the Kosmos, infinity, squeezed into this singular moment in this singular space. They are Aether. And they are winning.

Erebus writhes in front of them, its limbs flailing and melting from its body as it begins to shrink in on itself. Its torso disappears into the dark portal behind it, then its shrieking head, until only its tentacles remain, grasping desperately at the railings and decking. One slams down into the weakening asphalt and a deep crack streaks from one side of the bridge to the other like lightning.

A shuddering beneath them, ground giving way. The alignment of energies splinters and snaps as their bodies jolt with a sudden drop, and the boundless power they were channeling is lost to the raging storm.

Blake grabs Layna by both arms and hauls her across his body just as the piece of bridge she was standing on tumbles into the water below. She is only herself again, and she tries contending with the sudden emptiness that is left behind. She and Blake turn to find that the cracks in the asphalt caused by their battle have spread and broken through to the concrete foundation. The bridge between the universes is crumbling, and it will not hold for much longer.

The boy has climbed onto the side railing, but his fingers slip in the torrential rain as he tries to make his way toward them. The light closes in behind him, with only yards of weakening pavement remaining between the two portals. Layna knows instinctively that they can't allow them to meet, particularly not with Erebus still on the bridge.

Layna looks back at the dark portal and sees Erebus' gaping mouth reemerging as it grips the railings and pulls itself forward.

First, the boy.

She grabs Blake by the hand and they run toward the boy, hopping across chunks of the concrete as it caves beneath their feet. They both leap for the railing just as a large slab falls away, leaving their feet dangling in the air. Layna gets a foothold on the railing and Blake pulls himself up next to her. He is closer to the boy, and he grabs hold of him. The light portal is just behind them now and Layna knows it's time.

You can save them both.

"Blake!" she yells. He turns to face her and she has a moment of pause. She can't stand to say goodbye after they just found each other again. But she has no choice. She looks into his eyes for strength one last time as she says, "You have to go through at the same time. Don't give up."

Before launching herself across the gap toward the other side of the collapsing bridge, she sees the split second of recognition on his face—the panic and anguish—and she wishes it wasn't going to be the last image she held of him. She barely makes it across the divide, catching the broken ledge just beneath her arms.

"Layna, no! It's supposed to be me!" Blake shouts from behind her. Layna knows he can't come after her. Not without releasing either his grip on the railing or on the boy. She pulls herself up and draws her aetherblade as Blake's cries are lost to the wind and the rain.

Don't look back.

She approaches the swirling darkness, slicing through two of the last three tentacles as Erebus watches her, screeching with rage. The portal is sucking its monstrous frame back in now, and Layna can feel its pull on her own body. Erebus knows it's lost, and Layna can sense it seething at her, yearning to destroy her. So, she will let it.

"Come and get me then, you ugly shit," she whispers as she sheathes her weapon.

Erebus releases its final grip on their world to reach for her, to pull her into the darkness. The tentacle slides toward her as a series of images flash across her mind—her house, her school, the ocean, the faces of all her friends and family, Nyx, and Blake. She shuts her eyes and holds the last image of his face in her mind. The one where his smile still reached his eyes. She feels the tentacle wrap around her waist and she lurches forward. It takes everything in her not to fight the grip of death as terror and the will to live tear through her. *I don't want to die.*

But the tug on her stops abruptly, and she stumbles forward from the sudden lack of momentum. She opens her eyes to find Blake in front of her, his aetherblade drawn as the piece of tentacle that was wrapped around her waist disintegrates into the air.

Blake's eyes are fierce as he pulls her to him and kisses her, urgent, and yet unhurried. His lips linger longingly on hers for seconds they don't have. And then, he turns and jumps, disappearing as the remnants of Erebus slither into the darkness with him.

Layna drops to her knees.

She blinks, but the space before her is still empty. Her arms still reach for him, her lips still feel the warmth of his kiss. But he isn't there. Her chest is collapsing, caving in on itself like a chasm is opening up inside of her. She wants to scream, but there is no air.

He's not gone. He can't be gone. The darkness is inches from her, but she doesn't move, she can't move. *I have to go in after him.*

"Hemera! Hemera!"

She hears it from behind her. It doesn't matter. She needs to get Blake back. She needs to go through the portal after him.

"Please, help me!" the boy shouts in Kosmoli.

Layna turns to see him standing on the last ragged ledge on the other side of the bridge, his back pressed against the light.

"I can't get home without you!" he cries.

The light inches forward, pushing him even closer to the edge. His foot slips on the wet pavement.

Layna rises numbly to her feet. There are yards of open air between them. She looks back at the darkness where Blake disappeared. She doesn't know what would happen if she went through, how she could get him back. But how can she keep going forward?

Save Blake or save the universe.

With an agonized scream, she turns away from the darkness, pouring her pain into strength. Willing her body to keep moving.

Just this one last thing, then you can be done. Then it can be over.

She wipes the rain from her eyes, takes a running start, and leaps. She sails across the empty space between the portals just as the boy loses his footing and jumps forward into the air toward her. They aren't going to make it through.

The world slows down, lightning etching through the air around them, raindrops suspended as Layna flies forward and realizes what she must do. The only chance they might still make it back. There will be no second chances.

She gathers all the light inside of her—her hope, her dreams, her love for her family both Naut and human, her will to succeed—and holds onto it as she slams into the boy midair and latches onto him. And then they are both falling toward the steel and concrete debris as it sinks into the water below. With every last ounce of her strength, every last flicker of her Aether, she pours her whole self into this final purpose, this one last lucy-bomb.

She aims her will down toward the wreckage and releases the targeted explosion. The shockwave rebounds back up toward them, and then they are flying through the air in the other direction. Back toward the portal. She pulls the boy in close, shuts her eyes, and prays.

The back of her eyelids explodes with brightness and she grips even harder to the little body in her arms as they fall endlessly through nothingness. Then abruptly, she lands.

It's quiet. Layna opens one eye and sees a deeply cracked golden dome above her. There is pain everywhere. And there is exhaustion unlike anything she's ever known. She is empty, her duty fulfilled. There is nothing left. The world shrinks around her, and her very last thought before she falls into oblivion is, *how could I be here anyway, if here isn't where you are?*

CHAPTER

"Why won't she wake up?" says a voice.

"We don't know what she experienced in the other dimension. Neither of them were supposed to make it out at all. At least not with their minds intact."

"Well, hers *seems* intact according to all these beepy machines, so shouldn't she wake up?"

"I don't know."

"Well, figure it out!"

Harkin, she thinks. She knows him. Knows his voice and his name. But how can she know him if she doesn't know herself? She tries to dig deeper, but she senses a pain buried there and stops. She doesn't want to know the source. She tries opening her eyes, but they won't budge. She feels weak, paralyzed. Like her body doesn't belong to her.

"Lord Lucien," says a third voice, "it's time we get back down there for the gathering. The Consulate must make a decision, with or without her input, I'm afraid."

"Thank you, Thaddeus. I will be there momentarily."

She knows these names too. She wants to call out to them for help, but nothing works. She's broken somehow.

"Stay here. I'll return shortly."

"Can't wait," the one named Harkin mutters.

It's followed by a long silence. She's not even sure Harkin is still there, until he clears his throat.

"Hey," he whispers, "if you're still in there, you've got to wake up. The Consulate is doing some weird-ass shit. They'd probably listen to you. Plus…well…I'd kind of prefer it if you didn't die."

How heartwarming, she thinks. She tries deciphering what his words could mean. Who is the Consulate, and what does she have to do with them? Why would they listen to her? Who *is* she?

"And…I know he wouldn't want you to die either. Blake would want you to live. So do it for him at least, okay?"

Blake. At the sound of his name, something dreadful opens up inside of her. A hot geyser of anguish vaporizing the breath in her lungs and the heart in her chest.

She hears an alarm and Harkin yelling, "Hey! Hey, someone help! You, get over here and make her start breathing again!"

She hears the shuffling of feet and feels hands on her, but the nothingness beckons, and she welcomes it back as a friend.

"It's me again," a strained voice murmurs. The familiarity of it pulls her back from the nothingness. "I know it's been a while. Came as soon as they let me up and about again. They weren't too pleased with me last time I barged in here, I guess. I'm a few doors down, sharing a room with Selene. She's driving me bloody mad," the voice says with a joyless chuckle. "But they don't have a ton of space here given…you know, the almost apocalypse. At least we got the Naut docs looking after us.

"Anyway, they said it might help for you to hear a friendly voice. I mean, if it's…if you're still…in there. What am I saying? Of course you're still in there. What do they know? Useless gits, the lot of them. Physically, you're healing quite well, they tell me…" He trails off. "You've just got to open your eyes, Layna. Can you do that for your old, rubbish Guide?"

Layna. That's right. That's her name. And this voice, it's so warm and comforting. It fills her with a melting sense of relief to hear it, like she wasn't sure if she ever would again. And then a face appears in her mind, along with a name. *Des.*

She feels elated at being able to remember him, even if it is just a glimpse. She needs to let him know she hears him. She yells his name, over and over, willing her lips to move. But she is still broken. Her body still isn't hers. It belonged to someone else before this. Or…many someones. And they're all gone now.

"Alright, back to bed with you," says a gruff woman's voice. "You can try again tomorrow."

Layna hears a heavy sigh, the screech of a chair, and the sound of crutches. *No, he's leaving.* She screams his name louder and louder inside her head. *Des, don't leave!*

She hears a low moan that she realizes must have come from her own lips.

"Layna?" she hears Des blurt from the doorway. The clacking of the crutches moves back toward her bedside. "Did you hear that?" he asks the woman.

She did it, Des heard her. *Now just do it again.* She senses her lips, her lungs, and tries to make everything work together, forcing the air out as she moves her mouth again. "Des," she croaks.

"Aye! Layna, I'm here! Come on, kiddo, open your eyes."

She hears the elation in his voice, and she wants to obey his command. But where are her eyes? She shifts her concentration, finding her eyelids and giving everything she has to force them open. She feels them flutter. Progress.

"Layna?" His hands are squeezing hers, and it gives her strength. She pushes her heavy lids up enough that the bright blur of the world stings her retinas. She blinks, trying to distinguish between the indistinct shapes around her. The darker blur closest to her makes a vigorous whooping sound as she becomes aware of the physical pain in the other parts of her reawakening body. There is a bandage on the side of her head and her arm is in a cast. She wiggles her toes, which crackle unpleasantly with the movement. But at least there is movement.

"Des…" she rasps. "What happened to me?"

Before he can respond, several other people descend on her, grabbing her arms and shining bright lights into her eyes. Someone pours something wet into them and the world comes into better focus. She looks past the doctors toward Des. Her friend, her protector…that's all she remembers of anything. He looks haggard and unwell, something dark lurking beneath the tears of relief in his eyes. A promise of pain if she looks too closely. So instead, she watches the doctors as they continue to prod her.

"Des, make them leave me alone," she moans, as she swipes feebly at the nearest hand.

Des smiles at her. "They're here to help. They'll make you feel better, alright?"

She gives a weak nod that feels like an earthquake, and she suddenly feels overwhelmingly fatigued. "Can I take a nap, Des?"

Des looks to the doctor examining Layna's bandaged head for affirmation and then replies softly, "Sure you can, love."

The words barely leave his lips before she nods off with a grateful sigh.

A light breeze caresses the back of her neck, causing her long, golden hair to dance around her. She sucks in a deep breath, relishing the fresh scents of the grass and the ocean. She is sitting at their spot on top of Lycabettus Hill, looking out over Athens at sunrise. She hears the crunching of feet over gravel behind her and breaks into a grin.

She looks over her shoulder to see Blake strolling toward her, a delighted smile playing on his lips and lighting up his eyes.

"Well, hi," she says.

"Hi back," he replies, as he settles down next to her and pulls her close.

"This is perfect," she says with a sigh. "I want to stay here with you forever."

"I know," he replies, as he kisses her forehead. "But sooner or later, you're going to have to face the world."

"No, I don't," Layna says, as she snuggles in closer and breathes in the musky scent of him. "I can't go back to that life. What's back there for me now?"

"Lots of things," he says, brightening. "Your mom, your friends, school…"

She turns her face up to him and wrinkles her nose like he would do.

"Okay," he says with a laugh. "Maybe not school, but all the things that come after school. College, traveling, kids, a whole long life to do whatever you want with."

"But I don't want a life without you," Layna murmurs as an unbearable ache grips her heart.

"You won't be without me. I'll always be with you. We're Hemera and Nyx, remember? Death couldn't separate us before. We found each other in another lifetime. I'll find you again, Layna…I promise." He kisses her softly, and without another word, he releases her and leaps from the edge of the hill into the growing darkness below.

"No, wait! Blake, don't leave me!" she cries, as the hole inside of her opens up again. "Blake!"

She bolts up in bed, right into someone's arms, and begins sobbing.

"It's alright, love," Des whispers. "You were just having a nightmare."

"No, Des," Layna sobs, grabbing fistfuls of his t-shirt in her hands as her mind tries to comprehend the truth. "I remember now. It's not a nightmare, is it? It's *real*. Blake is really gone. He's gone…I was right there and I…and I…" She can barely catch a breath, and the words dissolve into the nonverbal language of grief.

Des rocks her in his arms, trying to soothe her with the choked, whispered lie that everything is going to be alright.

CHAPTER

L ayna scratches underneath the itchy cast on her arm as she looks out the window at the trees flying by.

Caledon.

She never thought she'd see it again. But she can't bring herself to feel excitement. She can't feel much of anything anymore.

Since she woke up in the hospital in Athens a week ago, she has teetered on the edge of nothing. Like a star about to go supernova. That's what she is, a black hole waiting to be born. It's as though she jumped into the darkness with him. In a way, she did.

She's done her best to put the pieces of who she was back together again, but it feels superficial, empty. Like the core of her being that was Hemera disappeared along with Blake and Nyx. Not to mention that she was nearly stripped of the Tripartite Powers when she crossed back through that portal. Des has been working to rehabilitate her, but she's made little progress. She could barely port more than twenty feet by the time she was ready to go home. So after saying their goodbyes, she and Des boarded a plane, their party of four down to a party of two.

It feels impossible that Lady Anora is gone. Des was barely able to keep it together when he broke the news to her in the hospital. Layna still finds herself expecting Lady Anora to materialize by their side at any moment, with her knowing gaze, wise and kind and powerful as always. But Des grieves for her in his silent, tormented way, and it's the only thing that truly convinces her that Lady Anora really did die beneath the Dome that day.

All the Nauts grieve, together, and in their own private ways. Phoebe's death has torn Selene apart. She nearly killed Maven with her bare hands when she showed up at the hospital one day to try and make amends. Many of the recruits that Layna trained with are gone, including Zain and Zahra. The rest of Omega is alive thanks solely to Harkin. As soon as Layna and Blake disappeared into the boy's mind, Harkin ported Molimo, Aysel, and Selene out of the Dome, and then went back in for Des and Lucien. Aysel lost both of her legs below the knee. Taking them was the only way to stop the spread of darkness from the deep bites of the shadow snakes. She's healing quickly, as all the surviving Nauts are, but she still has an arduous rehabilitation ahead of her.

Thousands of Nauts and countless humans lost their lives in the Battle of the Seven Cities, as the Nauts now call it. The Order has been reduced to less than two-thirds of what it was before, but they have little to occupy their time as the umbrae have disappeared again. The instant Layna reappeared with the boy in her arms, all the umbrae and shadow snakes disappeared, the storm clouds dispersed, the eclipsed Nauts shone bright again, and all fell still.

The Consulate is certain that the disappearance of the umbrae is temporary. But they've entered new territory now. All their preparation and prophecies have led up to a moment that has come and gone. The universes still exist, the balance still holds, time miraculously marches on. And no one knows what lies in store for their world in this new future they've embarked upon. Layna can't help but wonder why she's still here when so many others died. When she's fulfilled her only purpose on this Earth. When no one thought she would even return.

After she woke up, Lucien called upon her to appear before the Consulate to tell them what happened in there. She told them she couldn't remember anything, but the truth is, she remembers it all. Every detail of their battle with Erebus, Blake bringing her back when she nearly lost herself in the darkness of her mind, everything she felt for him when her two lives collided for those brief, beautiful moments. She remembers what it felt like to become Hemera and Layna, Nyx and Blake, all at once. The power of the unity that filled her and has now left her so empty. She remembers everything, all too clearly, and it's hard enough to stop herself from reliving it every minute, let alone having to talk about it. Especially to Lucien, who has taken over the role of Senectus.

She's meant to return to the Consulate in a month's time to relay any memories that may have returned. And supposedly, to help decide what is to be done with the boy. Harkin was right about the Consulate being shady. They wouldn't give her a single straight answer on how he was doing or what happened to him after they fell through the portal together. Lucien assured her that he was alive and well, and being looked after by the Order. Layna attempted to reach the boy with her telesthesia, but she felt nothing other than utter exhaustion when she tried.

Their car turns left into a parking lot, and Layna catches the reflection in the passenger-side mirror that she barely recognizes as her own. The fresh, pink scar that stretches down the right side of her face. A forever reminder. The shadow snake only grazed her, but it barely missed her eye, leaving her with a blind spot in her peripheral vision. Another black hole in her world.

She turns away from the agonizing reflection and looks across at Des sitting behind the wheel. He offers a halfhearted smile as they pull into a parking spot outside the Caledon police station. They climb out of the car in silence, and Layna follows Des, who is off his crutches but still walks with a slight limp, over to the bench outside the entrance to wait.

Lucien used his oneirokinesis to return the surviving recruits to families with amended stories. It only took a few false implanted memories on Layna's behalf. Some faked hospital records. A phone call to her mother from the police suggesting they may have found her daughter who was recovering from amnesia. The report of a man who found a young girl close to death in an alleyway, took her to the hospital, and set about finding out who she was.

Layna watches the people come and go from the station with numb detachment. None of them will ever know who it was that saved them from near annihilation. What this world lost when Blake jumped into the darkness. What *she* lost. And arising from her deadened apathy is a bubbling of resentment toward the whole damn world.

She doesn't have to wait more than ten minutes before she sees her mother's car peeling around the bend. It barely comes to a stop before the passenger door opens and her mom stumbles out. She sees Layna and claps her hands over her mouth with a muffled sob. Jim comes around from the driver's side and they both run to Layna.

Layna stands just as they reach her, and she is enveloped in her mother's arms. The feel of her embrace, the familiar scent of her perfume, the sound of Jim's voice as he repeats her name over and over, it shatters the wall that had formed around her heart. She weeps into her mother's shoulder with relief and heartache, happiness and despair, as the three of them sink together to the ground. Maybe she's not dead inside after all.

She hears the creaking of the bench behind her, and her mom shouts over her shoulder, "Wait! Are you the one who found her?"

They all turn to look at Des, and he pauses in his attempted retreat. His eyes sparkle as they land on Layna. "Aye. I'm the one who found her."

Layna smiles at the meaning behind his words as Jim releases her and stands up. He crosses to Des in a giant leap and pulls him into an inescapable hug. "How can we ever thank you?"

"No trouble at all, brother," Des wheezes as he claps him on the back.

"Jim, dear, let him go. You don't want to crush our hero to death!" Layna's mom exclaims, smiling through her tears. She pulls away to look at Layna and caresses her face, pushing her hair gently behind her ears. It pains Layna to see how exhausted her mom looks, her cheeks gaunt and dark circles etched deeply beneath her eyes. Layna's been gone a month, but her mother has aged years since Layna last saw her, happy and laughing on the deck of the cruise ship. Layna can't bear to think of the pain that she put her through in those weeks. She wishes she could take it all back.

"Mom, I'm so sorry. I...I couldn't remember anything." It wasn't entirely a lie. A mom-friendly version of events.

Her mom laughs, and Layna's heart soaks up the wistful sound of it. "Always apologizing. You're back. My baby is back, and that's all that matters. I never stopped hoping," she says fiercely as she hugs her again.

After her mother refuses to take no for an answer, Des joins them for dinner that night. It's strange to have him sitting there at the dinner table with her mom and Jim, her two worlds colliding. But it also feels right. After all, he is her family now too and always will be. Thankfully, they all keep the conversation light, free of questions and comments in any way related to her 'accident' or the events thereafter. Mostly it's Jim and Des chatting like a couple of old friends while her mom steals grateful, furtive glances at Layna.

Moxie weaves in between Layna's legs under the table, meowing and nudging her with affection as she's been doing since Layna first stepped into the house. Layna spent a good fifteen minutes lavishing her with cuddles and ear scratches, but she gets the impression Moxie will never voluntarily leave her side again. Layna reaches down and tenderly scratches underneath her cat's chin as she feels her mother's eyes on her.

And then, she feels something else she hasn't felt since she woke up in the hospital. Gratitude. For the people around this table. For being able to bring her mother peace. For the smell of her home, the sound of Moxie purring at her feet, the taste of a home-cooked meal. It's something. And there will be more things, every day. She'll make sure of it. She will continue, she will survive, just like she promised him she would. Though she knows she will never be able to move on, for Blake, maybe she can try to move forward.

EPILOGUE

The world has gone batshit in the months since the almost-apocalypse. Conspiracy theorists have taken over social media, and the news channels apparently have nothing better to talk about than the theories they peddle. Manufactured viruses and secret foreign plots and biological weapons, treaties and traitors and God. *Blah, blah, blah.* At least crime rates are down and wars are basically on hold. They should just shut up and be grateful for the relative peace while it lasts. Layna picks up the remote and clicks the TV off as they begin to replay the footage from that day in the Seven Cities for the umpteenth time.

"I'm sick of watching that story. How about you, weirdo?" she asks Kat.

As usual, Kat gives no response from the hospital cot set up in the downstairs guest room of the Taveras home. It's been about three months now since she slipped into her coma. Hypoxic brain injury was the fancy term the doctors initially gave. Mrs. Taveras told Layna that

Kat was showing some improvement in the beginning, able to breathe and function on her own without life support after a few weeks. There were times when she even seemed awake. But at this point, the doctors have warned her that it is becoming less likely her daughter will ever emerge from the vegetative state. And even if she does, apparently there's no way of knowing how much damage was done in the time her brain was deprived of oxygen. Layna is thankful that Mrs. Taveras is just as stubborn as her daughter. Neither of them are ready to say goodbye to Kat just yet.

Though she's back at school, Layna still visits Kat almost every day, often dozing off in the chair next to her cot instead of doing her homework. She helps out as much as she can too. Even though the aide is there most of the day, Mrs. Taveras has a difficult time with Kat's little sister to look after. She is a tiny terror, always running in to jump on Kat and shake her awake so she can play. Kat is still hooked up to IV and monitors and not in the best state for roughhousing.

Layna leans back in the chair and tries concentrating on the physics book lying open in her lap. She stares at it with repugnance. The first month back at school has been a total nightmare. Everyone looks at her differently now, not only because of the hideous scar on her face, but because she is a walking soap opera. She can just hear the taglines. A once beautiful girl disfigured in a tragic accident that claimed the lives of her best friends and her 'crush', Hunter. Rescued by a dashing stranger after losing the memory of who she was. *Ugh.*

It disgusts and infuriates her to hear the gossip and the rumors. To see the looks of pity and curiosity. Her popularity survived only among the drama-parasites who clung to her, trying to suck up some of the tragedy for themselves. She tried dealing with it for a week or so. Until she punched some girl in the face who was trying to commiserate over losing Suzanne. Now everyone leaves her alone. It's better that way.

Layna gives up and slams her book closed. She's falling drastically behind already, but she isn't planning to go to college next year anyway. Plus she has zero interest in learning the B.S. they're teaching in her classes. How could she, after everything she's learned and seen and done? She's lost people, she's *killed* people. She defied the laws of physics and battled a goddamn cosmic entity inside a little boy's head to help save the universe. How can she find the space to care about the coefficients of static and kinetic friction between two surfaces?

Her guidance counselor recommended that she take some time off to deal with her trauma, but Layna refused. It isn't going to get any better, she knows that. At least she can try to distract herself being at school more than she can at home. Her mom suggested that she go back to Dr. Nettles, but when Layna disappeared for a day after the suggestion, she didn't bring it up again. Layna hadn't really disappeared, of course. She was in her room the whole time, but whenever she heard her mom come upstairs, she projected into the Ouroboros and hid there until her mom left.

She passed the time doing the rehabilitation program Des created for her. It was similar to the methods he used when they were first learning the Tripartite Powers. She was simply strengthening her dream muscles, regaining access to the Limits. And once she got better with her porting, she started visiting Des in North Carolina. He inherited the house along with everything in it. Except for the Dream Book, which passed unsolicited through the Ouroboros to the secret compartment in Lucien's home in Melbourne at the moment of Lady Anora's death.

Des didn't look good the first time she showed up. He presented himself in a bathrobe, his blond hair and beard were several inches too long for tame society, and he smelled of stale liquor. The house was in no better condition than he was, with putrid fast-food containers everywhere and belongings scattered haphazardly about. Layna had no doubt he was obsessively reading and rereading all of Lady Anora's objects in the same way he had after losing Darcie. Layna helped him tidy up the house and tried her hand at giving him a much-needed haircut. She started visiting him almost daily after that.

She still hasn't told him what happened in the other dimension, and he hasn't pushed it. They mostly keep the conversation light and future focused. Sometimes they just sit on the porch for hours waiting for the sun to come up without speaking more than a few empty words about the sea or the weather. Sometimes they play the Beatles. Sometimes they even play Seether. But the two empty porch chairs haunt them both, and in ways, Layna thinks it hurts them more to spend time together. But the pain is bittersweet, and it's better than the emptiness that fills most of her days.

A couple of weeks ago, Selene showed up. She said she needed a change of scenery and didn't know where else to go. She's taken up the guest room Layna once stayed in. The extra company has been good for Des, and for Layna too. Although, Selene and Des still manage to find the energy to bicker like children from time to time. They've both been helping Layna get back up to speed in the Tripartite Powers, and Selene has been giving her more training in the Aetherem. Despite the fact that it might all be useless.

Selene told them a lot of Nauts were feeling lost. They spend hours in the Ouroboros just waiting to sense an umbra out there somewhere. But it's so rare now that it's become more like a hunting hobby than a defensive tactic. When they do show up, they usually don't even stick around long enough for a fight. Layna is certain it's just a regrouping. She's starting to regain her telesthetic sense again, and it crackles like constant static in the back of her mind. Even now, she can sense it. Something just on the edge of awareness, something screaming from the depths of darkness, seeking a way back in. Erebus is still out there, and she doesn't think it's done with them yet.

But there are moments when she wonders if she's imagining it all. Giving herself some sense of purpose that doesn't really exist. Now that they've saved the universe from the foretold annihilation that dictated all of their days since the beginning of history, why are Nauts even still here? What happens now?

The sun is setting outside. It's Thursday, which means take-out and movie night at home. Jim moved in to be there to support Julianne when Layna went missing, and his buoyant presence has helped to ease Layna back into a life that no longer feels like her own. Though still no mention of the proposal that Layna happened to witness on the ship that day, and no ring on her mom's finger.

Layna stands up and stretches, then walks to her friend's bedside. "See you tomorrow, Kat," she says with a sigh. She leans down to give her a kiss on the forehead and gets a biting electric shock.

"Ow, jeez! These machines are making you electrified," she mutters, rubbing her lip.

She walks to the door and prepares for the drawn-out goodbye with Mrs. Taveras, complete with at least twelve hugs and prayers of thanks. But before she can leave the room, she hears a loud gasping behind her, followed by an alarm bell. She spins on her heel and cries out as she sees Kat sitting up, eyes wide open and searching. She is sucking in breaths as though she's tasting air for the first time.

"Kat!" Layna wails. She moves toward her but is shoved backward by the aide pouring his large self into the room.

"Layna!" Kat croaks, her voice like sandpaper. The aide tries to get her to lie down but she flails wildly against him.

"She's hysterical, I need to calm her down," the aide says, as he raises a syringe, shooting liquid out of the tip.

"*No,* quack!" Kat screeches as she frees her arm and knocks the syringe from his hand.

Layna stifles a half-sob, half-laugh, as she watches her best friend speaking, moving, *not* braindead. Kat is back. Things will be better now. Life may be more than bearable. "I'm here, Kat!" she cries.

Kat turns her face in the direction of Layna's voice, her eyes still unfocused, the look in her gaunt features both frantic and intensely determined.

"Layna!" she gasps. "He's still alive!"

ACKNOWLEDGEMENTS

My utmost thanks again go to the Dream Team for your continued support and advice, and for keeping me sane while I navigate this writing and publishing journey. I am so lucky to have you all by my side.

Thank you to my editor, Ceri Savage, for your meticulous work on this book and for all the positive feedback. Thank you to Anna for your enthusiastic assistance with event planning and marketing, for being so generous with your time, and for being one of my dearest friends. Thanks to Jimmy for the marketing guidance, to my beta readers, and to all my family and friends who read *A Dance of Storm and Starlight* and overwhelmed me with the generous outpouring of love and encouragement. I may have written the words, but you all are the heart and soul of this story.

And a final, massive thanks to all my readers for buying these books. Telling you this story is a dream come true for me. I'm so grateful that you decided to stick with Layna and Blake on their journey, and I hope you will come back for the next and final installment.

About the Author

K.A. Vanderhoef grew up in Rockland County, New York and spent a good portion of her childhood exploring imaginary worlds co-created with her triplet sisters or otherwise found between the pages of a book. She holds a Bachelor of Arts in Psychology from Quinnipiac University and a law degree from Seton Hall University School of Law. She started writing speculative fiction and poetry while in law school, and her ardor for the hobby has only increased during her years working as an attorney, as one must always maintain the balance of light and dark in life. She currently lives in a peaceful lake community in Ringwood, New Jersey with her cat, Moxie.

Made in the USA
Middletown, DE
15 November 2021